The Collected
Supernatural and Weird
Fiction of
Hugh Walpole
Volume 2

The Collected Supernatural and Weird Fiction of Hugh Walpole Volume 2

One Novel 'The Killer and the Slain' and Thirteen Short Stories of the Strange and Unusual Including 'Seashore Macabre. A Moment's Experience', 'The Staircase', 'Miss Morganhurst', 'The Snow' and 'The Faithful Servant'

Hugh Walpole

LEONAUR

The Collected
Supernatural and Weird
Fiction of
Hugh Walpole
Volume 2
One Novel 'The Killer and the Slain' and Thirteen Short Stories of the Strange and
Unusual Including 'Seashore Macabre. A Moment's Experience', 'The Staircase', 'Miss
Morganhurst', 'The Snow' and 'The Faithful Servant'
by Hugh Walpole

FIRST EDITION

Leonaur is an imprint of Oakpast Ltd

Copyright in this form © 2018 Oakpast Ltd

ISBN: 978-1-78282-766-5 (hardcover)
ISBN: 978-1-78282-767-2 (softcover)

http://www.leonaur.com

Publisher's Notes

The views expressed in this book are not necessarily
those of the publisher.

Contents

The Whistle

Mrs. Penwin gave one of her nervous little screams when she saw the dog.

'Oh, Charlie!' she cried. 'You surely haven't bought it!' and her little brow, that she tried so fiercely to keep smooth, puckered into its customary little gathering of wrinkles.

The dog, taking an instant dislike to her, sank his head between his shoulders. He was an Alsatian.

'Well . . .' said Charlie, smiling nervously. He knew that his impulsiveness had led him once more astray. 'Only the other evening you were saying that you'd like a dog.'

'Yes, but *not* an Alsatian! You *know* what Alsatians are. We read about them in the paper every day. They are simply not to be trusted. *I'm* sure he looks as vicious as anything. And what about Mopsa?'

'Oh, Mopsa . . .' Charlie hesitated. 'He'll be all right. You see, Sibyl, it was charity really. The Sillons are going to London as you know. They simply can't take him. It wouldn't be fair. They've found it difficult enough in Edinburgh as it is.'

'I'm sure they are simply getting rid of him because he's vicious.'

'No, Maude Sillon assured me. He's like a lamb—'

'Oh, Maude! She'd say anything!'

'You know that you've been wanting a companion for Mopsa—'

'A companion for Mopsa! That's good!' Sibyl laughed her shrill little laugh that was always just out of tune.

'Well, we'll try him. We can easily get rid of him. And Blake shall look after him.'

'Blake!' She was scornful. She detested Blake, but he was too good a chauffeur to lose.

'And he's most awfully handsome. You can't deny it.'

She looked. Yes, he was most awfully handsome. He had lain down,

7

his head on his paws, staring in front of him, quite motionless. He seemed to be waiting ironically until he should be given his next command. The power in those muscles, moulded under the skin, must be terrific. His long wolf ears lay flat. His colour was lovely, here silvergrey, there faintly amber. Yes, he was a magnificent dog. A little like Blake in his strength, silence, sulkiness.

She turned again to the note that she was writing.

'We'll try him if you like. Anyway, there are no children about. It's Blake's responsibility—and the moment he's tiresome he goes.'

Charlie was relieved. It hadn't been so bad after all.

'Oh, Blake says he doesn't mind. In fact, he seemed to take to the dog at once. I'll call him.'

He went to the double windows that opened into the garden and called: 'Blake! Blake!'

Blake came. He was still in his chauffeur's uniform, having just driven his master and the dog in from Keswick. He was a very large man, very fair in colouring, plainly of great strength. His expression was absolutely English in its complete absence of curiosity, its certainty that it knew the best about everything, its suspicion, its determination not to be taken in by anybody, and its latent kindliness. He had very blue eyes and was clean-shaven; his cap was in his hand, and his hair, which was fair almost to whiteness, lay roughly across his forehead. He was not especially neat but of a quite shining cleanliness.

The dog got up and moved towards him. Both the Penwins were short and slight; they looked now rather absurdly small beside the man and the dog.

'Look here, Blake,' said Charlie Penwin, speaking with much authority, 'Mrs. Penwin is nervous about the dog. He's your responsibility, mind, and if there's the slightest bit of trouble, he goes. You understand that?'

'Yes, sir,' said Blake, looking at the dog. 'But there won't be no trouble.'

'That's a ridiculous thing to say,' remarked Mrs. Penwin sharply, looking up from her note. 'How can you be sure, Blake? You know how uncertain Alsatians are. I don't know what Mr. Penwin was thinking about.'

Blake said nothing. Once again and for the hundred-thousandth time both the Penwins wished that they could pierce him with needles. It was quite terrible the way that Blake didn't speak when expected to, but then he was so wonderful a chauffeur, so good a driver, so excellent a mechanic, so honest—and Clara, his wife, was an admirable cook.

'You'd better take the dog with you now, Blake. What's his name?'

'Adam,' said Charlie.

'Adam! What a foolish name for a dog! Now don't disturb Clara with him, Blake. Clara hates to have her kitchen messed up.'

Blake, without a word, turned and went, the dog following closely at his heels.

Yes, Clara hated to have her kitchen messed up. She was standing now, her sleeves rolled up, her plump hands and wrists covered with dough. Mopsa, the Sealyham, sat at her side, his eyes, glistening with greed, raised to those doughy arms. But at sight of the Alsatian he turned instantly and flew at his throat. He was a dog who prided himself on fighting instantly every other dog. With human beings he was mild and indifferently amiable. Children could do what they would with him. He was exceedingly conceited, and cared for no one but himself.

He was clever, however, and hid this indifference from many sentimental human beings.

Blake with difficulty separated the two dogs. The Alsatian behaved quite admirably, simply restraining the Sealyham and looking up at Blake, saying, 'I won't let myself go here although I should like to. I know that you would rather I didn't.' The Sealyham, breathing deeply, bore the Alsatian no grudge. He was simply determined that he should have no foothold here.

Torrents of words poured from Clara. She had always as much to say as her husband had little. She said the same thing many times over as though she had an idiot to deal with. She knew that her husband was not an idiot—very far from it—but she had for many years been trying to make some impression on him. Defeated beyond hope, all she could now do was to resort to old and familiar tactics. What was this great savage dog? Where had he come from? Surely the mistress didn't approve, and she wouldn't have the kitchen messed up, not for anybody, and as Harry (Blake) very well knew nothing upset her like a dog-fight, and if they were going to be perpetual, which knowing Mopsa's character they probably would be, she must just go to Mrs. Penwin and tell her that, sorry though she was after being with her all these years, she just couldn't stand it and would have to go, for if there was one thing more than another that really upset her it was a dog-fight and as Harry knew having her kitchen messed up was a thing that she couldn't stand. She paused and began vehemently to roll her dough. She was short and plump with fair hair and blue eyes like her husband's. When excited, little glistening beads of sweat appeared on her forehead. No one in this world knew whether Blake was fond of her or no. Clara Blake least of all. She wondered perpetually; this uncertainty and her cooking were her two principal interests in life. There were times when Blake seemed very fond of her indeed, others when he appeared not to be aware that she existed.

All he said now was: 'The dog won't be no trouble,' then went out, the dog at his heels. The Sealyham thought for a moment that he would follow him, then, with a little sniff of greed, settled himself down again at Clara Blake's feet.

The two went out into the thin misty autumn sunshine, down through the garden into the garage. The Alsatian walked very closely beside Blake as though some invisible cord held them together. All his life, now two years in length, it had been his instant principle to attach himself to somebody. For, in this curious world where he was, not his natural world at all, every breath, every movement, rustle of wind, sound of voices, patter of rain, ringing of bells, filled him with nervous alarm. He went always on guard, keeping his secret soul to himself, surrendering nothing, a captive in the country of the enemy. There might exist a human being to whom he would surrender himself. Although he had been attached to several he had not, in his two years, yet found one to whom he could give himself. Now as he trod softly over the amber and rosy leaves he was not sure that this man beside whom he walked might not be the one.

In the garage Blake took off his coat, put on his blue overalls, and began to work. The dog stretched himself out on the stone floor, his head on his paws, and waited. Once and again he started, his pointed ears pricked, at some unexpected sound. A breeze blew the brown leaves up and down in the sun, and the white road beyond the garage pierced like a shining bone the cloudless sky.

Blake's thoughts ran, as they always did, with slow assurance. This was a fine dog. He'd known the first moment that he set eyes on him that this was the dog for him. At that first glance something in his heart had been satisfied, something that had for years been unfulfilled. For they had had no children, he and Clara, and a motorcar was fine to drive and look after, but after all it couldn't give you everything, and he wasn't one to make friends (too damned cautious), and the people he worked for were all right but nothing extra, and he really didn't know whether he cared for Clara or no. It was so difficult after so many years married to tell. There were lots of times when he couldn't sort of see her at all.

He began to take out the sparking-plugs to clean them. That was the worst of these Heldsons, fine cars, as good as any going, but you had to be for ever cleaning the sparking-plugs. Yes, that dog was a beauty. He was going to take to that dog.

The dog looked at him, stared at him as though he were saying something. Blake looked at the dog. Then, with a deep sigh, as though some matter, for long uncertain, were at last completely settled, the dog rested again his head on his paws, staring in front of him, and so fell asleep. Blake, softly whistling, continued his work.

A very small factor, in itself quite unimportant, can bring into serious conflict urgent forces. So, it was now when this dog Adam came into the life of the Penwins.

Mrs. Penwin, like so many English wives and unlike all American wives, had never known so much domestic power as she desired. Her husband was of course devoted to her, but he was for ever just escaping her, escaping her into that world of men that is so important in England, that is, even in these very modern days, still a world in the main apart from women.

Charlie Penwin had not very many opportunities to escape from his wife and he was glad that he had not, for when they came he took them. His ideal was the ideal of most English married men (and of very few American married men), namely, that he should be a perfect companion to his wife. He fulfilled this ideal; they were excellent companions, the two of them, so excellent that it was all the more interesting and invigorating when he could go away for a time and be a companion to someone else, to Willie Shaftoe for instance, with whom he sometimes stayed in his place near Carlisle, or even for a day's golf with the Rev. Thomas Bird, rector of a church in Keswick.

Mrs. Penwin, in fact, had never quite, in spite of his profound devotion to her, never entirely captured the whole of her husband—a small fragment eternally escaped her, and this escape was a very real grievance to her. Like a wise woman she did not make scenes—no English husband can endure scenes—but she was always attempting to stop up this one little avenue of escape. But most provoking! So soon as one avenue was closed another would appear.

She realised very quickly (for she was not at all a fool) that this Alsatian was assisting her husband to escape from her because his pres-

11

ence in their household was bringing him into closer contact with Blake. Both the Penwins feared Blake and admired him; to friends and strangers they spoke of him with intense pride—'What we should do without Blake I can't think!'—'But aren't we lucky in *these* days to have a chauffeur whom we can completely trust?'

Nevertheless, behind these sentiments, there was this great difference, that Mrs. Penwin disliked Blake extremely (whenever he looked at her he made her feel a weak, helpless and idiotic woman), while Charlie Penwin, although he was afraid of him, in his heart liked him very much indeed.

If Blake only were human, little Charlie Penwin, who was a sentimentalist, used to think—and now, suddenly, Blake *was* human. He had gone 'dotty' about this dog, and the dog followed him like a shadow. So close were they the one to the other that you could almost imagine that they held conversations together.

Then Blake came in to his master's room one day to ask whether Adam could sleep in his room. He had a small room next to Mrs. Blake's, because he was often out late with the car at night and must rise very early in the morning. Clara Blake liked to have her sleep undisturbed.

'You see, sir,' he said, 'he won't sort of settle down in the outhouse. He's restless: I know he is.'

'How do you know he is?' asked Charlie Penwin.

'I can sort of feel it, sir. He won't be no sort of trouble in my room, and he'll be a fine guard to the house at night.'

The two men looked at one another and were in that moment friends. They both smiled.

'Very well, Blake. I don't think there's anything against it.'

Of course, there *were* things against it. Mrs. Penwin hated the idea of the dog sleeping in the house. She did not really hate it; what she hated was that Blake and her husband should settle this thing without a word to her. Nor, when she protested, would her husband falter. Blake wanted it. It would be a good protection for the house.

Blake discovered a very odd whistle with which he called the dog. Putting two fingers into his mouth he called forth this strange note that seemed to penetrate into endless distance and that had in it something mysterious, melancholy and dangerous. It was musical and inhuman; friends of the Penwins, comfortably at tea, would hear this thin whistling cry coming, it seemed, from far away beyond the Fells, having in it some part of the Lake and the distant sea tumbling on Drigg

12

sands, and of the lonely places in Eskdale and Ennerdale.

'What's that?' they would say, looking up.

'Oh, it's Blake calling his dog.'

'What a strange whistle!'

'Yes, it's the only one the dog hears.'

The dog did hear it, at any distance, in any place. When Blake went with the car the Alsatian would lie on the upper lawn whence he could see the road, and wait for his return.

He would both see and hear the car's return, but he would not stir until Blake, released from his official duties, could whistle to him— then with one bound he would be up, down the garden, and with his front paws up against Blake's chest would show him his joy.

To all the rest of the world he was indifferent. But he was not hostile. He showed indeed an immense patience, and especially with regard to the Sealyham.

The dog Mopsa attempted twice at least every day to kill the Alsatian. He succeeded in biting him severely, but so long as Blake was there Adam showed an infinite control, letting Blake part them although every instinct in him was stirred to battle.

But, after a time, Blake became clever at keeping the two dogs separate; moreover, the Sealyham became afraid of Blake. He was clever enough to realise that when he fought the Alsatian he fought Blake as well—and Blake was too much for him.

Very soon, however, Blake was at war not only with the Sealyham but with his wife and Mrs. Penwin too. You might think that the words 'at war' were too strong when nothing was to be seen on the surface. Mrs. Blake said nothing, Mrs. Penwin said nothing, Blake himself said nothing.

Save for the fights with the Sealyham there was no charge whatever to bring against the Alsatian. He was never in anyone's way, he brought no dirt into the house, whenever Charlie Penwin took him in the car he sat motionless on the back seat, his wolf ears pricked up, his large and beautiful eyes sternly regarding the outside world, but his consciousness fixed only upon Blake's back, broad and masterly above the wheel.

No charge could be brought against him except that the devotion between the man and the dog was, in this little house of ordered emotions, routine habits, quiet sterility, almost terrible. Mrs. Blake, as her husband left her one night to return to his own room, broke out:

'If you'd loved me as you love that dog I'd have had a different life.'

13

Blake patted her shoulder, moist beneath her night-dress.

'I love you all right, my girl,' he said.

And Mrs. Penwin found that here she could not move her husband.

Again, and again she said:

'Charlie, that dog's got to go.'

'Why?'

'It's dangerous.'

'I don't see it.'

'Somebody will be bitten one day and then you *will* see it.'

'There's a terrible lot of nonsense talked about Alsatians. . . .'

And then, when everyone was comfortable, Mrs. Blake reading her *Home Chat,* Mrs. Penwin her novel, Mrs. Fern, Mrs. Penwin's best friend, doing a 'crossword,' over the misty dank garden, carried, it seemed, by the muffled clouds that floated above the Fell, would sound that strange melancholy whistle, so distant and yet so near, Blake calling his dog.

For Blake himself life was suddenly, and for the first time, complete. He had not known, all this while, what it was that he missed, although he had known that he missed something.

Had Mrs. Blake given him a child he would have realised completion. Mrs. Blake alone had not been enough for his heart. In this dog he found fulfilment because here were all the things that he admired—loyalty, strength, courage, self-reliance, fidelity, comradeship, and above all, sobriety of speech and behaviour. Beyond these there was something more—love. He did not, even to himself, admit the significance of this yet deeper contact. And he analysed nothing.

For the dog, life in this dangerous menacing country of the enemy was at last secure and simple. He had only one thing to do, only one person to consider.

But of course, life is not so simple as this for anybody. A battle was being waged and it must have an issue. The Penwins were not in Cumberland during the winter. They went to their little place in Sussex, very close to London and to all their London friends. Mrs. Penwin would not take the Alsatian to Sussex. But why not? asked Charlie. She hated it, Mrs. Blake hated it. That, said Charlie, was not reason enough.

'Do you realise,' said Mrs. Penwin theatrically, 'that this dog is dividing us?'

'Nonsense,' said Charlie.

'It is not nonsense. I believe you care more for Blake than you do for me.' She cried. She cried very seldom. Charlie Penwin was uncomfortable, but some deep male obstinacy was roused in him. This had become an affair of the sexes. Men must stand together and protect themselves or they would be swept away in this feminine flood. . . .

Blake knew, Mrs. Blake knew, Mrs. Penwin knew, that the dog would go with them to Sussex unless some definite catastrophe gave Mrs. Penwin the victory. As he lay on his bed at night, seeing the grey wolf-like shadow of the dog stretched on the floor, Blake's soul for the first time in its history trembled at the thought of the slight movement, incident, spoken word, sound, that might rouse the dog beyond his endurance and precipitate the catastrophe. The dog was behaving magnificently, but he was surrounded by his enemies. Did he know what hung upon his restraint?

Whether he knew or no, the catastrophe arrived, and arrived with the utmost, most violent publicity. On a sun-gleaming russet October afternoon, on the lawn, while Charlie was giving Blake instructions about the car, and Mrs. Penwin put in also her word, Mopsa attacked the Alsatian, Blake ran to separate them, and the Alsatian, sharply bitten, bewildered, humiliated, snapped and caught Blake's leg between his teeth. A moment later he and Blake knew, both of them, what he had done. Blake would have hidden it, but blood was flowing. In the Alsatian's heart remorse, terror, love, and a sense of disaster, a confirmation of all that, since his birth, knowing the traps that his enemies would lay for him, he had suspected, leapt to life together.

Disregarding all else he looked up at Blake.

'And that settles it!' cried Mrs. Penwin, triumphantly. 'He goes!'

Blake's leg was badly bitten in three places; they would be scars for life. And it was settled. Before the week was out the dog would be returned to his first owners, who did not want him, who would give him to someone else who also, in turn, through fear or shyness of neighbours, would not want him. . . .

Two days after this catastrophe Mrs. Blake went herself to Mrs. Penwin.

'My husband's that upset . . . I wouldn't care if the dog stays, Mum.'

'Why, Clara, you hate the dog.'

'Oh, well, Mum, Blake's a good husband to me. I don't like to see him . . .'

'Why, what has he said?'

'He hasn't said anything, Mum.'

15

But Mrs. Penwin shook her head. 'No, Clara, it's ridiculous. The dog's dangerous.'

And Blake went to Charlie Penwin. The two men faced one another and were closer together, fonder of one another, man caring for man, than they had ever been before.

'But, Blake, if the dog bites *you* whom he cares for . . . I mean, don't you see, he really *is* dangerous. . . .'

'He wasn't after biting me,' said Blake slowly. 'And if he *had* to bite somebody, being aggravated and nervous, he'd not find anyone better to bite than me who understands him and knows he don't mean nothing by it.'

Charlie Penwin felt in himself a terrible disloyalty to his wife. She could go to . . . Why should not Blake have his dog? Was he for ever to be dominated by women? For a brief, rocking, threatening moment his whole stable ordered world trembled. He knew that if he said the dog was to remain the dog would remain and that something would have broken between his wife and himself that could never be mended.

He looked at Blake, who with his blue serious eyes stared steadily in front of him. He hesitated. He shook his head.

'No, Blake, it won't do. Mrs. Penwin will never be easy now while the dog is there.'

Later in the day Blake did an amazing thing. He went to Mrs. Penwin.

During all these years he had never voluntarily, himself, gone to Mrs. Penwin. He had never gone unless he were sent for. She looked at him and felt as she always did, dislike, admiration, and herself a bit of a fool.

'Well, Blake?'

'If the dog stays I'll make myself responsible. He shan't bite nobody again.'

'But how can you tell? You said he wouldn't bite anyone before, and he did?'

'He won't again.'

'No, Blake, he's got to go. I shan't have a moment's peace while he's here.'

'He's a wonderful dog. I'll have him trained so he won't hurt a fly. He's like a child with me.'

'I'm sure he is. Irresponsible like a child. That's why he bit you.'

'I don't make nothing of his biting me.'

'You may not, but next time it will be someone else. There's something in the paper about them every day.'

'He's like a child with me.'

'I'm very sorry, Blake. I can't give way about it. You'll see I'm right in the end. My husband ought never to have accepted the dog at all.'

After Blake had gone she did not know why, but she felt uneasy, as though she had robbed a blind man, or stolen another woman's lover. Ridiculous! There could be no question but that she was right.

Blake admitted that to himself. She was right. He did not criticise her, but he did not know what to do. He had never felt like this in all his life before, as though part of himself were being torn from him.

On the day before the dog was to go back to his original owners, Blake was sent into Keswick to make some purchases. It was a soft bloomy day, one of those North English autumn days when there is a scent of spices in the sharp air and a rosy light hangs in shadow about the trees. Blake had taken the dog with him, and driving back along the Lake, seeing how it lay a sheet of silver glass upon whose surface the islands were painted in flat colours of auburn and smoky grey, a sudden madness seized him. It was the stillness, the silence, the breathless pause. . . .

Instead of turning to the right over the Grange bridge he drove the car straight on into Borrowdale. It was yet early in the afternoon; all the lovely valley lay in gold leaf at the feet of the russet hills and no cloud moved in the sky. He took the car to Seatoller and climbed with the dog the steep path towards Honister.

And the dog thought that at last what he had longed for was to come to pass. He and Blake were at length free; they would go on and on, leaving all the stupid, nerve-jumping world behind them, never to return to it. With a wild, fierce happiness such as he had never yet shown, he bounded forward, drinking in the cold streams, feeling the strong turf beneath his feet, running back to Blake to assure him of his comradeship. At last he was free, and life was noble as it ought to be.

At the turn of the road Blake sat down and looked back. All round him were hills. Nothing moved; only the stream close to him slipped murmuring between the boulders. The hills ran ranging from horizon to horizon, and between grey clouds a silver strip of sky, lit by an invisible sun, ran like a river into mist. Blake called the dog to him and laid his hand upon his head. He knew that the dog thought that they two had escaped for ever now from the world. Well, why not? They could walk on, on to the foot of the hill on whose skyline the mining-hut stood like a listening ear, down the Pass to Buttermere, past the lake, past Crummock Water to Cockermouth. Then there would be a train. It would not be difficult for him to get work. His knowledge of cars (he had a genius for them) would serve him anywhere. And Clara? She was almost invisible, a white tiny blob on the horizon. She would find someone else. His hand tightened about the dog's head. . . .

For a long while he sat there, the dog never moving, the silver river spreading in the sky, the hills gathering closer about him.

Suddenly he shook his head. No, he could not. He would be running away, a poor kind of cowardice. He pulled Adam's sharp ears; he buried his face in Adam's fur. He stood up, and Adam also stood up, placed his paws on his chest, licked his cheeks. In his eyes there shone great happiness because they two were going away alone together.

But Blake turned back down the path, and the dog, realising that there was to be no freedom, walked close behind him, brushing with his body sometimes the stuff of Blake's trousers.

Next day Blake took the dog back to the place whence he had come.

Two days later, the dog, knowing that he was not wanted, sat watching a little girl who played some foolish game near him. She had plump bare legs; he watched them angrily. He was unhappy, lonely, nervous, once more in the land of the enemy, and now with no friend.

Through the air, mingling with the silly laughter of the child and other dangerous sounds, came, he thought, a whistle. His heart hammered. His ears were up. With all his strength he bounded towards the sound. But he was chained. Tomorrow he was to be given to a Cumberland farmer.

Mrs. Penwin was entertaining two ladies at tea. This was the last day before the journey south. Across the dark lawns came that irritating, melancholy whistle, disturbing her, reproaching her—and for what?

Why, for her sudden suspicion that everything in life was just ajar—one little push and all would be in its place—but would she be married to Charlie, would Mrs. Planty there be jealous of her pretty daughter, would Miss Tennyson, nibbling now at her pink piece of icing, be nursing her aged and intemperate father . . .? She looked up crossly—

'Really, Charlie . . . that must be Blake whistling. I can't think why now the dog's gone. To let us know what he thinks about it, I suppose . . .' She turned to her friends. 'Our chauffeur—a splendid man—we *are* so fortunate. Charlie, do tell him. It's such a hideous whistle any-way—and now the dog is gone . . .'

The Faithful Servant

No writer of stories should ever point a moral. I know that very well. Nor is it exactly a moral that I am pointing this time. In telling you about Mrs. Rayson and the negro, I am calling your attention to something that in all probability you have not noticed—inanely, that if you, in your own private life, pursue a virtue, a crime, a habit, a taste far enough, it brings you into contact with the strangest persons—and not, in general, living ones. And when I say 'living' I mean individuals obeying, for a brief period, the physical laws of this momentary existence.

All this is a pompous and wordy introduction to Mrs. Rayson, who was never pompous, although she was often wordy. *Whatever* she was, she was the last person in the world you would expect to find in warm friendship with a Negro wearing a primrose-coloured cap and bright-blue collar. Yet so was. And the word that united them was Fidelity.

Mrs. Rayson had been for a great many years, housekeeper to Frederick Rowlandson, Esquire, of Salt House, Polchester. Rowlandson, whom I knew well, deserves a whole book to himself. He was the only human being in our town who truly merited the name of Connoisseur, and, in fact, he was famous for his collection of pictures far beyond our town. At the big Winter Exhibitions at Burlington House, you would often read in the catalogue that a Reynolds or a Matisse or a Rembrandt drawing had been lent by 'Frederick Rowlandson, Salt House, Polchester, Glebeshire.'

He was a large, fat man, untidy, with mild blue eyes and a drooping moustache. He inherited his fortune from his father, who had invented some kind of toothpaste. Salt House was a hideous building, erected by Rowlandson Senior at the very worst period of Victorian taste: it stood in a sheltered valley only a mile or so outside Polchester. The inside of this ugly building was simply plastered with oils and drawings.

No one knew where young Rowlandson had got his taste from. The old man had none, but, a widower for the last twenty years of his life, he adored his boy, his only child, and let him do as he pleased. Young Rowlandson began to buy pictures somewhere about 1880, when Manet, Cézanne and the rest were still derided in their own country, and almost unknown in England. His first important purchase was an Ingres drawing, a male nude, and it hung over his study mantelpiece until the day of his death. Many people in Polchester thought it improper, no fig-leaves being anywhere indicated. He had been to Harrow and King's College, Cambridge, and it was at King's that he made a friendship with Michael Testy, one of the best art critics England has ever had. From then on, Testy advised him about his purchases.

In twenty years Rowlandson learnt a lot. His personal preference was for Italian Primitives and Old Master drawings, but his collection was most catholic. Not only catholic, but confused. You could never tell what you would see next! All along the wall of the main staircase were Constable drawings, dozens of them, lovely and sparkling with misted English fire, but directly after them, on the top landing, were Dufys and Légers and Braques. His big Italian pictures were, however, together and separate in the big drawing-room. He had a grand Tintoretto *Dethronement* and a superb Titian female head. Over the mantelpiece of the small drawing-room hung the Quentin Matsys that is, with Mrs. Rayson, the subject of this story.

Mrs. Rayson came to Rowlandson as his housekeeper when he was quite a young man. She must have been rather pretty then, although no one, I am sure, suggested anything improper between them. Rowlandson, apparently, had no 'affairs.' He lived only for his pictures—and Mrs. Rayson possessed a husband, a loafer, who appeared and disappeared and was at last killed in the war.

She did not, I suspect, keep her looks very long. She grew stout and was always untidy. Her face was pleasant, but stupid. She was, in fact, a stupid woman and was not, I am sure, a very good housekeeper. The house never looked very clean or disciplined. The maids seemed happy, but independent, and Frank Gunther, Rowlandson's chauffeur, was as cheerful, round-faced a man as you'd ever see, but his uniform was not smart, nor his grand cars very clean.

Everything and everyone concerned with Salt House was careless and disorderly, including Rowlandson, but Rowlandson seemed to prefer it thus.

Mrs. Rayson adored him. When I knew him she was middle-aged

and shapeless. She had agreeable light-brown hair, always a trifle disorderly; she had the pleasant, rather meaningless, smile of a peasant who is happy but does not bother to think why, and her voice was soft and friendly. She was a terrific talker and no respecter of persons. She adored Rowlandson, but thought him a crazy child who should be indulged by her, because she loved him. She resented that he should spend so much money on pictures. Every time that he went to London or Paris, she knew that more pictures would arrive at the house, and she hated the men she vaguely called 'these dealers' so intensely that it was lucky for them that they never paid Rowlandson a visit. She would, I am sure, have put poison in their soup. Michael Testy sometimes came to stay and she would have hated him if she could, but no one could hate him—he was so very amiable, generous and unmalicious.

She ruled Salt House like an untidy queen: she reminded me, in fact, very strongly of the White Queen in *Alice*. She tried to make an ally of me in the picture-buying question.

'You know, sir, he's got far more already than the house can hold, and, as I tell him again and again, he doesn't know what he *has* got in the top rooms, all piled against the wall they are. Why doesn't he sell some of them? I ask him that and he says he can't bear to part with them, which seems to me pure foolish as he never looks at them. And there's lots wants doing to the house and I don't think it's right with all these unemployed and the Germans as unfriendly as they are.' Then a really lovely smile transfigured her round, comfortable face:

'But there. It makes him happy and that's the main thing.'

There was, however, one picture that she liked. This was the Quintin Matsys of which I have already spoken. This picture had a romantic history. It represented a wealthy merchant or Town Councillor or Court official, dressed in a rich fur gown. He was staring in front of him, and against the lower part of his gown was a crown of thorns, to the right of him were some trees and, on the left, a negro in a primrose-coloured rap and wearing a bright-blue collar. This negro was looking anxiously at the councillor.

Now this picture, a most brilliant example of Matsys at his best, was part of a large altar-piece that, until the end of the eighteenth century, had been the glory of some Flemish church. No one living had any knowledge of the picture, but it was supposed that it represented the Crucifixion and that these two figures were part of the watching crowd. The church had been destroyed by fire, and a monk, escaping, had saved this part of the picture. This monk hid afterwards lived with a family in England and, in return for their kindness to him, had given them the painting. This same family had sold it to Rowlandson.

It made, however, a very complete thing in itself. The colour was gloriously rich; the fur of the coat, the dark green of the trees, the brown of the negro's face, and the richness of his blue collar—these were so brilliant that the whole painting was alive, deep in its profundity and reality Rowlandson called it *The Faithful Servant*, and once you had heard that, you could not believe that it could be anything else. The most lovely feature of it was the gaze of the Negro at his master. His thick lips were a little apart; his countenance expressed ardently his fidelity, and his anxiety—his anxiety as to what his master would do, or rather as to the effect that the scene would have on him.

You felt that the servant knew his mister so well that he realised how moving a moment this was for him. It might alter his life! Would he not even now perhaps expose himself by some public protest? The wonderful thing in the picture was the complete absorption of the servant in his master He had no thought, no eyes, for the general scene. He was waiting to follow his master wherever he might go. It was absurd, of course, to suppose that Mrs. Rayson saw all this in the picture She did not see it as a picture at all, but the negro represented a principle to her that she completely understood. Just so would she too behave were her master in any danger.

'You know,' Rowlandson would say, with that fat chuckle especially his, 'that is the only picture in the house Mrs. Rayson approves of. It tells her some kind of story that she can understand.'

And Mrs. Rayson said to me herself:

I don't know anything about pictures, sir—only I like what I do like, if you understand what I mean. But there, sir, that picture I *do* understand. There are some in the world, I believe, won't hold with black folk, but that black servant, even though he *has* got thick lips, was a good man once, whoever he was. And he's as alive to me as if I'd known him. That will sound silly to you, sir, but it's true all the same.'

I said it didn't sound silly to me at all.

And now I come to the harrowing part of my story, for Rowlandson, quite suddenly, and without any warning to anybody, married. He was married in a register office in London and, after a fortnight's holiday abroad, brought his wife home.

Polchester has all the faults, prejudices, provincialism of other Cathedral towns, but, if you have lived there for a long time, you do, most certainly, develop a pride and a warm affection for it. The Cathedral is so solemn, the old houses with their enclosed gardens so really English, the sea is so near, the moors beyond the town's walls are so open and free. I would not say that we citizens are altogether a loving brotherhood: we have our gossip, our spite, our malice like the rest of the world. And we have also a corporate sense and care for one another, and have a certain pride in one another.

Now, of Rowlandson we were always especially proud. He was our only international figure, unless our Bishop might be considered one. Never, since the days of Harmer John the Dane, had we possessed anyone who lived ardently for beauty and, as we thought, was selfless in his pursuit of it. We had never contemplated his marrying anyone. He seemed to care very little for women and there had never been, concerning him, a breath of scandal. We felt that, because of his passion for art, he was free of that maddening, disappointing, enchanting, baffling poison, sexual passion. When we heard that he had married, we could not believe it, and then, when we knew that it was true, we did hope that he had married wisely.

The very moment that we saw Julia Rowlandson, we all knew that he had married most unwisely. I shall never understand why he did it—there are dark places in all our hearts—but I suppose that she, for a brief moment, beguiled his senses and caught him before he could fly into safety.

Julia Rowlandson was not even pretty. She was small and soft and fluffy. She had cold blue eyes, a turned-up nose and a false smile. I am not prejudiced. She was as selfish and cold-hearted a creature as I shall ever know. She was, I think, about thirty years of age, and Rowlandson was a wonderful catch for her.

At first, he was, for some unknown reason, very proud of her. He said to me, one evening, talking rather like a bashful schoolboy:

'What luck! I'm no chicken and I'm no beauty. To think that Julia should care for me! And it's just what I need. Someone to pull this house together, tidy everything up. She's a marvellous manager.'

That Julia was! She immediately set about putting things to rights. She had her qualities. The house changed under her hand. She gave charming little dinner-parties. Rowlandson was tidied up as well as the house, and efficiency was everywhere. But how the servants hated her! In these democratic days, it is wonderful to me that there is anyone left who can look on servants *as* servants. Just as we art, most of us, paid to do a job for someone or other, so are they paid to do a job for us. We are all in the same boat and we should all be friends together, working for the same good cause. But Julia had. the old-fashioned ideas. Her servants were her slaves and that was the beginning and end of the arrangement.

It was from plump, good-natured Frank Gunther that I first heard. I could not believe that he could be so venomous.

'I would leave tomorrow, but chauffeurs' jobs are hard to get and I've been with Mr. Rowlandson for years and years, and there's no one I think higher of. But she's a holy terror, she is. She'll keep me waiting for hours and hours when one word could save it. She'll send me into the town for nothing at all, when a word on the telephone would get her what she wants. She speaks to me like a dog and it's the same with all the servants.'

There were tears in his eyes. I thought he was going to blubber like a child from sheer rage. Julia's selfishness was a marvellous thing to witness. A spoilt, selfish woman is something that no man can rival. And about Julia there was a self-satisfaction for which there were no grounds whatever. She was not beautiful, not clever, not kindly, not gracious. She needed a criminal assault to bring her to her senses.

And so here these two women were, Mrs. Rayson and Julia Rowlandson.

One afternoon, when it was all over, I had a full and sufficient account of the whole business from Mrs. Rayson's own lips, one wintry afternoon, when the snow was falling like lazy afterthoughts across the misted window. I would like to give the story in Mrs. Rayson's own words, but I could never, I fear, catch her fat, reminiscent chuckle. And there was more, of course, in her story than she herself saw.

There is an exciting novel, I fancy, in the relations between those two women while they were together in that house—but it is the business of the short story to catch a moment, a shadow at a window, a horse tumbling in the street, an uplifted glass, a cherry-tree in bloom, the smell of a soiled shirt, the padded walk of a hunting cat—any of these is all that a short story needs. *This* story exists, I fancy, at the exact moment when the sunlight fades from the room and the negro's face is blotted out.

But first there were these two women in the house.

I am sure that Mrs. Rayson dedicated herself, from the moment that Julia entered the house, to perfect service. She did not in the very least resent her master's marriage. All that she wanted was that he should be happy, and—who knows?—she may for a long time past have felt that she was not herself as efficient as she ought to be. She was determined to give Mrs. Rowlandson, whoever she might be, the loyalty and devotion that she gave to her master.

But, of course, she could not. One glance at Julia and you would know that everything Mrs. Rayson was and stood for would infuriate her spirit—but most of all that Mrs. Rayson had something she had not, a loving, faithful heart. Not that Julia knew that, she thought that she had everything. But we can sense our loss and be maddened by it, simply because someone else says, 'Goodbye then.'

Mrs. Rayson surrendered the keys of the house and she soon saw that she had surrendered everything else. The house had always been human—untidy, but human. Now Mrs. Rayson lost her humanity,

'It was an awful thing, sir. In three days it was as though I hadn't a stomach, if you'll pardon me, sir.'

It was Julia's especial gift to turn veins and arteries into wires and strings. At the end of the first week, Julia told Mrs. Rayson what she thought of her. . . .

'She was right, sir, in some of the things she said. I've never been very orderly. I have a good laugh and then promptly forget something I ought to have remembered. Mr. Rowlandson was rather like that himself, sir.'

Julia told her:

'How you've been housekeeper here so long, I can't imagine. You're thoroughly inefficient. No wonder the house was in the mess it was.'

And then, Julia hated the pictures! I think she resented the money Rowlandson had spent on them, but not for Mrs. Rayson's reason. Mrs. Rayson thought that he would have enjoyed life more had he not spent his money so foolishly. Julia wanted the money for herself. She was as greedy as a hungry cat. She knew what the Titian and Tintoretto were worth. And to think that she might be spending that wasted money herself!

Especially she hated the Matsys. The councillor's wise reflective gaze infuriated her, and the negro was a negro. She did everything she could to have it removed. She failed.

Within two months, Mrs. Rayson was her bitter enemy.

'I hated her as I've never hated any mortal. In fact, she was the first person, I think, I ever *did* hate!'

But she hated her because she was making Rowlandson unhappy'. Or was she? Rowlandson was terribly proud of his Julia, and, although he was uncomfortable now, disliked to be tidy, hated the interruptions and the dinner-parties, yet—how he was proud of her!

After a time, Julia herself was unhappy. It was not her idea to live in this small provincial place, miles from London. She found us all the dreariest lot. Not quite all of us. She began to flirt. Most of our young men at that time were not very exciting, but there *were* one or two: Henry Tattersall, Maurice Fleming, Charles Farley. Soon, it became obvious to everyone in the town, save Rowlandson, that Maurice Fleming was the one. This selection on her part proved how exceedingly common and stupid Julia was. Maurice was stout and smart. Julia liked men to be stout. Within my hearing, she said:

'Thin men are awful. You can feel their bones.' I myself am thin as a rake.

You certainly could not feel Fleming's bones. I doubt if he had any. He was well-dressed and had a clever crimson sports car—the regular thing. He was as vain, and selfish as Julia, but he was flattered by her liking for him. He was rather old news to the younger ladies of Polchester. They were now continually together and Mrs. Rayson was horrified. She believed in fidelity quite fanatically

Then, one morning, Julia told Mrs. Rayson to take the Matsys down from the wall and hide it somewhere in the attic.

'"Has the master ordered it?" I asked her. Oh no, of course not, he didn't know anything about it and wouldn't miss it anyway. "Wouldn't miss it?" said I. "That's all you know. Why, it's the pride and pleasure of his life," I said. Then she gets as red as a turkey-cock and stands up straight on her high heels (she wears high heels because she's so short and can't bear not to be as tall as other people), and says, "Now don't you be impertinent. I've had enough of you. Take that picture down." And I reply, "Not without master's orders," and didn't we just glare at one another! Almost insane it was.'

Mrs. Rayson was not the kind of person given to hallucinations, but it did seem to her, just then, that the negro in the picture moved.

'I'd got as fond of him as anything by that time, sir, and that woman abusing him only made me care for him more. And suddenly I was so angry I wasn't seeing quite straight—if you understand me, sir—I seemed to see the whole of him, not just his head and neck, stepping right out of the picture, with his primrose coat, the same as his cap, and tights on, blue just like his collar. He was a strong fellow if ever I see one, with arms would kill an ox. All imagination, sir, but you'll have sworn he looked at his master to ask him a question. All imagination, and there I was, a moment later, seeing Madam walk out majestic-like on her high heels and nearly slip on the door with them. It was almost as though the negro gave her a push when she wasn't looking.'

And the next thing was that Mrs. Rayson found a note from young Fleming under a pincushion on Julia Rowlandson's dressing-table. She should not, I suppose, have read it, but instinctively she felt that it was against her master's safety, something that endangered his happiness. I myself have never seen that note, but I understand that it began with 'darling' and had something about 'holding you in my arms again.'

It was quite enough for Mrs. Rayson. She was not shocked through moral sensitiveness, she always wanted people to be happy in any way that pleased them. But she was shocked to the very centre of her being by the infidelity. Julia Rowlandson had not been married more than three months and now here she was—'darling . . . in my arms again.' She felt quite sick. She was unwell. She had to sit down. She saw very quickly that, with this note, she could deal her mistress a nasty blow. She had only to show the note to her master. . . . But what effect would it have on *him?* He would be unhappy, ashamed, and, in the end, would do nothing at all. Her knowledge of him was perfect, Rowlandson was no good at a crisis. If he knew of his wife's infidelity, his life would be poisoned at the source. He would hate her, despise her, resent her, and continue to live with her.

On the other hand, it would be a triumph for Mrs. Rayson. She would have Julia Rowlandson henceforth where she wanted her. And—best of all—she would be first with her master again.

She fought, I believe, that dim January afternoon, the battle of her life. She was not greatly accustomed to battles. Her life had been run on a very simple plane. But now—on the one hand, a selfish, triumphant revenge, but with it her master's misery. On the other hand, subjection to a woman whom now she not only hated but despised with every warm impulse beating from her heart. To be married to her master and, within three months, to betray him. What do you think of that, ladies and gentlemen.?

She went, she has told me, on that late afternoon, into the room where the Matsys was. She did not switch on the light but watched it as the firelight leapt up and down its surface.

It was there that she fought her battle, fought it walking about the room, her hands clenched together, looking at the picture, seeing the dark face of the Negro, the thick lips open, the serious devoted eyes turned to the Councillor—this face, now so familiar to her, leaping in and out of darkness as the flames leapt.

How she longed to hear him speak! If only he would say a word! She knew well enough that he would understand her longing for revenge. He could revenge himself well enough on anyone who hurt his master! She could just fancy his animal rage, his cry of fury, the force with which that terrific body (for she knew that it was terrific) would leap upon the enemy. But to hurt his master for the sake of revenge! No, that, she realised as the fire died, he would never do. He would never, never do.

And so, at last she left the room, her decision made. She would say nothing about the note. After this she felt a physical disgust for Julia Rowlandson that was like an illness. . . .

'As when you have a fever, sir, your head burning and your feet icy and everything feeling twice its size when you touch it.'

She hated even to look at her and, unimaginative as she was, she fancied that the dry, sarcastic mouth of the councillor in the Matsys curled a little in additional contempt.

It was not perhaps altogether imagination, for Julia's hatred of the Matsys grew to a frenzy. She made a terrible scene one night about it. Rowlandson told me months later. . . .

'A strange thing. It was the negro she couldn't bear.'

Mrs. Rayson's temptation meanwhile continued.

'It never left me for a moment, digging at me. Just to say a word to the master, showing him the note which, rightly or wrongly, I'd kept. She was a careless slut and that I'll call her, even after what's happened. Just to show him the note! But It wouldn't have been right—sort of betraying my trust; at least, that's how I looked at it.'

Then came the catastrophe. One morning Rowlandson asked her into his sanctum. This is a small room that has always seemed to me one of the most beautiful I know anywhere. Here he has hung his Italian primitives, Venetian, Sienese, little pictures gleaming with gold, flashing with the wings of angels, deep with that old faded rose of cloth and hanging so especially satisfying—yes, angels and oxen, and tiny, white winding roads and plum-coloured hills, with the Virgin and Child eternally worshipped.

Here, most awkwardly and with a desperate embarrassment, Rowlandson told Mrs. Rayson that she would have to go. He could scarcely, I am sure, form his sentences:

'Dreadfully sorry . . . most unfortunate . . . after all these years . . . but my wife and yourself . . . don't seem to get along . . . don't know whose fault. . . . .' Something like that. The tears, quite frankly, flowed down Mrs. Rayson's plump cheeks. She had never been one to hide her feelings. It was the end of everything for her. Rowlandson was her child, her love, her care, her possession, her very self. The end of everything.

And now the temptation to show him the note must have been almost overpowering. A terrible longing desire, weakness of the will. She did not yield.

She hurried to her room that had, for all those years, been her home, that Rowlandson, ages ago, had hung with half a dozen pre-Raphaelite drawings—'because she liked pictures with a story.' She cried and dried her eyes. She knew that for her life was over, truly and honestly, as though she had died.

So, to the *moment* of this story. I have it, of course, only second-hand. A moment in the afternoon of that same day, a sunny day, with that early spring warmth that comes to Glebeshire often in January like an unexpected kiss on the cheek. The sun was just dropping behind the hill. In five minutes the room would be in dusk. Mrs. Rayson was saying goodbye to the Matsys, her bonnet on her head, her cape with the bugles, her shiny black gloves. She would not sleep another night in the house where she was not wanted.

Rowlandson had come to her earlier in the afternoon, taken her hand in his, looked at her like a witless man, and said desperately; 'Go home, . . .I'll come to see you. . . . I'll find a solution,' It was almost like the parting of lovers—these two very plain, elderly people saying goodbye.

But there no solution. Mrs. Rayson knew that well enough. So, there she stood crying in front of the Matsys. She cried very easily—at the sound of a band, at a reported gracious act of Queen Mary's (she put Queen Mary next to Rowlandson in her heart), at a stray dog with something tied to its tail, at any wedding or funeral.

She stared at the negro with his primrose cap and bright-blue collar. He had never seemed more adoring—faithful man Whatever he'd done he must be a good man, and the councillor was lucky. She said goodbye to her friend the negro, through the half-open door, she heard Julia Rowlandson coming down from the upper floor, *click, click, click* with her high heels. She held her breath, lest she should be found there. She wanted to leave the house without saying a word to anyone—only the negro.

'Goodbye, goodbye.'

The sun sank behind the hill. The room was in a sun-grey dusk.

What was the negro doing? Had he at last, for the first time in these many hundred years, removed his gaze from the councillor? Did someone, dark thick, heavy, brush her shoulders? Had someone crossed the floor?

Was there, in the lit door-space, for an instant, a flash of primrose and blue?

This at least is true.

There was a horrible sound of a slip, a scramble, a piercing cry, a crash ..

Mrs. Rayson found Julia Rowlandson in the hall at the bottom of the stairs, her neck broken. She had slipped on those high-heeled shoes; the stairs were steep.

'Very easily done,' the coroner said—'dangerous, these steep stairs.'

The house soon dropped back to its comfortable untidiness again. Mrs. Rayson was no more efficient than she had been before. Rowlandson was happier, I sometimes thought, as though he now realised what he had almost lost. I overheard Mrs. Rayson once say to someone:

'I had a nasty time once—the worst I *ever* had. I don't know what I'd have done if a friend hadn't helped me.'

Julia was as though she had never been alive. She never *had* been alive. We exist by the strength of the spirit that is within us.

Mr. Oddy

This may seem to many people an old-fashioned story; it is perhaps for that reason that I tell it. I can recover here, it may be, for myself something of the world that is already romantic, already beyond one's reach, already precious for the things that one might have got out of it and didn't.

London of but a few years before the war! What a commonplace to point out its difference from the London of today and to emphasise the tiny period of time that made that difference!

We were all young and hopeful then, we could all live on a shilling a year and think ourselves well off, we could all sit in front of the lumbering horse 'buses and chat confidentially with the omniscient driver, we could all see Dan Leno in Pantomime and watch Farren dance at the Empire, we could all rummage among those cobwebby streets at the back of the Strand where Aldwych now flaunts her shining bosom and imagine Pendennis and Warrington, Copperfield and Traddles cheek by jowl with ourselves, we could all wait in the shilling queue for hours to see Ellen Terry in *Captain Brassbound* and Forbes-Robertson in *Hamlet,* we could all cross the street without fear of imminent death, and above all we could all sink ourselves into that untidy, higgledy-piggledy, smoky and beery and gas-lampy London gone utterly and for ever.

But I have no wish to be sentimental about it; there is a new London which is just as interesting to its new citizens as the old London was to myself. It is my age that is the matter; before the war one was so *very* young.

I like, though, to try and recapture that time, and so, as a simple way to do it, I seize upon a young man; Tommy Brown we will call him. I don't know where Tommy Brown may be now; that Tommy Brown who lived as I did in two very small rooms in Glebe Place, Chelsea, who enjoyed hugely the sparse but economical meals provided so elegantly by two charming ladies at 'The Good Intent' down by the river, that charming hostelry whence looking through the bow windows you could see the tubby barges go floating down the river, and the thin outline of Whistler's Battersea Bridge, and in the small room itself were surrounded by who knows what geniuses in the lump, geniuses of Art and Letters, of the Stage and of the Law.

For Tommy Brown in those days life was Paradisal.

He had come boldly from Cambridge to throw himself upon London's friendly bosom; despite all warnings to the contrary he was certain that it would be friendly; how could it be otherwise to so charming, so brilliant, so unusually attractive a young man? For Tommy was conceited beyond all that his youth warranted, conceited indeed without any reason at all.

He had, it is true, secured the post of reviewer to one of the London daily papers; this seemed to him when he looked back in later years a kind of miracle, but at the time no miracle at all, simply a just appreciation of his extraordinary talents. There was also reposing in one of the publishers' offices at that moment the manuscript of a novel, a novel that appeared to him of astonishing brilliance, written in the purest English, sparkling with wit, tense with drama.

These things were fine and reassuring enough, but there was more than that; he felt in himself the power to rise to the greatest heights; he could not see how anything could stop him, it was his destiny.

This pride of his might have suffered some severe shocks were it not that he spent all of his time with other young gentlemen quite as conceited as himself. I have heard talk of the present young generation and its agreeable consciousness of its own merits, but I doubt if it is anything in comparison with that little group of twenty-five years ago. After all, the war has intervened—however young we may be and however greatly we may pretend, this is an unstable world and for the moment heroics have departed from it. But for Tommy Brown and his friends the future was theirs and nobody could prevent it. Something pathetic in that as one looks back.

Tommy was not really so unpleasant a youth as I have described him—to his elders he must have appeared a baby, and his vitality at least they could envy. After all, why check his confidence? Life would do that heavily enough in its own good time.

Tommy, although he had no money and no prospects, was already engaged to a young woman, Miss Alice Smith. Alice Smith was an artist sharing with a girl friend a Chelsea studio, and she was as certain of her future as Tommy was of his.

They had met at a little Chelsea dance, and two days after the meeting they were engaged. She had no parents who mattered, and no money to speak of, so that the engagement was the easiest thing in the world.

Tommy, who had been in love before many times, was certain, as he told his friend Jack Robinson so often as to bore that gentleman severely, that this time at last he knew what love was. Alice ordered him about—with her at any rate his conceit fell away—she had read his novel and pronounced it old-fashioned, the severest criticism she could possibly have made, and she thought his reviews amateur. He suffered then a good deal in her company. When he was away from her he told himself and everybody else that her critical judgment was marvellous, her comprehension of all the Arts quite astounding, but he left her sometimes with a miserable suspicion that perhaps after all he was not going to do anything very wonderful and that he would have to work very hard indeed to rise to her astonishing standards.

It was in such a mood of wholesome depression that he came one beautiful April day from the A.B.C. shop where he had been giving his Alice luncheon, and found his way to an old bookshop on the riverside round the corner from Oakley Street. This shop was kept by a gentleman called Mr. Burdett Coutts, and the grand associations of his name gave him from the very first a sort of splendour.

It was one of those old shops of which there are, thank God, still many examples surviving in London, in which the room was so small and the books so many that to move a step was to imperil your safety. Books ran in thick, tight rows from floor to ceiling everywhere, were piled in stacks upon the ground and hung in perilous heaps over chairs and window ledges.

Mr. Burdett Coutts himself, a very stout and grizzled old man enveloped always in a grey shawl, crouched behind his spectacles in a far corner and took apparently no interest in anything save that he would snap the price at you if you brought him a volume and timorously enquired. He was not one of those old booksellers dear to the heart of Anatole France and other great men who would love to discourse to you of the beauties of *The Golden Ass,* the possibility of Homer being a lady, or the virtues of the second *Hyperion* over the first. Not at all; he ate biscuits which stuck in his grizzly beard, and wrote perpetually in a large worm-eaten ledger which was supposed by his customers to contain all the secrets of the universe.

It was just because Mr. Coutts never interfered with you that Tommy Brown loved his shop so dearly. If he had a true genuine passion that went far deeper than all his little superficial vanities and egotisms, it was his passion for books—books of any kind.

He had at this time no fine taste—all was fish that came to his net. The bundles of Thackeray and Dickens, parts tied up carelessly in coarse string, the old broken-backed volumes of Radcliffe and Barham and Galt, the red and gold Colburn's Novelists, all these were exciting to him, just as exciting as though they had been a first Gray's *Elegy* or an original *Robinson Crusoe*.

He had, too, a touching weakness for the piles of fresh and neglected modern novels that lay in their discarded heaps on the dusty floor; young though he was, he was old enough to realise the pathos of these so short a time ago fresh from the bursting presses, so eagerly cherished through months of anxious watching by their fond authors, so swiftly forgotten, dead almost before they were born.

So, he browsed, moving like a panting puppy with inquisitive nose from stack to stack with a gesture of excitement, tumbling a whole racket of books about his head, looking then anxiously to see whether the old man would be angry with him, and realising for the thousandth time that the old man never was.

It was on this day, then, rather sore from the arrogancies of his Alice, that he tried to restore his confidence among these friendly volumes. With a little thrill of excited pleasure, he had just discovered a number of the volumes born of those romantic and tragedy-haunted 'Nineties.' Here in little thin volumes were the stories of Crackanthorpe, the poems of Dowson, the *Keynotes* of George Egerton, *The Bishop's Dilemma* of Ella d'Arcy, *The Happy Hypocrite* of Max Beerbohm.

Had he only been wise enough to give there and then for that last whatever the old man had asked him for it he would have been fortunate indeed, but the pennies in his pocket were few—he was not yet a book collector, but rather that less expensive but more precious thing, a book adorer. He had the tiny volume in his hand, when he was aware that someone had entered the shop and was standing looking over his shoulder.

He turned slowly and saw someone who at first sight seemed vaguely familiar, so familiar that he was plunged into confusion at once by the sense that he ought to say 'How do you do?' but could not accurately place him. The gentleman also seemed to know him very well, for he said in a most friendly way, 'Ah, yes, the "Nineties," a very fruitful period.'

Tommy stammered something, put down the Max Beerbohm, moved a little, and pulled about him a sudden shower of volumes. The room was filled with the racket of their tumbling, and a cloud of dust thickened about them, creeping into eyes and mouth and nose.

'I'm terribly sorry,' Tommy stammered, and then, looking up, was sorry the more when he saw how extremely neat and tidy the gentleman was and how terribly the little accident must distress him.

Tommy's friend must have been between sixty and seventy years of age, nearer seventy perhaps than sixty, but his black hair was thick and strong and stood up *en brosse* from a magnificent broad forehead. Indeed, so fine was the forehead and the turn of the head that the face itself was a little disappointing, being so round and chubby and amiable as to be almost babyish. It was not a weak face, however, the eyes being large and fine and the chin strong and determined.

The figure of this gentleman was short and thick-set and inclined to stoutness; he had the body of a prize-fighter now resting on his laurels. He was very beautifully clothed in a black coat and waistcoat, pepper-and-salt trousers, and he stood leaning a little on a thick ebony cane, his legs planted apart, his whole attitude that of one who was accustomed to authority. He had the look of a magistrate, or even of a judge, and had his face been less kindly Tommy would have said good day, nodded to Mr. Burdett Coutts, and departed, but that was a smile difficult to resist.

'Dear me,' the gentleman said, 'this is a very dusty shop. I have never been here before, but I gather by the way that you knock the books about that it's an old friend of yours.'

Tommy giggled in a silly fashion, shifted from foot to foot, and then, desiring to seem very wise and learned, proved himself only very young and foolish.

'The "Nineties" are becoming quite romantic,' he said in his most authoritative voice, 'now that we're getting a good distance from them.'

'Ah, you think so!' said the gentleman courteously; 'that's interesting. I'm getting to an age now, I'm afraid, when nothing seems romantic but one's own youth and, ah, dear me! that was a very long time ago.'

This was exactly the way that kindly old gentlemen were supposed to talk, and Tommy listened with becoming attention.

'In my young day,' his friend continued, 'George Eliot seemed to everybody a magnificent writer: a little heavy in hand for these days, I'm afraid. Now who is the God of your generation, if it isn't impertinent to enquire?'

Tommy shifted again from foot to foot. Who was the God of his generation? If the truth must be told, in Tommy's set there were no Gods, only young men who might be Gods if they lived long enough.

'Well,' said Tommy awkwardly, 'Hardy, of course—er—it's difficult to say, isn't it?'

'Very difficult,' said the gentleman.

There was a pause then, which Tommy concluded by hinting that he was afraid that he must move forward to a very important engagement.

'May I walk with you a little way?' asked the gentleman very courteously. 'Such a very beautiful afternoon.'

Once outside in the beautiful afternoon air everything was much easier; Tommy regained his self-confidence, and soon was talking with his accustomed ease and freedom. There was nothing very alarming in his friend after all, he seemed so very eager to hear everything that Tommy had to say. He was strangely ignorant too; he seemed to be interested in the Arts, but to know very little about them; certain names that were to Tommy household words were to this gentleman quite unknown. Tommy began to be a little patronising. They parted at the top of Oakley Street.

'I wonder if you'd mind,' the gentleman said, 'our meeting again? The fact is, that I have very little opportunity of making friends with your generation. There are so many things that you could tell me. I am afraid it may be tiresome for you to spend an hour or two with so ancient a duffer as myself, but it would be very kind of you.'

Tommy was nothing if not generous; he said that he would enjoy another meeting very much.

Of course, he was very busy and his spare hours were not many, but a walk another afternoon could surely be managed. They made an appointment, they exchanged names; the gentleman's name was Mr. Alfred Oddy.

That evening, in the middle of a hilarious Chelsea party, Tommy suddenly discovered to his surprise that it would please him very much to see Mr. Oddy walk in through the door.

Although it was a hilarious party Tommy was not very happy; for one thing, Spencer Russell, the novelist, was there and showed quite clearly that he didn't think Tommy very interesting. Tommy had been led up and introduced to him, had said one or two things that seemed to himself very striking, but Spencer Russell had turned his back almost at once and entered into eager conversation with somebody else.

This wasn't very pleasant, and then his own beloved Alice was behaving strangely; she seemed to have no eyes nor ears for anyone in the room save Spencer Russell, and this was the stranger in that only a week or so before she had in public condemned Spencer Russell's novels, utterly and completely, stating that he was written out, had nothing to say, and was as good as dead. Tonight, however, he was not dead at all, and Tommy had the agony of observing her edge her way into the group surrounding him and then listen to him not only as though he were the fount of all wisdom, but an Adonis as well, which last was absurd seeing that he was fat and unwieldy and bald on the top of his head.

After a while Tommy came up to her and suggested that they should go, and received then the shock of his life when she told him that he could go if he liked, but that he was not to bother her. And she told him this in a voice so loud that everybody heard and many people tittered.

He left in a fury and spent then a night that he imagined to be sleepless, although in truth he slept during most of it.

It was with an eagerness that surprised himself that he met Mr. Oddy on the second occasion. He had not seen Alice for two days. He did not intend to be the one to apologise first; besides, he had nothing to apologise for; and yet during these two days there was scarcely a moment that he had not to restrain himself from running round to her studio and making it up.

When he met Mr. Oddy at the corner of Oakley Street he was a very miserable young man. He was so miserable that in five minutes he was pouring out all his woes.

He told Mr. Oddy everything, of his youth, his wonderful promise, and the extraordinary lack of appreciation shown to him by his relatives, of the historical novels that he had written at the age of anything from ten to sixteen and found only the cook for an audience, of his going to Cambridge, and his development there so that he became Editor of *The Lion,* that remarkable but very short-lived literary journal, and the President of 'The Bats,' the most extraordinary Essay Club that Cambridge had ever known; of how, alas, he took only a third in History owing to the perverseness of examiners; and so on and so on, until he arrived in full flood at the whole history of his love for Alice, of her remarkable talents and beauty, but of her strange temper and arrogance and general feminine queerness.

Mr. Oddy listened to it all in the kindest way. There's no knowing where they walked that afternoon; they crossed the bridge and adventured into Battersea Park, and finally had tea in a small shop smelling of stale buns and liquorice drops. It was only as they turned homewards that it occurred to Tommy that he had been talking during the whole afternoon. He had the grace to see that an apology was necessary.

'I beg your pardon, sir,' he said, flushing a little, 'I'm afraid I have bored you dreadfully. The fact is, that this last quarrel with Alice has upset me very badly. What would you do if you were in my position?'

Mr. Oddy sighed. 'The trouble is,' he said, 'that I realise only too clearly that I shall never be in your position again. My time for romance is over, or at least I get my romance now in other ways. It wasn't always so; there was a lady once beneath whose window I stood night after night merely for the pleasure of seeing her candle outlined behind the blind.'

'And did she love you,' Tommy asked, 'as much as you loved her?'

'Nobody, my dear boy,' Mr. Oddy replied, 'loves you as much as you love them; either they love you more or they love you less. The first of these is often boring, the second always tragic. In the present case I should go and make it up; after all, happiness is always worth having, even at the sacrifice of one's pride. She seems to me a very charming young lady.'

'Oh, she is,' Tommy answered eagerly. 'I'll take your advice, I'll go this very evening; in fact, if you don't mind, I think it would be rather a good time to find her in now.'

Mr. Oddy smiled and agreed; they parted to meet another day.

On the third occasion of their meeting, which was only two days after the second, Tommy cared for his companion enough to wish to find out something about him.

His scene of reconciliation with his beautiful Alice had not been as satisfactory as he had hoped; she had forgiven him indeed, but given him quite clearly to understand that she would stand none of his nonsense either now or hereafter. The satisfactory thing would have been for Tommy there and then to have left her, never to see her again; he would thus have preserved both his pride and his independence; but, alas, he was in love, terribly in love, and her indignation made her appear only the more magnificent.

And so, on this third meeting with his friend he was quite humble and longing for affection.

And then his curiosity was stirred. Who was this handsome old gentleman, with his touching desire for Tommy's companionship? There was an air about him that seemed to suggest that he was some-one of importance in his own world; beyond this there was an odd sense that Tommy knew him in some way, had seen him somewhere; so, on this third occasion Tommy came out with his questions.

Who was he? Was he married? What was his profession, or was he perhaps retired now? And another question that Tommy would have liked to have asked, and had not the impertinence, was as to why this so late interest in the Arts and combined with this interest this so complete ignorance.

Mr. Oddy seemed to know a great deal about everything else, but in this one direction his questions were childish. He seemed never to have heard of the great Spencer Russell at all (which secretly gave Tommy immense satisfaction), and as for geniuses like Mumpus and Peter Arrogance and Samuel Bird, even when Tommy explained how truly great these men were, Mr. Oddy appeared but little impressed.

'Well, at least,' Tommy burst out indignantly, 'I suppose you've read something by Henry Galleon? Of course, he's a back number now, at least he is not modern if you know what I mean, but then he's been writing for centuries. Why, his first book came out when Trollope and George Eliot were still alive. Of course, between ourselves I think *The Roads,* for instance, a pretty fine book, but you should hear Spencer Russell go for it.'

No, Mr. Oddy had never heard of Henry Galleon.

But there followed a most enchanting description by Mr. Oddy of his life when he was a young man and how he once heard Dickens give a reading of *A Christmas Carol,* of how he saw an old lady in a sedan chair at Brighton (she was cracked, of course, and even then a hundred years after her time, but still he had seen it), of how London in his young day was as dark and dirty at night as it had been in Pepys' time, of how crinolines when he was young were so large that it was one of the sights to see a lady getting into a cab, of how in the music-halls there was a chairman who used to sit on the stage with a table in front of him, ring a bell and drink out of a mug of beer, of how he heard Jean de Reszke in *Siegfried* and Ternina in *Tristan,* and of how he had been at the first night when Ellen Terry and Irving had delighted the world with *The Vicar of Wakefield.*

Yes, not only had Mr. Oddy seen and done all these things, but he related the events in so enchanting a way, drew such odd little pictures of such unexpected things and made that old London live so vividly, that at last Tommy burst out in a volley of genuine enthusiasm: 'Why, you ought to be a writer yourself! Why don't you write your reminiscences?'

But Mr. Oddy shook his head gently: there were too many reminiscences, everyone was always reminiscing; who wanted to hear these old men talk?

At last when they parted Mr. Oddy had a request—one thing above all things that he would like would be to attend one of these evening gatherings with his young friend to hear these young men and women talk. He promised to sit very quietly in a corner—he wouldn't be in anybody's way.

Of course, Tommy consented to take him; there would be one next week, a really good one; but in his heart of hearts he was a little shy. He was shy not only for himself but also for his friend.

During these weeks a strange and most unexpected affection had grown up in his heart for this old man; he really did like him immensely, he was so kind and gentle and considerate.

But he would be rather out of place with Spencer Russell and the others; he would probably say something foolish, and then the others would laugh. They were on the whole a rather ruthless set and were no respecters of persons.

However, the meeting was arranged; the evening came and with it Mr. Oddy, looking just as he always did, quiet and gentle but rather impressive in some way or another. Tommy introduced him to his hostess, Miss Thelma Bennet, that well-known futuristic artist, and then carefully settled him down in a corner with Miss Bennet's aunt, an old lady who appeared occasionally on her niece's horizon but gave no trouble because she was stone deaf and cared only for knitting.

It was a lively evening; several of the brighter spirits were there, and there was a great deal of excellent talk about literature. Every writer over thirty was completely condemned save for those few remaining who had passed eighty years of age and ceased to produce.

Spencer Russell especially was at his best; reputations went down before his vigorous fist like ninepins. He was so scornful that his brilliance was, as Alice Smith everywhere proclaimed, 'simply withering.' Everyone came in for his lash, and especially Henry Galleon. There had been some article in some ancient monthly written by some ancient idiot suggesting that there was still something to be said for Galleon and that he had rendered some service to English literature. How Russell pulled that article to pieces! He even found a volume of Galleon's among Miss Bennet's books, took it down from the shelf and read extracts aloud to the laughing derision of the assembled company.

Then an odd thing occurred. Tommy, who loved to be in the intellectual swim, nevertheless stood up and defended Galleon. He defended him rather feebly, it is true, speaking of him as though he were an old man ready for the alms-house who nevertheless deserved a little consideration and pity. He flushed as he spoke, and the scorn with which they greeted his defence altogether silenced him. It silenced him the more because Alice Smith was the most scornful of them all; she told him that he knew nothing and never would know anything, and she imitated his piping excited treble, and then everyone joined in.

How he hated this to happen before Mr. Oddy! How humiliating after all the things that he had told his friend, the implication that he was generally considered to be one of England's most interesting young men, the implication above all that although she might be a little rough to him at times Alice really adored him, and was his warmest admirer. She did not apparently adore him tonight, and when he went out at last with Mr. Oddy into the wintry, rain-driven street it was all he could do to keep back tears of rage and indignation.

Mr. Oddy had, however, apparently enjoyed himself. He put his hand for a minute on the boy's shoulder.

'Goodnight, my dear boy,' he said. 'I thought it very gallant of you to stand up for that older writer as you did: that needed courage. I wonder,' he went on, 'whether you would allow me to come and take tea with you one day—just our two selves. It would be a great pleasure for me.'

And then, having received Tommy's invitation, he vanished into the darkness.

On the day appointed, Mr. Oddy appeared punctually at Tommy's rooms. That was not a very grand house in Glebe Place where Tommy lived, and a very soiled and battered landlady let Mr. Oddy in. He stumbled up the dark staircase that smelt of all the cabbage and all the beef and all the mutton ever consumed by lodgers between these walls, up again two flights of stairs, until at last there was the weather-beaten door with Tommy's visiting-card nailed upon it. Inside was Tommy, a plate with little cakes, raspberry jam, and some very black-looking toast.

Mr. Oddy, however, was appreciative of everything; especially he looked at the books. 'Why,' he said, 'you've got quite a number of the novels of that man you defended the other evening. I wonder you're not ashamed to have them if they're so out of date.'

'To tell you the truth,' said Tommy, speaking freely now that he was in his own castle, 'I like Henry Galleon awfully. I'm afraid I pose a good deal when I'm with those other men; perhaps you've noticed it yourself. Of course, Galleon is the greatest novelist we've got, with Hardy and Meredith, only he's getting old, and everything that's old is out of favour with our set.'

'Naturally,' said Mr. Oddy, quite approving, 'of course it is.'

'I have got a photograph of Galleon,' said Tommy. 'I cut it out of a publisher's advertisement, but it was taken years ago.'

He went to his table, searched for a little and produced a small photograph of a very fierce-looking gentleman with a black beard.

'Dear me,' said Mr. Oddy, 'he does look alarming!'

'Oh, that's ever so old,' said Tommy. 'I expect he's mild and soft now, but he's a great man all the same; I'd like to see Spencer Russell write anything as fine as *The Roads* or *The Pattern in the Carpet*.'

They sat down to tea very happy and greatly pleased with one another.

'I do wish,' said Tommy, 'that you'd tell me something about yourself; we're such friends now, and I don't know anything about you at all.'

'I'd rather you didn't,' said Mr. Oddy. 'You'd find it so uninteresting if you did; mystery's a great thing.'

'Yes,' said Tommy, 'I don't want to seem impertinent, and of course if you don't want to tell me anything you needn't, but—I know it sounds silly, but, you see, I like you most awfully. I haven't liked anybody so much for ever so long, except Alice, of course. I don't feel as though you were of another generation or anything; it's just as though we were the same age!'

Mr. Oddy was enchanted. He put his hand on the boy's for a moment and was going to say something, when they were interrupted by a knock on the door, and the terrible-looking landlady appeared in the room. She apologised, but the afternoon post had come and she thought the young gentleman would like to see his letters. He took them, was about to put them down without opening them, when suddenly he blushed. 'Oh, from Alice,' he said. 'Will you forgive me a moment?'

'Of course,' said Mr. Oddy.

The boy opened the letter and read it. It fell from his hand on to the table. He got up gropingly as though he could not see his way, and went to the window and stood there with his back to the room. There was a long silence.

'Not bad news, I hope,' said Mr. Oddy at last.

Tommy turned round. His face was grey and he was biting his lips. 'Yes,' he answered, 'she's—gone off.'

'Gone off?' said Mr. Oddy, rising from the table.

'Yes,' said Tommy, 'with Russell. They were married at a register office this morning.'

He half turned round to the window, put out his hands as though he would shield himself from some blow, then crumpled up into a chair, his head falling between his arms on the table.

Mr. Oddy waited. At last he said: 'Oh, I'm sorry: that's dreadful for you!'

The boy struggled, trying to raise his head and speak, but the words would not come. Mr. Oddy went behind him and put his hands on his shoulders.

'You know,' he said, 'you mustn't mind me. Of course, I'll go if you like, but if you could think of me for a moment as your oldest friend, old enough to be your father, you know.'

Tommy clutched his sleeve, then, abandoning the struggle altogether, buried his head in Mr. Oddy's beautiful black waistcoat.

Later he poured his heart out. Alice was all that he had; he knew that he wasn't any good as a writer, he was a failure altogether; what he'd done he'd done for Alice, and now that she'd gone—

'Well, there's myself,' said Mr. Oddy. 'What I mean is that you're not without a friend; and as for writing, if you only write to please somebody else, that's no use; you've got to write because you can't help it. There are too many writers in the world already for you to dare to add to their number unless you're simply compelled to. But there— I'm preaching. If it's any comfort to you to know, I went through just this same experience myself once—the lady whose candle I watched behind the blind. If you cared to, would you come and have dinner with me tonight at my home? Only the two of us, you know; but don't if you'd rather be alone.'

Tommy, clutching Mr. Oddy's hand, said he would come.

About half-past seven that evening he had beaten up his pride.

44

Even in the depth of his misery he saw that they would never have got on together, he and Alice. He was quickly working himself into a fine state of hatred of the whole female race, and this helped him—he would be a bachelor all his days, a woman-hater; he would preserve a glorious independence. How much better this freedom than a houseful of children and a bagful of debts.

Only, as he walked to the address that Mr. Oddy had given him he held sharply away from him the memory of those hours that he had spent with Alice, those hours of their early friendship when the world had been so wonderful a place that it had seemed to be made entirely of golden sunlight. He felt that he was an old man indeed as he mounted the steps of Mr. Oddy's house.

It was a big house in Eaton Square. Mr. Oddy must be rich. He rang the bell, and a door was opened by a footman. He asked for Mr. Oddy.

The footman hesitated a little, and then, smiling, said: 'Oh yes, sir, will you come in?'

He left his coat in the hall, mounted a broad staircase, and then was shown into the finest library that he had ever seen. Books! Shelf upon shelf of books, and glorious books, *editions de luxe* and, as he could see with half an eye, rare first editions and those lovely bindings in white parchment and vellum that he so longed one day himself to possess. On the broad writing-table there was a large photograph of Meredith; it was signed in sprawling letters, 'George Meredith, 1887.' What could this mean? Mr. Oddy, who knew nothing about literature, had been given a photograph by George Meredith and had this wonderful library! He stared bewildered about him.

A door at the far end of the library opened and an elegant young man appeared. 'Mr. Galleon,' he said, 'will be with you in a moment. Won't you sit down?'

The Adventure of the Imaginative Child

Young Chippet and I had many funny times together. Out of many adventures that we had I have chosen this affair that I have called 'The Adventure of the Imaginative Child' because of the strange figure who is its centre. I cannot hope to give any satisfactory explanation of John Borstal Clay. I am only stating the case as I saw it. There is, perhaps, no explanation of anybody in this strange and casual world. I sometimes think that the Potter simply throws odd pieces of material together and then lets come out of it what will. It takes more than Dr. Freud to explain John Borstal Clay.

One day in the middle of spring, when the trees were budding and the very streets humming their pleasure under the April sun, a Mr. Henry Fortescue Bumpus paid me a call. I had had so many strange visitors within the last few weeks that it was rather comforting to see anybody so completely normal as Mr. Bumpus. He was one of those little men who wear their clothes like armour, who are so cleanly shaven, save for a neat moustache, that their cheeks gleam like billiard balls, who are right and tight in their person, upon whose bodies there is no speck of dust, and upon whose souls there is no sign of any abnormal curiosities.

Mr. Bumpus, it was plain to see, was a man entirely without imagination, fifty-odd years or so, kind in the English fashion, making, one must suppose, a satisfactory income, having ten minutes' Müller exercises in his bedroom of a morning before the open window, abusing gently each day at breakfast the socialistic tendencies of the Labour Party, calling, in all probability, his wife 'mother,' and arranging what he was going to do with himself and his family on Bank Holiday months and months before the event. Mr. Bumpus, in fact, is what is known as the backbone of England. It was all the more deplorable, therefore, to see that he was in a state of very considerable distress.

When something distresses a man of Mr. Bumpus' type, he is like a lost dog with a tin can tied to his tail. He has no idea where to go, to whom to speak—above all, he has no one in the world with whom he can be intimate. With his wife he has lived so long and so complacently that possible intimacy between them lies buried deep 'neath layers of domestic dust. The friends of his own sex are only on billiard, golf, or drinking terms, and his children he probably approaches in alternate gusts of anger and sentimentality, boxing their ears one day and giving them too many chocolates the other. He knows, deep, deep down, that the world is a rum place, but it is his natural tradition to set up around himself a kind of Crystal Palace hung with dark green blinds, and to sit inside it, and although he may feel the warmth of the sun beating upon the glass and sometimes hear torrents of rain like thunder on the roof, he cheats himself into believing that there is no world outside, or that, if there is, like Noah in his Ark, he has been forbidden to encounter it.

All this long explanation is necessary for my story.

Chippet was just then away, engaged upon some affair of his own. My friend Borden and I consoled Mr. Bumpus to the best of our abilities. He sat down, pulling his trousers a little above his knees, laying his plump hands upon them, and looking forward at us with a pathetic eagerness, rather as an infant bird in the nest opens its beak for an expected worm.

'You're very young, gentlemen,' was the first thing he said.

'We are not so young as we look,' I replied, smiling at him encouragingly. 'At any rate, tell us what we can do for you, Mr. Bumpus, and if it's beyond our youth, you can be sure of our discretion, and we will not, of course, charge you a penny.'

'Oh, that's all right, that's all right,' he answered nervously, 'that's really quite all right. Lovely weather today, isn't it?'

'Spring,' said Borden very solemnly, 'is upon us. It is the period of the year when youth is at its best. We take your coming to us on such a spring-like day as the best of omens.'

'Yes, yes, quite so,' said Mr. Bumpus, gazing desperately around the room, suffering all the agonising terror of one who must speak of intimate matters to a couple of strangers to whom he has really never been properly introduced.

'It was a Mrs. Fleming,' he began at last, 'who recommended me to ask your advice. She told me that a few months ago you helped her in a serious domestic difficulty. It is a domestic difficulty of my own about which I have come to speak to you, but really you are so young——' He broke off and ended with a rather foolish smile. 'I might be your father, you see.'

I saw that this was the moment to exert our authority. 'Excuse me for speaking plainly, Mr. Bumpus,' I replied, 'physical age has nothing to do with this matter at all. We may be able to help you or we may not. Tell us your trouble, and we will see what we can do.'

'Well, it seems so foolish,' said Mr. Bumpus, 'to come to anybody about such a matter as this, but Mother is nearly distracted. She loves her children, gentlemen, with a devotion I have never seen equalled elsewhere. Mrs. Bumpus is one in a million.'

'Is it about your children that you wish us to help you?' I asked.

'In a way, yes,' he answered nervously, and then, taking courage apparently from Borden's muscular and thoroughly British appearance, he plunged straight in.

'Some three years ago a brother of mine, who lived in South Africa, was killed with his wife in a railway accident. He was my favourite brother, and left an only child. This was a boy, then nine years of age and now twelve. My brother, in his will, as though he had a premonition that something might happen to him, left the boy to us in case of any disaster, with a very handsome sum of money for his upbringing. Mrs. Bumpus and I were proud and delighted to assume solemn charge. The boy arrived just three years ago this very month, and became, of course, as one of our own. It is about this boy that I wish to consult you.'

He coughed, looked at us piteously as though he were begging us to tell him that no further information was needed. That, of course, we were unable to do, and we could only look at him with an intelligent and kindly interest.

'The boy's name,' he continued, 'is John Borstal Clay.' He repeated these words over again as a sort of solemn incantation. 'He was a bright little fellow, nice-looking, intelligent, and amusing. We sent him to Dulwich School.' He paused, then, leaning forward toward us, repeated with the greatest solemnity: 'That boy, gentlemen, is wrecking our beautiful home life.'

'Dear me,' Borden remarked, 'so young a boy and so wicked?'

'Not wicked,' said Mr. Bumpus hurriedly. 'I don't want to say a word against the child.'

'You must tell us the truth, Mr. Bumpus,' I said. 'We cannot possibly help you unless you tell us everything.'

'But it is just that,' said Mr. Bumpus, 'that is so difficult to tell. The boy's not a wicked boy—at least, not in the accepted form of wickedness—he doesn't steal nor tell lies.' Then again, with the utmost solemnity: 'He is not a real boy, gentlemen, at all. Not like any other boy in the whole world. We are afraid of him—all of us—and when you've seen him you will know why.'

This was very interesting, and I saw Borden, who likes boys and thoroughly understands them, lean forward and watch Mr. Bumpus with renewed interest. 'Would you mind telling us,' he asked, 'about the rest of the family? How many children have you?'

'Three,' said Mr. Bumpus, 'Emmeline, Gertrude, and little Percival.'

'What ages are they?' asked Borden.

'Emmeline is thirteen and a half, Gertrude is twelve, and Percival eight.'

'And are they also in terror of your nephew?'

'They are indeed,' said Mr. Bumpus. 'And yet it is hard to say why they are. If it were simply a case of John's being unkind to them or ill-treating them, it would be comparatively simple. You see, gentlemen, I loved my brother dearly, and what Mrs. Bumpus and I wish, above all things, is to be just.'

'If the boy is upsetting your family,' said Borden, 'why don't you send him to a boarding-school?'

'We did, sir,' said Mr. Bumpus. 'He went away to school for a term, but we were almost more uncomfortable when he was away from us than we were when he was with us. What we want,' he cried, 'is for John's attention to be directed toward somebody else. We shall have no peace until he loses interest in us. That is where I want your help.'

'Loses interest in you?' asked Borden. 'That's a strange phrase to use about a small boy of twelve.'

'I know it is,' repeated Mr. Bumpus, almost in agony, 'but when you see the boy you will understand what I mean. He is extraordinarily old for his age, and he knows much more about all of us than any boy has a right to know. He is not a wholesome boy.'

'Do you mean that he is a nasty-minded boy?' asked Borden. 'Does he tell your children nasty stories and put wrong ideas into their heads?'

'No, not in the accepted way,' said Mr. Bumpus, 'and yet he does tell them stories, too. But no, I can't explain what I mean. You must come and see him for yourself.'

'Then what you want us to do,' I summed up, 'is to turn this boy's attention from yourselves into some other channel?'

'That's it,' said Mr. Bumpus. 'Oh, if you only would, how happy and grateful we'd all be!'

The conversation ended in our making an agreement with Mr. Bumpus on our usual terms, namely, that if we were successful he should pay us a certain sum, and if we failed, only half of that sum.

The very next day I took tea with the Bumpus family. They lived in West Kensington, and their house was as right and tight as little Mr. Bumpus himself. Mrs. Bumpus was a charming, stout, friendly woman, considerably older, I should imagine, than her husband, with hair turning grey, rosy cheeks, and a voice like a kettle on the hob.

John was not present when I arrived, but the three Bumpus children were all there. They were the quietest, demurest children you ever saw. Emmeline and Gertrude would be stout and rosy-faced like their mother. Little Percival was in a velvet Fauntleroy suit, and was doing something with a set of bricks in a corner of the drawing-room. They presented a very happy, domestic picture, all of them talking in low tones, Emmeline stitching away at a small piece of cambric, Gertrude, who wore spectacles, reading a book, the clock ticking, the windows open to let in the beautiful evening sun, Mrs. Bumpus being kind and smiling at Borden and myself as though she had known us for years.

We had been there, I suppose, some half-hour when John came in. He came in very quietly, closing the door behind him, shook hands with us, took his place near the tea-table in the properest manner possible. He was a short, thick-set boy with a strangely foreign appearance. This arose, I think, partly from his jet-black hair, his deep black eyes, fringed with heavy dark eyelashes, and a rather sallow complexion, in which there was, nevertheless, the colour of excellent health. I noticed at once his hands, which were remarkably clean for a boy of his age, with well-kept nails and thin, beautiful fingers. He moved with admirable grace, not at all with the clumsy awkwardness of a boy of his age, and yet he was a quite natural boy, not effeminate, nor mannered, nor artificial. He said very little. Borden, after a time, began to talk to him, asked him questions about his school, whether he liked football, and so on, and to all this he replied politely, completely at his ease.

I soon noticed, however, that the family were all strangely disturbed at his appearance. Percival seemed to be no longer happy with his bricks, and Emmeline and Gertrude glanced nervously toward the tea-table, and an air of constraint crept into the comfort and homeliness of the scene. After a while John got up and walked very quietly over to Percival, knelt down on the carpet, and began to help him to arrange his bricks. Once or twice Mr. Bumpus glanced at us to see whether we noticed anything peculiar. Conversation halted. We ourselves felt awkward and uncomfortable. We were about to get up and go, but suddenly a wail from Percival drew all our attention.

'I don't want them that way!' he cried. 'That's a nasty way. I was building a cathedral.'

'All right,' said John quietly. 'Let's build a cathedral, then.'

'But I want to build my own cathedral,' Percival wailed. 'I don't like your cathedrals.'

'Now, now, Percy darling,' said Mrs. Bumpus, getting up and going toward him, 'it's very kind of John to help you.'

'I don't want John to help me,' said Percival, getting up and suddenly bursting into a flood of tears.

'Well, then, I won't help you,' said John, smiling.

Then, seated as he was on the floor, he looked up at Mrs. Bumpus, and that glance was the first revelation I had of what might be disturbing the tranquillity of the Bumpus family. It was the oldest glance I have ever seen a child bestow upon another human being—a strange glance to see in that young and innocent face. It seemed to say: 'Well, and what are you going to do about it? I know you better than you know yourself, and I want to see, just for my own amusement, to what lengths of folly you are likely to go.'

There may have been, of course, some imagination on my part; after events, however, were to prove to me that I was not far wrong. Percival was led from the room. John got up and came across to us. Mr. Bumpus tried to cover the uneasy effect of this little incident by saying in an unnatural, jocular tone: 'Well, my boy, and how's the work been today?'

'All right, Uncle Henry, thank you,' said John quietly. He looked at him as though he were going to say something more, then gave Borden and myself the strangest glance of amused curiosity, and left the room. No further allusion to him was made during the rest of our visit.

★★★★★★

We have in these days the habit of discussing in learned terms and all the latest German technique the psychology of children. By this parents are influenced, and become morbidly anxious about the ethical state of their little ones; friends are perpetually bored by discoveries made by anxious mothers of the new tendencies in their darlings' little souls; the only beings entirely uninfluenced by this modern movement are the children themselves. Children form the only portion of the earth's population entirely untouched by the development of so-called civilisation. Children, like their elders, are cruel, malicious, mean, treacherous, tyrannous, greedy, remorseless, selfish, but, unlike their elders, they make no sort of pretence of pretending that these unpleasant emotions are anything but what they are.

Ask a cherub of twelve and a half what during last term he did to another cherub aged nine and a half, and if he discovers that you are to be trusted, he will show you that the head-hunters of Borneo are not in it with him for the frank indulgence of cheerful cruelty. But, more than that, small boys live so entirely in a world of their own that we cannot begin to realise what they are really doing and thinking unless we become small boys ourselves, and we do not become small boys by sitting neatly dressed in amiable drawing-rooms and talking in dulcet tones to charming old aunts, but rather by going out boldly into the boy world, stealing all we can see, eating everything we can lay hands upon, being as cruel as possible to everybody weaker than ourselves, and allowing ourselves to be torn into very small pieces rather than betray a fragment of the truth about some friend whose possessions we would instantly lay hold upon had we a moment's opportunity.

There are some men and a few women who are often praised for 'never growing up'; these remain among the nastiest and most dangerous of their kind. On the other hand, there are some boys who grow up at once and are a great deal older than their elders. It was at first this that I supposed had happened to John Borstal Clay.

'He's simply,' I told myself, 'been living with grown-up people and is old before his time. The Bumpuses, on the other hand, are younger than they've any right to be, because they've allowed their imagination to die a natural death, and have developed such a strain of English prudery that they are quite incapable of seeing what's in front of their noses.'

For a week or two this explanation sufficed me. Borden and I, in the arrogance of our young hearts, agreed that it would be very easy to detach the youthful John's mind from the Bumpus family and to fix it upon something or someone else, even, if need be, upon ourselves. I suppose that there's no one in the world who dislikes boys of John's age more thoroughly than I do myself, but John was an exception. He had none of the noisy, greedy, unattractive habits of his kind. He did not interrupt his elders when they had just reached what they considered the earth-compelling portion of their narrative. He did not beg for food that would, he knew, be denied him unless he made a terrible noise. He was not uncleanly in ways that I need not more minutely define, and he watched life with a curiosity that was quite astonishing.

It was this last quality in him that gradually absorbed my attention. Nothing seemed to escape him. I soon saw that there was no foolishness or weakness in the Bumpus family that he had not observed, and from that I began to see why it was they were so anxious to be rid of him. We can support with comparative ease those friends of ours who realise only the weaknesses that we have not got, but so soon as anyone puts his finger upon even the tiniest of our real faults, we begin to dislike him and think that we had better have somebody kinder in his place.

John knew perfectly well that Emmeline was cultivating, as fast as she could, all the domestic virtues because she was lazy, and found that those same virtues brought in the quickest and most tangible rewards. She lived, so to speak, for aunts, uncles, cousins, and elderly friends. She ran messages, spoke in sweet tones, and loved to group herself at the feet of some short-sighted relative and lay her head against that relative's knee and look ecstatically comfortable. John knew that she was not comfortable, and if that particular relation did not speedily produce something in the way of a gift or an invitation, Emmeline grouped herself elsewhere.

Gertrude, on the other hand, was all for aestheticism. What she wanted to be was strange and peculiar, so that people coming to tea said to Mrs. Bumpus: 'That's an original child you've got there; she should do something when she grows up.' So, Gertrude was learning the piano in a quite excruciating fashion, was ready to recite *We are Seven* and *The Wreck of the Hesperus* on the slightest invitation, and very often on no invitation at all, and loved to sit on a small stool in the very middle of the drawing-room floor, staring in front of her, gazing into nothing. Little Percival was the only one of the family who pursued his gentle way without artificiality, but in his case, you could not but wish for a little affectation, his natural habits, manners, and customs being of the noisiest, most provocative kind.

Mrs. Bumpus was a sweet woman, with the intelligence of a very kind sheep. She just managed to get through the duties of the day without any actual disaster. These duties left her but little time for the development of her brain; she liked novels and read, on an average, one new one a day. She had never the slightest idea of the names of the authors of these novels, and had been known to read the same book three days after an earlier perusal without the slightest notion that she had ever met it before. She was, however, a very good woman, being far too stupid to be anything else. Mr. Bumpus adored her, not so much because she was good or sweet or kind, but because she was so stupid that he had no fear of anyone thinking her cleverer than himself.

Now, all these things John perfectly knew, and I soon perceived that he played with these qualities and defects, not apparently with any malicious intent, but only because he was so anxious to see what, in the circumstances, they would do. He would, for instance, ask Mrs. Bumpus very quietly where she thought Uruguay was. She would probably say hurriedly: 'Why, in Africa, dear.' He would say, 'Thank you,' very quietly, and then, days later, when relations and friends were gathered together, he would remark, still more quietly: 'Uruguay isn't in Africa, auntie—I looked it up in my atlas.'

Mrs. Bumpus was always terribly upset at any exposure of non-intelligence, it being her theory, studiously developed through many years, that she knew just as much about anything as a good woman had any right to know. Mr. Bumpus also was distressed, and would look at with surprise, saying: 'Why, surely, mother, you didn't say that Uruguay was in Africa, did you?' She would then be all in a flutter, and her eyes would fill with those large, warm tears that seemed to contain some composition of grease in them, so heavy and thick and slow were they.

With Emmeline, John had a glorious time, taking pleasure, but not a malicious pleasure, in betraying her to aunts and uncles and any others likely to be too easily captivated.

When Emmeline was nicely seated upon a cushion on the floor, her flaxen head resting against a bony knee, uttering in a soft dreamy voice, 'And now, auntie, please tell me what you were like as a little girl,' John would look at her with such a curious, inquisitive smile that the aunt, too, would wonder whether all were well, and instead of the natural impulse to burst into sentimental reminiscence there would come forth a rather snappy: 'Not now, child. After all, there can be very little about my youth that anyone would want to know.'

Also, when John was alone with Emmeline, he would say softly:

'Emmy, Uncle George is coming tomorrow; he is good for a box of chocolates, but not more than that. I shouldn't bother about him.' And Emmeline, who cheated herself, as we all do, into believing that she invariably acted from the purest and most beautiful motives, would get one of those nasty little glimpses into reality which kind friends in a temper sometimes give us, which are, indeed, almost the only link with reality that we have.

I need not emphasise this further. It will now be seen by anybody who is interested in the Bumpuses why they wanted to get rid of John.

At the end of the first fortnight I decided that I must get to know John better, and I asked Mr. Bumpus if he would have any objection to John's coming to spend a night with me in my little house in Westminster. Mr. Bumpus was delighted. 'I do hope,' he explained, 'that you don't think that we wish to be unkind to the child; it's simply that—that—well, to put it frankly, that he upsets the tempers of my wife and the children.'

'Yes, I understand that,' I answered, 'but what is still a puzzle to me is that you tell me that he upsets you as much when he's away from you as when he's with you. That, I confess, is a mystery to me.'

'It's a mystery to me, too,' said Mr. Bumpus. 'I think it's a little this way—that we feel as though he always had us in his mind and was thinking the worst of us. Not exactly that he dislikes us, you know, but if I may put it personally, suppose I'm dressing in the morning, and lose my collar-stud and go down on my knees after it, and am, just for the moment, in the condition that—well, you know what a man's like when he loses a collar-stud.'

'I do,' I assured him.

'Well, I feel as though John had watched me, even though he's as far away as Bilton, and ten to one I get a letter from him the next day with something in it that seems to me to hint ever so slightly at that very incident. Now, you'll say that's absurd. I dare say I'm over-sensitive about John—I think we all are—but it would have astonished you to have seen the numbers of letters that John liked to write while he was at Bilton. Boys of his age don't like writing letters, you know, but he seemed to enjoy it, and every letter made one a little uncomfortable some way. Now, all we want is for him to fix his attention upon somebody else. It really is most uncomfortable, feeling that a boy of his age is watching you all the time, and regards you rather like animals in the Zoo. Mrs. Bumpus doesn't like it, and although she wouldn't say an unkind word about the boy, and, indeed, never says an unkind word about anybody, still, she isn't comfortable when he's in the house, nor, for that matter, when he's out of it, and it's for her sake, more than my own, that I have asked your assistance.'

★★★★★★

That was a strange night when John came to stay. I shall never forget it. I lived in an old house in Westminster, just off Barton Street, under the very shadow of the Abbey—one of those old houses with crooked staircases, low-ceilinged rooms, and boards that creak at every step.

John arrived in time for an early dinner, and we went off to the pantomime at the Hippodrome, which that year had lasted from Christmas almost until Easter. I need have had no fear as to the reality of John's youth. It did one's heart good to see that little figure rocking about in his seat, laughing and shouting and crowing with that peculiar cockerel noise made by small boys when they're very happy. Nellie Wallace had only to appear for him to go into ecstasies, and when Lupino Lane vanished in and out of his numerous trapdoors, John was doubled and twisted with delight. Walking home afterward, as he said he preferred to do, he remained pure boy. 'Do you think,' he asked me, in that funny, hoarse voice of his, 'that Miss Wallace is really like that at home? Is she as ugly, do you think?'

'No,' I said, 'she's probably very beautiful. She is one of the few women in the world whom it pays to pretend to be as ugly as possible.'

'If she was more ugly still,' asked John, 'would she get more money?'

'Probably,' I answered.

'And if she was more ugly than that?' asked John.

I saw that there was no end to the heights and involutions of this enquiry, so I changed it to another one.

'Did you like the princess?' I asked him.

'Oh, yes,' he answered. 'She's the one I've seen the advertisements about, with all her teeth in a row. Don't you think it's a pity,' he continued, 'that when anybody is going to be a princess in the evening, she should be an advertisement in the daytime?'

'I really haven't thought about it,' I answered. 'It's very difficult for anybody to be a princess all the time.'

'Why?' asked John.

'Oh, I don't know,' I said; 'it's very exhausting.'

'Why?' asked John.

'Because you have to sit still, and be very proper, and dressed in your best.'

'Why?' asked John.

I am glad to say that at that moment we arrived at my Westminster home.

Now, as soon as we entered my old house and found our way up the dark staircase, John became another person. I cannot describe it better than by saying he was like a dog who sniffs a good smell somewhere close at hand. He did literally go round my sitting-room sniffing at the walls. He poked his small nose into every possible corner, and suddenly, to my amazement, flopped down on the floor and laid his ear to one of the boards.

'Good Heavens!' I said. 'What are you doing?'

'It's funny,' he answered, getting up slowly, not in the least disturbed. 'It's old. It's been here hundreds of years. Lots of things have happened in this room.'

'Yes,' I said, 'they have.'

'Nothing's ever happened in Uncle Henry's house,' he said. 'Not to Aunt Mary, nor Emmy, nor Gertrude, nor Percival. I hate Percival,' he added reminiscently.

He stood in a funny little way against the hearth, as though he were trying to balance himself on a rocking floor. 'I like you,' he said, smiling. 'Do you think it's wrong not to like Uncle Henry and the others? Because I don't like any of them.'

'No, I don't know that it's wrong,' I answered. 'If you don't like them, you had better go away and live with somebody else. With me, for instance.'

'Oh, no,' he answered. 'It's fun living with them. I can make them ratty in no time.'

'Well, it isn't right,' I said, 'to like making people uncomfortable who've been good to you.'

'They've only been good to me,' he said, 'because they'd be uncomfortable if they weren't.'

'Good Heavens!' I exclaimed. 'How old are you?'

'I'm twelve and a half,' he said, 'by years, but do you ever have that funny feeling, Mr. Johnson, as though you'd been a lot older really, and seen everything before, and knew just what was coming next?'

'I have known that,' I answered, speaking to him, in spite of myself, exactly as though he were my age, 'once or twice at moments, but only for a moment.'

'Well, I know it often,' he said. 'At school there's a master who's got a bad leg and he goes limping around. Well, I know I've seen him limping somewhere else a long while ago, and he was all in red and green.'

'Red and green?' I said.

'Yes,' said John, laughing just as he had laughed at Nellie Wallace, 'and it was so funny. He was a man everybody laughed at, and that's what he was there for, and he hit people on the head with a balloon.'

I was beginning to feel uncomfortable.

'Well, we won't talk about that now,' I said. 'Only look here, you mustn't do things that make your aunt and uncle unhappy. They've been kind to you, after all.'

'I don't want to make them unhappy,' he said, 'but they're so silly, and if you know that if you do something somebody else'll do something, and then you'll do something again, it's awfully jolly to make them do something.' After which explanation I took him down to the little dining-room and gave him something to eat. In the middle of supper, I said:

'You know, John, I oughtn't to be giving you supper. Little boys oughtn't to have supper just before they go to bed.'

'Why?' he asked.

'Because it makes them dream and talk in their sleep.'

'Oh, I always dream,' he said, 'every night. Last night I dreamt that Aunt Mary was a cow, a large, white cow with flowers on her head. It was a funny thing, but I was sorry for her last night. I'm never sorry for her in the daytime. But the one I really hate,' he added, becoming confidential, 'is Emmeline. Isn't it a silly name—Emmeline?'

'Yes,' I said, 'it is rather.'

'I sometimes feel,' he said, 'that I'd like to get Emmy into a corner and twist her hair round and round and round. She's a sucker-up.'

'Most girls are,' I answered.

'Why?' said John.

'Well, because they're not so strong and they can't hit back.'

'No, but they can pinch and bite,' said John. 'Emmy does when you're not looking.'

'And why,' I asked, 'do you write them so many letters when you're away? Most boys don't like writing letters.'

'It's such fun sometimes,' he answered, 'to write something that you know they won't expect. It's just as though I were at home with them and saw everything that they were doing.'

'If you didn't think of them anymore,' I said, 'and thought of someone else, wouldn't it be a bit of a change for you!'

'You see,' he answered very seriously, as though he were sixty years old, 'I like to have somebody to think about and to do things with— like playing draughts, you know.'

I took him up to bed and put him into a small dressing-room next to mine. He asked questions through the open door all the time he was undressing. 'I say, isn't this fun?' he called out. 'Is Miss Wallace married?' And then, 'Are you married? Have you got any children? Do you go to the theatre every night? I saw *Charley's Aunt* once. I like Nellie Wallace better. Don't you think it's a shame when you don't like cricket that you have to play? Have you got a boiler in your bath? We have at Uncle Henry's. Do you wear a nightshirt or pyjamas? Is this the first time you've ever had a boy in your house? Do you know all Aunt Mary's hair isn't real, and she can take some of it out when she likes?'

To all of which questions I attempted suitable answers. I had just put on my pyjamas, and was going to see him safely into bed, when he appeared in the doorway quite naked, and, with the most enchanting smile on his face, cried, 'Mr. Johnson, can you do this?' and was suddenly down on his hands, and started walking, feet in air, across my room. Midway he paused and, with a most amazing little chuckle, began to turn somersaults round and round and round.

I've always done my best to curb my too tempting imagination, and I intend in this case strictly to tell the truth, but something extraordinary occurred in that room as that little naked figure went tumbling from side to side. It was as though a light flashed through the air, the kind of reflection that a piece of glass, turned in the hand, throws upon the wall. He was not distinguishable as a human body. He was rather a piece of colour transmuting the whole place, as though, had I turned off the electric light, the beam would have passed glittering, now here, now there, objects in the room starting from the shadows as he touched them—strangest and most incommunicable of sensations, bringing me back, it seemed, to something that I had once known, promising me some future confirmation of something for which I had always hoped. I sat staring, scarcely venturing to breathe, lest the enchantment should break.

He stopped; with a kind of jerk he was on his feet in the middle of the floor, an ordinary naked smiling little boy. 'You can't do that, I bet, Mr. Johnson,' he said.

'No,' I replied, 'I'm much too old.'

'I'll never be too old,' he answered. He came across to me, held out his small and now very grubby hand, and with an air of infinite age and generations-past courtesy, said: 'Now I think I'll go to bed. I've enjoyed my evening very much.' And to his room he went......

★★★★★★

One of the most tiresome of Chippet's many tiresome relations was the old Dowager Countess of Pruxe. She was tiresome in all sorts of ways, one of them being that she had lived beyond her time, having had an elder sister who had been danced on Byron's knee (the only drawback to this story was the doubt, natural to any literary mind, as to whether Byron had ever dandled anyone under twenty on his knee). She was more inquisitive by nature than anyone else of her own sex in the British Isles. She was uglier than any human being had any right to be, and she was a bully. No one knew what her age was. She was a very distant cousin indeed of Chippet, but whether it was that she had nothing else to do, or that she really had taken a kind of liking to him, whatever her mysterious reasons might have been, she continued to come of a morning into our little office, sit upright on one of our smallest chairs, looking like an angry, over-painted cockatoo with an enormous Roman nose, and ask us all sorts of questions about our business and private affairs that she had, of course, no right to ask at all.

The trouble with her, Chippet said, was that she had too much imagination. We would have rid ourselves of her cantankerous company in no time at all had it not been that we dared not challenge her ever. Old though she was, she could be still a terrible enemy, and having no affection for the truth, and all the romantic anecdotage of very old age, she could ruin somebody's reputation in less time than it takes to poach an egg. She was marvellously vigorous, and always brought with her a miserable-looking, impoverished, pale-faced companion, who snored through her nose so disconcertingly that my only explanation of Lady Pruxe's engaging her was that she added to the general terror of the atmosphere and the old lady's dignity.

She came to the office the morning following John's visit to me, and, while she sat there, in her ugly, husky voice asked questions that Chippet did his best to avoid answering. She vaguely reminded me of someone. I looked at her again and again, but the connection would not come. Where had I seen somebody like her, or, at least, where had I heard that voice before, and who was it who took that curious, almost malicious interest in their fellow-beings' weaknesses? There was something, somebody.....

However, the increasing difficulty of the Bumpus case soon absorbed my attention again. I could see that the Bumpuses were beginning to regard us with suspicion, even as Mrs. Fleming had once done. Further than that, I could see that Bumpus himself disapproved of my liking for Johnny. I could not disguise that John was a million times more interesting to me than all the Bumpus children put together, and in the eyes of the Bumpus parents it became apparent that I was encouraging John in all his natural wickedness. Then with dramatic swiftness the crisis arrived. One night I was going to bed, and was standing at my bedroom window listening to the wind and the rain that came beating and howling up the little Westminster street and whirling away round the great walls of the Abbey, when my telephone bell rang. A moment later the trembling, agitated tones of Mr. Bumpus came through to me.

'Is that you, Mr. Johnson?'

'Yes,' I answered. 'What is it?'

'Is John with you?'

'John?' I said. 'No, why?'

'Oh, dear! I thought he might be, and Emmeline, too.'

'Emmeline?' I cried. 'What's she doing out at this time of night?'

'Oh, we don't know! We don't know!' wailed the voice at the other end. 'Would you mind coming round at once and helping us? We are in the greatest trouble.'

I detected in his voice the implication that I was considered largely responsible for the catastrophe. Of course, I hurried through the rain and arrived to find the Bumpus parents walking up and down their drawing-room literally wringing their hands and making unhappy little exclamations.

'Well, now, what is it?' I asked.

It was difficult at first to discover what it really was, but from the agitation that fell during the next quarter of an hour like a shower about my head, I discovered that John and Emmeline had slipped out of the house about half-past seven that evening, Mr. and Mrs. Bumpus being out at a dinner-party and the governess asleep over a novel. No one had discovered their absence until Mr. and Mrs. Bumpus, returning, went up to see whether they were quietly sleeping. They were not there. A maid in the house next door had seen them come out of the gate. After that there was no news.

During the whole of this, the look in the eyes of the poor little Bumpuses and the plaintive whine in their voices showed me that I was held entirely responsible for this horrible occurrence. What a night followed! All the policemen of London were out in the wind and rain. All the telephones were ringing in agitated convulsions, and by three in the morning I was held to be very little less than a murderer. By that time, I was myself so agitated, so wet in body and so exhausted in soul, that I had determined to give up the whole of our business, although now it was making such hopeful progress, and I was wishing that I had never thought so confidently to plunge into that most confused of all foreign countries, the psychology of one's fellow beings. Then as the clock struck four, and the tenth policeman was being offered a drink by the now tearful Mr. Bumpus, John quietly walked in, dragging with him a bedraggled, hysterical, dripping, but triumphant Emmeline.

Mrs. Bumpus, with a shriek of joy, threw her arms round the neck of her dripping daughter. An odd thing then occurred. Emmeline pushed her mother away, saying peevishly: 'Don't fuss me, mother. Can't you see I'm tired?'

John was not, of course, in the least perturbed. He seemed to be scarcely wet, his little overcoat, with its upturned collar, giving him a strangely grown-up appearance, his eyes watching us all with the same critical, amused, slightly scornful glance that by now I knew so well.

'Where have you been? Where have you been? Where have you been?' cried Mr. Bumpus, exactly like an excited clock striking the hour.

'We've been on Primrose Hill,' said John quietly.

'Glad to see it's all right, sir,' said the constable, finishing his whisky and preparing to depart.

'All right! All right!' cried little Bumpus, obviously now in a state of hysterics quite beyond his control. 'It's not all right—it's terrible!'

The constable looked a little confused. 'Well, if you want me in the morning, sir—' he said, and departed.

'Don't be so silly, father,' said Emmeline. 'John and I have had a wonderful time. We would have been back before, only we lost the way. There was a lovely old woman——'

But her father could do nothing but turn upon John. 'You're responsible for this!' he cried. 'Leading my daughter . . . . .'

'Not now, not now, dear,' interrupted Mrs. Bumpus. 'We're all so tired. I'm sure that we shall discuss it better in the morning.'

Next morning, at ten o'clock, I was summoned to a family conference. When I arrived, I found that I was, in the eyes of both Mr. and Mrs. Bumpus, the villain of the piece. It was still very uncertain what exactly Emmeline and John had done the night before. It appeared that John had tempted her with some story of meeting an old man on Primrose Hill who had bags of gold that he distributed for the asking. It seemed to me that it was very unlikely that Emmeline, a matter-of-fact child if ever there was one, would believe such a story as this, but more than anyone I've ever known, she was one who loved, beyond all else, the consciousness that she was getting something for nothing. John had had for a long time past a certain power over her, and I imagine that she was flattered by his so definitely pleading for her company. However, she went.

The interesting fact now about her was the fashion in which she returned. Already, so few hours after her adventure, it was plain she was entirely changed, or, rather, not changed, because no human being ever changes—simply this accident had brought to the surface qualities that no one had seen before. She was independent, scornful, and imaginative. She talked about a little man in a green cap, about three stars that had hit a tree, about the rain dancing in circles around a heap of stones, and about an old woman with a basket of apples who had offered her a silver bodkin.

'Bodkin?' cried her father, now terribly afraid his favourite daughter was completely out of her mind. 'There isn't such a thing.'

'That's what John said it was, father,' said Emmeline. 'He said he'd had one once just like it.'

'Well, where is it?' asked her father.

'The rain blew the old woman away,' said Emmeline. 'If I go out there another night, John says she's sure to give me one.'

After this, can it be doubted that the little Bumpus was in a frenzy of despair? He took me into his stuffy little study and there told me quite plainly what he thought of me.

'You come into this house,' he cried, 'with some cock-and-bull story about helping us in our trouble. You deliberately encourage the boy in all his worst faults, you help him to abduct my daughter and to turn her head crazy with mad fancies, and now I suppose you expect us to pay you seventy-five pounds and say "Goodbye, and thank you very much."'

'Not at all, Mr. Bumpus,' I answered. I will admit that I was feeling frightfully tired and dishevelled after my stormy night's experiences. 'If you want me to tell you what I think, it is that John has woken your daughter up to some semblance of real life, and if he is given time, he will wake the rest of your children. Give me another twenty-four hours, and I may yet succeed in my task.'

Poor little Bumpus could do nothing else. He was in despair. John might be removed, but how would that help matters? His influence over the family would be as strong as ever. Poor little Percival would be the next to be corrupted. Wake up all their imaginations, and Heaven knew what might happen. Why, even Mrs. Bumpus . . . . . And at this thought he burst suddenly into tears and sobbed like a child.

'I don't know what's happening!' he cried. 'The world used to be such a straightforward place.' You knew where you were, and things were either right or they weren't. The people, too. Now everything was upside down, and nobody was shocked any longer. If he lost his children, he didn't know what he'd do, and if they weren't going to respect him, then he had lost them, and so on and so on. He ended by turning upon me.

'I daresay to you, Mr. Johnson,' he said, 'this all seems very funny. You're one of this new generation who don't believe in God, and think the only thing to do is just what you want to do; but you're corrupting the young, and I tell you the next generation will have to pay for the sins of this one.'

'Excuse me, Mr. Bumpus,' I answered, with all the dignity I could, 'you didn't engage me to come here and talk morals and modern sociology. I daresay you're perfectly right in what you say. My business is to remove John's attention from your family, and if I don't succeed within the next twenty-four hours, I will admit myself beaten, and make no further demands upon either your time or your purse.'

I left him with all the dignity I could command, but it was all very well—I had not at that moment the slightest idea of how I was going to win my case. I felt a beaten man, and I tell you that I was pretty miserable and conscience-stricken over the whole affair. When I had gone a little way down the street, I heard someone running after me, and was caught up by John. He informed me that they were all so foolish that morning, and that it was too late to go to school, and that therefore he would accompany me to my office for an hour or two. I tried to get from him the explanation of last night's adventure.

'Well, you see,' he said, 'I've been wondering for a long time whether I couldn't do something with Emmeline, and suddenly it occurred to me that if I took her out in all the rain and lost her, it would be funny to see what she'd be like afterward.'

'That was very wrong, John,' I said.

'Why?' he asked.

'It's always very wrong,' I went on, 'to make people unhappy just for your own pleasure.'

'Why?' he asked.

'Well, of course it is,' I continued. 'What we're here for is to make people happy, not unhappy.'

'Who said so?' he asked.

'You want people to make you happy, don't you?' I asked.

'I don't care what they do,' he answered. 'I can be happy or unhappy all by myself.'

'But don't you mind what other people do or say?' I asked him.

'Why should I?' he asked.

'Other people can make you feel all sorts of things.'

'Why?' he asked.

'Well, because they're so close to you, and we're all mixed up together.'

'I'm not mixed up with anybody,' he answered. 'I just wanted to see what Emmeline would do, and what Uncle Henry would do, and what the policeman would do, and what you'd do. I haven't finished,' he ended, with a chuckle, 'seeing what Uncle Henry will do. I'm sure he'll do something silly. Emmeline's not so bad,' he added reflectively. 'If you tell her stories, she believes them.'

I will frankly admit that I was in despair when we entered the office. I was beginning, ever so slightly, to understand, in my own experience, why the Bumpuses were so anxious to be rid of John. I was beginning to wonder how long it would be before I myself would yearn to escape from that curious, inquisitive, sarcastic glance.

We entered the office and therein found Chippet, very bored indeed, and his distant cousin, Lady Pruxe.

'Good morning, Mr. Johnson,' she said, and as soon as she spoke I realised where it was that I had already heard that odd, husky voice. Other realisations were achieved at that same moment.

John gave a little gasp, and stood in the middle of the floor, staring. The old woman looked down from her chair and stared in return.

'Who's that strange boy?' she asked.

'A little friend of mine,' I answered, 'come in to pay us a visit.'

From that moment, you may believe it or no, as you please, the two never removed their eyes from each other's face.

'Come here, boy,' the old woman commanded.

John came over to her.

'What's your name?' she asked.

'John Borstal Clay,' he told her.

'Where have I seen you before?' she asked.

He shook his head.

'What do you wear all that jewellery for in the daytime?' he asked.

'Because I like to,' she replied.

'Why?' asked John.

'Because they're pretty,' she answered. He looked at her with that funny sarcastic glance of his, but this time there was something in his smile that I had never seen before, something of recognition, of acclaiming that at last he had found someone worthy of his companionship.

'Feel as though I'd seen you somewhere before,' she said slowly. But he was looking at the rings on her fingers.

'I know that green one,' he said, pointing, 'only I don't know where . . . . .' He shook his head. 'Somewhere, a long time ago.'

She looked at him queerly. 'That was given me by my husband,' she said slowly, 'sixty-three years ago, and it was in his family——' She broke off.

'You're a queer little boy,' she said. 'Will you come back to my house and have lunch with me?'

'Yes,' he answered. 'Have you got peacocks in your house?'

'No.'

'Why not?'

'We have peacocks in the country, not in London.'

'Why?'

'Oh, because they like to move about, and they make such a noise.'

'I like you,' he said, nodding his head confidently. 'You're more clever than the others.' Then he turned and saw the pale companion. I watched creep into his eyes just the expression, the malicious, inquisitive, humorous, sporting expression that I had once seen as he watched Emmeline, Gertrude, and little Percival, and I knew that he had found a new occupation. . . . . .

John Borstal Clay has taken up his permanent residence in the enormous gloomy house in Portland Place owned by the Dowager Countess of Pruxe. The old lady has already had four different companions during the three months of his stay there. She herself declares that she has a new joy in life. Many weeks ago, Mr. Bumpus paid the firm of Boniface and Company a cheque for one hundred and fifty pounds and wrote a little note expressing in the warmest terms his appreciation of our efforts on his behalf.

Seashore Macabre. A Moment's Experience

We had gone to our usual summer residence, a farm perched on the steep hill above Gosforth—Gosforth in Cumberland, where the Druid Cross is in the graveyard, so that foreigners come from the far ends of the earth to see it. For the rest the farm was hay and chickens' eggs, and wallflowers in hot dusty clusters under the narrow garden-wall, and the ducks walking into the kitchen, and Mrs. A—, the friendly, soft-hearted and deeply pessimistic farmer's wife, making cakes, hot and spicy, in the cavernous black oven.

But this incident, so clearly and sharply remembered, so symbolic, Mr. Freud perhaps would tell me, of all my older life, has nothing to do with the farm, except that it starts from there. It starts from there because on fine days we bicycled three miles into Seascale.

Seascale was the nearest seaside resort. It looked then as though one day it might become a true resort. It had long, lazy sands, a new golf course, a fine hotel, and there were little roads and lanes in and about that looked as though, with the slightest encouragement, they might become quite busy shop-haunted streets. Nevertheless, little roads and lanes now after thirty years they still are. Seascale has never taken that step upward into commercial prosperity that once perhaps was hoped for it. I myself am glad that it has not. It is the one place of my childhood that is not altered. The flat, passive sands are damp and wind-blown as they always were, the little station—sticky in the warm weather with a sort of sandy grit, damp in the wet weather like a soaked matchbox—stands just as it always did, as though with a rather stupid finger to its lip it were wondering whether it should go or stay.

No, not on the face of it a romantic place, Seascale—and yet to myself one of the romantic places of the world!

We bicycled—my father, my sister and I—while my mother and small brother were driven the three miles in a pony-trap. Then, if the weather permitted us, we spent the day on Seascale sands. We bathed in water that had always a chill on it quite special to itself, we ate ham sandwiches, hard-boiled eggs and gingerbreads under the shelter of the one small rock that the beach possessed (if that rock were not already occupied), and we read—my mother and father *The Egoist;* I—if priggish—*Le Rouge et le Noir,* if unpriggish, *Saracinesca.*

Now it happened that one day in the week was specially glorious to me; this was the day of my weekly pocket-money, threepence the amount, if not already owed for reasons of discipline, sin or back-answering. Now it also occurred that on the same day that I received my pocket-money was published the new number of a paper, yet I believe (and hope) in a flourishing condition—*The Weekly Telegraph.*

The *Weekly Telegraph* was my love and my dear, it cost, I think, only a penny. Its dry and rather yellow-tinted sheets (smelling of straw, liquorice and gunpowder, I fancy in reminiscence) held an extraordinary amount of matter, and especially they held the romantic short stories of Robert Murray Gilchrist, the serial narratives of young Mr. Phillips Oppenheim, and even, best of all as I remember it, *The Worldlings,* by Mr. Leonard Merrick. There were also 'Country Notes,' tinged deeply with Cumberland sights and sounds, jests, quips and oddities, ways of cleaning knives and forks, making pillow-slips and curing a child of the croup.

What I suppose I am trying to emphasise is the contrast of these happy simplicities with—well, reader (as Charlotte Brontë always said), be patient and you shall hear!

You can see me, small, spindle-shanked and wind-blown, while my family sat huddled beneath the one Seascale rock, struggling through the spidery sand to the little station, my threepenny piece damply clutched. It was, as I remember it, a day of bright, glittering sun and a high wind. I am at least certain of a general glitter in the heavens and fragments of burning sand about my eyes.

I fought my way up the slope, sand in my shoes, sand in my eyes, sand in my throat. I stood on the higher ground, rubbed the sand from my eyes and looked back to the distant plum-coloured hills where the Screes run down sheer to Wastwater and Gable rolls his shoulder. Then into the little station that burnt in the sun so that its paint sizzled. I asked for *The Weekly Telegraph.* I cannot remember what he was like who gave it to me, but I do know that I did not take two steps before I had opened the paper to see whether there were a Gilchrist 'Peakland' story, all about My Lady Swarthmore and tinkling spinets and a room darkly hung with tapestries, and some fair child working a picture in delicate silks. Yes, there it was! The horn was blowing through Elfland, the long slow sands below me were lit with mother-of-pearl, and there were mermaids near the shore. Mr. Oppenheim was also there—*A Prince of Swindlers*, Chap. XVII. 'As he walked down the steps of the Hôtel Splendide, wondering whether he should try his luck at the Tables or no, Prince Serge . . .' I drew a deep breath of satisfaction, took a step out of the station and almost collided with the wickedest human being it has ever been my luck to behold. Now, wicked human beings are rare! I have, I think, never beheld another. The majority of us are fools with or without a little knavery. This old man was, although, as you will see, I never exchanged a word with him, really wicked—capable, I am sure, of real, fine, motiveless villainy like Iago.

He was a little man, bent in the back, wearing a rather floppy black hat and carrying an umbrella. He had, I remember, a sallow complexion, a hooked nose, and a wart on his chin. I say I remember, but indeed he is as vivid to me as though he were standing by my side at this moment—which in fact he may be for all I know to the contrary.

And now, how strange what followed! As I have said, I almost stumbled on him. He stood aside and looked at me, and *I* looked at him! His look as I recall it was cold, sneering and mean-faced. Then he turned on his heel and, waving his bulging umbrella in the air, walked down the road.

Why, of all things in the world, did I follow him? I cannot imagine. I was on the whole a timid child, a good deal of a coward. Moreover, I had in my hand my adored *Weekly Telegraph* and was longing to read in it. Nevertheless, I followed him. Looking back across all those years it seems to me that a cloud passed over the sun as we walked along, that the walls of the houses shone with a less brilliant reflection, that a chill creeping little wind began to wander. That is doubtless imagination. What is true is that the little man walked without making any sound upon the road. He was wearing, I suppose, shoes soled in felt or something of the kind. What is also true is that I was drawn after him as though I were led by a string.

Now I have said that I knew him to be wicked. How did I know? Was it only the idlest fancy? At that time, I had but a child's knowledge of the world, and wickedness was far from my experience. The nearest to wickedness that I had then reached perhaps was the sight of a schoolfellow who had pulled the wings from a fly, or the lustful anger in the eyes of a schoolmaster beating one of my companions. Well, this little old man with the umbrella had something of that about him. Cruelty and meanness? Are there any other sorts of wickedness? I am sure that this little man could be both cruel and mean.

Did he know that I was following him? He must have heard my step. He gave no sign. With his head forward, his back bent, waving his umbrella, so under the windy sun he pursued his way.

Beyond the little town we reached paths soft in sand and with stiff sea-grasses sprouting there. We approached the sea and I fancy that the wind increased in volume, began to blow a hurricane. My heart was beating with terror, a sort of sickly pleasure, an odd mixture of daring and foreboding.

The little man came to a cottage knee-deep in sand, on the very edge in fact of a dune that ran down to a sea where waves were flinging in a succession of fiery silver wheels. Although the sun shone so brilliantly, the cottage looked dark and chill. There was, as I remember it, no warmth here, and the wind tugged at my trouser-legs. The little man vanished into the cottage. Clutching my *Weekly Telegraph,* I followed. And then—how did I have the courage? What spell was laid upon me so that I did something utterly against my nature? Or was it that my true nature was for once permitted the light?

In any case I paused, my heart hammering the little cottage as still as a picture. Then—I turned the handle of the door and looked in.

What I saw was a decent-sized kitchen with a yawning black oven, dressers—but on them no plates; windows—but uncurtained. In a rocking-chair beside the fire sat an old man, the very spit of the old gentleman I had followed. The room was dark, for the windows were small; it was lit by candles and the candles were placed, two at one end of a trestle, two at another. And on the trestle, lay a corpse.

I had never until that moment seen a dead person. This figure lay wrapped in white clothes; a white bandage was round his chin; his cheeks were waxen and yellow. So, he lay. There was a silence, as there should be, of the grave itself. The corpse, as, with horror clutching my throat, I more persistently gazed, was that of an old man, the image again of the old boy with the umbrella, of the old boy in the chair. Nothing stirred. I could hear the solemn tick of a clock.

But, in my agitation, unknowing, I held the door open. A sudden gust of wind rushed past me, and instantly—most horrible of all my life's recollections!—everything sprang to life. The little man whom

I had followed appeared at the head of the kitchen-stairs and, in the most dreadful way, he pointed his umbrella as though condemning me to instant death. The little man in the chair sprang out of his sleep, and I shudder now when I remember his loose eye with its pendulous lid and an awful toneless grin as he stepped towards me. But worst of all was the way in which the thin silver hair of the corpse began to blow and his grave-clothes to flutter.

The room was filled with the wind. Sand came blowing in. Everything was on the move; it seemed to me that the yellow-faced corpse raised his hand . . .

Screaming, I ran for my life. Stumbling, falling, bruising my knees, tearing my hands against the spiky grass, I frantically escaped.

A moment's experience—yes, but Mr. Freud might say—a lifetime's consequence.

The Staircase

It doesn't matter in the least where this old house is. There were once many houses like it. Now there are very few.

It was born in 1540 (you can see the date of its birth over the lintel of the porch, cut into the stone). It is E-shaped with central porch and wings at each end. Its stone is now, in its present age, weathered to a beautiful colour of pearl-grey, purple-shadowed. This stone makes the house seem old, but it is not old; its heart and veins are strong and vigorous, only its clothes now are shabby.

It is a small house as Tudor manor-houses go, but its masonry is very solid, and it was created by a spirit who cared that it should have every grace of proportion and strength. The wings have angle buttresses, and the porch rises to twisted terminals; there are twisted terminals with cupola tops also upon the gables, and the chimneys too are twisted. The mullioned windows have arched heads, and the porch has a Tudor arch. The arch is an entrance to a little quadrangle, and there are rooms above and gables on either side. Here and there is rich carving very fancifully designed.

It is set upon a little hill, and the lawn runs down to a small formal garden with box-hedges mounted by animals fancifully cut, a sun-dial, a little stone temple. Fields spread on either side of it and are bordered completely by a green tangled wood. The trees climb skywards on every side, but they are not too close about the house. They are too friendly to it to hurt it in any way. Over the arched porch a very amiable gargoyle hangs his head. He has one eye closed and a protruding chin from which the rain drips on a wet day, and in the winter icicles hang from it.

All the country about the house is very English, and the villages have names like Croxton, Little Pudding, Big Pudding, Engleheart and Applewain. A stream runs at the end of the lower field, runs through the wood, under the road, by other fields, so far as Bonnet where it becomes a river and broadens under bridges at Peckwit, the country town.

The house is called Candil Place and is very proud of its name. Its history for the last hundred years has been very private and personal. No one save myself and the house knows the real crises of its history, just as no one knows the real crisis of your history save yourself. You have doubtless been often surprised that neighbours think that such and such events have been the dramatic changing moments in your life—as when you lost your wife or your money or had scarlet fever—when in reality it was the blowing of a window curtain, the buying of a ship in silver, or the cry of a child on the stair.

So, it has been with this house which has had its heart wrung by the breaking of a bough in the wind, a spark flying from the chimney, or a mouse scratching in the wainscot. From its birth it has had its own pride, its own reserve, its own consequence. Everything that has happened in it, every person who has come to it or gone from it, every song that has been sung in it, every oath sworn in it, every shout, every cry, every prayer, every yawn has found a place in its history.

Its heart has been always kindly, hospitable, generous; it has had as many intentions as we have all had, towards noble ends and fine charities. But life is not so easy as that.

Its first days were full of light and colour. Of course, it was always a small house; Sir Mortimer Candil, who helped to create it, loved it, and the house gave him its heart. The house knew that he did for it what he could with his means; the house suffered with him when his first wife died of the plague, rejoiced with him when he married again so beautiful a lady, suffered with him once more when the beautiful lady ran away to Spain with a rascal.

There is a little room, the Priest's Room, where Sir Mortimer shut himself in and cried, one long summer day, his heart away. When he came out of there he had no heart any more, and the house, the only witness of that scene, put its arms about him, loved him more dearly than it had ever done, and mourned him most bitterly when he died.

The house after that had a very especial tenderness for the Priest's Room, which was first hung with green tapestry, and then had dark panelling, and then was whitewashed, and then had a Morris wall-paper, and then discovered its dark panelling again, changing its clothes but never forgetting anything.

But the house was never a sentimental weakling. It was rather iron-

73

ic in spirit because of the human nature that it saw and the vanity of all human wishes.

As to this business of human wishes and desires, the house has never understood them, having a longer vision and a quieter, more tranquil heart. After the experience that it has had of these strange, pathetic, obstinate, impulsive, short-sighted beings it has decided, perhaps, that they are bent on self-ruin and seem to wish for that.

This has given the house an air of rather chuckling tenderness.

Considering such oddities, its chin in its hand and the wood gathering round to listen, whether there should be anything worth listening to (for the house when it likes is a good story-teller), the eye of its mind goes back to a number of puzzling incidents and, most puzzling of all, to the story of Edmund Candil and his lady Dorothy, the events of a close summer evening in 1815, the very day that the house and its inhabitants had the news of Waterloo.

Sir Edmund Candil was a very restless, travelling gentleman, and all the trouble began with that.

The house could never understand what pleasure he found in all these tiresome foreign tours that he prosecuted when there was the lovely English country for him to spend his days in. His wife Dorothy could not understand this either.

There was a kind of fated air about them from the moment of their marriage. The house noticed it on their very wedding-day, and the Priest's Room murmured to the Parlour: 'Here's an odd pair!' and the Staircase whispered to the little dark Hall with the family pictures: 'This doesn't look too well,' and the Powder-Closet repeated to the Yellow Bedroom: 'No, this doesn't look well at all.'

They had, of course, all known Edmund from his birth. He was a swarthy, broad-shouldered baby, unusually long in the leg, and from the very beginning he was known for his tender heart and his obstinate will. These two qualities made him very silent. His tender heart caused him to be afraid of giving himself away, his obstinate will made him close his mouth and jut out his chin so that nobody could possibly say that his resolve showed signs of weakening.

He had a sister Henrietta, who was the cause of all the later trouble. The house never from the beginning liked Henrietta. It considered that always she had been of a sly, mean, greedy disposition. There is nothing like a house for discovering whether people are mean or greedy. Chests of drawers, open fireplaces, chairs and tables, staircases and powder-closets, these are the wise recipients of impressions whose confidence and knowledge you can shake neither by lies nor arrogances.

The house was willing to grant that Henrietta loved her brother, but in a mean, grasping, greedy manner, and jealousy was her other name.

They were children of a late marriage and their parents died of the smallpox when Edmund was nineteen and Henrietta twenty-one. After that Henrietta ruled the house because Edmund was scarcely ever there, and the house disliked exceedingly her rule. This house was, as I have said, a loyal and faithful friend and servant of the Candil family. Some houses are always hostile to their owners, having a great unreasoning pride of their own and considering the persons who inhabit them altogether unworthy of their good fortune. But partly for the sake of Sir Mortimer, who had created and loved it, and partly because it was by nature kindly, and partly because it always hoped for the best, the house had always chosen only the finest traits in the Candil character and refused to look at any other.

But, if there is one thing that a house resents, it is to be shabbily and meanly treated. When a carpet is worn, a window rattling in the breeze, a pipe in rebellion, a chair on the wobble, the house does everything towards drawing the attention of its master. This house had been always wonderfully considerate of expense and the costliness of all repair. It knew that its masters were not men of great wealth and must go warily with their purposes, but, until Henrietta, the Candils had been generous within their powers. They had had a pride in the house which made them glad to be generous. Henrietta had no such pride. She persisted in what she called an 'adequate economy,' declaring that it was her duty to her brother who drove her, but as the house (who was never deceived about anything) very well knew, this so-called 'economy' became her god and to save money her sensual passion.

She grew into a long bony woman with a faint moustache on her upper lip and a strange, heavy, flat-footed way of walking. The Staircase, a little conceited perhaps because of its lovely banisters that were as delicate as lace, hated her tread and declared that she was so common that she could not be a Candil. Several times the Staircase tripped her up out of sheer maliciousness. The Store-room hated her more than did any other part of the house. Every morning she was there, skimping and cheese-paring, making this last and doing without that, wondering whether this were not too expensive and that too 'outrageous.' Of course, her maidservants would not stay with her. She found it cheapest to engage little charity-girls, and when she had them she starved them. It is true that she also starved herself, but that was no virtue; the house would see the little charity-girls crying from sheer hunger in their beds, and its heart would ache for them.

This was of course to some degree different when Edmund came home from his travels, but not very different, because he was always considerably under his sister's influence. He was soft-hearted and she was hard, and, as the house very well knew, the hard ones always win.

Henrietta loved her brother, but she was also afraid of him. She was very proud of him but yet more proud of her domination over him. When he was thirty and she thirty-two she was convinced that he would never marry. It had been once her terror that he should, and she would lie awake thinking one moment of the household accounts and the next of wicked girls who might entrap her brother. But it seemed that he was never in love; he returned from every travel as virgin as before.

She said to him one morning, smiling her rather grim smile: 'Well, brother, you are a bachelor for life, I think.'

It was then that he told her that he was shortly to marry Miss Dorothy Preston of Cathwick Hall.

He spoke very quietly, but, as the armchair in the Adam Room noticed, he was not quite at his ease. They were speaking in the Adam Room at the time, and this armchair had only recently been purchased by Edmund Candil. The room was not known then as the Adam Room (it had that title later) but it was the room of Edmund's heart. The fireplace was in the Adam style and so were the ceiling, and the furniture, the chairs, the table, the sofa, the commode Edmund had had made for him in London.

Very lovely they were, of satin-wood and mahogany, with their general effect of straight line but modified by lovely curves, delicate and shining. In the centre of the commode was a painted vase of flowers, on the ceiling a heavenly tracing of shell-like circles. Everywhere grace and strength and the harmony of perfect workmanship.

This room was for Edmund the heart of England, and he would stand in it, his dark eyes glowing, fingering his stock, slapping his tight thigh with his riding-whip, a glory at his heart. Many things he had brought with him from foreign countries. There was the Chinese room, and the little dining-room was decorated with Italian pictures. In his own room that he called the Library there was an ink-horn that had been (they said) Mirabeau's, a letter of Marie Antoinette's, a yellow lock cut from the hair of a mermaid and some of the feathers from the head-dress of an African chieftain. Many more treasures than these. But it was the Parlour with the fine furniture bought by him in London that was England, and it was of this room that he thought when he was tossing on the Bay of Biscay or studying pictures in Florence or watching the ablutions of natives in the Sacred River.

It was in this room that he told his sister that he intended marriage. She made no protest. She knew well enough when her brother's mind was made up. But it was a sunny morning when he told her, and as the sun, having embraced merrily the box-hedge peacocks and griffins, looked in to wish good-morning to the sofa and the round shining satin-wood table that balanced itself so beautifully on its slim delicate legs, it could tell that the table and chairs were delighted about something.

'What is it?' said the sun, rubbing its chin on the window-sill.

'There's a new mistress coming,' said the table and chairs.

And, when she came, they all fell at once in love with her. Was there ever anyone so charming and delicate in her primrose-coloured gown, her pretty straw bonnet and the grey silk scarf about her shoulders? Was there ever anyone so charming?

Of course, Henrietta did not think so. This is an old story, this one of the family relations greeting so suspiciously the new young bride, but it is always actual enough in its tragedy and heartbreak however often it may have happened before.

Is it sentimental to be sorry because the new Lady Candil was sad and lonely and cried softly for hours at night while her husband slept beside her? At that time at least, the house did not think so. Possibly by now it has grown more cynical. It cannot, any more than the humans who inhabit it, altogether be unaware of the feeling and colour of its time.

In any case the house loved Dorothy Candil and was deeply grieved at her trouble. That trouble was, one must realise, partly of her own making.

Her husband loved her, nay, he adored her with all the tenderness and tenacity that were part of his character. He adored her and was bored by her: as everyone knows, this is a most aggravating state of feeling. He thought her beautiful, good, amiable and honest, but he had nothing at all to say to her. For many a man she would have been exactly fitting, for it was not so much that she was stupid as that she had no education and no experience. He gave her none of these things as he should have done. Nor did he realise that this life, in the depths of English country, removed from all the enterprise and movement of the town, removed also by the weather from any outside intercourse for weeks at a time, was for someone without any great resources in herself depressing and enervating.

And then she was frightened of him. How well the house understood this! It too was, at times, afraid of him, of his silences, his obstinacy and easy capacity of semi-liveliness, a sensitiveness that his reticence forbade him to express.

How often in the months that followed the marriage did the house long to advise her as to her treatment of him. The sofa in the parlour was especially wise in such cases. Long before it had been covered with its gay cherry-coloured silk it had been famous among friends and neighbours for its delicacy in human tactics.

There came a morning when Lady Candil sat on a corner of it, her lovely little hand (she was delicate, slim, fragile, her body had the consistency of egg-shell china) clenching the shining wood of its strong arm for support, and a word from her would have put everything right. The sofa could feel the throbbing of her heart, and looking across to the thick, stiff, obstinate body of her husband, longed to throw her into his arms. But she could not say the word, and the mischanced moment became history for both of them. Had they not loved so truly it might have been easier for them; as it was, shyness and obstinacy built the barrier.

And of course, Henrietta assisted. How grimly was she pleased as she sat in her ugly old russet gown, pretending to read Lord Clarendon's History (for she made a great pretence of improving her mind), but in reality, listening to the unhappy silences between them and watching for the occasion when a word from her to her brother would skilfully widen the breach. For she hated poor Dorothy. She must in any case have done so out of jealousy and disappointment, but Dorothy was also precisely the example in woman whom she most despised. A weak, feckless, helpless thing whose pretty looks were an insult!

Then Dorothy felt her peril and rose to meet it. The house may have whispered in her ear!

Yes, she rose to meet it, but, as life only too emphatically teaches us, it is no good crying for the moon—and it is no good, however urgent we may be, begging for qualities that we have not got. She had a terrible habit of being affectionate at the wrong time. A kind of fate pursued her in this. He would return from his afternoon's ride, pleasantly weary, eager for his wife and happy in the thought of a little romantic dalliance, and she, fancying that he would not be disturbed, would leave him to snore beside the fire. Or a neighbour squire would visit him and he be off with him for the afternoon and she feel neglected. Or he would be absorbed in a newsletter with a lively account of French affairs and she choose that moment to sit on his knee and tug his hair.

Dorothy was in truth one of those unfortunate persons—and they are among the most unfortunate in the world—who are insensitive to the moods and atmospheres of others. These err not through egotism nor stupidity, but rather through a sort of colour-blindness so that they see their friend red when he is yellow and green when he is blue. Neither Dorothy nor Edmund had any gift of words.

So, a year and a half after his marriage, Edmund, with an ache in his heart, although he would own this to nobody, went once again to foreign parts. The house implored him not to go: he almost heard its protests.

On one of his last evenings there—a windy spring evening—he came in from a dark twilight walk, splashed with the mud of the country paths, the sense of the pale hedgerow primroses yet in his eye, the chatter of birds in his ear, and standing in the hall heard the William and Mary clock with the moon and stars, the banisters of the staircase, the curtains of the long hall window whisper to him:

'Don't go! Don't go! Don't go!'

He stood there and thought: 'By Gemini, I'll not leave this!' Dorothy came down the stairs to greet him and, seeing him lost in thought, stole upstairs again. In any case he had taken his seat in the coach, and his place in the packet-boat was got for him by a friend in London.

'Don't go!' said the portrait of old Uncle Candil.

He strode upstairs and Dorothy was reading *Grandison* by the fire, and although her heart was beating with love for him, was too timid to say so.

So, to foreign parts he went again and, loving her so dearly, wrote letters to her which he tore up without sending lest she should think him foolish—such being the British temperament.

How the house suffered then, that Dorothy should be left to the harsh economies of sister Henrietta. Henrietta was not a bad woman, but she was mean, selfish, proud and stupid. She was also jealous. Very quickly and with little show of rebellion Dorothy submitted to her ways. If true love is in question absence does indeed make the heart grow fonder, and Dorothy thought of her husband night, morning, and night again.

She was snubbed, starved, and given a thorough sense of her insufficiencies. It is surprising how completely one human being can convince another of incompetence, ignorance and silly vanity if they be often alone together and one of them a woman. Women are more wholehearted than men in what they do, whether for good or ill, and Henrietta was very whole-hearted indeed in this affair.

She convinced Dorothy before her husband's return that she was quite unworthy of his love, that he found her dull and unresponsive, that he was deeply disappointed in the issue of his marriage, and that she had deceived him most basely. You may say that she was a poor-spirited little thing, but she was very lonely, half-starved, and her love made her defenceless.

The appetite grows with what it feeds on, and Henrietta found that 'educating Dorothy,' as she called it, was a very worthy and soul-satisfying occupation. Dorothy began to be frightened, not only of herself and of Henrietta but of everything around her, the house, the gardens, the surrounding country.

The house did its utmost to reassure her. When she lay awake in her bed at night the house would hush any noise that might disturb her, the furniture of her room, the hangings above her bed, the old chest of Cromwell's time, the Queen Anne wardrobe, the warming-pan, the fire-irons that had the heads of grinning dogs, the yellow rug from Turkey, the Italian lamp beside her bed, they all crowded about her to tell her that they loved her. After a while she was conscious of their affection. Her bedroom and the parlour were for her the happiest places in the house, the only places indeed where she was not afraid.

She did not know that they were saying anything to her—she had not that kind of perception—but she felt reassured by them, and she would lock herself into her bedroom and sit there for hours thinking of her husband and wondering where he might be.

She became so painfully aware of Henrietta that she saw her when she wasn't there. She saw her always just around a corner, behind a tree, on the other side of the rose-garden wall, peering over the sun-dial, hiding behind the curtain. She became a slave to her, doing all that she was told, going where she was bid. The house considered it a disgusting business.

One evening she broke into a flash of rebellion.

'Edmund loves me!' she cried, her little breasts panting, her small hands clenched. 'And you hate me! Why do you hate me? I have never done you any harm.'

Henrietta looked at her severely.

'Hate! Hate! I have other things to do—and if he loves you, why does he stay so long away?'

Ah! why indeed? The house echoed the question, the very floors trembling with agitation. The stupid fool! Could he not see the treasure that he had? Did he think that such glories were to be picked up anywhere, any day, for the asking? The fire spat a piece of coal on to the hearthrug in contempt of human blindness.

When the time arrived at last for Edmund's return, Dorothy was in a fitting condition of miserable humility. Edmund did not love her. He was bored with her too dreadfully. But indeed, how could he love her? How could anybody love her, poor incompetent stupid thing that she was! And yet in her heart she knew that she was not so stupid. Did Edmund love her only a little she could jump all the barriers and be really rather brilliant—much more brilliant than Henrietta, who was certainly not brilliant at all. It was this terrible shyness that held her back, that and Henrietta's assurance that Edmund did not love her. And indeed, he did not seem to. It was but too likely that Henrietta was right.

As the time approached for Edmund's return Henrietta was in a fine bustle and the house was in one too. The house smiled contemptuously at Henrietta's parsimonious attempts to freshen it up. As though the house could not do that a great deal better than Henrietta ever could! Bees-waxing the floors, rubbing the furniture, shining up the silver—what were these little superficialities compared with the inner spiritual shake that the house gave itself when it wanted to? A sort of glow stole over windows, stairs and hall; a silver shine, a richer colour crept into the amber curtains, the cherry-coloured sofa; the faces in the portraits smiled, the fire-irons glittered, the mahogany shone again. Edmund had been away too long; the house would not let him go so easily next time.

The night before his return Dorothy did not sleep, but lay there, her eyes burning, her heart thickly beating, determining on the bold demonstrative person she would be. She would show Henrietta whether he loved her or no. But at the thought of Henrietta she shivered and drew the bed-clothes closely about her. She seemed to be standing beside the bed, illumined in the darkness by her own malignant fires, her yellow skin drawn tightly across the supercilious bones, her hands curving over some fresh mean economy, her ridiculous head-dress wagging like a mocking spirit above her small red-rimmed eyes. Yes, if only Henrietta were not there . . .

And the old chest murmured softly: 'If only Henrietta were not there . . .'

The post-chaise came up to the door darkly like a ghost, for it had been snowing all day and the house was wrapped in silence. The animals on the box-tree hedge stood out fantastically against the silver-grey of the evening sky, and the snow fell like the scattering feathers of a heavenly geese-flock.

Edmund stepped into the hall and had Dorothy in his arms. At that moment they knew how truly they loved one another. He wondered as he flung his mind back in an instant's retrospect over a phantasmagoria of Indian Moguls, Chinese rivers and the flaming sunsets of Arabia how it could be that he had not known that his life was here, here with his beloved house above him, his adored wife in his arms. His head up like a conqueror's, he mounted the stairs, almost running into his wonderful parlour, to see once again the vase of flowers on the commode, the slender beautiful legs of his chair, the charming circles of his delicate ceiling. 'How could I have stayed away?' he thought. 'I will never leave this again!'

And that night, clasped in one another's arms, they discovered one another again: shyness fled and heart was open to heart.

Nevertheless, there remained Henrietta. Would you believe that one yellow-faced old maid could direct and dominate two normal healthy creatures? You know that she can, and is doing it somewhere or other at this very moment. And all for their good. No one ever did anything mean to anyone else yet save for their good, and so it will be until the end of this frail planet.

She told Edmund that she had been 'educating Dorothy.' He would find her greatly improved; she feared that her worst fault was Hardness of Heart. Hardness of Heart! A sad defect!

During those snowy days Henrietta tried to show her brother that no one in the world truly loved him but herself. She had shown him this before and found the task easy; now it was more difficult. Dorothy's shyness had been melted by this renewed contact; he could not doubt the evidence of his eyes and the many little unconscious things that spoke for her when she had no idea that they were speaking. Now they rode and walked together and he explained to her how *he* was, how that at a time his thoughts would be far, far away in Cairo or Ispahan and that she must not think that he did not care for her because he was dreaming, and she told him that when he had frightened her she had been stupid, but that now that he frightened her no longer she would soon be brilliant. . . . So, Henrietta's task was difficult.

And then in the spring, when the daffodils blew among the long grasses and the white violets were shining in the copse, a chance word of hers showed her the way. She hated Dorothy now because she suspected that Dorothy was planning to be rid of her. The fear that she would be turned out of the house never left her, and so, as fear always does, it drove her to baser things than belonged truly to her nature. She hinted that in Edmund's absence Dorothy had found a neighbouring squire 'good company.' And there had been perhaps another or two . . . MEN . . . At that word every frustrated instinct in Henrietta's body turned in rebellion. She had not spoken before she believed it true. She had this imaginative gift, common to lonely persons. She was herself amazed at the effect of her words on Edmund. If she had ever doubted Edmund's love for his wife (and she had not really doubted it) she was certain of the truth at last. Dorothy . . . Dorothy . . . His stout body trembled; his eyes were wounded; he turned from his sister as though he were ashamed both of her and of himself. After that there was no peace.

It was now that the house wondered most deeply at these strange human beings. The little things that upset them, the odd things that, at a moment, they would believe! Here, for instance, was their Edmund, whom they so truly admired, loving his Dorothy and entirely trusting her. Now, at a moment's word from a sour-faced virgin, there is a fire of torment in his heart. He looks on every male with an eager restless suspicion. While attempting to appear natural he watches Dorothy at every corner and counters in his mind her lightest word.

'Why,' said the Italian lamp (which from its nationality knew everything about jealousy) to the Cromwellian chest, 'I have never known so foolish a suspicion,' to which the Cromwellian chest replied in its best Roundhead manner: 'Woman . . . the devil's bait . . . always has been . . . always will be.'

He attacked his sister again and again. 'With whom has she been? Has she ever stayed from the house a night? What friends has she made?'

To which Henrietta would indignantly reply: 'Brother, brother. What are you about? This jealousy is most unbecoming. I have suggested no impropriety . . . only a little foolishness born of idleness.'

But it did not need time for Dorothy to discover that something was once again terribly amiss.

This strange husband of hers, so unable to express himself—she had but just won him back to her and now he was away again! With the courage born of their new relationship she asked him what was the trouble. And he told her: 'Nothing. . . . Nothing! Nothing at all! Why should there be trouble? You are for ever imagining . . .' And then looked at her so strangely that she blushed and turned away as though she were indeed guilty. Guilty of what? She had not the least idea. But what she did know was that it was dear sister Henrietta who was responsible, and now, as May came with a flourish of birds and blossom and star-lit nights, she began to hate Henrietta with an intensity quite new to her gentle nature.

So, with jealousy and hatred, alive and burning, the house grew very sad. It hated these evil passions and had said long ago that they ruined with their silly bitterness every good house in the world. The little Chinese cabinet with the purple dragons on its doors said that in China everything was much simpler—you did not drag a situation to infinity as these sluggish English do, but simply called Death in to make a settlement—a much simpler way. In any case the house began to watch and to listen with the certainty that the moment was approaching when it must interfere.

Jealousy always heightens love, and so, if Edmund had loved Dorothy at the first, that cool, placid anticipation was nothing to the fevered passion which he now felt. When he was away from her he longed to have her in his arms, covering her with kisses and assuring her that he had never doubted her, and when he was with her he suspected her every look, her every word. And she, miserable now and angry and ill, could not tell what possessed him, her virtue being so secure that she could not conceive that anyone should suspect it. Only she was well aware that Henrietta was to blame.

These were also days of national anxiety and unrest; the days when Napoleon jumping from Elba alighted in France and for a moment promised to stay there. Warm, stuffy, breathless days, when everyone was waiting, the house with the rest.

On the staircase one summer evening Dorothy told Henrietta something of her mind. 'If I had my way,' she ended in a shaking rage, 'you would not be here plotting against us!'

So that was it! At last Henrietta's suspicions were confirmed. In a short while Dorothy would have her out of the house; and then where would she go? The thought of her desolation, loneliness, loss of power, gripped her heart like a cat's claws. The two little charity-girls had a time of it during those weeks and cried themselves to sleep in their attic that smelt of mice and apples, dreaming afterwards of strong lovers who beat their mistress into a pulp.

'Give me proof!' said Edmund, so bitterly tormented. 'If it is true, give me proof!'

And Henrietta answered, sulkily: 'I have never said anything,' and a window-sash fell on his fingers and bruised them just to teach him not to be so damnable a fool.

Nevertheless, Henrietta had her proof. She had been cherishing it for a year at least. This was a letter written by a young Naval Lieutenant, cousin of a neighbouring squire, after he had danced with Dorothy at a Christmas ball. It was only a happy careless boy's letter, he in love with Dorothy's freshness, and because he was never more than a moment in any one place, careless of consequences. He said in his letter that she was the most beautiful of God's creatures, that he would dream of her at sea, and the rest. Dorothy kept it. Henrietta stole it. . . .

The day came when the coach brought the news of the Waterloo victory. On that summer evening rockets were breaking into the pale sky above the dark soft shelter of the wood; on Bendon Hill they were waiting for dark to light the bonfire. You could hear the shouting and singing from the high-road. The happiness at the victory and the sense that England was delivered blew some of the cobwebs from Edmund's brain; he took Dorothy into the garden and there, behind the sun-dial, put his arms around her and kissed her.

Henrietta, watching the rockets strike the sky from her window, saw them, and fear, malice, loneliness, greed, hurt pride and jealousy all rose in her together. She turned over the letter in her drawer and vowed that her brother should not go to bed that night before he had heard of it.

'Look out! Look out!' cried her room to the rest of the house. 'She will make mischief with the letter. We must prevent her . . .'

'She has done mischief enough,' chattered the clock from the hall. 'She must be prevented . . .' whistled the chimneys. Something must be done and at once. But how? By whom?

She is coming. She stands outside her door, glancing about the dim sunset passage. The picture of Ranelagh above her head wonders—shall it fall on her? The chairs along the passage watch her anxiously as she passes them. But what can they do? Each must obey his own laws.

Stop her! Stop her! Stop her! Edmund and Dorothy are coming in from the garden. The sun is sinking, the shadows lengthening across the lawn. One touch on his arm: 'Brother, may I have a word?' and all the harm is done—misery and distress, unhappiness in the house, separation and loneliness. Stop her! Stop her!

All the house is quivering with agitation. The curtains are blowing, the chimneys are twisting, the tables and chairs are creaking: Stop her! Stop her! Stop her!

The order has gone out. She is standing now at the head of the staircase leading to the hall. She waits, her head bent a little, listening. Something seems to warn her. Edmund and Dorothy are coming in from the garden. The fireworks are beginning beyond the wood, and their gold and crimson showers are rivalling the stars.

Henrietta, nodding her head as though in certainty, has taken her step, some roughness in the wood has caught her heel (was it there a moment ago?), she stumbles, she clutches at the balustrade, but it is slippery and refuses to aid her. She is falling; her feet are away in air, her head strikes the board; she screams, once and then again; a rush, a flash of huddled colour, and her head has struck the stone of the hall floor.

How odd a silence followed! Dorothy and Edmund were still a moment lingering by the door looking back to the shower of golden stars, hearing the happy voices singing in the road. Henrietta was dead and so made no sound.

But all through the house there was a strange humming as though everything from top to bottom were whispering.

Everything in the house is moving save the woman at the bottom of the stairs.

Lilac

Frederick Anstey moved the Rodin Balzac a little so that the light of the spring evening should catch the strong curve of the nose and the high broad lines of the forehead.

'Marvellous!' he murmured, as though he had never seen it before. 'And he put a lot of extra work into this one. In fact, there's not two of them alike. The one Mr. Bernard Shaw has . . .'

'Yes,' said Mr. Litehouse cautiously. 'If only it weren't so like Lloyd George. I should never be able to get it out of my head. "Why, it's the image of Lloyd George," was the very first thing my wife said when she came in to see it yesterday. And you can't deny. . . . Two hundred guineas, did you say?' he asked with sudden suspicion, as though Frederick Anstey might have forgotten what he *had* said.

'Two hundred,' said Frederick, smiling his round rubicund smile that was, he knew, bad for business but he never could check it. Bad for business because when a customer saw it he concluded instantly that Frederick was a creature of no stamina and could be easily beaten down.

'All right, I'll take it,' said Mr. Litehouse suddenly. (Five minutes before he had declared quite firmly that nothing would induce him to buy it.) 'That is if I can take it away now in my car—at once. I want to show it to somebody.' (You could always tell a true collector by his insistence on taking things with him, as though the object would disappear the moment his back was turned.)

'Of course, you can,' said Frederick, his whole body smiling now. Then he was grave and sincere. It wouldn't do (for the hundredth time he told himself) to look as though selling the Balzac had pleased him. His gesture must be that if Mr. Litehouse didn't buy it, someone else would in half a minute!

Mr. Litehouse wouldn't allow it to be wrapped up. He ordered it to be carried at once into his car, and there, on the back seat, Balzac sat with Mr. Litehouse's bony and beautifully dressed person beside him, looking out on to the busy London streets as though he didn't care a damn.

'Sold the Balzac,' Frederick said carelessly to Pecking, whose attitude always was that no one save himself could sell anything.

'Litehouse?' asked Pecking.

Frederick nodded.

'Too good for him. . . . Still, he's got some fine things. It's only snobbery of course. Doesn't know one thing from another.'

'Lucky for us,' said Frederick, laughing.

'You look cheerful,' said Pecking resentfully. 'Come into a fortune?'

'No,' said Frederick. 'Expect it's the spring weather.'

He knew that it was not, or at least only a little. It had been a wonderful day and now the evening was lovely, but he regarded the selling of the Balzac as an omen. And he needed good omens, for in a quarter of an hour's time he was going to ask Lily Brocket to marry him. Everything helped. The Balzac helped. The spring evening helped. And if she refused him, nothing would be of any use at all!

He went into the farther room where the Zzierzcky pictures hung. This was the first Zzierzcky show in London and it had been a wonderful success. Nearly every picture had sold. A success of snobbery of course. The people who liked the pictures hadn't been able to afford to buy them: the people who had bought them had most certainly not liked them. Zzierzcky was very modern indeed. His landscapes were entitled 'Pond in Snow,' 'The Mountain Pass,' 'Winter Sunlight' and so on, but unless you were the kind of person who was ready for anything in pictures, you would never guess what the pictures were about. Nevertheless, they had grown on Frederick during the month of their exhibition. He had, in the last three years, explained so many modern pictures to so many stupid and reluctant people that he had come to have modern tastes himself.

When he had come first to the Gallery he had actually thought Dawson a good painter! Now Dawson made him sick. Or would have done had he not a kindly feeling for Dawson. That was his trouble, that he had a kindly feeling for almost everyone. He was a very modest, kindly-hearted little man, and had he ever considered what he was (which he never did) he would have wished fervently that he was anything else in the world.

But that was his trouble, that no one ever took him seriously. It had not been a real trouble (because formerly he had not taken himself seriously) until he had fallen in love with Lily Brocket. He wanted her to take him seriously. If she did not he might as well go and drown himself. And then at the thought of that he couldn't help but smile. The picture of his going to drown himself was so very absurd.

While he was washing his hands in the little cupboard off the passage and peering at himself in the glass, he hated, for the hundred-thousandth time, his round rosy face. It was the face of an infant, a good-natured infant who had just enjoyed a good feed from its bottle! Anything less distinguished! And his body too, round and short, thick in the leg, short in the arm. Who could take seriously such a body? The only thing he could do with it was to keep it clean and neat. . . .

He shrugged his shoulders, wiped his hands with a kind of careful ceremony on the towel and then forgot about himself. He never could think about himself for long. Something would keep breaking in; a joke or a meal, a pretty girl, or selling a picture, a game of golf (which he enjoyed and played very badly) or meeting a friend. He was an ordinary dull kind of fellow like thousands of others. That was what he thought of himself. He *could* not imagine what Lily saw in him.

But perhaps she saw nothing at all. This thought came to him as he put on his overcoat; so awful was it that for a moment his heart stopped beating. When it came to it you could not tell with a girl, could you? You could never tell what a girl was thinking. Were she really fond of him would she not have married him a year ago? There was, of course, her old father, that ridiculous old man of skin and bone, with his greed and rheumatism and voice like a mouse in the wainscot.

She said that she couldn't leave him, but couldn't she? Ah, that was the question. Wouldn't she leave him if she really loved Frederick? How was Frederick to tell?

No, all he knew about it was that he adored her, could not live without her. That was the old hackneyed phrase, but in his case, it was real and authentic. In spite of his chubby face and passion for seeing the cheerful side of everything, if Lily married someone else—that ridiculous tobacconist, for instance—he, Frederick, would decline and die—and no one in the whole world would care a halfpenny!

Lord! what melancholy thoughts for so lovely an evening! He was walking up Duke Street, and every shop was a little magic of fire and splendour, and overhead the sky swam in a mist of blue and silver light. People did not look at the sky enough in London. They walked with their noses straight in front of them or hurried like nervous rabbits or talked to their friends.

Perhaps he himself would not now have looked at the sky had it not been for his love of Lily. But spring was in the air and pushing up through the very pavement. You could almost, were your fancy poetic enough, detect violets in the corners of the grey stone and primroses clustered in the doorways.

Five minutes later he was thinking of nothing but Lily. She was waiting for him at the corner of the Green Park, the entrance near the Ritz corner, and they moved away down the Park in the direction of Buckingham Palace, at first not speaking.

'What a lovely evening!' she said softly. She was herself lovely in her little grey hat and silver-grey coat, with her rosy cheeks, black, black eyes and her way of moving as though she loved the world and couldn't have enough of it.

Someone had given her a bunch of primroses. She had pinned them into her coat. He was instantly jealous.

'Who gave you those primroses?' he asked huskily.

'Never *you* mind,' she answered him, laughing. And then, lest she should have hurt him, she added hastily: 'It was old Mr. Deering. He's always doing something kind.'

'Oh, is he?' said Frederick scornfully. 'Old man of his age. He ought to be thinking of the next world.'

'Now look here,' she said, putting her hand on his arm; his body trembled at her touch. 'Don't let's waste time talking of old nothings like Mr. Deering. We haven't got a minute. I oughtn't to have come, really, but I knew you'd be so disappointed. Aunt Clara's turned up unexpectedly from Brighton. There's no one in the house but father, and he's got one of his toothaches. I've simply got to go straight back.'

There was rage in Frederick's heart, passionate hatred of Aunt Clara, bitter disappointment, a sense that life had once again dealt him a knockdown blow, a physical pain about his heart, an impulse to rage at Lily like a maniac, tear her hat from her head and trample on her bunch of primroses—and a surprising, incredible desire to break down and cry like a child.

She felt at once his bitter, desperate disappointment, pressed her hand into his arm, and, in a voice more loving than any that she had ever used to him before, said:

'Fred, dear . . . you're not more disappointed than I am. It's a rotten shame. I never dreamt of Aunt Clara coming. It's just like her. It's our luck. I'm wretched about it.'

And she was! He knew at once that she meant what she said; he knew that she cared for him, and in that knowledge the filmy silver sky, the dazzling friendly lights, the dark, obscure trees danced and turned and danced again and his eyes were dim.

'See here, Lily,' he said, turning her towards him so that she looked into his eyes. 'I love you. You know I do. I've loved you for two years, and now I love you so that it eats me up. It does truly. You've got to marry me. I've asked you before. Three times I've asked you, but never like tonight. It's so serious that I can't live . . . I can't live . . . if you don't. . . .'

Her face was tender, maternal, gravely anxious, as she looked at him. 'Yes, Fred . . . I know . . . but there's father.'

'Damn your father,' he answered (and she saw that tonight there was something new in his face, something really desperate). 'Isn't he seventy-six? Are our lives to be ruined for an old man like that? Isn't it a wicked thing for an old man to stop two people's lives . . .?'

'But you don't understand—'

'I do understand, perfectly. You've told me again and again. And I tell you that if you're going to let your father interfere any longer, I'll never see you again after to-night. This is the last time. I can't stand it. . . . It isn't fair.'

'No; it isn't fair,' she answered him frankly. 'I've been thinking that for a long time. It isn't fair to you and it isn't fair to me, really.'

He felt an impulse of intense irritation and exasperation.

'Well, then, if it isn't fair, it's got to be ended. . . . Are you going to marry me?'

'But there's father—'

'Father can come and live with us. I've told you so over and over again.' He looked at her, tears in his eyes. He saw everything—sky and trees and coloured lights—in a trembling mist. 'If you loved me,' he said, his voice shaking, 'you wouldn't have hesitated. I might have known. It's because you don't love me that you can talk about your father.'

She shook her head, looking at him with great tenderness. 'It isn't as easy as that, Fred. It isn't indeed. . . . But it isn't fair either. . . . You're right there. I tell you what I'll do.'

He looked at her with new hope. His eyes cleared. The Park seemed suddenly to have a scent of flowers.

'I've got to go, but I'll write a line, telling you what I feel, and I'll send it along by Alfred to Garland Square. Before ten anyway. That's the best I can do, really it is, Fred.'

'A note?' he said, bewildered.

'Yes; saying how I feel. I'll settle it tonight. There are things I can say better in a letter. I'll send it by Alfred before ten. . . . Goodbye. I've got to run.'

And she was gone, without a pressure of the hand, without another word, swallowed up by the Park as though she had never been.

He stayed there, staring in front of him; then, after a minute or two, started on his way home. He didn't know what to think. No, but he was hopeful, more hopeful than he had ever been before. And, whatever way it might go, tonight would settle it. Whatever way it might go!

At the thought that it might go the wrong way his body shrank within its clothes as though a giant hand were compressing it. Supposing she should say no! Oh, suppose . . . He was nearly killed by a car, a voice shouted at him, lights flashed and danced, he was on the farther pavement. A lucky escape; but if she refused him he might as well be dead.

She didn't mean to, though. She wouldn't put him to all the agony of suspense, hours of it, if she meant to refuse him. But perhaps she thought that it would be kinder that way. Couldn't bear to hurt him by telling him . . . He walked on blindly, seeing nothing, hearing nothing and, before he knew anything about it, he was at his door.

Garland Square is one of those little Squares that have been dropped like pools of quiet and comfort here and there about London. They say that they are doomed, that modern traffic, modern I-don't-know-what, must drive them away. If that is true, then some of the most beautiful things in the world are doomed.

Garland Square is small and its railed-in garden is like a green napkin laid out between the old dove-grey houses. Round the green square flowers blow according to the seasons, daffodils, purple and white lilac; it is best in the spring; in the summer such flowers as there are are hidden by the dark thick green of the trees and bushes. The trees are haunted by the birds, who use the grass as their promenading ground by right immemorial. There is at one end the statue of an eighteenth-century gentleman in a tie-wig, with a cocked hat and a handsome frill to his waistcoat. There are some green benches.

The inhabitants of the houses in the Square have, of course, a key to the garden—no one else in the world—and the old gardener, who has a beard just like his broom, regrets bitterly that, in these days, the inhabitants of the houses have gone down so dreadfully in 'class.' He belongs to the fine old days when 'class' mattered, when a gentleman *was* a gentleman. Now everybody is a gentleman, or nobody if you look at it his way.

Frederick's house was Number Ten and had been, like several others, divided into flats. They were not flats of the splendid West End order. There was no lift; you walked up the fine eighteenth-century stone staircase and then, if your room was high up, as Frederick's was, a further smaller staircase, and then a small corkscrew staircase most difficult to manoeuvre if, like Mr. Bendish in the room opposite to Frederick, you came back early in the morning, wine having made your heart so glad that you sang aloud and disturbed everyone. Poor Bendish! He didn't care for wine, as he often told Frederick. He didn't care very much for whisky, but what were you to do when you were all alone in the world and one girl after another refused to marry you? He had proposed, he told Frederick, to twenty within the last year. It wasn't true (what the newspapers were always saying) that an Englishwoman would marry any man who asked her.

Frederick's room could not, by any sort of courtesy, be called a flat. It was simply a bed-sitting-room, and a woman (Mrs. Marl) came in the morning, gave him his breakfast and cleaned up. He shared her with Bendish and the Russell Greens.

He could have afforded quite easily a real flat, but the house was so grand, the Square so beautiful and so quiet, the neighbourhood so good and old Lady Cannon (who lived on the ground floor and whose house it was) so aristocratic, that he was lucky to be there. He loved his room, his view, his neighbourhood; only marriage with Lily would persuade him to depart.

He was standing now, his window flung up, looking out over the Square. Behind him his room told him that it was glad that he was back. He had two Chinese rugs, some good pieces of old furniture, and three pictures—an oil by Paul of a lady with a white face and a green nose, a sketch by Duncan Grant and a drawing of a music-hall by Sickert. He had had no taste when he had first come to this room, five years ago, but the picture-gallery had educated him, educated him, Lily said, to liking everything that was ugly. She couldn't understand the lady with the green nose. After all, people didn't have green noses, whatever light you saw them in. It was their only real difference of opinion.

But he was not thinking of that now. As he leaned out of the window there came to him quite unmistakably the scent of lilac. It could not in reality be. There was no lilac in bloom in the gardens, and yet he smelt the lilac and seemed, as he leaned out, to see through the grey-moth-like evening the sky above the Square broken into soft shreds and patches of blue, and bushes of dim purple lilac staining the air with its colour, a cloud of shadowy radiance.

He knew that he was cheating himself and yet he urged himself to be cheated. The belief acting against knowledge that the lilac was there seemed to be linked with his dramatic anticipation of his fate. His heart was thumping, his throat hot and dry, his body suddenly tired with a rather pleasant fatigue; he was in short like a man waiting for his sentence of execution. And yet surely nothing very terrible could happen to him on so lovely an evening as this. All the world was beautiful, and the Rodin Balzac which he had so successfully sold, the soft Duncan Grant landscape (amber and rose its colouring), the Square with its sense of spring, its scent of lilac, all these beautiful things seemed to come together and assure him that his fate must be a kind one.

He was aware of the door opening and, turning, saw Bendish there.

Bendish was a large, stout, rumpled man with little blue eyes, grey untidy hair, and a small pouting mouth. He seemed to be always asking for your indulgence, wondering whether you would scold him or no. There was something eternally unsatisfactory about him, which was perhaps why girls had so often refused to marry him. Their maternal feelings were roused by his helplessness, their practical self-protection alarmed by his irresponsibility, and so he was still a bachelor.

'I say, have you got a hammer?' he asked.

'Yes,' said Frederick, turning back into the room. 'I think so.' As he turned back he was convinced that Lily would accept him, and the room blazed with light and the pictures danced.

'You look as though you'd come into a fortune,' said Bendish rather resentfully. Anstey, after all, was a very ordinary little fellow, and yet he seemed to be always in luck, while himself . . .

Frederick rummaged in the cupboard, standing on his toes because he was short and the hammer was probably on the top shelf. Bendish, looking at his broad back, the strong sturdy strain of his body as he raised his arms, and something gay and independent about the set of his round, closely cropped bullet-head, suddenly liked him very much and, liking him, felt happier.

He had himself a decision that he must, that evening, come to a decision that all the week he had been evading. To escape from the thought of it he had come in to borrow a hammer (it was true that there *was* a hunting picture to hang). Now he was more cheerful, and when Frederick, the hammer in his hand, turned and showed his rosy, flushed face, he said quite amiably: 'Thanks. Lovely evening, isn't it?'

They both turned to the window.

'Bit nippy with the window open,' said Bendish.

'Funny thing,' said Frederick, 'I've been thinking I could smell lilac. Of course, it's impossible. But an evening like this makes you imagine things.'

Bendish never imagined anything, so he said nothing.

'Made a good sale this afternoon,' the little man went on. 'Head of Balzac by Rodin. Sold it to that fellow Litehouse, the big tobacco man. He's collecting pictures and things. Doesn't know anything about art, but we look after him—see he doesn't get anything rotten, you know.'

'Much better,' said Bendish gloomily, 'if he gave his money to children's hospitals or something like that.'

'Oh, I don't know,' said Frederick, suddenly irritated, because nothing exasperated him so much as this very popular sentiment; 'it would be an awful world if there weren't any beautiful things in it, and who'd go on making beautiful things if nobody ever bought them?'

'I don't see that,' said Bendish. 'Pictures are only a luxury.'

But he couldn't quarrel with Frederick; there was something in his easy, quite uncomplacent good-nature that made him difficult to quarrel with. Frederick, on his side, had a very strong impulse to tell Bendish all about Lily. Lily was around him, inside him, everywhere. His heart was still hammering, his cheeks were hot, his throat was dry. It would be a relief to tell Bendish, and ask him what he thought of the chances, to gain encouragement perhaps in opposition to his own fears. But no, it was no use to tell Bendish anything. He was only interested in himself.

Bendish looked at him curiously. 'I believe you've been making money at racing,' he said. 'You do have all the luck. I've noticed it before.' He felt, himself, a temptation to tell Anstey about his problem. There was something about Anstey tonight. . . . But Anstey would only advise him to do what he didn't want to do.

'No,' said Frederick, 'I never have any luck with horses. I always lose.' Never any luck? Would he have luck with Lily? Even now she was making up her mind. It might be that she was, at this very moment, writing her letter.

'Dear Fred, I want to tell you—'

His heart seemed to knock him right over. It wouldn't have surprised him at all to find himself flat on the floor! To steady himself, he put his hand on Bendish's arm. At the touch the two men seemed to come into some new relation with one another. Bendish was a lonely fellow. No one ever seemed to need him or put themselves out to see him. Bendish was greatly moved. But all he said was, gruffly: 'Well, I must go and hang that picture.' By the door he added: 'Thanks for the hammer.'

Frederick said: 'That's all right. Come in any time you like.'

He was alone again: the house was utterly still about him.

Bendish had done something to him; he had made him see how desperate, how abandoned, how hopelessly ruined he would be did Lily refuse him. He would be like Bendish, only worse. Bendish's loose, stout, uncared-for figure seemed to be a prophecy of his later self refused by Lily. He would go down and down . . .

Standing now in the middle of his room he saw nothing. The room seemed to be filled with a warm, clinging, smelly fog. Deserted by Lily, all the little devils that were always waiting in attendance (he could see them, hideous naked little demons squatting on their hams) would have their way with him. And their way would be a bad one. He was no saint (he little knew how few his sins were in comparison with many of his companions) and he would yield, he would yield. . . . He would go over to Paris with Prentiss or Solomon. He would take Miss Geary (what Miss Geary wanted of him had always been perfectly obvious) out to supper. He would . . .

He pressed his hands to his forehead, sat down, wretched misery overwhelming him. He could not smell any lilac now, but the room was so stuffy that he must go out. He must go out or his head would burst and scatter his brains (such as they were) about the floor. If he went out (the temptation suddenly came to him) he might in another moment be at Lily's door. A taxi would take him there in no time. But that he must not do. It would be breaking all the rules of restraint that he had ever formulated for himself, and, worse than that, he would be driving Lily to some sort of forced decision which would in all probability be exactly the wrong one. But the temptation was fearful. It was exactly as though a little devil in a shiny top-hat and a frock-coat were leading him (he could feel the touch of the little pudgy hand) straight out of his door.

He got his hat, his coat and his stick and went out. He stood in the little passage and listened. No sound. Not even Bendish knocking nails into his wall. But he knew instinctively that Bendish had not really wanted the hammer. What he had wanted was Frederick's help about something. He had come in for company. He had his own especial troubles. Yes, after all, we were all alike. All in the soup together and the best thing that we could do was to help one another. He went carefully down the corkscrew staircase—he seemed to be slightly drunk—and, in the lower passage, almost collided with someone. It was dark here almost always, but this evening something of this miraculous spring had pushed through.

A faint pale glow suffused everything, the shabby yellowed print of Victoria receiving the news of her Succession, an umbrella stand, an old chair with a red-plush seat to it. Standing near to the chair, her hand resting upon it as though to support herself, was young Mrs. Russell Green. The Russell Greens were acquaintances of Frederick rather than friends. A very young couple who loved one another apparently but were for ever quarrelling. They had been quarrelling now, it seemed, for at once Mrs. Russell Green, on seeing Frederick, whispered: 'Oh, Mr. Anstey, I can't stand any more of it. I can't, indeed. I'm going to my mother this very night.'

She was, he saw, in a very agitated state, her hand to her heart, her eyes furious and miserable, staring at him as though she couldn't see him at all.

'What's the matter?' he asked. Their conversation had the oddest urgency and whispering conspiracy about it, as though they were, the two of them, plotting to murder someone.

'The matter is,' she whispered frantically, 'that he's just insulted me more than I can stand. Yes, more than I can stand. I've stood enough. I didn't marry him for this sort of thing. I've told him often enough that if he did it again I'd leave him. And now he's done it.'

'What's he done?' Frederick asked. He could smell the lilac once more. Certainly, it was lilac. Coming in from the Square and stealing up the stairs.

'He's been out with that Marchmont girl again. All last evening, when he said that he was with the Berys. He wasn't with the Berys at all. He's confessed it.'

Frederick understood, as though some special agent had whispered it to him, that this was really serious. If she went off now, in her hat and coat as she was, out of the house, she might never return. A burst of temper and jealousy and the Russell Green life was ruined for ever. He must persuade her into the flat again. He must, if it cost him his life. Once more, as with the Balzac and poor old Bendish, there seemed a fateful omen in this—if Mrs. Russell Green left the house Lily would refuse him.

'I shouldn't take it too seriously,' he whispered. 'You know he loves you, whatever he does. I don't suppose he meant any harm.'

'Harm! What do you call harm? If that Marchmont girl . . . And lying to me, too! I've told him again and again I'll stand anything, but not lies. No, never!'

He touched her arm with his hand. She was trembling, but his touch seemed to steady her. She leant a little towards him. She liked him. She had always liked him. Nice, kind little man. She realised him now, stolid and kind, wanting to help her. And realising him, she liked men better. She saw her own Walter with a little bit of Frederick Anstey stuck on to him.

'I shouldn't,' Frederick said, 'do anything drastic on such a lovely evening.'

Lovely evening! That was about the silliest thing she had ever heard! Nevertheless, there was something in it. She was a sentimental girl and she loved Walter Russell Green more than all the world and everything in it. She caught Frederick's hand.

'What does he tell me lies for?' she went on in an agonised whisper. 'That's what I want to know. I could stand anything but that. And such silly lies. He's always found out and he knows it.'

'Everyone tells lies,' whispered Frederick. 'One can't help it. We all do. And what does it matter when you know he loves you? Anyone can see it.'

Yes, he did. Of that she was quite sure. At the thought of the way that he loved her, of his past goodness, tenderness and incredible childish charm, she softened. She wanted to soften. She had wanted it all the time.

'Go back,' said Frederick. 'Don't leave tonight. See how it is in the morning.'

She looked at the door, sniffed, sighed.

'Very well, then. I'll give him another chance. But it's the last.' She nodded, pushed her Yale key into the door and vanished.

He shook his head. Perhaps in a moment she would be out again. He waited, half expecting the door to open and a furious figure to emerge, but nothing happened. Silence and the spring evening. He went down to the main hall, which had still, at the bottom of its stone staircase, an air and a grandeur. The floor was paved in black and white squares; there was a large empty fireplace, and over it hung what Frederick had always supposed to be a young ancestor of Lady Cannon's— a handsome boy in a blue suit with a fine gold sword at his side.

'I wonder,' thought Frederick, looking at him, 'whether you ever proposed to a lady who couldn't make up her mind if she'd accept you or no . . . I'm sure you did not. . . . You are too good-looking. Any woman would have accepted you at sight.'

He still hesitated, glancing at the door as though it held special temptation for him. He must not go out: he would be off at once to Lily. That would anger her. Everything would be ruined. . . .

But the door pulled at him! Its strong dark face seemed to urge him: 'Come and open me! Slip outside. It is such a delicious evening.'

Then the door, to his astonishment, opened. The light spread softly towards him, he saw the white stone steps, the shining surface of the pavement, the dark trees beyond. Old Lady Cannon stood there, leaning against the door as though she would fall.

He went quickly towards her and she said with a little gasping sigh: 'Oh, Mr. Anstey. . . . I'm a little faint . . . please.'

He supported her, standing there by the open door, and it was strange to him, having her in his arms, to feel the absolute frailty of her body, something so sparse and fragile that it was difficult to believe that it could still exist. She always wore the same clothes, a black bonnet, a shiny black dress, a round silver locket on her heart, long black gloves, all very old-fashioned and quaint; she was a figure that everyone stared at in the street.

She was very small in stature, with a little white peaked face in which were set large anxious eyes. Frederick did not know her very well. She could be haughty and superior. She let the rooms of her house through an agent, and Frederick might never have known her at all had it not been that she had asked his advice on two occasions about family pictures that she wished to sell. One of them, a very charming little Romney, had fetched an excellent price.

He had never entered the rooms where she lived. He was to enter them now.

She gave him the oddest, dry little smile. 'I'm sorry,' she said. 'I beg your pardon. I fear that I shall have to ask you to assist me. I'm not very well. My maid is out.' Then she added, speaking with great difficulty: 'They want so much freedom in these days.'

He almost carried her across the hall: she felt in the pocket of her black dress and gave him the key. They went through the little passage into a vast cold drawing-room, and here he placed her in an old deep chair covered with faded brocade near the wide empty fireplace. How cold the room was and, after he had settled her and looked about him, how empty and desolate!

He could see on the faintly yellow walls the marks where pictures had been hanging. There were still some pictures left, faint and beautiful under the electric light.

She said: 'Will you please turn the light off again? . . . And my smelling salts, if you please. On that table!'

He switched the light off and at once the great room was beautiful. From the high wide windows, a lake of pale colour spread over the old red carpet, the little tables, the old shabby gilt chairs. A clock struck the hour with a lovely silver tone as though it welcomed the evening.

She lay back, her bonnet on the table beside her, sniffing at the salts, her head turned away from him. He could not see her face. He was sitting stiffly on a gilt chair near to her.

'Can't I get you some brandy?' he asked gently. 'Is there something I can do for you?'

But she did not answer. Her thin arm in its long black glove had fallen to her side. He waited. He did not wish to disturb her. A certain deference that he had been trained from his babyhood to feel for the English aristocracy kept him silent. Our English snobbery, and yet not quite that. He felt, in the presence of an old lady like this, all the romance and colour of the English past. They said that the past didn't matter anymore, that even to think of people belonging to this class or another was vain and empty-headed. Well, he *was* empty-headed then! This old lady had something that neither he nor Lily would ever have, and it was some beautiful thing with dignity, history, courage in it. Courage! The old lady needed it, he was sure. Looking cautiously about the dim empty room, he felt an air of poverty and hardship. She should not be poor, receiving the rents for all the rooms in her house, and yet she was poor. There was some mystery here. He sat there, not venturing to move. He would stay there a little while, lest she needed somebody. He thought that she was asleep.

The door was a little open and the farther door was open too. He could hear the chatter of the old clock in the hall.

He fell asleep. . . .

When he awoke he was fearfully cold. For a moment he could not remember where he was. Then it all came to him. At once his heart began to hammer again in his breast. Suppose that a letter had come while he slept. He could still see the figure in the chair, quite motionless. She also was sleeping.

Confusedly, things crowded about him—the Balzac, old Bendish, Mrs. Russell Green, the old lady. All omens for Lily; omens of life, too. All these ways life could go—the artist perfecting his beautiful work and then selling it to a man like Litehouse who cared for it only because it cost him money; if Lily refused him, the aimless, decaying life of Bendish; if Lily accepted him, perhaps the quarrelling, jealous life of marriage; and at last, at the end, this old age, nothing left save the past, all gone, all empty, all the fire and stress as though it had never been. Those were the ways that life could take.

But he was no very great philosopher. For an instant only the fantasy of this strange mystery had danced before his eyes. Now it was gone. Lily. Lily . . . Oh, Lily, my darling, darling!

He got up very carefully from his chair, stole across the floor, moved into the dusky hall. There was the letter-box hanging like a malicious chin from the dark surface. Trembling so that he could scarcely stand, he went, opened it. There, shimmering white, was a letter. He saw that it was addressed to himself and was in Lily's handwriting.

Now his agony was upon him. He had to summon to his rescue every power that he had ever known. His forehead was damp with sweat. He took out his handkerchief and mopped it. He tore the envelope, letting it fall to the ground. In her big, sprawling handwriting, so precious to him, he read:

Dearest Fred,

I want you to know that I love you and will marry you tomorrow, if you want me to. My mind was made up this afternoon (it has always really been made up), but I wouldn't tell you in that hurry, and then father . . .

He read no more. All the world was singing. He flung open the hall door, and a great flood of lilac seemed to salute him and in the dusk, he saw the clustered bushes burning purple.

Miss Morganhurst

It may be that in future years when critics and commentators look back upon the European War, one of the aspects of it that will seem to them strangest will be the attitude of complete indifference that certain people assumed during the course of it. Indifference! That is an inefficient word. It is not too strong to say that hundreds of men and women in London during those horrible years were completely unconscious, save on the rare occasions when rationing or air-raids forced them to attend, that there was any war at all. There were men in clubs, women in drawing-rooms . . . old maids and old bachelors . . . . . .old maids like Miss Morganhurst.

How old Miss Morganhurst really was, for how long she had been raising her lorgnette to gaze scornfully at Society, for how many years now she had been sitting down to bridge on fine sunny afternoons with women like Anne Carteledge and Mrs. Mellish and Mrs. Porter, for how many more years she had lived in No. 30 flat at Hortons she alone had the secret—even Agatha, her sour and confidential maid, could not tell.

No one knew whence she came; years ago some young wag had christened her the "Morgue," led to that diminutive by the strange pallor of her cheeks, the queer bone-cracking little body she had. and her fashion of dressing herself up in jewellery and bright colours that gave her a certain sort of ghastliness. She had been for years an intimate of all sorts of sets in London: no one could call her a snob—she went just everywhere, and knew just everyone; she was after two things in life—scandal and bridge—and whether it were the old Duchess of Wrexe's drawing-room (without the Duchess of course) or the cheapest sort of provincial tea-party, she was equally at home and satisfied. She was like a ferret with her beady eyes—a dressed-up ferret. Yes, and like the "Morgue" too, a sniff of corruption about her somewhere.

People had said for many years that she was the best bridge-player in London and that she lived by her winnings. That was, I daresay, true enough. Her pale face looked as though it fed on artificial light, and her over-decorated back was always bent a little, as though she were for ever stooping over a table.

I've seen her play bridge, and it's not a sight one's likely to forget—bent almost double, her hooky fingers of a dull yellow loaded with rings pointing towards some card and her eyes literally Hashing fire. Lord! how these women played! Life and death to them truly . . . no gentle card-game for *them*. She was a woman who hated sentiment; her voice was hard and dry, with a rasp in it like the movement of an ill-fitting gate. She boasted that she cared for no human being alive, she did not believe in human affection. Her maid, Agatha, she said, would cut her throat for two pence; but, expecting to be left something in the will, stayed on savagely hoping.

It is hard, however, for even the driest of human souls to be attached to nothing. Miss Morganhurst had her attachment—to a canine fragment of skin and bone known as Tiny-Tee. Tiny-Tee was so small that it could not have been said to exist had not its perpetual misery given it a kind of spasmodic liveliness. It is the nature of these dogs to shiver and shake and tremble, but nothing ever lived up to its nature more thoroughly than Tiny-Tee. Miss Morganhurst (in her own fierce rasping way) adored this creature. It never left her, and sat on her lap during bridge shuddering and shivering amongst a multitude of little gold chains and keys and purses that jangled and rattled with every shiver.

Then came the war, and it shook the world to pieces. It did not shake Miss Morganhurst.

For one bad moment she fancied that bridge would be difficult and that it might not be easy to provide Tiny-Tee with her proper biscuits. She consulted with Mrs. Mellish and Mrs. Porter, and after looking at the thing from every side they were of opinion that it would be possible still to find a "four." She further summoned up Mr. Nix from the "vasty deeps" of the chambers and endeavoured to probe his mind. This she did easily, and Mr. Nix became quite confidential. He thoroughly approved of Miss Morganhurst, partly because she knew such very grand people, which was good for his chambers, and partly because Miss Morganhurst had no kind of morals and you could say anything you liked. Mr. Nix was a kindly little man and a diplomatic, and he suited himself to his company; but he did like sometimes to be quite unbuttoned and not to have "to think of every word."

With Miss Morganhurst you needn't think of anything. She found his love of gossip very agreeable indeed; she approved, too, of his honourable code. You were safe with him. Not a thing would he ever give away about any other inhabitant of Hortons. She asked him about the food for Tiny-Tee, and he assured her that he would do his best. And the little dinners for four? . . . She need not be anxious.

After which she dismissed the war altogether from her mind. It would, of course, emphasize its more unagreeable features in the paper. That was unfortunate. But very soon the press cleverly discovered a kind of camouflage of phrase which covered up reality completely. "The honourable gentleman, speaking at Newcastle last night, said that we would not sheathe the sword until—" "Over the top! those are the words for which our brave lads are waiting——" "Our offensive in these areas inflicted very heavy losses on the Germans and resulted in the capture of important positions by the Allied troops."

It seemed that Miss Morganhurst read these phrases for a week or two, and easily persuaded herself that the war was non-existent. She was happy that it was so. It appears incredible that anyone could have dismissed the war so easily, but then Miss Morganhurst was surely impenetrable.

I have heard different explanations given by people, who knew her well, of Miss Morganhurst's impenetrability. Some said that it was a mask, assumed to cover and defeat feelings that were dangerous to liberate; others, that she was so selfish and egoistic that she really did not care about anybody. This is the interesting point about Miss Morganhurst. Did she banish the war entirely from her consciousness and give it no further consideration, or was she, in truth, desperately and with ever-increasing terror aware of it and unable to resist it?

She gave no sign until the very end; but the nature of that end leads me to believe that the first of the two theories is the correct one. People who knew her have said that her devotion to that wretched little canine remnant proves that she had no heart, but only a fluent sentimentality. I believe it to have proved exactly the opposite. I believe her to have been the cynic she was because she had, at some time or other, been deeply disappointed. She had, I imagine, no illusions about herself, and saw that the only thing to be, if she were to fight at all, was ruthless, harsh, money-grubbing, and, above all, to bury herself in other people's scandal. She was, I rather fancy, one of those women for whom life would have been completely changed, had she been given beauty or even moderate good looks. As life had not given her that, she would pay it back. And after all, life was stronger than she knew. . . .

She did not refuse to discuss the war, but she spoke of it as of something remotely distant, playing itself out in the sands of the Sahara, for instance. Nothing stirred her cynical humour more deeply than the heroics on both sides. When politicians or kings or generals got up and said before all the world how just their cause was and how keen they were about honour and truth and self-sacrifice, and how certain they were, after all, to win, Miss Morganhurst gave her sinister, villainous chuckle.

She became something of a power during the bad years, when the air-raids came and the casualties mounted higher and higher, and Roumania came in only to break, and the Russian revolution led to the sinister ghoulishness of Brest-Litovsk. People sought her company. "We'll go and see the 'Morgue,'" they said; "she never mentions the war." She never did; she refused absolutely to consider it. She would not even discuss prices and raids and ration-books. Private history was what she cared for, and that generally on the scabrous side, if possible. What she liked to know was who was sick of who, why so-and-so had Left such-and-such a place, whether X—— was really drinking, and why Z—— had taken to cocaine. Her bridge got better and better, and it used to be a real trial of strength to go and play with her in the untidy, over-full, over-garish little flat. The arrival of the Armistice was, I believe now, her first dangerous moment. She was suddenly forced to pause and consider; it was not so easy to shut her eyes and ears as it had been, and the things that she had, against her will, seen and heard were now, in the new silence, insistent. She suddenly, as I remember noticing about this time, got to look incredibly old.

Her nose seemed longer, her chin hookier, her hands bonier, and little brown spots like sickly freckles appeared on her forehead.

Her dress got brighter and brighter. She especially affected a kind of purple silk, I remember.

The Armistice seemed to disappoint her. It would have done us people a lot of good to get a thorough trouncing, I remember her saying. What would have happened to herself and her bridge had we had that trouncing I don't think she reflected. So far as one could see, she regarded herself as an inevitable permanency. I wonder whether she really did. She developed, too, just about this time, an increased passion for her wretched little dog. It was as though, now that the war was really nearing its close, she was twice as frightened about that animal's safety as she had been before. Of what was she afraid? Was it some ghostly warning? Was it some sense that she had that fate was surely going to get her somewhere, and that now that it had missed her through air-raids it must try other means? Or was it simply that she had more time now to spend over the animal's wants and desires?

In any case she would not let the dog out of her sight unless on some most imperative occasion. She trusted Agatha, but no one would take so much care as one would oneself. The dog itself seemed now to be restless and alarmed as though it smelt already its approaching doom. It got, so far as one could see, no pleasure from anything. There were no signs that it loved its mistress, only it did perhaps have a sense that she could protect it from outside disaster. Every step, every word, every breath of wind seemed to drive its little soul to the very edge of extinction—then, with shudderings and shiverings and tremblings, back it came again. They were a grim pair, those two. Christmas came and passed, and the world began to shake itself together again. That same shaking was a difficult business, attended with strikes and revolutions and murder and despair; but out of the chaos prophets might discern a form slowly rising, a shape that would stand for a new world, for a better world, a kindlier, a cleaner, honester. . . .

But Miss Morganhurst was no prophet. Her sallow eyes were intent on her bridge-cards—so, at least, they appeared to be.

After the catastrophe, I talked with only one person who seemed to have expected what actually occurred. This was a funny old thing called Miss Williams, one of Miss Morganhurst's more shabby friends—a gossip and a sentimentalist—the last person in the world as I would have supposed to see anything interesting.

However, this old lady insisted that she had perceived, during this period, that Miss Morganhurst was "keeping something back."

"Keeping what back?" I asked. "A guilty secret?"

"Oh, not at all," said Miss Williams. "Dear me, no. Dahlia wouldn't have minded anything of that kind. No, it's my belief she was affected by the war long before any of us supposed it, and that she wouldn't think of it or look at it because she knew what would happen if she did. She knew, too, that she was being haunted by it all the time, and that it was all piling up, ready, waiting for the moment. . . . I do hope you don't think me fantastical—"

I didn't think her "fantastical" at all, but I must confess that when I look back I can see in the Miss Morganhurst of these months nothing but a colossal egotism and greed.

However, I must not be cruel. It was towards the end of April that fate was suddenly tired of waiting, took her in hand, and finished her off.

One afternoon when, arrayed in a bright pink tea-gown, she was lying on her sofa, taking some rest before dressing for dinner, Agatha came in and said that her brother was there and would like to see her. Now Miss Morganhurst had a very surprising brother—surprising, that is, for her. He was a clergyman who had been for very many years the rector of a little parish in Wiltshire. So little a parish was it that it gave him little work and less pay, with the result that he was, at his advanced age, shabby and moth-eaten and dim, like a poor old bird shut up for many months in a blinded cage and let suddenly into the light. I don't know what Miss Morganhurst's dealings with her brother had been, whether she had been kind to him or unkind, selfish or unselfish; but I suspect that she had not seen very much of him. Their ways had been too different, their ambitions too separate. The old man had had one passion in his life, his son, and the boy had died in a German prison in the summer of 1918. He had been, it was gathered, in one of the more unpleasant German prisons. Mr. Morganhurst was a widower, and this blow had simply finished him—the thread that connected him with coherent life snapped, and he lived in a world of dim visions and incoherent dreams.

He was not, in fact, quite right in his head.

Agatha must have thought the couple a strange and depressing pair as they stood together in that becoloured and becrowded room, if, that is to say, she ever thought of anything but herself. Poor old Morganhurst was wearing an overcoat really green with age, and his squashy black hat was dusty and unbrushed.

He wore large spectacles, and his chin was of the kind that seems always to have two days' growth upon it. The bottoms of his trousers were muddy, although it was a dry day. He stood there uneasily twisting his hat round and round in his fingers and blinking at his sister.

"Sit down, Frederick," said his sister. "What can I do for you?"

It seemed that he had come simply to talk to her. He was going down to Little Roseberry that evening, but he had an hour to spare. The fact was that he was besieged, invaded, devastated by horrors of which he could not rid himself.

If he gave them to someone else might they not leave him? At any rate he would share them—he would share them with his sister. It appeared that an officer, liberated from Germany after the Armistice, had sought him out and given him some last details about his son's death.

These "details" were not nice. There are, as we all know, German prisons and German prisons. Young Morganhurst seemed to have been sent to one of the poorer sort. He had been rebellious and had been punished; he had been starved, shut up for days in solitary darkness . . . . . . at the end he had found a knife somewhere and had killed himself.

The old man's mind was like a haystack, and many details lost their way in the general confusion. He told what he could to his sister. It must have been a strange meeting: the shabby old man sitting in one of those gaudy chairs trying to rid himself of his horror and terror and, above all, of his loneliness. Here was the only relation, the only link, the only hope of something human to comfort him in his darkness; and he did not know her, could not see how to appeal to her or to touch her . . . she was as strange to him as a bird of paradise. She on her side, as I now can see, had her own horror to fight. Here at last was the thing that throughout the war she had struggled to keep away from her. She knew, and she alone, how susceptible she was! But she could not turn him away; he was her brother, and she hated him for coming—shabby old man—but she must hear him out.

She sat there, the dog clutched shivering to her skinny breast. I don't suppose that she said very much, but she listened. Against her will she listened, and it must have been with her as it is with some traveller when, in the distance, he hears the rushing of the avalanche that threatens to overwhelm him. But she didn't close her ears. From what she said afterwards one knows that she must have heard everything that he said.

He very quickly, I expect, forgot that he had an audience at all. The words poured out. There was some German officer who had been described to him and he had grown, in his mind, to be the very devil himself. He was a brute, I daresay; but there are brutes in every country. . . .

"He had done simply nothing—just spoken back when they insulted him. They took his clothes off him—everything. He was quite naked. And they mocked him like that, pricking him with their swords. . . . They put him into darkness . . . . a filthy place, no sanitation, nothing. . . . They twisted his arms. They made him imagine things, horrible things. When he had dysentery they just left him. . . . They made him drink . . . forced it down his throat. . . ."

How much of it was true? Very little, I daresay. Even as the old man told it details gathered and piled up.

"He had always been such a good boy. Very gentle and quiet—never any trouble at school. . . . I was hoping that he would be ordained, as you know, Dahlia. He always loved life . . . one of the happiest boys. What did they do it for? He hadn't done them any harm. They must have made him very angry for him to say what he did—and he didn't say very much. . . . And he was all alone. He hadn't any of his friends with him. And they kept his parcels and letters from him. I'd just sent him one or two little things. . . ."

This, more than anything else, distressed the old man: that they'd kept the letters from the boy. It was the loneliness that seemed to him the most horrible of all.

"He had always hated to be alone. Even as a very little boy he didn't like to be left in the dark. He used to beg us. . . . Night-lights, we always left night-lights in his room. . . . But what had he done? Nothing. He had never been a bad boy. There was nothing to punish him for."

The old man didn't cry. He sniffed and rubbed his eyes with the back of his hand, and once he brought out a dirty handkerchief. The thing that he couldn't understand was why this had happened to the boy at all. Also, he was persecuted by the thought that there was something still that he could do. He didn't know what it might be, but there must be something. He had no vindictiveness. He didn't want revenge. He didn't blame the Germans. He didn't blame anybody.

He only felt that he should "make it up to his boy" somehow.

"You know, Dahlia," he said, "there were times when one was irritated by the boy. I haven't a very equable temper. No, I never have had. I used to have my headaches, and he was noisy sometimes. And I'm afraid I spoke sharply. I'm sorry enough for it now—indeed, I am. Oh, yes! But, of course, one didn't know at the time. . . ."

Then he went back to the horrors. They would not leave him, they buzzed about his brain like flies. The darkness, the smell . . . the smell, the filth, the darkness. And then the end! He could not forget that. What the boy must have suffered to come to that! Such a happy boy! . . . Why had it happened? And what was to be done now?

He stopped at last and said that he must go and catch his train. He was glad to have talked about it. It had done him good. It was kindly of Dahlia to listen to him. He hoped that Dahlia would come down one day and see him at Little Roseberry. It wasn't much that he could offer her. It was a quiet little place, and he was alone, but he would be glad to see her. He kissed her, gave her a dim bewildered smile, and went.

Soon after his departure Mrs. Mellish arrived. It is significant of Mrs. Mellish's general egotism and ignorance that she perceived nothing odd in Miss Morganhurst! Just the same as she always was. They talked bridge the next afternoon. Bridge. Four women. What about Norah Pope? Poor player. That's the worst of it. Doesn't see properly and won't wear glasses. Simply conceit. But still, who else is there? Tomorrow afternoon. Very difficult. Mrs. Mellish admits that on that particular day she was preoccupied about a dress that she couldn't get back from the dressmakers. These days. What has come to the working-classes? They don't care. They don't care. Money simply of no importance to them. That's the strange thing. In the old days you could have done simply everything by offering them a little more.....
... But not now. Oh, dear no! ... She admits that she was preoccupied about the dress, and wasn't noticing Dahlia Morganhurst as she might have done. She saw nothing odd. It's my belief that she'll see nothing odd at the last trump. She went away.

Agatha is the other witness. After Mrs. Mellish's departure she came in to her mistress. The only thing that she remarked about her was that "she was very quiet." Tired, I supposed, after talking to that Mrs. Mellish. And then her old brother and all. Enough to upset anyone.

Miss Morganhurst sat on the edge of her gaudy sofa looking in front of her. When Agatha came in she said that she would not dress just yet. Agatha had better take the dog out for a quarter of an hour. The maid wondered at that because that was a thing that she was never allowed to do. She hated the animal. However, she pushed its monstrous little head inside its absurd little muzzle, put on her hat and went out.

I don't know what Miss Morganhurst thought about during that quarter of an hour, but when at the end of that time Agatha returned, scared out of her life with the dog dead in her arms, the old lady was sitting in the same spot as before. She can't have moved. She must have been fighting. I fancy, against the last barrier—the last barrier that kept all the wild beasts back from leaping on her imagination.

Well, that slaughtered morsel of skin and bone finished it. The slaughtering had been the most natural thing in the world. Agatha had put the creature on the pavement for a moment and turned to look in a shop window. Some dog from the other side of the street had enticed the trembling object. It had started tottering across, uttering tiny snorts of sensual excitement behind its absurd muzzle. A Rolls-Royce had done the rest. It had suffered very little damage, and, laid out on Miss Morganhurst's red lacquer table, it really looked finer

110

than it had ever done. Agatha, of course, was terrified. She knew better than anyone how deeply her mistress had loved the poor trembling image. Sobbing, she explained. She was really touched, I think—quite truly touched for half a minute. Then, when she saw how quietly Miss Morganhurst took it, she regained her courage. Miss Morganhurst said nothing but "Yes." Agatha regained, with her courage, her volubility. Words poured forth. She could needs tell *Madame* how deeply, deeply she regretted her carelessness. She would kill herself for her carelessness if *Madame* preferred that. How she could! *Madame* might do with her what she wished. . . .

But all that Miss Morganhurst said was "Yes."

Miss Morganhurst went into her bedroom to dress for dinner, and Tiny-Tee was left, at full length in all her glory, trembling no longer, upon the red lacquer table.

Agatha went downstairs for something, spoke to Fanny, the portress, and returned. Outside the bedroom door, which was ajar, she heard a strange sound, like someone cracking nuts, she described it afterwards. She went in. Miss Morganhurst, her thin grey hair about her neck, clad only in her chemise, was sitting on her bed swinging her bare legs. At sight of Agatha she screeched like a parrot. As Agatha approached she sprang off the bed and advanced at her—her back bent, her fingers bent talon-wise. A stream of words poured from her lips. Every horror, every indecency, every violation of truth and honour that the war had revealed through the press, through books, through letters, seemed to have lodged in that brain. Every murder, every rape, every slaughter of innocent children, every violation of girls and old women—they were all there. She stopped close to Agatha and the words streamed out. At the end of every sentence, with a little sigh, she whispered—"I was there! I was there! . . . I've seen it."

Agatha, frozen with horror, remained; then, action coming back to her, she fled—Miss Morganhurst pursued her, her bare feet pattering on the carpet. She called Agatha by the name of some obscure German captain.

Agatha found a doctor. When they returned Miss Morganhurst was lying on her face on the floor in the darkness, hiding from what she saw. "I was there, you know," she whispered to the doctor as he put her to bed.

She died next day. Perhaps, after all, many people have felt the war more than one has supposed. . . .

Sentimental but True

1

Mrs. Comber had no idea where it came from. She had been sitting on the green, sloping cliff at Rafiel, a fishing village on the south coast of Cornwall, looking at the sea, and suddenly it came up to her.

'Came' is perhaps an inaccurate word—'rolled' or 'tumbled' would describe more nearly its motion, although even then one conveys no sense of its sudden, abrupt halt, a check so sharp that it seemed as though the dog must, by the force of it, be tumbled backwards.

It had come so suddenly from nowhere that Mrs. Comber of course expected that, in a moment, someone (its master or mistress) would turn the corner and summon it down the hill. But the minutes passed and no one came, and the sun continued to blaze out of burning blue into burning blue, and little Rafiel lay on its back down in the valley behind the hill and simmered, and the dog sat there motionless, frozen into amazement at the vision of Mrs. Comber.

Mrs. Comber knew very little about dogs, but she knew enough to be sure that there was no other dog in the world quite like this one.

He might have been, were he smaller, a Yorkshire terrier, or, were he very, very much larger, a sheep-dog. He had, too, a dash of Skye. He was small but remarkably square, so square that he bore a distinct resemblance to the popular conception of a sea-captain. Hair that was turned up at the ends of it into little curls by the wind fell all about him—over his eyes, spreading into an American sharp-pointed beard under his chin, making his legs like the legs of an Eskimo, waving in frantic agitation all round his stump of a tail. His nose, like a wet black button, and his mouth, with an under-lip that went back in rather a melancholy curve, were his most certain features, but his eyes, when his hair allowed you to see them, were a beautiful melting brown.

Perhaps the most amazing thing about him was that the second half of his body was quite different from the first half, being broader and thicker, so that he seemed to have been the complete result of two divided dogs—and these two had been rather badly glued together.

He looked at Mrs. Comber and then he laughed. He gave two short, sharp barks and wagged his stump of a tail.

Mrs. Comber was large and highly coloured. Her face was stout and good-natured; her eyes appealed to you as though they said, 'I know that I'm silly and stupid and scatter-brained, but do try to find something to like in me.'

She liked to wear purple or bright green or red; she always looked untidy and a little dusty; she was always in a breathless hurry, hastening to do something that she had forgotten, and so forgetting something that she ought already to have done. She loved to be liked, and therefore seized at any sign of goodwill, but she always made advances too quickly, was flung back, and, with tears, determined that she'd never make advances to anyone again, and then made them again immediately.

Her husband was stupid, conventional, self-opinionated, and an entirely self-satisfied man, who took his wife for granted, and thought she was lucky to be allowed to serve his wants. He was a master at Moffatt's, a school not far from Rafiel, and there he had been during twenty years of his life, and would be in all probability for twenty years more. He liked food and golf and bridge and arguments and putting people in their places. He despised his wife in her sentimental moments and disliked her in her careless ones, but on the whole, he found her useful.

Mrs. Comber had felt lonely and just a little depressed. Certainly, this fine weather was very wonderful, and it was a great deal better— oh, yes! A *great* deal better—than that miserable wet time that they had had during their first days in Rafiel, but it *did* mean that her husband disappeared every morning with his golf-clubs and was no more seen until the evening, when he was too tired to talk.

No one, up at the *pension* where they were staying, appealed to her except a girl, Miss Salter, who was at the present moment occupied with a young man who was expected very shortly to propose.

So, in spite of her protestations, Mrs. Comber was lonely. Up at the villa she said, 'I can't tell you how delightful it is just pottering about by myself all about the little place. One gets to know the villagers so well. They are always so glad to see one, so friendly, it's quite like home. I've never enjoyed myself so much.'

But the honest truth was that Mrs. Comber longed for company. As the wife of a schoolmaster she had during the greater part of the year more than enough of her fellow-creatures. One might have supposed that solitude would be pleasant for a little time. So, in theory it was. During the heat and battle of term-time, to be alone seemed the most fortunate of destinies. But now in practice—now!

Mrs. Comber looked at the blue sea and the green cliffs and longed for conversation, affection, the positive proof that there was someone in the world—scoundrel or vagabond, it did not matter—who was at that moment desiring her company.

Well, the dog desired it. Of that there could be no possible doubt. His brown eyes, through the tangled hair, gazed at Mrs. Comber with the utmost devotion. Then, his whole body quivering, his lip drew back and he grinned, the most pathetic, urgent, wheedling grin.

Down upon the black rocks far below, the gulls, like flakes of snow, hovered and wheeled, rose and fell. The sea broke into crisp patterns along the shore; its lazy murmur mingled with the hum of bees behind her, among the honeysuckle.

Round the point the Rafiel fishing-boats, with their orange sails, stole as though bent on some secret, nefarious business.

Mrs. Comber, who was emotional and completely at the mercy of fine weather and a coloured world, felt that her heart was full. She drew the dog towards her.

2

Seven o'clock struck suddenly down in the valley, and Mrs. Comber ceased her conversation with the dog and pulled herself together.

Meanwhile, she had told the dog everything. She had explained to him that apparently hopeless paradox that, although one was longing for peace and quiet, yet nevertheless one hated solitude. She explained to him all the disadvantages of having to do with schools most of one's life, and at the same time gave him to understand that she was not complaining, and that many poor people had much worse times, and that most of her troubles came from the difficulties of her own temperament, from her impetuosity and clumsiness and bad memory for detail.

The dog understood every word of it.

He had a way of sitting with one of his back legs stretched out in a straight line from his body, so that he seemed more certainly than ever to be compounded of two different dogs. His brown eyes gazed sadly out to sea, but every now and again he bent forward and licked her hand. She had now no sense, when she had finished her impetuous disclosures, of shame because she had been too garrulous, too intimate, too confiding. The dog could have listened to a great deal more.

He followed closely at her side as she walked down the hill. She had still, at the back of her brain, a confused sense that his master would suddenly appear round the corner. She would be very sorry when he was taken away from her.

He ran on in front of her, ran back, jumped upon her, showed himself in every way delighted at the afternoon's events. When he ran, he ran like a rabbit with his stump of a tail in the air, his head down, his ears flapping, and his legs scattering.

The evening scents stole out upon the air. The little square harbour was starred and crossed with reflected lights—blue and brown and grey. The crooked streets flung voices from one corner to another and one evening star came out.

Mrs. Comber climbed the opposite hill up to Sea View Villa, and still the dog was with her.

At one of the little cottages she stopped for a moment to speak to Mr. Tregatta, known in the village by the title of 'Captain.' Captain Tregatta, although he was sixty-two, looked not a day more than forty. He was short and square, with the compact, buttoned look that years in the navy give a man. He had retired now and received a small pension weekly.

He lived for two things—his son and music—and he had talked a good deal to Mrs. Comber about both of these things. His son was in a hosier's in Bristol, and he had not, during the last five years, found time to come and pay his father a visit, and had quite plainly expressed his wish that his father should not come and visit him. So, his father had waited, and now, as Mrs. Comber knew, the son was at last coming home.

'Tomorrer,' said the captain, as he gave Mrs. Comber good evening, 'tomorrer the lad's comin', bless 'is 'eart. "Inconvenient, dad, though it is," 'e writes to me, "I wouldn't disappoint 'ee"—no, nor 'e wouldn't, bless 'ee.'

'I'm sure I'm very glad,' said Mrs. Comber, a little doubtfully, wondering whether the reality of this reluctant son from a Bristol hosier's would be quite so glorious as the anticipation. She liked the little captain better than anyone in Rafiel. He had a mild blue eye, a most sentimental heart, and he was lonely.

115

'That's a nice little dawg,' eyeing Mrs. Comber's shaggy admirer, who was sitting now with his leg out and his lip in.

'Yes,' said Mrs. Comber eagerly. 'I don't know whom it belongs to. It just came along and attached itself to me. Dogs are so confiding, aren't they? And, really, it's a nice little creature. Yes—well, if you hear of anyone who's lost one, Captain Tregatta. Goodnight.'

She climbed the hill and did hope, as she went, that the son would not turn out too dreadfully disappointing—five years in a hosier's shop could make such a difference.

It was then, as the hideous front of Sea View Villa shone horribly before her, that she first seriously confronted the question of the dog. He, she could perceive, had no question at all as to what she would do with him, and his confidence alone would have made it difficult for her to dismiss him.

But she knew, assuredly, without any question of his attitude to her, that she could not leave him. It might be only for to-night. Probably in the morning someone would come and claim him. But tonight she must keep him.

Then, as she drew nearer Sea View Villa, she knew that she would need all her courage. Had she been of the type that perpetually accuses Fate she would have taken this moment as only another instance of the way that she was for ever driven into the ludicrous. Other human beings passed through life gathering what they desired, achieving their aims, always, to the end, preserving their dignity. But she—

Years ago, when she had first married Freddie Comber, she had told herself that, whatever happened, for his sake as well as her own, she must henceforth never be absurd.

And since then, beyond her agency, without any action on her part, she was driven again and again into ridiculous situations. She was always being driven into them. Things that others could achieve without danger were, for her, beset with difficulties. Always the laughing audience, always that amused anticipation 'that Mrs. Comber would put her foot into it.'

Well, for herself, she might perhaps endure it, but Freddie did hate it so. He hated it, and he showed her that he hated it.

Now, once again, when an ordinary person could arrive with perfect security at a *pension* with a strange dog, Mrs. Comber knew that, for herself, it would be a position of danger and insecurity. Freddie liked dogs—of his own discovering—but he would hate this one. The others, with the exception of Miss Salter, would see in it 'another of

Mrs. Comber's funny ways.' Mrs. Pentaglos, the head of Sea View Villa, would be kind and polite, but she would disapprove.

For an instant Mrs. Comber hesitated. Then, remembering that long exchange of intimacies on the cliff, she marched boldly forward.

3

She had hoped that, on this one occasion, Fortune would favour her, would permit her to creep round at the back with the dog and put him in the outhouse, then gradually, at her own time, she might explain to them his presence. But no. How like Fortune's treatment of her! There, to her horror, she saw them all, taking their last glimpse at a magnificent sunset, sitting in the little green strip of garden.

She could not escape them. Freddie, just returned from golf, was standing, in radiant glow from the sunset, enormous, important, in the fullest of plus fours.

She heard him say, 'You can take my opinion for what it is worth, Mrs. Cronnel. I don't pretend to be one of these brainy fellows.'

She'd heard him say that so often before. Mrs. Cronnel, always fat and yellow, but now under the sunset positively golden, was filling a large easy-chair and was looking up into Freddie Comber's face with rapt attention. Miss Bride and Miss Salter, two young ladies who were rivals for the hand of Mr. Salmon, the only bachelor resident at Sea View Villa, were saying bitter things to one another in a sprightly and amiable manner.

All these people turned at the sound of Mrs. Comber's feet upon the gravel and saw her, flushed, untidy, agitated, with a strange dog at her side. Mrs. Cronnel, who for obvious reasons hated Mrs. Comber, cried, with a shrill scream, 'Oh! a dog!'

Otherwise there was silence.

Mrs. Comber, laughing nervously, came forward.

'Oh! I didn't know you'd all be here; that is, I might have guessed that you'd all be looking at the sunset—so natural—but here you all are. Yes, I've found a dog, such a dear little thing, and it would come all the way with me, although I did try to send it back. I *did* really. But you know what dogs are, Mrs. Cronnel.' (Mrs. Cronnel, who detested dogs, obviously, from her expression, declined to have any knowledge of them whatever.) 'I hadn't the heart, I hadn't really. Isn't he jolly? A Yorkshire, I think, only he's rather large. He's so hairy I think I shall call him Rags.'

Mrs. Comber paused.

Mrs. Cronnel said, with a cruel little smile, 'Rather a commonplace name for a dog, Mrs. Comber.'

Mrs. Comber laughed nervously. 'Oh, do you think so? Perhaps it is.'

Then there was a long pause. The dog looked at them all and understood at once that he was not likely to be very popular there. But he had, in all probability, been received doubtfully before on other occasions. He was brave; he smiled at them all, wagged his tail, went into the middle of them, pretended to see an enemy, growled; rolled on his back, finally sat up, and, with one ear back, lifted his blackberry nose towards Mr. Comber with the most amiable of interrogations.

Freddie Comber looked at him, then across at his wife. 'What a cur!' he snapped, and vanished.

Mrs. Comber slowly coloured, and a little smile, intended for bravery, but too struggling and fugitive for success, came and passed.

They all saw it, and even in Mrs. Cronnel's dry heart there was sympathy. Miss Salter fell on her knees before the dog.

'You darling! You really are! Oh, Mrs. Comber, how splendid of you to find him! I know Mrs. Pentaglos won't mind. He can be kept in the stable. And he looks as good as gold. I *know* he's adorable.'

To all the women, as they stood there with the dusk coming up about them, there came the thought that men were beasts, that women must band together, that no woman in the world could ever be as cruel as Mr. Comber had been. For the moment they came together—Miss Bride and Miss Salter, Mrs. Comber and Mrs. Cronnel.

'I knew you'd all love him,' said Mrs. Comber, in an ecstasy.

4

Freddie Comber was one of those men who say a thing by accident and then afterwards cling to what they have said as though it were the key-note of their lives. He liked dogs—he had always liked them.

Had Mrs. Cronnel found the dog, or had even his own Mrs. Comber brought it to him at a propitious moment—when he was flushed with success at golf or billiards or argument—he would in all probability have taken the dog to himself, acclaimed it as his own find, petted and indulged it.

But his wife had arrived at a moment when he was explaining the world to sympathetic listeners, she had looked foolish and frightened—the dog had been condemned.

He had called the dog a cur in public, therefore must the dog always be a cur. His wife had been foolish about the dog in the beginning, therefore must she always be considered foolish. The dog was a nuisance, his wife was a fool—so must things remain.

He regarded Rags, therefore, with exceeding disgust, and the secret affection that he felt for him in his heart only spurred him to further obstinate exhibitions of his disgust.

At any rate, the dog must be a wastrel of the very worst description, because nobody came to claim him. It was obvious to any intelligent person that his former owner had desired anxiously to be rid of him. Probably the dog had some horrible disease or infirmity. Probably he had a vicious temper and bit children and horses. Drowning was much the best thing.

'I know a bit about dogs,' he would say a hundred times a day, 'and if ever there was a cur—'

Secretly, in his heart, he admired it. With the other inhabitants of Sea View Villa Rags had instantly won his way.

He was a dog of the most engaging character in the world and of an amazing intuition. He realised, for instance, that what Mrs. Cronnel liked was for people to be deferential to her, to listen and to admire. He therefore lay at her feet and looked up at her golden locks with the burning eyes of a devout adorer. He never practised upon her his humour, of which he had a vast store. She did not understand humour.

He kept his humour for Miss Salter, in whom it lay dormant, waiting for encouragement. Miss Salter had been too anxiously engaged in landing Mr. Salmon to see anything in a very humorous light, but Rags restored to her the funny side of things and was never serious with her for a moment.

To Mrs. Pentaglos he paid the deference that is due to the head of an establishment, to one who may dismiss you in an instant into an outhouse if she so pleases. He was always very staid and respectful to Mrs. Pentaglos.

But it was to Mrs. Comber only that he gave his heart.

The two of them discovered during the weeks that they were together a thousand things that they had in common. They were really very alike in many ways, except that the dog had far more adapted himself much more swiftly to the atmosphere about him. Comber herself perceived this. She saw that the dog at Sea View was a very different dog from the dog down in Rafiel. At the v was ordinary, amusing on the surface. He did little tricks; he in an amiable manner on the grass; he allowed himself to be petted by Miss Salter or Mrs. Pentaglos. Down in the narrow little streets of the village he was a dog of importance and also a dog of mysterious perceptions and intuitions.

Mrs. Comber felt that, with the dog at her side, she was more at home among those cobbles, bending roofs, sudden glimpses of blue water, and clustered fishing-boats than she ever was alone. Rags knew every inhabitant; he selected the good from the bad, the worthy from the unworthy; he was treated with a deference by the other dogs of the place that was remarkable indeed, for the dogs of Rafiel were a wild and savage race.

To Mrs. Comber the effect of it all was astonishing—it was as though the dog were, through all these weeks, explaining the place to her. She felt it—the mysterious, subtle life of it—so poignantly that the knowledge that in another week or two she must be uprooted from it all and go back to her commonplace, workaday Moffatt's—little boys, mutton underdone, Freddie overdone—seemed to her, through these glorious hours, an incredible disaster.

She couldn't go back—she couldn't go back. Then, coming to herself, she laughed. Had she not lived that life for all these past years? Could one always expect holiday?

Then also, perhaps, if the dog had so lightened this place for her ↄ would also lighten Moffatt's in the same way. She must take him k—she *must* take him back. Would Freddie allow it? He *must* allow ﹒is time she would have her way.

˥all the Rafiel natives Rags liked best Captain Tregatta. The little d an affection for all animals, but perhaps it was because he ﹒ed more truly than any other inhabitant the Rafiel spirit that ﹒ him so much. They had always, when they were together, ﹒ most complete understanding. Captain Tregatta did not ﹒ary to speak to Rags as he would to an ordinary dog. ﹒t needed.

﹒, indeed, almost resented a feeling that she had when ﹒ both that she was 'out of it.'

ﹶke young Tregatta from Bristol. He would go no— ﹒would neither bark nor smile, wag nor quiver. He

﹒ot like the young man either. He was thin, with ﹒eyes and a pallid cheek. His ears stood out from ﹒ patronised and sneered at his father. He always

ɔˉ
re-
act,
Mrs.
Villa
lla he
played

120

'washed his hands' as he came towards Mrs. Comber, and obviously found it very difficult to refrain from saying, 'And what can I do for you today, madam?'

They stood, all four, outside Captain Tregatta's cottage. Young Tregatta said:

'Well, it 'as been a fine day, ma'am.'

'Yes,' said Mrs. Comber, who was always at her most voluble when she was in company that she disliked. 'It has—really wonderful; so much colour and sun. I—'

'My boy's had a fine outing today, haven't yer, John? We went and picnicked up along to Durotter, us and the Simpsons and Mrs.—'

'All right, father,' the young man interrupted. 'Stow it. Stupid day, I call it.'

He caught Rags's eye. Rags was regarding him with a cold and haughty malevolence. He bent down and snapped his fingers. '*Goo'* dog—*goo'* doggie! Come along then.'

Rags did nothing, but continued to stare. Mrs. Comber wished them good night and passed up the hill. How she disliked the young man! The captain had a wistful look; she was sure that the son had been a great disappointment. What a horrid mess towns could make of a man!

5

And now was she horribly driven in upon her climax. Never in all her married life before had she so eagerly desired a request to be granted by Freddie. Never before had she faced the approaching moment of demand with such sinkings of the heart.

They had only another three days before they must return to Moffatt's, and with every instant of the swiftly vanishing time the spell of Rafiel increased. Could she take Rags back with her to her daily life, then she would seem to be taking with her some of the adorable things that belonged to Rafiel. He would remind her of some of the most precious moments of her life.

But, indeed, of himself now he had contrived to squeeze himself into her heart. Whatever part she might play to herself, God knew that for many years that heart had been empty. But Rags had wanted it and had taken it.

She watched Freddie's every movement now to give her a clue to his probable answer. Golf had been well with him during these last days; he was in a good temper. Had Mrs. Comber been able to hide her feelings, had she managed to surprise him suddenly with her request, at the last moment, on the eve of departure, she might have won. But she was no diplomatist. She showed him by her fluttering agitation that there was something that she wanted to ask him, and she showed him that she was afraid, already, lest he should refuse.

That determined him at once. He *would* refuse. These little opportunities of displaying his authority were of great value. Every husband ought to refuse his wife at least once a month. He would certainly refuse.

The moment came. It was the last night but one of their holiday, and Freddie was undoing his collar before the looking-glass. The head of the stud had allowed itself to be bent and the collar refused to move.

Of course, Mrs. Comber chose this unpropitious moment for her petition. It was odd that she should feel seriously about it, but her throat was quite dry and her heart was beating furiously.

'Freddie!'

'Yes? Confound it!'

'Freddie!'

'Well?'

'I wonder—I've been thinking—it's occurred to me—'

The stud broke, the collar was off, but what was one going to do in the morning? There was no other stud with a large enough head, and on the very day when there would be so much to see to—

'Hang it! Well?'

'I'm so sorry, dear. Perhaps I'll be able to find another. What I was going to say, to ask you, was whether—if you wouldn't very much mind—whether—he wouldn't be in the way, really no trouble at all, and it would make such a difference to me—and I think you'd like him after a time; it would be so nice for the boys, too, and there *is* that kennel—'

'What *are* you talking about?'

He had turned and faced her, his cheeks still flushed with the exertion of the stud.

'Well'—Mrs. Comber's voice trembled a little—'it's only Rags. I thought, if you didn't dreadfully mind, if I might—if we might—take him back with us to Moffatt's; it would make *such* a difference to me. I've got to love this place so, you know, and you'll think it very silly of me, but if I had Rags with me at Moffatt's—well, I know you'll think it just like my usual silliness, but I should feel as though I had taken a bit of this place with me.'

Freddie had said no word, only stood there, staring at her, and fingering, absent-mindedly, his stud. Her allusion to the place had suddenly surprised some curious feeling, right down deep in him, that he too had loved this Rafiel, had had the best of days here, would be immensely sorry to leave it. And this sudden feeling angered him. What was he doing with feelings of that kind?

He was quite ashamed, and resenting his shame, laid the discomfort of it to his wife's charge, and beyond her to the dog. The dog! The mongrel!

His wife wanted the dog at Moffat's. She was terrified lest he should refuse. He was master. He was a man. No more of this miserable sentiment for him. He would show her.

'Once for all,' he said, glowering at her, 'you can put that out of your mind. I've hated the dog from the first; it's a beastly mongrel, and the sooner it's drowned the better.'

'But, Freddie—'

'Not another word will I utter. I'm a man who means what he says.'

'Please, just listen. He—'

'No more. I've got to get undressed. You must get rid of the dog.'

She saw that it was final—that, and how much else? For, as he stood there, denying her this simple thing, as he looked at her so angrily, so cruelly, she knew, once and for all, that all her love for him was gone, had been gone indeed for many years past. She would in the future care for him in a protecting, motherly way; she would always be a good wife to him, but no more passion, no more colour, no more poetry.

She turned away and lay by his side that night as though he were suddenly a stranger. In the morning it was almost more than she could bear, the joy that Rags, coming to meet her, flung upon her. He curved round until his tail was nearly in his mouth; he bared his teeth; his stump of a tail, with hair branching out of it on every side until it looked like a Christmas-tree, almost wagged itself from his body. It was very early, before breakfast. Down the hill they went into the little village, all sparkling with morning freshness, the little quay reeking with fish, the cobbles glittering with silver scales.

She turned the corner and came out on to the path that runs above the little harbour. The boats, blue and green, lay in rows and, beyond and above them, the little white cottages stole up the hill into all the misty brightness of a summer morning. A haze was over the sea, so that it came quite suddenly out of nowhere, white and blue on to the rocks.

The abandon and reality of the beauty of it all came up to Mrs. Comber, but she seemed to have no place in it. The future of her life, how dreary, how purposeless! Not even Rags to comfort her! For the first time since her marriage she rebelled—hotly, fiercely rebelled. Why should she not leave Freddie? Why should she be the only one in the world to do without things? Why *need* she suffer so? It was the hardest, sharpest, cruellest moment of her life.

Little Captain Tregatta turned the corner. Rags ran forward to meet him, jumped upon him, licked his hand. But Captain Tregatta's face was sad, his shoulders drooped, he looked old.

'Good marnin', ma'am.'

'Good morning,' said Mrs. Comber.

'Lovely day. Yes, indeed, if you're in tune for it; but there's nothing like lovely weather for making you melancholy if you're out of sorts.'

His distress touched her at once.

'I'm sorry if something's the matter,' she said.

'Oh! it's silly. Only my boy. ''E goes back to Bristol today, and 'e's glad to go. Yes, 'e is—I knaws it. And 'e'll never come back, I knaw that, too. All this time I've been 'appy thinking that 'e cared for me—maybe 'e was a bit busy, but 'e cared all the same—and now I knaws 'e doesn't—I knaws it; and now all the day will be without somethin', always. It's a long time to be waitin', doing nothing, thinking of nothing.'

Rags, with his back legs before his front ones, sat hunched up, looking at the sea.

As she felt the glory of the morning the idea came to her—it flashed upon her.

'Captain Tregatta,' she said hurriedly, 'I'm going away tomorrow—I can't take the dog with me. It wouldn't do in a school, you know. Would you look after him for me? Keep him here with you so that he'll be here when I come back next summer. I've loved Rafiel so, and I feel that if I knew you were both here together I would feel as though I'd got a link with the place—both of you together here.'

'I will, ma'am,' he said. 'Certainly, I will. 'E'll be 'ere for yer when yer come back to us, as I hope yer will.' Then, with a little sigh of satisfaction, 'Yes. That's correct.'

Mrs. Comber thanked him. She waited, tried to say more, but failed.

They all three looked out to sea. Cries and bells came up to them from the village. Suddenly Mrs. Comber, very red in the face, caught Rags's body in her arms, gave him one hug, and then thrust him into the captain's hands.

'There—take him—take him. You two together will be splendid to think of. Goodbye—goodbye. I'm feeling too silly for words. Good-bye—goodbye—goodbye.'

She went, almost running, down into the flashing village, past the fish, the smells, the gossip, the cobbles—up the hill to Sea View Villa.

She did not turn or stay, but in her heart, there was that picture of the dog and the man—both of them wanting her to come back.

She had staked her claim in Rafiel after all.

Portrait in Shadow

Mr. K— told me this story one wet day in Cumberland. He did not tell it me all in one piece: the first part of it I had as we walked in soaking rain from Braithwaite to Buttermere, the second part that same evening over a fire in the Buttermere Inn, and he finished it for me next day on our tramp under a mellow September sun into Ennerdale. We had met three days before in Keswick; we were both looking for the right kind of companion. The week that we then spent together seemed to promise a good and strong friendship but, alas, K— died in the following year, of pneumonia. I have concealed his name because he would himself have wished it. He had a charming and most original talent, but some kind of delicacy and mistrust of himself, also, I fancy, a constitutional ill-health which all his life pursued him, and thirdly a comfortable income, prevented him from making the mark that he should have done. In all his forty-eight years he published only three little books; one of them, a slight but most brilliant Venetian story, had some success.

However, in these days, with the rush, roar and confusion of letters, a very delicate and fugitive talent such as his has not, I fear, a great chance of survival.

In appearance K— was tall, slim, and fragile. He had eyes of a very bright blue and eyebrows that were almost white, so faint in colour were they. He had a charming nervous smile and never seemed to be quite sure what to do with his legs and his arms.

But it was his voice that was beautiful. How can I describe it? Anyone who knew it will hear the echo of it so long as life lasts. It had a cadence of reminiscence as though it were best pleased to speak of the past. The timbre was marvellous, very lightly pitched and yet as clear as a bell across water. He was the least affected of men, yet he had a way of lingering over a beautiful word as though he hated to let it go.

His shyness, his humour, good-fellowship, almost childish gratitude for being liked, all these things made up his charm, and yet there was more than these—some special goodness of spirit, perhaps, that put him a little apart from other men.

This was his story. I have tried to give it as though he were himself telling it. The point about it is that it should have happened to K— of all people in the world. There are men I know to whom such an incident would have been nothing at all. It would have been forgotten as soon as it occurred. To K— it was epochal, transforming. The man with the hair *en brosse,* the room with the picture, these were part of his life for ever after.

It happened (said K—) more than twenty years ago. Before the war—the way we date everything now. I had come down from Oxford and was very uncertain as to my next step. I had some means of my own, you see, and I was an orphan. I have been an orphan nearly all my life.

I had been brought up by an uncle who lived in Leeds, but he died while I was at Oxford, and it was then that an aunt of mine became my friend. The odd thing about this aunt was that she was only some five years older than myself. She was my father's youngest sister, fifteen years younger than he. My father married when he was twenty, and I was his only child. I did not see much of this aunt until my uncle died. She lived with a rather tyrannical, selfish father in London. Then at almost the moment when my uncle died her father died also, and that seemed to bring us together. We were both quite alone in the world.

But she was in a worse position than I, for she had almost no means. She was perfectly charming. I can't possibly give you any idea of her charm. She was slight, fair, most delicately made, full of zest for life, a zest that she had never been able to fulfil. She had always had the very dullest time.

She was a child in many ways, taking everything with an eager intensity and quite surprisingly ignorant of the world. As a matter of fact, I was that also. I had never been strong, had been driven by a quite invincible shyness into a remote life of my own. I wanted to make friends but did not know how to make them. So, when we discovered one another, it was wonderful for both of us. Almost the first thing I wanted to do was to take her abroad and give her a splendid holiday. She had never been out of England.

The thought of the holiday excited her tremendously. I can see her now, sitting in a dingy room of the London house, leaning on the table after breakfast, her fragile body shaking with enthusiasm, a fog slurring the lines of the street beyond the window, the sordid remains of the meal all about her, as she cried:

'Oh, but how wonderful! . . . France, Spain, Italy . . .!'

In the end it was Spain, and, of all mad things, the North of Spain in August. I know that we were crazy, and you may be sure that every-one told us that we were. The North of Spain! August! and you must remember that before the war Spain was by no means the sanitary and clinical paradise that its splendid 'Turismo' has lately succeeded in making it.

Yes, everyone said that we were mad, but it was the Sun that we both wanted. We found that we were completely agreed about that. My aunt had never had any sun at all. She had never been really warm. Northern Spain in August—yes, we would be certain to be warm!

So off we went. What an enchanting journey we had! We found that we were perfect travelling companions. The perfect travelling companion! Isn't he or she practically an impossibility? As with mar-riage, you may compromise, and nine out of ten times you do. Is it your fault or the other's? Surely not your own, for you start out with such splendid confidence as to your own character. And, to the very last, it isn't your own character that seems to have failed. Aside from one or two little irritabilities you have been perfect, but the other—! You had no idea before you started of the weaknesses, the selfish-ness, the odd, exasperating tricks, the refusal to agree to the most obvious course, the insistence on unimportant personal rights! No, it has most certainly *not* been your fault; and yet, in retrospect, are there not suddenly exposed certain flecks, little blemishes in your own personality that you had never suspected?

Forgive me for emphasising the obvious, but this very question of companionship plays its important part in the little story. For my aunt and myself were the most perfect companions. We simply found, as the days passed and all those little accidents, upsets, surprises, turned up their innocent faces, as they always do on such an expedition, that we were only more and more suited to one another. We liked the same things but had our different points of view, we were amused by the same nonsense, exhilarated by the same drama, enriched by the same beauty.

My aunt's sure perception and lovely sense of humour threw a light about her as a flower is lit by the shaking glitter of a neighbour-ing fountain. She had that iridescence, that eternal possibility of some beautiful surprise. And yet what a child she was! She had indeed seen nothing of life at all, and every moment of her day was a wonder and an amaze.

Well, we reached San Sebastian, and the heat was terrific. It was then that for the first time I knew a moment of alarm. This was indeed heat as I had never known it, and I lay, that first night in the San Sebastian hotel, naked on my bed while the sweat poured in streams off my body. My aunt, however, I discovered next morning, was in no way inconvenienced by it. She was ready, she declared, for anything!

I was determined to discover some small place by the sea that should be for us characteristically Spanish but quiet and beautiful. Quiet, you know, is not Spain's most eminent characteristic! I asked the porter of the hotel, and he spoke to me at once of the little resort of Z—, a charming place, he said, over the hills, quiet and beautiful. Strange to think that it was from the round plump features of the porter of that San Sebastian hotel that, in such commonplace words, I first heard of a spot that would never, from that moment, leave me again!

I spoke of it to my aunt and she enthusiastically agreed! How little we both of us knew to what we were going!

At that time a small clumsy railway ran over the mountains to the sea. Into the fearfully hot, exceedingly democratic carriage we climbed! We had chosen an evening train that we might escape the heat of the day. We were embedded in a cheerful clump of eager, friendly people, two priests, an old and a young one, three pretty girls, a stout farmer, a clerk. I can see them all now as though they were still with me, as perhaps they are! I knew some Spanish. There are no people at the same time so friendly and so uninterfering as the Spaniards! Their hospitality is prodigious, their pride and sensitiveness also. They are gay, but never to abandon, and one of their mysteries is that they should at the same time be so kind to children and so cruel to animals.

The heat, I suppose (for that carriage *was* hot!), sent me into a kind of trance. I saw my companions after a while as trees walking, and the coloured haze that fell in an ever-deepening purple bloom about the hills seemed to tell me that I was entering a new country.

There is little twilight in this country—soon all was dark beyond our windows, and when at last we had arrived we stepped down into mystery. About us, in the little station, I remember, was the sharp scent of some strange unknown flower and the dry sandy whisper of the sea. No breeze, and a sky stiff with the most silver stars I had ever seen.

But it was in the morning that, on waking, we realised the splendour into which we had stepped. It is the charm of Z— that it lies, surrounded with woods, backed by mountains, in a kind of delicious privacy, as though that especial piece of sea were its own creation and separate possession. The beach is in fact large, but the black rocks that run out on either side to protect it give it a natural aristocracy, as though it were a beach preserved during many, many years by some lordly and beneficent owner for the pleasure of his friends.

Not that it was deserted or sacred with a sort of Crusoe loneliness. Far from it. As we looked out on it that morning (we had slept late) all the brilliantly striped tents—green, purple, red, yellow—were unfolding and from every side, down the hill, the bathers, all wrapped in dressing-gowns as gay as flower-beds, were advancing. I believe that even now, you know, that Spanish custom of coloured dressing-gowns on the beaches is preserved.

Well, but when we saw it all more completely we had both the same sensation. Z— was like a flower shining at the heart of dark leaves, for all the brilliance of light and colour was enfolded by the dark woods, darker than any woods that we had ever seen.

'It must be terrible in rain and storm,' said my aunt with a little shiver, and then I, looking more closely, fancied that some of the old houses that bordered the woods were of the order of the storm and the wind, old and green, with gardens along whose paths the leaves thickened and in whose hedges no birds sang. This light in this darkness! That was Z—!

Only this was curious—on that very first morning, the two of us walking out towards the beach together, I noticed, from all the others, the very house, the house that still so often seems to invite me within its doors,—a gate, rather shabby, a garden-path, some beds thick with dark-red flowers, a front of faded brown, and a bright green door with a silver knocker. It was, I think, the bright green and the silver of the knocker that attracted me. The knocker sparkled in the sun, and even as we looked the door opened and an old lady and gentleman, the old lady in a large black hat and leaning on a stick, walked out. We passed on.

Reaching the beach, it seemed to our young and inexperienced souls that we had attained Paradise. The water came rolling in, trembling in crystal lights, green like a bird's wing; the tents of crimson and gold were grander and more lordly than anything that we had ever imagined for a beach.

Undressing under a rock on the Cornish coast was the nearest to them that we knew. Don't imagine, though, that there was anything stiff or ceremonial about the life here. For a week at least, we were as happy and care-free as any two in the world. I knew some Spanish, my aunt could smile and nod her head and look the friend of all the world, which, for that moment, she was.

Yes, we had the happiest week of our lives. We had never conceived such a sun, such colour, such laughter, such freedom from interference, such willingness on the part of everyone that we should be at home.

Then, on a lovely morning, sometime between seven and eight, bathing alone, I encountered a gentleman in the water. He was, judging by his head, a very jolly gentleman indeed.

He shouted that it was a lovely morning, that the water was perfect. I called back in my funny Spanish that he couldn't possibly say enough about it or do it any sort of justice.

It was, I think, my funny Spanish that won him, for, coming out of the sea at the same time as myself, he said that he supposed that I was English or American. Now that should have told me something, for the Spaniards, the *right* Spaniards, are the most courteous people in the world and never press into the privacy of anyone.

But I never gave that a thought. I liked him at once. Standing there in the new morning sun, the water dropping from him in crystal drops, he was as handsome a man as I've ever seen—more handsome, I sometimes think, than anyone else in the world. What was he like? I don't know, except that his hair stood up stiffly *en brosse,* even then when it was soaked with water. Its colour was raven black, his body bronze. He had a small mole underneath one eye. We talked, and he made me lose my accustomed shyness. He had always a great deal to say and he found everything amusing. He told me at once his name— Ramon Quintero. He was staying with relations. He had been here a fortnight. He liked English people. How well I spoke Spanish! Oh yes, I did. My accent was very attractive.

At breakfast I told my aunt about him. Later that morning while we sat under our crimson tent, eating grapes, he was introduced to her. I know now that she fell in love with him at once, and that from that moment some thin, almost invisible cloud obscured our own relationship.

What a commonplace it is nowadays to remark that we are all as lonely in this life as Crusoe on his island, but it is true enough. On the instant that I introduced Ramon Quintero (robed, I remember, at the moment in a purple dressing-gown, his face of shining bronze, his blue eyes sparkling with an amusement that seemed always to be more directed against himself than anyone else) to my aunt, I lost for ever the only really close intimacy with another human being that I have ever known or, I fancy, ever will know.

Remember that my aunt and I had only reached any sort of true companionship during the last week; there had not been time enough for a real basis of trust, fond though we were growing of one another. Had fate given us another two months—! But it did not. Does it not often seem to break something that is *almost* completed?—shrugging its shoulders, saying: 'Oh, well, this is disappointing. I thought it would turn out better. I'll smash this and start again.'

In any case she was not, I suppose, sure enough of herself. She fancied, perhaps, that I should think her foolish. . . . But I don't know. *I don't know.* That's what, after all this time, makes me so unhappy. Yes, even now. I'm telling you the story perhaps only that I may clear it up a little more to myself in the telling.

Such a child as she was, but not more of a child than I. Quintero must at once have put me right out of account as someone not worth considering. That is why the sequel must have astonished him!

I don't wonder now on looking back that she fell in love with him at sight. My only wonder is that I should have been such a fool as not to have noticed it, but I knew very little about life or human beings at that time. I was quite incredibly ignorant.

The other figure in the story now appears—Sancho Panza. He was obviously Sancho to anyone coming to Spain for the first time, although Ramon Quintero was most certainly no Don Quixote. He was round and fat like a tub, with a jolly laughing face, and he had all Sancho's proper equipment of proverbs, love of food and drink, a passion for display, a wife, to whom he was apparently devoted, very much in the background, and a passionate affection for his friend and master, Quintero. He was supposedly Quintero's secretary, although he never wrote any letters so far as I could see. He did everything for him—a great many things of which I was probably at the moment not in the least aware. He ran messages, endured every kind of insult, was Quintero's utterly faithful hound.

On the very first day of our acquaintanceship he mentioned my sister.

'My aunt,' I said.

'Your aunt? Impossible!'

I explained.

He spoke only Spanish. Quintero spoke only Spanish. That was one reason why I never dreamed of an intimacy between himself and her. How could there be? Which showed how little, how sadly little, I knew about love and lovers. Quintero was teaching her Spanish on that very first day.

Then Sancho said:

'So lovely and unmarried!'

'Yes,' I said.

'And rich? All the English are rich.'

'Rolling,' I answered. It was a joke, my answer, and, as it turned out, a deadly one.

I should have resented his impertinence, but it was impossible to resent anything that Sancho said or did. He meant so well to everyone.

The next thing that occurred was that we visited the house. I see now—oh, how many things I see!—that that had been arranged by the two of them. I can see her now as, coming over to me on the verandah of the hotel, laying her hand on my shoulder, she said:

'Mr. Quintero has asked us to go to tea tomorrow afternoon!'

'How do you know?' I said, laughing. 'You can't understand a word he says.'

'Oh yes, I can,' she answered.

I should have known by the way she said that that she had already moved worlds away from me. With what a speed, with what force of a sweeping whirlwind, this thing must have caught her! She was not one, as the sequel shows, to love idly or lightly. Had she been, there would have been no story in this. This was the way, I can see now, that she had always dreamt that love would come—in a foreign land, colour and loveliness on every side of her, and the handsomest, kindest, tenderest hero at her feet! Any girl's dream! How often in that ugly London house, with a cross father inside and the rain outside, she must have cherished just such dreams! Unlike Desdemona, she could not listen to his tales of peril and adventure, but with every word of Spanish that he taught her she crept closer to him, he had her in his possession more securely.

'Of course, we'll go,' I said. 'Quintero's a good fellow. I like him. Where does he live?'

Well, he was staying in that very house with the bright green door and the silver knocker! As we walked up the garden path the world closed in darkly about us. Spain is a noisy country; this house was as still as the grave. But my impressions of that first visit are an odd

133

conflict of silence and sound. The background did not accord with the actors in front of it. In an old room hung with a green wall-paper painted with golden bees we had tea. The two old people, relations of Quintero's, were there, Sancho Panza, my aunt and myself. Quintero was 'the life of the party.' He was brilliant; he was perfect. Merry, kind, full of ridiculous stories, considerate of everyone. How we laughed! We sang songs to an old cracked piano while the two old people sat and nodded their heads with approval like two gentle and very ancient mandarins. To all the noise the house made no response. Beyond the windows were the shadows of the trees, and through the trees the glory of the summer sun came so dimly that it flung a pale glow. Somewhere a bird twittered in a cage.

Then they said that we must see 'The Picture.' We climbed a fine old staircase that creaked with our steps, passed ghostly cabinets crowded with ghostly china, and then found ourselves in a room hung with red curtains, containing only a bookcase, a table, an old green silk settee, and some chairs as furniture, and there, the only ornament of the walls, was an amazing picture. I don't know how good a picture it was. I am no connoisseur. It represented a young man in eighteenth-century dress, standing against a dark background of porticoes, a fountain, shadowy trees. With head erect he stood smiling. His smile was as fascinating and as mysterious as the Gioconda's. He was young, fiery with energy and the pride of life. He was on tiptoe for any adventure. His beauty (for he was beautiful) resided in his eagerness, his almost impertinent self-confidence. While I looked I thought to myself, 'What a splendid friend to have!' and then, moving to another part of the room, the light changed for me, there came some twist in the lip, some evil glint in the eyes, and I said: 'He is a rogue, a rascal—I wouldn't trust him a yard.' Then, moving back again, all my confidence in him returned.

'That's odd,' I remember saying, but, looking round, found only the stout and smiling Sancho with me.

'Where are the others?'

'They have gone into the garden.'

I thought nothing of that. I was absorbed by the picture. I stayed there twenty minutes looking at the picture. Friend or rogue? Good man or base? To be trusted or to be fled from?

I did not know then. I do not know now.

We went to the house on many more occasions. We had tea and dinner there. Many of Quintero's friends came. Time passed with enchanting swiftness. The weather was lovely. The waves turned with caressing, loving lightness on the gold sand. The beach was covered with the brilliant shining tents, with hundreds of naked bronze babies; the women walked selling their biscuits, offering lottery tickets, crying the delights of the Tombola; evening after evening sank from crystal blue into grape-dark skies, and the mornings glittered like fire.

But suddenly I wasn't happy. Why? I didn't know. I wanted to go away, but my aunt grew pale at the hint. She had never been so happy anywhere in her life as here. I detected in her a strange kind of fierceness. I realised with a flash why I was unhappy. She and I had lost touch with one another. We were never alone any more. We had no longer any confidences. I brooded sometimes, but I was too young, too inexperienced, to find a solution—I knew that we loved one another as deeply as ever. What had occurred?

Then I began to hear things about Quintero. Speaking Spanish, I made friends easily, friends outside the Quintero circle. I found that Quintero was not approved of. He was a waster, an adventurer, something of a rascal. Oh, a jolly fellow of course! Grand company. But not to be trusted. Beware of him. Don't lend him money. A dangerous man about money. And yet there was nothing very definite. They told me frankly that there was nothing actually against him. Perhaps he was not bad, only—what was his occupation? On what did he live? And there were stories from Madrid. . . .

I wanted to speak to her about him and I had not the courage. She was so happy. She moved like the spirit of good fortune. I noticed— poor fool that I was—a kind of ecstasy of happiness in her eyes, in her laughter. But I guessed nothing. I only knew that we were never alone together, and I wanted to go away. . . .

Then, in a moment, in a blinding second of revelation, the catastrophe crashed. Blinding! That is my only excuse, that I had no chance of preparation, no time for thought.

One lovely morning I went down alone to the beach and came, without warning, upon Quintero and Sancho Panza. I came upon them in the middle of a fearful and appalling row. I caught a glimpse— as you see a face in a flash of lightning—of Quintero in a temper. It was a fine sight, something grand and elemental about it. He looked as though he could have caught the beach, tents and babies and all, into his fist and thrown it, crumpled to nothing, into the sea. He gave me one glance and, without a word, strode off.

Sancho was in a rage too. He was quivering like a jelly in his bathing-dress, a very ludicrous sight. He was too angry to measure his words. With real foreign abandon he flung himself on me. There were no words adequate for Quintero. Had he not slaved for him, endured every insult, served him as no other man? . . . and now to be cheated . . . . .money . . . fair wages . . . I caught here and there fragments of his fury.

'And you look out!' He grasped my arm. 'You say she's your aunt. Well, whatever she is, he's got her. In another day or two he'll be off with her, money and all. . . . What will *you* look like, my friend?'

I gazed at him bewildered. I had, I remember, a *sticky* sense of being bogged. I felt perhaps as a fly may feel when, dancing aimlessly, its spidery feet catch the fly-paper, its shrill buzz like the twanging of a thin wire. . . . But I didn't utter a sound. I simply stared at him. His contempt for me was boundless, aided perhaps by the consciousness of his coming contempt for himself for giving his beloved friend away. He had wondered how long it would be before I would see it. My aunt—or whatever she was—had been crazy about Quintero from the first instant. That was no new thing. Quintero was used to it. In ordinary he let them go. He was not in reality greatly interested in women. But this time it was different. He had liked her, she was pretty, only a child—and then he was low in funds. He had always intended to make a safe marriage. My aunt was 'rolling'—I had said so. It was myself, it seemed, who had been the trouble. At first, she had said that she must tell me everything. At least that is what they thought that she meant, for one of the great difficulties throughout had been her ignorance of Spanish on one side and his of English on the other. But he had convinced her that it would be wiser to tell me after the deed was done. To warn me would only disturb me, burden me with a sense of responsibility. In any case everything was arranged. In three days' time they were to be married in San Sebastian. . . .

'But she hasn't a penny!' was the cry on my lips. I don't know now what held me back. The beginning, maybe, of that uncertainty that has haunted me all my life after.

Well, I was in an agony of distress. I use that word deliberately. It *was* an agony, like the fiercest toothache or the first pain of a broken arm. For so many men it would have meant nothing at all. They would have gone to her and said: 'Look here, my dear, what's all this about your running away with a Spaniard? All nonsense. . . . He's a rogue and a vagabond. I'm not going to hear of it.' But it is the point of this story that neither she nor I could take anything lightly. This was the first big crisis of both our lives. If only it had come a little later when we knew one another better! But I walked down that beach simply feeling that I had been for ever and ever betrayed! I had lost, in one jeering glance from that Spaniard, the only loving intimacy I had ever known in my life. She might have told me. Oh! she might have told me!

And then, passion rising in me, my only thought was that I would at once prevent it. He was marrying her for her money—the old, old story—and she hadn't a penny! I had a wild, savage, childish, boyish pleasure in thinking that now I could have my revenge, that now I could make her unhappy. That wickedness—for such selfish angry cruelty is perhaps the wickedest thing our heart can know—rose round the light and happiness of those last weeks as the dark trees closed in on the golden beach and the bright jade water. I would not waste an instant. I would show my power.

I was, of course, on the outside edge of the story, completely justified. Here was my poor little friend, ignorant utterly of life, in the hands of an adventurer, whom I, by a casual careless remark, had led into thinking her wealthy.

It was my plain duty to put things right. *That* on the outside—the *heart* of the affair was quite other.

Miserable, angry, blinded as though the sand had risen in a storm about my eyes, I hastened, almost running, to the house.

I remember the stillness and quietness when I had closed the gate and was alone on the garden-path. Something in that stillness made me pause as though a voice out of those thick trees whispered to me: 'This isn't what you think. Go back and wait! . . . Go back!' It was all dim in that garden, the rumble of the sea rocking through the trees, the sunlight shimmering in shadow and little sudden patterns of brilliant light. That garden tried to hold me, but I wouldn't be held. I knocked on the silver knocker. When the servant came I asked for Quintero. He was an old bent man, that servant, with a bald patch on his head like a nutmeg-grater. He too seemed to say before he let me in: 'Won't you stop a moment, sir, and think it over.'

He took me up the old creaking stairs and led me into the room with the picture. Then went softly out, closing the door behind him. Well, left alone, I looked at the picture, looked at it as though I had never seen it before.

At first, standing in a kind of raging despair, wanting only to get at Quintero as quickly as might be, charge him with treachery, strike him in the face, do anything that would relieve me, I thought that the young man smiled at me. He was wearing cherry-coloured breeches and a coat of white satin. He smiled at me as a friend, and the whole bare room seemed to be warm with his young honesty. 'Trust me!' he seemed to say. 'This is fair. Give me my opportunity. I never meant anything so truly.'

Then, in my restlessness, moving to another part of the room, his face grew shifty, his eyes narrow, his mouth curled. He seemed to disdain my simplicity, to laugh at my poor attempt at good conduct. Sometimes I think that light can do everything with pictures. Maybe there is no final value in any work of art, it is only our view that gives the estimate.

In any case I moved back to my first position again and suddenly determined to leave the thing alone, at least to wait and judge it more quietly. His honest eyes looked in mine. He seemed to nod approval. 'You'll find that best,' he seemed to say.

And then, with another shift, I was back to the other view again. This was a rascal! You could see it in his shifting eyes, the narrowness of his forehead . . . Why! Just the fellow to marry a poor girl for her money and then to discard her because she hadn't any!

The door opened, and Quintero came in.

He advanced to me, his hand out, his face all smiles. And I, seeing the picture in the bad light, behaved with all the melodrama that a boy can use.

'You blackguard!' I cried.

'I know. Of course, I am,' he said, 'But why?'

It was then that, oddly enough, I had the impulse to leave them alone, let them do as they wished and go. The picture was smiling at me. 'What right have you to interfere with other lives? And it may be that I am a finer fellow than you are!'

I think that at that time he may have been, and that she was finer too.

But I turned my back on the picture and told him what I thought of him. I used fine language. He was carrying off a young girl for her money. He didn't love her.

'How do you know that I don't love her?'

He seemed now to be years older than before, and his voice was cold with a sick distaste.

'Because it's only for her money that you are taking her.'

'How do you know?'

'Because I know what you are. Everyone knows.'

Then he threw himself on me. He literally fell on to me, caught my throat with his hands, and we began the silliest, most childish rough-and-tumble. We were both young and strong. We fell about the floor, knocking the chairs over. I tore his shirt open and grabbed at his bare flesh; his long sinewy hand was strangling me. We fell together. He lay on top of me, and our hearts thumped together. We lay there panting in a kind of truce, and at last I gasped out:

'But you don't know—the best of it—she hasn't a penny.'

He raised himself and stared down into my face. We looked at one another, calmly, quietly, as though we loved one another. Our hands rested, palm against palm. I think that I had an odd awareness then that this was all a mistake, that if I had let them go on with it, helped them, been their friend, it would have been the most tremendous success—and for all three of us. But it was too late. I had taken the step in the wrong direction. Even if I could draw back he would not. For, resting his hand on my heart, looking down on me, he said:

'So, she lied.'

I swore, panting, that she had not, that it had been my own foolish joke.

But he got up. I also scrambled to my feet.

'She has nothing?'

I said nothing.

'My last chance gone.' And, oddly enough, I'll swear to you that I believed then, and I believe now, that it was not of money at all that he was thinking. Had she, in some innocent ingenuous way that he could not possibly understand, suggested to him that she was rich? Was it that he, like Hamlet with Ophelia, suddenly believed her treacherous, and that, believing in someone for the first time, he was for the first time deceived?

In any case I swear that it was not the money that disappointed him. Something deeper . . . He looked at me with hatred and contempt. No one, before or since, has ever so utterly despised me.

He conducted a short cross-examination as a judge might with his prisoner.

'She told you—about us?'

'Not a word.'

'She did. You have been laughing at me—both of you.'

'I tell you that I had no idea. I never saw. I was blind.'

'Yes, you might be. You are too simple for anything. All the same—you are a pair. I have been a fool for the first time—to be taken in by two English . . .' He broke off and added to himself, as I well remember, 'And to believe in an idyll—to think that once—only five minutes ago—I thought life could be like that.'

And then he burst out:

'She has nothing—not a penny?'

'Not a penny.'

He stopped then, looking at me with a sombre brooding as though he were taking a last look at something very beautiful. Then he added: 'Too good for me—the whole thing. Sentimental. I always knew it.'

He tossed his head as though he had come to a decision.

'Wait here,' he said, like a master to a servant. He left the room. I remained, trying to tidy myself, but feeling that I had, in some way or another, committed some great treachery. He quickly returned. He gave me a letter.

'That is for her,' he said.

I went out.

Well, then, what do you make of it? I lost the only great thing in my life, a relationship in bud, promising every sort of beauty and friendship. I have been afraid, since then, of making a relationship.

My aunt loved him until she died five years later. When I gave her that letter she died, died to all the new life that was just beginning for her. She became an old maid. After our return to England she shut herself up in the country somewhere. She died in the second year of the war, of pneumonia.

And Quintero? That is the oddest thing. I saw him again only last year, in the rooms at Monte Carlo. He was fat, ugly, peevish. I recognised him by the little mole under his left eye. We talked a little in quite a friendly fashion. Only, at the very last, he said, looking over my shoulder into distance:

'You should have let us go away. It was my only chance. I loved her quite sincerely.'

'Why did you care for what I said? I was only a boy. And if you loved her why did the fact that she had nothing make you let her go?'

'It was not that.' He looked at me oddly. It was as though he were uncovering, for a moment, his lost self. 'I had been all along afraid of my fine feelings—so unusual to me, you know. The only ones of my life. I've never had them again. You came in and gave me the opportunity to be my natural self. But she might have made me . . .' He laughed and turned away.

So, she was lost and I was lost and he was lost. And if I had let her go? He was a rascal. He would have broken her heart. Or perhaps he would not. No one is altogether a rascal. And in any case, she would have had her glorious time, a week, a month, a year . . .

What right have we ever to take things into our own hands? And how do we know? Rascal or no, doesn't it depend on where we ourselves stand?

The Man Who Lost His Identity

The essential point about this story is to prove how eagerly and readily one's friends will join in a game or a plot if the object thereof is to make some other human being miserable and uncomfortable. In saying this I am by no means the cynic that I appear. I have tremendous belief in human nature, and am perpetually surprised at the heroisms, unselfishness, and touching gratitude shown so often against desperate odds by my fellow mortals. But it is not surprising that we should all enjoy a game, and if that game involves the lowering in the general estimation of some unfortunate—why, then, the higher go ourselves.

Do not think that Pritchard, the hero of this story, could really be called unfortunate. Before this adventure he was a fairly happy man, the self-satisfied bachelor, and after it—well, you shall see, if you read far enough, how happy he was after it.

My attention was first drawn to Pritchard by the visit of a little man, Meening, to our office. He was a fellow member of the Rococo Club, and there I had met him on various occasions. He was one of those little men who can attract attention only by being constantly at your side. For months and months, you hear them speak, see them move, watch them eat, listen to their sighs, their laughter, and perhaps their tears, but are nevertheless unaware that they exist. Then one day, after their persistent company, you exclaim, 'Why, who's that?' and in a leisurely kind of way you take steps to discover. So, when Meening came to our office (I was alone there at the time), I could only vaguely remember his name, and, I am afraid, called him Menzies throughout the whole of our first interview, although he quite often in his weak, supplicating voice corrected me. The point was that Meening had become engaged to Pritchard's sister, that she was a dear little woman (according to Meening, devoted to him), and that he was the happiest man in the world except for one thing, and that thing was Pritchard.

Miss Pritchard was apparently dominated by her brother, and not only was she so dominated, but all the Pritchard family, mother and father, other sisters, brothers, aunts and cousins, were in the same case. What was the matter, I enquired, with this domination? Was Henry Pritchard a bully? No, indeed, he was not. He was a kindly, good-natured, amiable man of forty or so; he had apparently been clever in his own way, had made a lot of money during the war, with ships or something of the kind, and had had the good sense to save it, and now did no work at all, went about the world, discursive, amiable, and desperately complacent. I gathered from Meening—who, a gentle little man by nature, nevertheless spoke with some bitterness about his future brother-in-law—that Henry Pritchard was the most complete and devastating egoist yet known to history—Napoleon, Frederick the Great, and Catherine of Russia were nothing to him in this respect. The fact was that poor little Meening simply did not think that he would be able to marry Miss Pritchard unless some change were made in Henry Pritchard's character, and yet marry Miss Pritchard of course he must.

It appeared that Henry Pritchard was very fond of his sister, and intended to see a great deal of her after her marriage, and neither Miss Pritchard nor Meening had character enough to keep him out of the way. 'You see,' said Meening in his mild little voice, 'it has really come to this. If I hear very much more from Henry of how fine he is, how clever, how rich, how handsome, or how well he played Rugby football fifteen years ago, or why it is that he likes eggs scrambled rather than boiled, of the fun that he gets from using a certain sort of brown polish on his shoes that nobody else has yet discovered, of the extraordinary morning in his life in which he discovered that his hair looked much better without a parting than with one, there will be one day a very nice murder somewhere in the direction of Chelsea, and Daisy will be a widow almost before she's realised that she's a bride!'

Little Meening has quite a sense of humour in his own particular way, and real pain and suffering lent vigour to his remarks. 'You see,' he went on, 'I understand that you and your two friends have undertaken a number of cases of just this kind—removing people who are tiresome, changing their characters, and making them see life differently. Of course, I don't want any harm to happen to Henry—Daisy would never forgive me—but you're so clever that I thought you might think of something. Tell me your terms; I am sure money will be no trouble.'

'This is our general custom,' I explained to him. 'I must meet your future brother-in-law, consider the case for a week, and then, if I have a plan that promises success, I will tell you. Then you pay me seventy-five pounds down and then another seventy-five if I succeed within a reasonable period.'

He sighed with relief. 'You've already taken a weight off my mind,' he said. 'I am sure you will think of something, and then not only will I be grateful to you for the rest of my life, but the whole Pritchard family, and perhaps Henry himself.' He spoke more truly than he knew.

Shortly after this I made Henry Pritchard's acquaintance. He was a bullock of a man, one of those Englishmen who, having worshipped athletics in their youth, have in middle age allowed their muscles to run to fat. He must have been six feet three or four in height, and he was as broad as he was tall. He had one of those big round bullet heads with snub nose, large smiling mouth, and eyes looking for ever Narcissus-wise at their own likeness. He was something of a dandy in his dress, and wore bright ties that represented on different days of the week various athletic clubs which had the honour of his genial membership. Genial he was: he not only slapped you on the back in the first five minutes of your meeting him, but roared with laughter at nothing at all, and then, drawing your arm through his, became instantly loudly confidential about some exciting matter connected with himself. I had luncheon with him and Meening at the Rococo Club.

In the first five minutes he explained to everyone within a hundred miles' radius that he liked his steak not exactly underdone, but very nearly so, and that he found that, in his experience, sauces always spoiled a fine piece of meat, that of course other people might disagree with him, but that that really didn't matter, because that was the sort of man he was—he had always been like that since quite a kid. 'The fact is,' he said, putting his hand on my shoulder and shaking his heavy sides at me, 'that I am not quite like other fellows here. I know exactly what I want and why I want it. I attribute my success in life,' he went on quite frankly, 'to that very thing. You may not believe it about me, but many people have noticed that in my whole make-up, if I may say so, I never hesitate, but go straight for a thing and take it. And when I have got it I keep it,' he ended with a roaring laugh, gripping my shoulder with so tight a hold that he almost lifted me from the ground. Our lunch was all like that; neither Meening nor I said very much, but we listened and admired and remembered. By the end of the meal I had conceived a plan.

What attracted me quite frankly in this case was neither Meening nor Pritchard nor the addition of a hundred and fifty pounds to our income. We were doing very well now, and might pick and choose among our clients; the point was that I saw here an opportunity of settling an interesting question that had for a long time past intrigued me. The point was just this: Can a human being, if sufficient persuasion be brought to bear upon him, be led to believe that he is not himself, but somebody else? And I mean, of course, a quite normal human being, not in ill-health in any way, and in full possession of such faculties as God has given him.

★★★★★★

Within a week after my first meeting with Henry Pritchard I had evolved my plan. This case was different from any other we had had, because it needed for its successful issue the collaboration of several of our friends. We had always considered it rather a point of honour that our office should, so to speak, do its own dirty work, and Chippet and Borden and I had generally found ourselves equal to our task. But in this affair outside help was inevitable. I had better, perhaps, describe events just as they occurred. One afternoon, about tea-time, Pritchard was relaxing his enormous body in an enormous chair in the Rococo Club, reading a newspaper, when a man whom I will call Brown came up to him and said: 'Hullo, Forrester! I am glad to see you. Where have you been? I haven't seen you for ages.'

Now, Pritchard had never seen this man before. He was a nice-looking ordinary Englishman, just the sort of man whom Pritchard would naturally like. Pritchard, as I already have said, was the most genial of men, so he looked up smiling from his paper and remarked amiably: 'Sorry, you've got the wrong man.'

Brown laughed. 'My dear Guy,' he said, 'what's the matter with you? It's true that we haven't met for eighteen months, but don't be silly. I want to talk to you.'

Pritchard said rather more brusquely: 'I am very sorry, sir, you've made some mistake; I have never seen you in my life before.'

Brown also stiffened. 'Look here, Guy, are you tight or something? Don't be a silly ass. I want to thank you for all you did for Everett; you're really wonderful, the way you take trouble——'

Pritchard's sense of his own dignity began to suffer. He rose slowly from his chair and, looking Brown full in the face, said quite sternly: 'You are wrong, sir; you are mistaking me for somebody else,' and

145

walked, with great pomposity, away.

He was, I think, made a little uncomfortable by this episode, because, as it appeared, there was somebody else about the place very like himself, and he had always fancied that there was no one like himself anywhere. Next morning, passing the derelict ruins of Devonshire House just where the buses stop, he felt himself tapped on the shoulder. He turned round and found himself confronted by a little dapper man with an eyeglass, a complete stranger. 'Hullo, Forrester!' said this little man in a shrill piping voice. 'I am glad to see you. Where on earth have you been all this time?'

Pritchard looked at him very haughtily. 'I beg your pardon,' he said. 'You've made some mistake.'

But the little man clutched his arm.

'Don't be an ass, Forrester,' he piped. 'You haven't forgotten Monte Carlo. I am Bennett.'

'I don't care the devil who you are,' answered Pritchard. 'I have never seen you before in my life, and I——'

But Bennett did not relax his hold. 'Look here,' he cried—and his voice was one that in its shrillness would always attract attention in a public place—'I have got to speak to you. I have been wanting to see you for weeks. That business of Emily Clay is all settled.'

Pritchard roughly shook him off. 'I tell you, sir, I don't know you!' he almost shouted, and turned fiercely down Piccadilly. He was angry, he was furious. There must be somebody in London exactly like him. Twice in two days! What an extraordinary thing, and why had it never happened before? And how could there be anybody exactly like him? He had never seen anybody in the least like him anywhere. He brooded about it all day. That night he was dining with the Pritchard family. He gave them a full account of the affair; they couldn't, of course, understand it.

'You know, it's awful!' he cried to his mother. 'If there's a fellow going about London just like me, he may be buying things at shops, leading a disgraceful life, or anything. No one's ever heard of such a thing, and it isn't as though I was just like anybody else.'

'No, dear, it isn't,' his mother assured him. All the family assured him of the same thing.

Two nights later, finding himself unexpectedly free, he dined at his club and went to that amusing musical comedy, *The Girl with Bobbed Hair.* During the first interval he went out to have a drink. There was rather a crowd at the bar, and a man, pushing past him to order something, turned round and cried: 'Hullo! Why, if it isn't old Guy!'

This was serious. Pritchard looked at the man. He looked a very nice fellow indeed, thick-set, clear-eyed, jolly, with no nonsense about him. The thing was past a joke. Pritchard took his drink and led this stranger gently aside. 'May I have a word with you, sir?' he said.

The man stared at him in amazement. 'A word with me? My dear Guy, don't touch that drink—you've had enough already.'

Pritchard stood over him, gazing into his face with intense seriousness. 'Will you listen to me a moment?' he said. 'My name is Pritchard—Henry Pritchard. I have chambers in Half Moon Street. I have never seen you in my life before. Within the last week two men, complete strangers to me, have addressed me as Guy Forrester; they apparently know me well. There is obviously someone in London who is exactly like me. I am sure you will do me the courtesy to believe that I am telling you the precise truth.'

The other man stared back at him, his face absolutely bewildered. 'Look here, Guy,' he said, 'don't be an ass. I know you were annoyed with me at Wimbledon the other day, and I suppose you've got some game on now to pay me off. I am sorry about the other day, but it was a crazy thing to double on that hand of yours when you knew that I hadn't any hearts.'

Pritchard, holding himself in control with great difficulty, replied: 'I assure you, sir, that I have never seen you in my life before tonight. Would you mind telling me who you think I am?'

'Who I think you are?' the other man answered. 'Well, if you want to go on with this silly game, I'll inform you. You're Guy Forrester, and I am Anthony Bellows, with whom, three winters ago, you went out to St. Moritz, who gave you some good shooting last autumn, who wrote to you ten days ago asking where you were, whose letter you never answered, and who, weakling though he is, will give you the rottenest hiding in your life if you don't drop this silly nonsense and come to your senses!' He was laughing—obviously a charming fellow—and he meant every word that he said.

Pritchard, in an agony, began: 'I assure you——' when another man came up and touched Bellows on the arm, saying:

'The bell's gone, old man. We've got to trample on millions of people to get back to our places so we'd better go.'

'You'll hear from me in the morning, Guy,' Bellows said. 'It's a poor joke—not a bit funny,' and he went off.

Pritchard went back to his chambers. This was the most awful

147

thing that had ever happened to him. There were several letters for him on his dining-room table. He felt a great sense of relief when he picked them up; they were all addressed to Henry Pritchard, Esq. He walked up and down the room, thinking the whole thing out. First, there was somebody in London exactly resembling him; this somebody was plainly a very agreeable fellow whom people were delighted to see. Pritchard was no fool, and he realised that these three men who had spoken to him had addressed him with an eagerness and a cordiality that was not the manner with which his own friends greeted him. We go on from year to year so thoroughly accustomed to our own habits and ways of life that it is very difficult to realise that they could ever be otherwise.

Pritchard was at heart, like most Englishmen, a sentimentalist. He adored to be liked, and at one time, in earlier days, he had been extremely popular; but he had known, although he had never confessed it to himself, that of late years the increased geniality and heartiness of his own manner had covered up a little the absence of heartiness in the manner of others. All great egoists are subjectively suspicious of themselves; they have built up a great wall of defence around their personality and conditions, and at all costs this wall has to be kept absolutely intact. Let the tiniest hole appear and the whole edifice crumbles instantly, and then has at once feverishly to be built up again. Every post, every little implied criticism, every chance encounter, is a desperate danger. Pritchard, although he would never admit it for a moment, had during the last few years been feeling the loneliness of the middle-aged man whose value to the outside world is diminishing.

It was, in fact, quite a long time since anybody, whether in the club or the street or the theatre, had addressed him eagerly with excited anticipation. Alone in the silence of his room that night he faced several facts about himself. He had liked extremely the look of that man Bellows at the theatre—just the sort of man he did approve; it seemed a shame that here was the opportunity of a friendship exactly of the right kind offered to him in London, and yet at the same time forbidden to him. Why did not men of the Bellows type come up to him, Pritchard, in that sort of way? Could it be possible that there was something wrong with him?

Let the true egoist once start on the broad road of self-suspicion, and there's no end to his horrible discoveries. Could it be that his own dear family were sometimes bored with him and wanted him elsewhere? Could it be—worst suspicion of all—that he sometimes talked too much about himself? He had, he told me afterwards, very little sleep that night. For a man of Pritchard's habit that means a great deal.

There next occurred a piece of marvellous luck for our firm. I had, as I think you will agree, laid my plans very carefully, but my final crowning success does not lie to my credit. Towards seven o'clock one evening, soon after these events, I was walking down the Haymarket, when I encountered a great friend of mine, Miss Helen Freed, one of the prettiest and nicest girls in London. She was a girl who led one of those modern independent lives at which our most up-to-date novelists are always hinting terrible things, whereas there is nothing terrible about them at all, but only a pleasant freedom and an honest disregard of Victorian silliness. I asked Helen where she was going. She told me that she was intending to have a bite of something somewhere, and afterwards would join a girl friend at the theatre.

At that very moment—and surely these things are arranged by an all-watching and often benevolent Providence—Pritchard passed us, stopped one instant to look at the posters outside His Majesty's Theatre, and then vanished down the steps into the Carlton Grill. It was then that I had my inspiration. 'Do you want to have a little fun,' I asked Helen, 'and to do some good at the same time?'

Of course, she did. Without being at all priggish about it, these were her two objects in life. Then I quickly explained things to her, told her about Bellows and Brown, informed her of the imagined Guy Forrester's supposed position and attributes, assured her that Pritchard was, behind his absurdities, a thorough gentleman, that no harm could possibly come to her, and that much good might be the result. Of course, she hesitated, and I think that if the evening had not been lovely, the Haymarket crammed with that spirit of romance and adventure that London, in spite of its grime and the County Council, continually provides, she would not have taken the risk. In the light of after events there was, I fancy, one other inducement—she had looked at Pritchard as he stood for a moment near the theatre. You know how quick women are to make up their minds.

I think there was something about him that she liked from that very first glance. She went into the Carlton Grill—she had often been there before—and was ushered with much friendliness to a table. She looked at Pritchard for a quarter of an hour; that decided her. She told me afterwards that, in spite of his health and ruddiness, he looked helpless and desolate. She was touched by him, in a way, of course, that no man ever would have been; it was her maternal instinct. Just as Pritchard had finished his sole and was wondering gloomily why it was that in these days he was so often alone, he heard a charming voice: 'Guy, my dear, how lovely to see you, and alone, too, you, the most popular man in London! What a piece of luck!'

So, it had happened again! A shiver ran down Pritchard's spine, but he was not now unprepared, as on the other occasions he had been. Moreover, looking up, he saw one of the prettiest girls ever constructed by Nature (in the main), but also with a little assistance from art. He had the wildest temptation to succumb to the whole thing, to allow himself just for half an hour to be this charming Forrester, the most popular man in London, and to ask this girl to sit down beside him and to continue to smile at him in that perfectly charming way. He did stammer, 'Oh, won't you sit down?' and then, when she did so, because he was a very honest man, he tried half-heartedly to explain.

'You've made a mistake,' he began, his heart thumping as he spoke, 'but never mind—at least, never mind for a moment. I think you'd be interested to hear about the mistake. It's a most extraordinary thing,' he went on, stammering a bit. 'I don't want you to bother about that—at least, what I mean is that if you do bother about it you won't talk to me any longer.' And then he broke off because a waiter approached, and Miss Freed gave the waiter to understand that she would have the rest of her meal at this table; she had met an old friend.

'My dear Guy,' she said, 'I don't know what you're talking about; you look quite upset. But it is the luckiest thing in the world that I should get you alone like this, with a chance of telling you that I think you were simply splendid about poor Lance. That you should have taken all that trouble about a man whom you scarcely know, simply because—well, because you've got a certain liking for me, I suppose—is flattering, to say the least.' And then, as Pritchard tried to interrupt: 'No, don't say anything about it. I know—I've heard from lots of people—it's the hardest thing in the world to get a job for anybody these days, and the trouble you must have taken about Lance is simply marvellous, and I'll never forget it.'

This was indeed awful for an honest man. Oh, how he wished—how fervently he wished—that he had taken trouble about Lance, whoever Lance might be! But, indeed, it was a long time, as he now too clearly perceived, since he had taken any trouble about anybody.

'Look here,' he said urgently, staring at her beauty and dreading the moment when that light of pleasure and gratitude must fade from her beautiful eyes, 'do believe me, do listen to me. I can't let you praise me for things I haven't done. You've made a mistake. It's happened to me several times lately. There's some man going about London who's exactly like me—he must be my very image. I'd like to be him if I could, but I can't if I'm not, can I?'

Helen Freed laughed, so that several people at tables nearby looked up and smiled; she was extremely charming when she laughed. 'Guy,' she said, when she'd recovered a little, 'are you doing this for a bet, or are you trying to tell me that you want to be by yourself this evening, or what is it? We've always been honest with one another, and we may as well go on being honest now.'

'Oh, I am being honest—I am indeed!' he cried. 'I tell you what I say is true. My name is Henry Pritchard, and I live in Half Moon Street. I have never seen you before, although I wish to Heaven I had. I don't know your name nor anything about you, but—but I'll be Forrester or anyone else you like, I'll take credit for any good deed in the world, if only you'll stay for a little and talk to me!'

She looked very serious then, and answered in a voice full of tender kindliness: 'I don't know what your game is, Guy, but whatever it is, I'm with you. You've got some reason for this, I suppose, and if you like to be a mysterious man in Half Moon Street for the rest of our meal—why, go ahead. As a matter of fact,' she went on confidentially, 'I have often thought what fun it would be to take on somebody else's character for a little. I have imagined myself all sorts of people at different times, so while I eat my chicken you shall pretend to be somebody else, and if I like the person you pretend to be, I'll pretend to be somebody else, too; it will be most refreshing for both of us.'

How delighted he was! How eagerly he began to tell her all about himself—what a famous footballer he had once been, how cleverly he had made his money and kept it instead of losing it, as most people did, of how nice his family was, but of how strangely, during the last few years, things had seemed in some odd way to go wrong with him, of how he was very often alone now, and of how he was beginning to wonder whether, after all, in some mysterious way it might be his own fault, and then of this extraordinary thing that had happened to him— of how four people had spoken to him in the last ten days as though he were somebody else, and of how pleased these people had been to meet him, more pleased, he was beginning to think, than anyone had been for a long time to meet the real him that was Henry Pritchard.

They sat there for an hour at least, Helen Freed treating him with a wonderful mixture of attention and kindliness, with just a hint in her smiling eyes that of course this was only a game, quite an amusing one and entirely novel. Then she had to go. She was late as it was; she must meet her friend.

'You'll see me again?' he said. 'You will, won't you?'

'See you again!' she cried. 'You're really extraordinary tonight, Guy. Is there ever a time when I'm not delighted to see you? Come and lunch with me tomorrow—you know, the same old rooms, 18a Walpole Street, Chelsea, one o'clock.'

'But I don't know your name,' he said in an agony. 'I don't really. It isn't a game. I have told you nothing but the truth. I have never seen you in my life before, but, Heaven helping me, it isn't the last time I do!'

She turned to him as she was about to go up the stairs. 'Well, you shall have your way,' she said, laughing. 'We'll play the game to the end. My name is Helen Freed—with two "ee's," not with an "a", as you once spelled it; spelling was never your strong point, Guy.' And she was gone.

Poor Pritchard had no sleep at all that night. He walked his room trying to invent pieces of poetry, and when he could see through the thick intoxicating haze that surrounded him, puzzled again and again as to how he could keep her, as to whether he couldn't in reality continue to be this strange Guy Forrester. Impossible things seem so possible at three o'clock in the morning.

He arrived at Walpole Street half an hour too early, walked down as far as the Town Hall and back again, turned off towards the river and then back once more, and then at last, trembling with a deep and really humble excitement, he climbed a flight of stairs and rang a bell. Her room was very pretty. He knew nothing about pictures, but here, in love as he was, the water-colour drawings and the orange sofa, the amber bowl with its roses, enchanted him; he was in a land of magic. She came in happier to see him than anyone had ever hitherto been. A moment later he was kissing her. He did not know how it had happened; he did not think that he had never seen her before yesterday, and she did not know it, and she did not think it either.

'And now,' he said, standing away from her, 'it's Henry Pritchard who is asking you to marry him, it's Henry Pritchard, it's Henry Pritchard, it's Henry Pritchard. I don't know anything about you except that I love you, and that I believe that you love me, and surely whether my name is Pritchard or Forrester doesn't matter. If it's Forrester's character you care for, then I'll have Forrester's character; I'll be just what he was, and then I'll be better than that because he isn't married to you and I shall be.'

'Wait a moment!' she cried. 'We can't go as fast as that. I don't know you at all, and you don't know me.'

'You don't know me?' he returned fiercely. 'Why, you told me yesterday that you'd known me for years, that I was the best friend you had, that you were terribly grateful. If you don't know me, what about Lance, for whom I got a job the other day? Why were you so glad to see me if you don't know me?'

'I was glad to see you,' she answered, 'because I had never seen you in my life before, and you'll never want to see me again because I behaved disgracefully, and am ashamed of myself, and glad, too, because if I hadn't behaved disgracefully I never would have spoken to you and never would have had the happiest hour of my life. And now you'd better go, and I shan't be surprised if you cut me the next time we meet.'

He asked her then to explain, and she did. She didn't know, of course, the whole of the affair; all she knew was what I'd told her in the Haymarket. At her mention of my name he was more than ever bewildered. He knew me scarcely at all, and he could not conceive what I had to do with his affairs, but dimly saw that there was a plot. He realised at least that there was no Guy Forrester, and mixed with the relief at that, there was, as he tried clumsily to explain to me afterwards, an odd sort of regret; he was beginning to like Forrester—at least, he was beginning to like the attitude to Forrester that other people had.

But it says, I think, a great deal for his amiable character that he bore no malice against anybody. How could he? He was so terribly in love that he could think only well of all the world. If somebody had played a practical joke upon him, perhaps after all he had deserved it. He explained to her that he had been too much alone lately, and that perhaps that had forced him to think too much about himself. With the *naïveté* of a child he declared: 'It isn't about myself that other people want to hear; they want to talk about themselves.'

'I want to hear you talk about yourself,' she told him, 'for weeks and weeks.'

'Yes,' he answered with, for him, amazing perspicacity, 'but when we've been married a year you won't want to.'

'Well, let's get married and see,' she said.

It is scarcely necessary to add that little Meening paid our firm the second seventy-five pounds without a murmur.

On Pritchard's mantelpiece there is a photograph of a man; a pleasant, smiling face he has. When people ask him who this is, he says: 'Oh, that's Guy Forrester—my best friend.' But he doesn't know who it is. He found it one day in a photographer's shop. But it has just that kindly, good-natured, jolly expression that Guy Forrester is certain to have had.

The Snow

The second Mrs. Ryder was a young woman not easily frightened, but now she stood in the dusk of the passage leaning back against the wall, her hand on her heart, looking at the grey-faced window beyond which the snow was steadily falling against the lamplight.

The passage where she was led from the study to the dining-room, and the window looked out on to the little paved path that ran at the edge of the Cathedral green. As she stared down the passage she couldn't be sure whether the woman were there or no. How absurd of her! She knew the woman was not there. But if the woman was not, how was it that she could discern so clearly the old-fashioned grey cloak, the untidy grey hair and the sharp outline of the pale cheek and pointed chin? Yes, and more than that, the long sweep of the grey dress, falling in folds to the ground, the flash of a gold ring on the white hand. No. No. NO. This was madness. There was no one and nothing there. Hallucination . . .

Very faintly a voice seemed to come to her: 'I warned you. This is for the last time. . . .'

The nonsense! How far now was her imagination to carry her? Tiny sounds about the house, the running of a tap somewhere, a faint voice from the kitchen, these and something more had translated themselves into an imagined voice. 'The last time . . .'

But her terror was real. She was not normally frightened by anything. She was young and healthy and bold, fond of sport, hunting, shooting, taking any risk. Now she was truly *stiffened* with terror—she could not move, could not advance down the passage as she wanted to and find light, warmth, safety in the dining-room. All the time the snow fell steadily, stealthily, with its own secret purpose, maliciously, beyond the window in the pale glow of the lamplight.

Then unexpectedly there was noise from the hall, opening of

doors, a rush of feet, a pause and then in clear beautiful voices the well-known strains of 'Good King Wenceslas.' It was the Cathedral choir boys on their regular Christmas round. This was Christmas Eve. They always came just at this hour on Christmas Eve.

With an intense, almost incredible relief she turned back into the hall. At the same moment her husband came out of the study. They stood together smiling at the little group of muffled, becoated boys who were singing, heart and soul in the job, so that the old house simply rang with their melody.

Reassured by the warmth and human company, she lost her terror. It had been her imagination. Of late she had been none too well. That was why she had been so irritable. Old Doctor Bernard was no good: he didn't understand her case at all. After Christmas she would go to London and have the very best advice. . . .

Had she been well she could not, half an hour ago, have shown such miserable temper over nothing. She knew that it was over nothing and yet that knowledge did not make it any easier for her to restrain herself. After every bout of temper she told herself that there should never be another—and then Herbert said something irritating, one of his silly muddle-headed stupidities, and she was off again!

She could see now as she stood beside him at the bottom of the staircase, that he was still feeling it. She had certainly half an hour ago said some abominably rude personal things—things that she had not at all meant—and he had taken them in his meek, quiet way. Were he not so meek and quiet, did he only pay her back in her own coin, she would never lose her temper. Of that she was sure. But who wouldn't be irritated by that meekness and by the only reproachful thing that he ever said to her: 'Elinor understood me better, my dear'? To throw the first wife up against the second! Wasn't that the most tactless thing that a man could possibly do?

And Elinor, that worn elderly woman, the very opposite of her own gay, bright, amusing self? That was why Herbert had loved her, because she was gay and bright and young. It was true that Elinor had been devoted, that she had been so utterly wrapped up in Herbert that she lived only for him. People were always recalling her devotion, which was sufficiently rude and tactless of them.

Well, she could not give anyone that kind of old-fashioned sugary devotion; it wasn't in her, and Herbert knew it by this time.

Nevertheless, she loved Herbert in her own way, as he must know, know it so well that he ought to pay no attention to the bursts of temper. She wasn't well. She would see a doctor in London . . .

The little boys finished their carols, were properly rewarded, and tumbled like feathery birds out into the snow again. They went into the study, the two of them, and stood beside the big open log-fire. She put her hand up and stroked his thin beautiful cheek.

'I'm so sorry to have been cross just now, Bertie. I didn't mean half I said, you know.'

But he didn't, as he usually did, kiss her and tell her that it didn't matter. Looking straight in front of him, he answered:

'Well, Alice, I do wish you wouldn't. It hurts, horribly. It upsets me more than you think. And it's growing on you. You make me miserable. I don't know what to do about it. And it's all about nothing.'

Irritated at not receiving the usual commendation for her sweetness in making it up again, she withdrew a little and answered:

'Oh, all right. I've said I'm sorry. I can't do any more.'

'But tell me,' he insisted, 'I want to know. What makes you so angry, so suddenly?—and about nothing at all.'

She was about to let her anger rise, her anger at his obtuseness, obstinacy, when some fear checked her, a strange unanalysed fear, as though someone had whispered to her, 'Look out! This is the last time!'

'It's not altogether my own fault,' she answered, and left the room.

She stood in the cold hall, wondering where to go. She could feel the snow falling outside the house and shivered. She hated the snow, she hated the winter, this beastly, cold dark English winter that went on and on, only at last to change into a damp, soggy English spring.

It had been snowing all day. In Polchester it was unusual to have so heavy a snowfall. This was the hardest winter that they had known for many years.

When she urged Herbert to winter abroad—which he could quite easily do—he answered her impatiently; he had the strongest affection for this poky dead-and-alive Cathedral town. The Cathedral seemed to be precious to him; he wasn't happy if he didn't go and see it every day! She wouldn't wonder if he didn't think more of the Cathedral than he did of herself. Elinor had been the same; she had even written a little book about the Cathedral, about the Black Bishop's Tomb and the stained glass and the rest. . . .

What was the Cathedral after all? Only a building!

She was standing in the drawing-room looking out over the dusky ghostly snow to the great hulk of the Cathedral that Herbert said was like a flying ship, but to herself was more like a crouching beast licking its lips over the miserable sinners that it was for ever devouring.

As she looked and shivered, feeling that in spite of herself her temper and misery were rising so that they threatened to choke her, it seemed to her that her bright and cheerful fire-lit drawing-room was suddenly open to the snow. It was exactly as though cracks had appeared everywhere, in the ceiling, the walls, the windows, and that through these cracks the snow was filtering, dribbling in little tracks of wet down the walls, already perhaps making pools of water on the carpet.

This was of course imagination, but it was a fact that the room was most dreadfully cold although a great fire was burning and it was the cosiest room in the house.

Then, turning, she saw the figure standing by the door. This time there could be no mistake. It was a grey shadow, and yet a shadow with form and outline—the untidy grey hair, the pale face like a moon-lit leaf, the long grey clothes, and something obstinate, vindictive, terribly menacing in its pose.

She moved and the figure was gone; there was nothing there and the room was warm again, quite hot in fact. But young Mrs. Ryder, who had never feared anything in all her life save the vanishing of her youth, was trembling so that she had to sit down, and even then, her trembling did not cease. Her hand shook on the arm of her chair.

She had created this thing out of her imagination of Elinor's hatred of her and her own hatred of Elinor. It was true that they had never met, but who knew but that the spiritualists were right, and Elinor's spirit, jealous of Herbert's love for her, had been there driving them apart, forcing her to lose her temper and then hating her for losing it? Such things might be! But she had not much time for speculation. She was preoccupied with her fear. It was a definite, positive fear, the kind of fear that one has just before one goes under an operation. Someone or something was threatening her. She clung to her chair as though to leave it were to plunge into disaster. She looked around her everywhere; all the familiar things, the pictures, the books, the little tables, the piano were different now, isolated, strange, hostile, as though they had been won over by some enemy power.

She longed for Herbert to come and protect her; she felt most kindly to him. She would never lose her temper with him again—and at that same moment some cold voice seemed to whisper in her ear: 'You had better not. It will be for the last time.'

At length she found courage to rise, cross the room and go up to dress for dinner. In her bedroom courage came to her once more. It was certainly very cold, and the snow, as she could see when she looked between her curtains, was falling more heavily than ever, but she had a warm bath, sat in front of her fire and was sensible again.

For many months this odd sense that she was watched and accompanied by someone hostile to her had been growing. It was the stronger perhaps because of the things that Herbert told her about Elinor; she was the kind of woman, he said, who, once she loved anyone, would never relinquish her grasp; she was utterly faithful. He implied that her tenacious fidelity had been at times a little difficult.

'She always said,' he added once, 'that she would watch over me until I rejoined her in the next world. Poor Elinor!' he sighed. 'She had a fine religious faith, stronger than mine, I fear.'

It was always after one of her tantrums that young Mrs. Ryder had been most conscious of this hallucination, this dreadful discomfort of feeling that someone was near you who hated you—but it was only during the last week that she began to fancy that she actually saw anyone, and with every day her sense of this figure had grown stronger.

It was, of course, only nerves, but it was one of those nervous afflictions that became tiresome indeed if you did not rid yourself of it. Mrs. Ryder, secure now in the warmth and intimacy of her bedroom, determined that henceforth everything should be sweetness and light. No more tempers! Those were the things that did her harm.

Even though Herbert were a little trying, was not that the case with every husband in the world? And was it not Christmas time? Peace and Good Will to men! Peace and Good Will to Herbert!

They sat down opposite to one another in the pretty little dining-room hung with Chinese woodcuts, the table gleaming and the amber curtains richly dark in the firelight.

But Herbert was not himself. He was still brooding, she supposed, over their quarrel of the afternoon. Weren't men children? Incredible the children that they were!

So, when the maid was out of the room she went over to him, bent down and kissed his forehead.

'Darling . . . you're still cross, I can see you are. You mustn't be. Really you mustn't. It's Christmas time and, if I forgive you, you must forgive me.'

'You forgive me?' he asked, looking at her in his most aggravating way. 'What have you to forgive me for?'

Well, that was really too much. When she had taken all the steps, humbled her pride.

She went back to her seat, but for a while could not answer him because the maid was there. When they were alone again she said, summoning all her patience:

'Bertie dear, do you really think that there's anything to be gained by sulking like this? It isn't worthy of you. It isn't really.'

He answered her quietly.

'Sulking? No, that's not the right word. But I've got to keep quiet. If I don't I shall say something I'm sorry for.' Then, after a pause, in a low voice, as though to himself: 'These constant rows are awful.'

Her temper was rising again; another self that had nothing to do with her real self, a stranger to her and yet a very old familiar friend.

'Don't be so self-righteous,' she answered, her voice trembling a little. 'These quarrels are entirely my own fault, aren't they?'

'Elinor and I never quarrelled,' he said, so softly that she scarcely heard him.

'No! Because Elinor thought you perfect. She adored you. You've often told me. I don't think you perfect. I'm not perfect either. But we've both got faults. I'm not the only one to blame.'

'We'd better separate,' he said, suddenly looking up. 'We don't get on now. We used to. I don't know what's changed everything. But, as things are, we'd better separate.'

She looked at him and knew that she loved him more than ever, but because she loved him so much she wanted to hurt him, and because he had said that he thought he could get on without her she was so angry that she forgot all caution. Her love and her anger helped one another. The more angry she became the more she loved him.

'I know why you want to separate,' she said. 'It's because you're in love with someone else. ('How funny,' something inside her said. 'You don't mean a word of this.') You've treated me as you have, and then you leave me.'

'I'm not in love with anyone else,' he answered her steadily, 'and you know it. But we are so unhappy together that it's silly to go on .. ....silly. . . . The whole thing has failed.'

There was so much unhappiness, so much bitterness, in his voice that she realised that at last she had truly gone too far. She had lost him.

She had not meant this. She was frightened and her fear made her so angry that she went across to him.

160

'Very well then . . . I'll tell everyone . . . what you've been. How you've treated me.'

'Not another scene,' he answered wearily. 'I can't stand any more. Let's wait. Tomorrow is Christmas Day . . .'

He was so unhappy that her anger with herself maddened her. She couldn't bear his sad, hopeless disappointment with herself, their life together, everything.

In a fury of blind temper, she struck him; it was as though she were striking herself. He got up and without a word left the room. There was a pause, and then she heard the hall door close. He had left the house.

She stood there, slowly coming to her control again. When she lost her temper, it was as though she sank under water. When it was all over she came once more to the surface of life, wondering where she'd been and what she had been doing. Now she stood there, bewildered, and then at once she was aware of two things, one that the room was bitterly cold and the other that someone was in the room with her.

This time she did not need to look around her. She did not turn at all, but only stared straight at the curtained windows, seeing them very carefully, as though she were summing them up for some future analysis, with their thick amber folds, gold rod, white lines—and beyond them the snow was falling.

She did not need to turn, but, with a shiver of terror, she was aware that that grey figure who had, all these last weeks, been approaching ever more closely, was almost at her very elbow. She heard quite clearly: 'I warned you. That was the last time.'

At the same moment Onslow the butler came in. Onslow was broad, fat and rubicund—a good faithful butler with a passion for church music. He was a bachelor and, it was said, disappointed of women. He had an old mother in Liverpool to whom he was greatly attached.

In a flash of consciousness, she thought of all these things when he came in. She expected him also to see the grey figure at her side. But he was undisturbed, his ceremonial complacency clothed him securely.

'Mr. Fairfax has gone out,' she said firmly. Oh, surely, he must see something, feel something.

'Yes, Madam!' Then, smiling rather grandly: 'It's snowing hard. Never seen it harder here. Shall I build up the fire in the drawing-room, Madam?'

'No, thank you. But Mr. Fairfax's study . . .'

'Yes, Madam. I only thought that as this room was so warm you might find it chilly in the drawing-room.'

This room warm, when she was shivering from head to foot; but holding herself lest he should see . . . She longed to keep him there, to implore him to remain; but in a moment, he was gone, softly closing the door behind him.

Then a mad longing for flight seized her, and she could not move. She was rooted there to the floor, and even as, wildly trying to cry, to scream, to shriek the house down, she found that only a little whisper would come, she felt the cold touch of a hand on hers.

She did not turn her head: her whole personality, all her past life, her poor little courage, her miserable fortitude were summoned to meet this sense of approaching death which was as unmistakable as a certain smell, or the familiar ringing of a gong. She had dreamt in nightmares of approaching death and it had always been like this, a fearful constriction of the heart, a paralysis of the limbs, a choking sense of disaster like an anaesthetic.

'You were warned,' something said to her again.

She knew that if she turned she would see Elinor's face, set, white, remorseless. The woman had always hated her, been vilely jealous of her, protecting her wretched Herbert.

A certain vindictiveness seemed to release her. She found that she could move, her limbs were free.

She passed to the door, ran down the passage, into the hall. Where would she be safe? She thought of the Cathedral, where tonight there was a carol service. She opened the hall door and just as she was, meeting the thick, involving, muffling snow, she ran out.

She started across the green towards the Cathedral door. Her thin black slippers sank in the snow. Snow was everywhere—in her hair, her eyes, her nostrils, her mouth, on her bare neck, between her breasts.

'Help! Help! Help!' she wanted to cry, but the snow choked her. Lights whirled about her. The Cathedral rose like a huge black eagle and flew towards her.

She fell forward, and even as she fell a hand, far colder than the snow, caught her neck. She lay struggling in the snow and as she struggled there two hands of an icy fleshless chill closed about her throat.

Her last knowledge was of the hard outline of a ring pressing into her neck. Then she lay still, her face in the snow, and the flakes eagerly, savagely, covered her.

Sarah Trefusis

1

Sarah Trefusis lived, with her mother, in the smallest house in March Square, a really tiny house, like a box, sandwiched tightly between two fat buildings, but looking, with its white paint and green doors, smarter than either of them. Lady Charlotte Trefusis, Sarah's mother, was elegant, penniless and a widow; Captain B. Trefusis, her husband, had led the merriest of lives until a game of polo carried him reluctantly from a delightful world and forced Lady Charlotte to consider the problem of having a good time alone on nothing at all. But it may be said that, on the whole, she succeeded.

She was the best-dressed widow in London, and went everywhere, but the little house in March Square was the scene of a most strenuous campaign, every day presenting its defeat or victory, and every minute of the day threatening overwhelming disaster if something were not done immediately. Lady Charlotte had the smallest feet and hands outside China, a pile of golden hair above the face of a pink-and-white doll. Staring from this face, however, were two of the loveliest, most unscrupulous of eyes, and those eyes did more for Lady Charlotte's precarious income than any other of her resources. She wore her expensive clothes quite beautifully, and gave lovely little lunches and dinners; no really merry house-party was complete without her.

Sarah was her only child, and, although at the time of which I am writing she was not yet nine years of age, there was no one in London better suited to the adventurous and perilous existence that Fate had selected for her. Sarah was black as ink—that is, she had coal-black hair, coal-black eyes, and wonderful black eyelashes. Her eyelashes were her only beautiful feature, but she was, nevertheless, a most remarkable looking child. "If ever a child's possessed of the devil, my dear Charlotte," said Captain James Trent to her mother, "it's your precious daughter—she *is* the devil, I believe."

"Well, she needs to be," said her mother, "considering the life that's in store for her. We're very good friends, she and I, thank you."

They were. They understood one another to perfection. Lady Charlotte was as hard as nails, and Sarah was harder. Sarah had never been known to cry. She had bitten the fingers of one of her nurses through to the bone, and had stuck a needle into the cheek of another whilst she slept, and had watched, with a curious abstracted gaze, the punishment dealt out to her, as though it had nothing to do with her at all. She never lost her temper, and one of the most terrible things about her was her absolute calm. She was utterly fearless, went to the dentist without a tremor, and, at the age of six, fell downstairs, broke her leg, and so lay until help arrived without a cry. She bullied and hurt anything or anybody that came her way, but carried out her plans always with the same deliberate abstraction as though she were obeying somebody's orders. She never nourished revenge or resentment, and it seemed to be her sense of humour (rather than any fierce or hostile feeling) that was tickled when she hurt anyone.

She was a child apparently without imagination, but displayed, at a very early period, a strangely sharpened perception of what her nurse called "the uncanny." She frightened even her mother by the expression that her face often wore of attention to something or somebody outside her companions' perception.

"A broomstick is what she'll be flying away on one of these nights, you mark my word," a nurse declared. "Little devil, she is, neither more or less. It isn't decent the way she sits on the floor looking right through the wall into the next room, as you might say. Yes, and knows who's coming up the stairs long before she's seen 'em. No place for a decent Christian woman, and so I told her mother this very morning."

It was, of course, quite impossible to find a nurse to stay with Sarah, and, when she arrived at the age of seven, nurses were dismissed, and she either looked after herself or was tended by an abandoned French maid of her mother's, who stayed with Lady Charlotte, like a wicked, familiar spirit, for a great number of years on a strange basis of confidante, fellow-plunderer, and sympathetic adventurer. This French maid, whose name was, appropriately enough, Hortense, had a real affection for Sarah "because she was the weeckedest child of 'er age she ever see." There was nothing of which Sarah, from the very earliest age, did not seem aware. Her mother's gentlemen friends she valued according to their status in the house, and, as they "fell off" or "came on," so was her manner indifferent or pleasant.

For Hortense she had a real respect, but even that improper and brazen spirit quailed at times before her cynical and elfish regard. To say of a child that there is something "unearthly" about it is, as a rule, to pay a compliment to ethereal blue and gold. There was nothing ethereal about Sarah, and yet she was unearthly enough. Squatting on the floor, her legs tucked under her, her head thrust forward, her large black eyes staring at the wall, her black hair almost alive in the shining intensity of its colour, she had in her attitude the lithe poise of some animal ready to spring, waiting for its exact opportunity.

When her mother, in a temper, struck her, she would push her hair back from her face with a sharp movement of her hand and then would watch broodingly and cynically for the next move. "You hit me again," she seemed to say, "and you *will* make a fool of yourself."

She was aware, of course, of a thousand influences in the house of which her mother and Hortense had never the slightest conception. From the cosy security of her cradle she had watched (with hostile irritation) the friendly spirit who had accompanied her entrance into this world. His shadow had, for a long period, darkened her nursery, but she repelled, with absolute assurance. His kindly advances.

"I'm not frightened. I don't, in the least, want things made comfortable for me. I can get along very nicely, indeed, without you. You're full of sentiment and gush—things that I detest—and it won't be the least use in the world for you to ask me to be good, and tender, and all the rest of it. I'm not like your other babies."

He must have known, of course, that she was not, but, nevertheless. He stayed. "I understand perfectly," He assured her. "But, nevertheless, I don't give you up. You may be, for all you know, more interesting to me than all the others put together. And remember this—every time you do anything at all kind or thoughtful, every time you think of anyone or care for them, every time you use your influence for good in any way, my power over you is a little stronger, I shall be a little closer to you, your escape will be a little harder."

Oh, you needn't flatter yourself," she answered Him. "There's precious little danger of *my* self-sacrifice or love for others. That's not going to be my attitude to life at all. You'd better not waste your time over me."

She had not, she might triumphantly reflect, during these eight years, given Him many chances, and yet He was still there. She hated the thought of His patience, and somewhere deep within herself she dreaded the faint, dim beat of some response that, like a warning bell across a misty sea, cautioned her. "You may think you're safe from Him, but He'll catch you yet."

"He shan't," she replied. "I'm stronger than He is."

2

This must sound, in so prosaic a summary of it, fantastic, but nothing could be said to be fantastic about Sarah. She was, for one thing, quite the least troublesome of children. She could be relied upon, at any time, to find amusement for herself. She was full of resources, but what these resources exactly were it would be difficult to say. She would sit for hours alone, staring in front of her. She never played with toys—she did not draw or read—but she was never dull, and always had the most perfect of appetites. She had never, from the day of her birth, known an hour's illness.

It was, however, in the company of other children that she was most characteristic. The nurses in the Square quite frankly hated her, but most of the mothers had a very real regard for Lady Charlotte's smart little lunches; moreover, it was impossible to detect Sarah's guilt in any positive fashion. It was not enough for the nurses to assure their mistresses that from the instant that the child entered the garden all the other children were out of temper, rebellious, and finally unmanageable.

Nonsense, Janet, you imagine things. She seems a very nice little girl."

"Well, ma'am, all I can say is, I won't care to be answerable for Master Ronald's behaviour when she *does* come along, that's all. It's beyond belief the effect she 'as upon 'im.

The strangest thing of all was that Sarah herself liked the company of other children. She went every morning into the garden (with Hortense) and watched them at their play. She would sit, with her hands folded quietly on her lap, her large black eyes watching, watching, watching. It was odd, indeed, how, instantly, all the children in the garden were aware of her entrance. She, on her part, would appear to regard none of them, and yet would see them all. Perched on her seat she surveyed the garden always with the same gaze of abstracted interest, watching the clear, decent paths across whose grey background at the period of this episode the October leaves, golden, flaming, dun, gorgeous and shrivelled, fell through the still air, whirled, and with a little sigh of regret, one might fancy, sank and lay dead.

The October colours, a faint haze of smoky mist, the pale blue of the distant sky, the brown moist earth, were gentle, mild, washed with the fading year's regretful tears; the cries of the children, the rhythmic splash of the fountain throbbed behind the colours like some hidden orchestra behind the curtain at the play; the statues in the garden, like fragments of the white bolster clouds that swung so lazily from tree to tree, had no meaning in that misty air beyond the background that they helped to fill. The year, thus idly, with so pleasant a melancholy, was slipping into decay.

Sarah would watch. Then, without a word, she would slip from her seat, and, walking solemnly, rather haughtily, would join some group of children. Day after day the same children came to the garden, and they all of them knew Sarah by now. Hortense, in her turn also, sitting, stiff and superior, would watch. She would see Sarah's pleasant approach, her smile, her amiability. Very soon, however, there would be trouble—some child would cry out; there would be blows; nurses would run forward, scoldings, protests, captives led away weeping ... and then Sarah would return slowly to her seat, her gaze aloof, cynical, remote. She would carefully explain to Hortense the reason of the uproar. She had done nothing—her conscience was clear. These silly little idiots. She would break into French, culled elaborately from Hortense, would end disdainfully—"*mais, voilà*"—very old for her age.

Hortense was vicious, selfish, crude in her pursuit of pleasure, entirely unscrupulous, but, as the days passed, she was, in spite of herself, conscious of some half-acknowledged, half-decided terror of Sarah's possibilities.

The child was eight years old. She was capable of anything; in her remote avoidance of any passion, any regret, any anticipated pleasure, any spontaneity, she was inhuman.

Hortense thought that she detected in the chit's mother something of her own fear.

3

There used to come to the garden a little fat red-faced girl called Mary Kitson, the child of simple and ingenuous parents (her father was a writer of stories of adventure for boys' papers); she was herself simple-minded, lethargic, unadventurous, and happily stupid. Walking one day slowly with Hortense down one of the garden paths, Sarah saw Mary Kitson engaged in talking to two dolls, seated on a bench with them, patting their clothes, very happy, her nurse busy over a novelette.

Sarah stopped.

"I'll sit here," she said, walked across to the bench and sat down. Mary looked up from her dolls, and then, nervously and self-consciously, went back to her play. Sarah stared straight before her.

Hortense amiably endeavoured to draw the nurse into conversation.

"You 'ave 'ere ze fine garden," she said. "It calls to mind my own Paris. Ah, the gardens in Paris!"

But the nurse had been taught to distrust all foreigners, and her views of Paris were coloured by her reading. She admired Hortense's clothes, but distrusted her advances.

She buried herself even more deeply in the paper. Poor Mary Kitson, alas! found that, in some undefinable manner, the glory had departed from her dolls. Adrian and Emily were, of a sudden, glassy and lumpy abstractions of sawdust and china. Very timidly she raised her large, stupid eyes and regarded Sarah. Sarah returned the glance and smiled. Then she came close to Mary.

"It's better under there," she said, pointing to the shade of a friendly tree.

"May I?" Mary said to her nurse with a frightened gasp.

"Well, now, don't you go far," said the nurse with a fierce look at Hortense.

"You like where you are?" asked Hortense, smiling more than ever. "You 'ave a good place?" Slowly the nurse yielded. The novelette was laid aside.

Impossible to say what occurred under the tree. Now and again a rustle of wind would send the colours from the trees to short branches loaded with leaves of red gold, shivering through the air; a chequered, blazing canopy covered the ground.

Mary Kitson had, it appeared, very little to say. She sat some way from Sarah, clutching Adrian and Emily tightly to her breast, and always her large, startled eyes were on Sarah's face. She did not move to drive the leaves from her dress; her heart beat very fast, her cheeks were very red.

Sarah talked a little, but not very much. She asked questions about Mary's home and her parents, and Mary answered these interrogations in monosyllabic gasps. It appeared that Mary had a kitten, and that this kitten was a central fact of Mary's existence. The kitten was called Alice.

"Alice is a silly name for a kitten. I shouldn't call a kitten Alice," said Sarah, and Mary started as though in some strange, sinister fashion she were instantly aware that Alice's life and safety were threatened.

From that morning began a strange acquaintance that certainly could not be called a friendship. There could be no question at all that Mary was terrified of Sarah; there could also be no question that Mary was Sarah's obedient slave. The cynical Hortense, prepared as she was for anything strange and unexpected in Sarah's actions, was, nevertheless, puzzled now.

One afternoon, wet and dismal, the two of them sitting in a little box of a room in the little box of a house, Sarah huddled in a chair, her eyes staring in front of her, Hortense sewing, her white, bony fingers moving sharply like knives, the maid asked a question:

"What do you see—Sar-ah—in that infant?"

"What infant?" asked Sarah, without moving her eyes.

"That Mary with whom now you always are."

"We play games together," said Sarah.

"You do not. You may be playing a game she does nothing. She is terrified—out of her life."

"She is very silly. It's funny how silly she is. I like her to be frightened."

Mary's nurse told Mary's mother that, in her opinion, Sarah was not a nice child. But Sarah had been invited to tea at the confused, simple abode of the Kitson family, and had behaved perfectly.

"I think you must be wrong, nurse," said Mrs. Kitson. "She seems a very nice little girl. Mary needs companions. It's good for her to be taken out of herself."

Had Mrs. Kitson been of a less confused mind, however, had she had more time for the proper observation of her daughter, she would have noticed her daughter's pale cheeks, her daughter's fits of crying, her daughter's silences. Even as the bird is fascinated by the snake, so was Mary Kitson fascinated by Sarah Trefusis.

"You are torturing that infant," said Hortense, and Sarah smiled.

4

Mary was by no means the first of Sarah's victims. There had been many others. Utterly aloof herself from all emotions of panic or terror, it had, from the very earliest age, interested her to see those passions at work in others. Cruelty for cruelty's sake had no interest for her at all; to pull the wings from flies, to tie kettles to the tails of agitated puppies, to throw stones at cats, did not in the least amuse her. She had once put a cat in the fire, but only because she had seen it play with a terrified mouse. That had affronted her sense of justice. But she was gravely and quite dispassionately interested in the terror of Mary Kitson. In later life a bull-fight was to appear to her a tiresome affair, but the domination of one human being over another, absorbing. She had, too, at the very earliest age, that conviction that it was pleasant to combat all sentiment, all appeals to be "good," all soft emotions of pity, anything that could suggest that Right was of more power than Might.

It was as though she said, "You may think that even now you will get me. I tell you I'm a rebel from the beginning; you'll never catch me showing affection or sympathy. If you do you may do your worst."

Beyond all things, her anxiety was that, suddenly, in spite of herself, she would do something "soft," some weak kindness. Her power over Mary Kitson reassured her.

The fascination of this power very soon became to her an overwhelming interest. Playing with Mary Kitson's mind was as absorbing to Sarah as chess to an older enthusiast. Her discoveries promised her a life full of entertainment; if, with her fellow-mortals, she was able, so easily, "to do things," what a time she would always have. She discovered, very soon, that Mary Kitson was, by nature, truthful and obedient, that she had a great fear of God, and that she loved her parents. Here was fine material to work upon. She began by insisting on little lies.

"Say our clocks were all wrong, and you couldn't know what the time was."

"Oh, but—"

"Yes, say it."

"Please, Sarah."

"Say it. Otherwise I'll be punished too. Mind, if you don't say it, I shall know."

There was the horrible threat that effected so much. Mary began soon to believe that Sarah was never absent from her, that she attended her, invisibly, her little dark face peering over Mary's shoulder, and when Mary was in bed at night, the lights out, and only shadows on the walls, Sarah was certainly there, her mocking eyes on Mary's face, her voice whispering things in Mary's ears.

Sarah, Mary very soon discovered, believed in nothing, and knew everything. This horrible combination, naturally, affected Mary who believed in everything and knew nothing.

"Why should we obey our mothers?" said Sarah. "We're as good as they are."

"Oh, *no*," said Mary, in a voice shocked to a strangled whisper. Nevertheless, she began, a little, to despise her confused parents. There came a day when Mary told a very large lie indeed; she said that she had brushed her teeth when she had not, and she told this lie quite unprompted by Sarah. She was more and more miserable as the days passed.

No one knew exactly the things that the two little girls did when they were alone on an afternoon in Sarah's room. Sarah sent Hortense about her business, and then set herself to the subdual of Mary's mind and character. There would be moments like this: Sarah would turn off the electric light, and the room would be lit only by the dim shining of the evening sky.

"Now, Mary, you go over to that corner—that dark one—and wait there till I tell you to come out. I'll go outside the room, and then you'll see what will happen."

"Oh, no, Sarah, I don't want to."

"Why not, you silly baby?"

"I—I don't want to."

"Well, it will be much worse for you if you don't."

"I want to go home."

"You can after you have done that."

"I want to go home now."

"Go into the corner first."

Sarah would leave the room and Mary would stand with her face to the wall, a trembling prey to a thousand terrors. The light would quiver and shake, steps would tread the floor and cease, there would be a breath in her ears, a wind above her head. She would try to pray, but could remember no words. Sarah would lead her forth, shaking from head to foot.

"You little silly. I was only playing."

Once, and this hurried the climax of the episode, Mary attempted rebellion.

"I want to go home, Sarah."

"Well, you can't. You've got to hear the end of the story first."

"I don't like the story. It's a horrid story. I'm going home."

"You'd better not."

"Yes, I will, and I won't come again, and I won't see you again. I hate you! I won't! I won't!"

Mary, as she very often did, began to cry. Sarah's lips curled with scorn.

"All right, you can. You'll never see Alice again if you do."

"Alice?"

"Yes, she'll be drowned, and you'll have the toothache, and I'll come in the middle of the night and wake you."

"I—I don't care. I'm go-going home. I'll t-t-ell M-other."

"Tell her. But lookout afterwards, that's all."

Mary remained, but Sarah regarded the rebellion as ominous. She thought that the time had come to put Mary's submission really to the test.

5

The climax of the affair was in this manner. Upon an afternoon when the rain was beating furiously upon the window-panes and the wind struggling up and down the chimney, Sarah and Mary played together in Sarah's room; the play consisted of Mary shutting her eyes and pretending she was in a dark wood, whilst Sarah was the tiger who might at any moment spring upon her and devour her, who would, in any case, pinch her legs with a sudden thrust which would drive all the blood out of Mary's face and make her "as white as the moon."

This game ended, Sarah's black eyes moved about for a fresh diversion; her gaze rested upon Mary, and Mary whispered that she would like to go home.

"Yes, you can," said Sarah, staring at her, "if you will do something when you get there."

"What?" said Mary, her heart beating like a heavy and jumping hammer.

"There's something I want. You've got to bring it me."

Mary said nothing, only her wide eyes filled with tears.

"There's something in your mother's drawing-room. You know, in that little table with the glass top where there are the little gold boxes with the silver crosses and things. There's a ring there—a gold one with a red stone—very pretty. I want it."

Mary drew a long, deep breath. Her fat legs in the tight, black stockings were shaking.

"You can go in when no one sees. The table isn't locked, I know, because I opened it once. You can get and bring it to me tomorrow in the garden."

172

"Oh," Mary whispered, "that would be stealing."

Of course, it wouldn't. Nobody wants the old ring. No one ever looks at it. It's just for fun."

"No," said Mary, "I mustn't."

"Oh, yes, you must. You'll be very sorry if you don't. Dreadful things will happen. Alice——"

Mary cried softly, choking and spluttering and rubbing her eyes with the back of her hand.

"Well, you'd better go now. I'll be in the garden with Hortense tomorrow. You know, the same place. You'd better have it, that's all. And don't go on crying, or your mother will think I made you. What's there to cry about? No one will eat you."

"It's stealing."

"I dare say it belongs to you, and, anyway, it will when your mother dies, so what *does* it matter? You *are* a baby! "

After Mary's departure Sarah sat for a long while alone in her nursery. She thought to herself: "Mary will be going home now and she'll be snuffling to herself all the way back, and she won't tell the nurse anything, I know that. Now she's in the hall. She's upstairs now, having her things taken off. She's stopped crying, but her eyes and nose are red. She looks very ugly. She's gone to find Alice. She thinks something has happened to her. She begins to cry again when she sees her, and she begins to talk to her about it. Fancy talking to a cat. . . ."

The room was swallowed in darkness, and when Hortense came in and found Sarah sitting alone there, she thought to herself that, in spite of the profits that she secured from her mistress she would find another situation. She did not speak to Sarah, and Sarah did not speak to her.

Once, during the night, Sarah woke up; she sat up in bed and stared into the darkness. Then she smiled to herself. As she lay down again she thought:

"Now I know that she will bring it."

The next day was very fine, and in the glittering garden by the fountain, Sarah sat with Hortense, and waited. Soon Mary and her nurse appeared. Sarah took Mary by the hand and they went away down the leaf-strewn path.

"Well?" said Sarah.

Mary quite silently felt in her pocket at the back of her short, green frock, produced the ring, gave it to Sarah, and, still without a word, turned back down the path and walked to her nurse. She stood there, clutching a doll in her hand, stared in front of her, and said nothing. Sarah looked at the ring, smiled, and put it into her pocket.

At that instant the climax of the whole affair struck, like a blow from someone unseen, upon Sarah's consciousness. She should have been triumphant. She was not. Her one thought as she looked at the ring was that she wished Mary had not taken it. She had a strange feeling as though Mary, soft and heavy and fat, were hanging round her neck. She had "got" Mary for ever. She was suddenly conscious that she despised Mary, and had lost all interest in her. She didn't want the ring, nor did she ever wish to see Mary again.

She gazed about the garden, shrugged her thin, little, bony shoulders as though she were fifty at least, and felt tired and dull, as on the day after a party. She stood and looked at Mary and her nurse; when she saw them walk away she did not move, but stayed there, staring after them. She was greatly disappointed; she did not feel any pleasure at having forced Mary to obey her, but would have liked to have smacked and bitten her, could these violent actions have driven her into speech. In some undetermined way Mary's silence had beaten Sarah. Mary was a stupid, silly little girl, and Sarah despised and scorned her, but, somehow, that was not enough; from all of this, it simply remained that Sarah would like now to forget her, and could not. What did the silly little thing mean by looking like that? "She'll go and hug her Alice and cry over it." If only she had cried in front of Sarah that would have been something.

Two days later Lady Charlotte was explaining to Sarah that so acute a financial crisis had arrived "as likely as not we shan't have a roof over our heads in a day or two."

"We'll take an organ and a monkey," said Sarah.

"At any rate," Lady Charlotte said, "when you grow up you'll be used to anything."

Mrs. Kitson, untidy, in dishevelled clothing, and great distress, was shown in.

"Dear Lady Charlotte, I must apologise—this absurd hour—but I—we—very unhappy about poor Mary. We can't think what's the matter with her. She's not slept for two nights—in a high fever, and cries and cries. The doctor—Dr. Williamson—*really* clever—says she's unhappy about something. We thought—scarlet fever—no spots—can't think—perhaps your little girl—"

"Poor Mrs. Kitson. How tiresome for you. Do sit down. Perhaps Sarah—"

Sarah shook her head.

"She didn't say she'd a headache in the garden the other day?"

Mrs. Kitson gazed appealingly at the little black figure in front of her.

"Do try and remember, dear. Perhaps she told you something?"

"Nothing," said Sarah.

"She cries and cries," said Mrs. Kitson, about whose person little white strings and tapes seemed to be continually appearing and disappearing.

"Perhaps she's eaten something?" suggested Lady Charlotte.

When Mrs. Kitson had departed. Lady Charlotte turned to Sarah.

"What have you done to the poor child?" she said.

"Nothing," said Sarah. "I never want to see her again."

"Then you *have* done something?" said Lady Charlotte.

"She's always crying," said Sarah, "and she calls her kitten Alice," as though that were explanation sufficient.

The strange truth remains, however, that the night that followed this conversation was the first unpleasant one that Sarah had ever spent; she remained awake during a great part of it. It was as though the hours that she had spent on that other afternoon, compelling, from her own dark room, Mary's will, had attached Mary to her. Mary was there with her now, in her bedroom. Mary, red-nosed, sniffing, her eyes wide and staring.

"I want to go home."

"Silly little thing," thought Sarah. "I wish I'd never played with her."

In the morning Sarah was tired and white-faced. She would speak to no one. After luncheon she found her hat and coat for herself, let herself out of the house, and walked to Mrs. Kitson's, and was shown into the wide, untidy drawing-room, where books and flowers and papers had a lost and strayed air as though a violent wind had blown through the place and disturbed everything.

Mrs. Kitson came in.

"*You*, dear?" she said.

Sarah looked at the room and then at Mrs. Kitson. Her eyes said: "*What* a place! *What* a woman! *What* a fool!"

"Yes, I've come to explain about Mary."

"About Mary?"

"Yes. It's my fault that she's ill. I took a ring out of that little table there—the gold ring with the red stone—and I made her promise not to tell. It's because she thinks she ought to tell that she's ill."

"*You* took it? *You* stole it?" Before Mrs. Kitson's simple mind an awful picture was now revealed. Here, in this little girl, whom she had preferred as a companion for her beloved Mary, was a thief, a liar, and one, as she could instantly perceive, without shame.

"You *stole* it?"

"Yes; here it is." Sarah laid the ring on the table.

Mrs. Kitson gazed at her with horror, dismay, and even fear.

"Why? Why? Don't you know how wrong it is to take things that don't belong to you?"

"Oh, all that!" said Sarah, waving her hand scornfully. "I don't want the silly thing, and I don't suppose I'd have kept it, anyhow. I don't know why I've told you," she added. "But I just don't want to be bothered with Mary anymore."

"Indeed, you won't be, you wicked girl," said Mrs. Kitson. "To think that I—my grandfather's—I'd never missed it. And you haven't even said you're sorry."

"I'm not," said Sarah quietly. "If Mary wasn't so tiresome and silly, those sort of things, wouldn't happen. She *makes* me do them."

Mrs. Kitson's horror deprived her of all speech, so Sarah, after one more glance of amused cynicism about the room, retired.

As she crossed the Square she knew, with happy relief, that she was free of Mary, that she need never bother about her again. Would *all* the people whom she compelled to obey her hang round her with all their stupidities afterwards? If so, life was not going to be so entertaining as she had hoped. In her dark little brain already was the perception of the trouble that good and stupid souls can cause to bold and reckless ones. She would never bother with anyone so feeble as Mary again, but, unless she did, how was she ever to have any fun anymore?

Then, as she climbed the stairs to her room, she was aware of something else.

"I've caught you, after all. You *have* been soft. You've yielded to your better nature. Try as you may you can't get right away from it. Now you'll have to reckon with me more than ever. You see you're not stronger than I am."

Before she opened the door of her room she knew that she would find Him there, triumphant.

With a gesture of impatient irritation, she pushed the door open.

The Killer and the Slain

PART 1

1

I, John Ozias Talbot, aged thirty-six years and three months, being in my perfectly sane mind, wish to write down this statement.

I do so entirely and solely for my own benefit and profit—in fact, for the quietening of my disturbed mind. It is most improbable that anyone other than myself will read this document but should anything happen to me and I die without destroying this writing, I wish the reader, whoever he or she may be, to realise fully that no one could conceivably be of a more complete mental sanity and honest matter-of-fact common sense than I am at this moment.

It is because I wish to show this self-evident fact to myself and, if need be, to the whole world (after my death) that I write this down. There will be many minute and apparently insignificant facts and de-tails in this record because *circumstantial facts* are in this matter the thing! I have suffered during these preceding months certain expe-riences so unbelievable that were I *not* sane, and were many of the facts not so commonplace, my sanity might be doubted. It is *not* to be doubted. I am as sane as any man in the United Kingdom.

Because in the course of this narrative I confess to a crime this document will be kept in the greatest possible secrecy. I have no desire to suffer at the hand of the common hangman before I need. That I do not myself *feel* it to be a crime matters nothing, I am afraid, to the Law. One day, when the important elements in such matters are taken into account rather than the unimportant, justice will be better served. But that time is not yet.

I was born in the little seaside town of Seaborne in Glebeshire on January 3rd, 1903. I am married and have one son aged ten. I inherited

177

my father's business of Antique and Picture Dealer. I am the author of four books, a *Guide to Glebeshire* and three novels—*The Sandy Tree* (1924), *The Gridiron* (1930) and *The Gossip-monger* (1936). The last of these had some success. I was born in a bedroom above the shop, which is in the High Street and has, from its upper windows, a fine view of the sea and the now neglected and tumbledown little harbour.

I was the only child of my parents and adored by them. Some have said that they spoiled me. It may be so. I worshipped my mother but had always a curious disaffection to my father. This was partly, I can see now, physical. He was an obese and sweaty man and would cover my face with wet slobbery kisses when I was small, and this I very greatly disliked. My mother, on the other hand, was slight and dapper in appearance, and the possessor of the most beautiful little hands I have ever seen on any woman. Her voice was soft and musical, marked with a slight Glebeshire accent. She had something of the gipsy in her appearance and liked to wear gay colours.

I remember especially a dress made of some foreign material—silk of many brilliant shades—that I used to love, and I would beg her to show it me as it hung in the cupboard in the bedroom. My father, when they woke in the morning, would always go downstairs to get breakfast ready (he worshipped my mother), and then my mother would take me into her bed and I would lie in her arms. Never, until I married, did I know such happiness.

My father was successful in his little business—successful, that is to say, for those easier, more comfortable days—and we lived very pleasantly. His great passion was for the buying of old and apparently worthless pictures. He would clean them with the hope that something by a Master might be discovered. He did, indeed, make one or two discoveries—a Romney portrait and an Italian Pietà by Piombo, were two of his successes. But his main business was with visitors and tourists. He visited all the local sales and sometimes went quite far afield.

We lived quietly and knew few people. My mother was fastidious about people and I have inherited that from her.

At this point I must say something about my own personality and character because so much of what afterwards happened depends on that. I will try to be honest, although honesty is never easy when we write about ourselves. We naturally incline to our own favour. But I have always trained myself to consider myself objectively and am possibly given overmuch to self-criticism.

I have been always of a reserved nature, careful to say no more than I truly feel and to confide only in those I trust and thoroughly know. My father's sentimentality affected me unpleasantly, and the love that I felt for my mother did not need expression.

From my very early years I have been considered cold and undemonstrative, but in reality I have always longed for affection although I have found it difficult to believe that anyone could in real fact be fond of me—this not because I do not know that there are many things in me worthy of affection, but because I have seen, during my life, so many false emotions, so many bitter betrayals of people by one another, and have realised that most men and women express more than they feel and mean less than they say. I have tried very earnestly to avoid this fault in myself.

I suppose that I must confess myself a prude, and this same prudery has lost me many contacts that I might otherwise have made. The sexual life of man has always seemed to me ugly and dangerous, and only to be redeemed by real and abiding love. The conventional life of man with man regarding the physical side of things has been, and is, repellent to me.

And yet God knows I have longed again and again for friendship and companionship and have blamed myself bitterly for not obtaining it more easily. Another reason for my reserve is that I have had one ceaseless ambition—namely, to be generally recognised as a good writer. Not a great one—that I long ago realised I should never be. But I have wanted to be one of the writers of my time whose work is generally known. It is *good* work, better by far than the writings of many who have been generally acclaimed, but it has had a quality of rareness and peculiarity that has hindered its general popularity. And then I must regretfully admit that my sense of humour is small. Life seems to me to be altogether too serious, especially during the last anxious twenty years, to admit of much humour!

I have always shrunk from boisterousness, violence and noise. I love soft voices (such as that possessed by my dear mother), courteous ways, good manners in argument, consideration of others. The cheerful, hail-fellow, slap-on-the-back sort of man I have never been able to abide.

I can be exceedingly obstinate and tenacious of purpose. When an idea is deeply rooted in my mind I find it impossible to reject. I like to be allowed to go my own way without interference and I detest enquiries into my personal affairs.

179

God knows this is not a pleasant self-portrait and I can blame no one for wishing to see the last of me, and yet I have, I think, qualities of honesty, courage, affection and fidelity that are valuable.

I had better here say something about my personal appearance, as that is of the utmost importance in these peculiar circumstances. I will not describe myself as I am at this moment, for reasons to be seen later, but rather as I was two years ago.

I was, and am, five foot eleven inches in height. I was slender and yet not meagre. My hair was plentiful, dark brown in colour and apt to be untidy owing to my dislike of filthy things like brilliantine: my eyes grey, and my eyebrows faint, my nose neither large nor small, my lips thin and nervous if I am agitated or worried, and my chin rather in-determinate. My hands free of hair (my body, apart from my head, has little hair). Although when clothed I appear slim, without my clothes I had, two years ago, the evidences of a slight tendency to stoutness. And here I must mention a possible over-delicacy as to my being seen by anyone unclothed. I attribute this to my having been a day boy and, since my school time, I have mixed very little with men.

I shall never forget my horror when, one morning entering my room without knocking, an aunt, a noisy careless creature, saw me nude in my bedroom. I was at that time a boy of about fifteen.

I might have made a good thing of my business had I been able to put my whole heart into it. My father had trained me well and I have a natural love for rare and beautiful things. But my mind was for ever on my writing, and had it not been for my wife, I should, I fear, have lost everything. I owe her a great deal for this and many other things.

I am not a religious man although recent fearful events have led me to reconsider many of my earlier views. If there *is* a God, I pray Him to forgive my many years of disobedience and to lift, if it may be so, this dreadful present burden from my shoulders.

2

I met for the first time James Oliphant Tunstall on my very first day at the Seaborne Grammar School. (This was in 1913.) I was a boy of ten years of age and, of course, dreadfully shy and nervous at this, my first day at school. I remember it as though it were yesterday, and indeed because it was the hour of my first meeting James Tunstall, it may be said to be the most important day of my life.

During the morning nothing much occurred. I was placed with several other new boys in a class some way up the school. We were the *bright* new boys and James Tunstall was not among them. He was in a lower form. I remember very well the master of my form—Oxley was his name—for he had a passionate love for literature and was the first human being to make Chaucer and Shakespeare, and even Milton, understandable to me. He was a long, thin man with a long, thin nose, and a habit of sniffing as though an unpleasant odour were somewhere lurking. But how he *adored* Shakespeare!

We were let out for recreation at midday and it was in the playground on that sharp September morning that I first saw James Tunstall. Anyone would have noticed him before the other new boys, just as in later life he was always the first to be recognised anywhere. He was exactly my height but even then, filled out sturdily and broadly. Whereas I was sallow-complexioned he was rosy and brown in colour, with rounded cheeks. Even then his eyebrows were thick above his bright sparkling eyes.

He was always laughing, joking, calling out, on the move. As a small boy (he was the same age as myself, born in the same month) he was friendly to all the world. I suppose, to use modern rather cheap terms, you would say he was an extrovert. I was an introvert. But there was more in it than that. He used his breeziness and heartiness to cover his secret designs. Even then, at ten years of age, he was plotting how he could use everybody and everything to his own advantage. He was helped, of course, by the fact that he never had any morals whatever.

When I first saw him he was standing in the middle of the stone yard telling some story to a group of other boys, and although he was only a new boy, he had already fascinated them and they were laughing and joking with him as though he had been at the school for years. I didn't want to approach the group but I had to. Even at that very first moment he fascinated me and even at that very first moment I hated him.

He said again and again, in after years, that he had always liked me—even at that first encounter. And I think, in a strange sort of way, that was true—liked me and patronized me.

Now if there is one thing stronger in me than another it is my hatred of being patronized. Patronage of one human being by another seems to me despicable. It is true, I suppose, that the patroniser does not sometimes know that he is patronizing. That makes it worse, for it argues a secret arrogance and conceit, an arrogance of the soul.

In any case, from the first Tunstall patronised and mocked me. This does not mean that he was not pleasant to me. He, as he laughingly said afterwards, from the very first took me under his wing. He called me 'Jacko,' a name that naturally revolted me. 'You know, Jacko,' he said to me many years later, 'I'll never forget how you looked that first morning at the old school—with your anxiety and politeness and helplessness. You were the most tempting object for anyone to rag, and where you'd have been if I hadn't protected you I can't imagine.'

Protect me in a sort of way he did, but for me in a very shaming kind of way. He was popular, of course; I was not so much unpopular as negative and colourless. When a boy twisted my arm or kicked my behind, Tunstall would come up, laughing, and say: 'Stop that. Jacko's under my protection. Didn't you know?' And because he was strong and stoutly built, and everyone liked him, people did let me alone. But the other boys caught up the horrid name, Jacko, from him. How I detested it! It was as though I were a monkey.

I very soon discovered that Tunstall was up to every kind of trick and broke all the rules, but he was popular with the masters as well as with the boys, and he had, then as later, an open, hearty, smiling manner. He was always in good spirits and had great ingenuity in the carrying-out of his secret plans. He was lazy and I often did his work for him. It wasn't as though I were frightened of him exactly, and yet I can see now that there was some sort of secret fear mixed in my feelings about him. Not so much fear, perhaps, as a consciousness of some bond between us. He felt that as well as I.

I have mentioned the word fear. I will admit at once that I am not brave and have never been so. One of the first things to exasperate me in Tunstall was his apparent fearlessness. It seemed that he was afraid of nothing, but I am not really sure that this was so. There was, I fancy, a lot of false bravado mixed up with it.

But I must get on, for I have much to tell—how much I didn't properly perceive when I began.

One summer term at the Grammar School an episode occurred which I fancy affected all my after life—and it changed my nervous dislike of Tunstall into positive hatred. I have spoken already of my sensitiveness to any sort of personal exposure. This was always with me a kind of spiritual passion.

On a certain day in the week the town salt-water baths were reserved for our school. They were formed from part of the sea, but the actual bathing-pool was enclosed in an especial pavilion. We boys undressed all together in a long kind of reserved corridor. I was extremely sensitive of undressing before others, and while most of the boys were quite careless about the matter and ran about the place naked, I was always careful to slip on my bathing-trunks before taking off my shirt.

One afternoon a number of boys, including Tunstall, were undressing near me when someone mocked me and called me rude names. Then they all teased me. I was standing with only my shirt on when, quite unexpectedly, Tunstall whipped my shirt off, snatched my bathing-trunks away from me, and then pranced round me laughing and gesticulating. The others joined in and formed a ring round me while I stood, trembling all over, my hands folded in front of me. My folded hands annoyed them and they pulled them away, and I don't know what would have happened had not a master been seen approaching. Then, laughing and shouting, they jumped into the water.

It will be difficult for many people to understand the deep and lasting effect that this trivial little incident had upon my character. These things cannot be explained even now when Freud and Jung have done so much to reveal us to ourselves. I felt as though I had been deeply and publicly shamed, and my original shyness and reticence were doubly reinforced.

The affair was, however, made worse for me by what followed. As, after our bath, we walked up to the school, Tunstall joined me. He was in radiant health and spirits. He put his arm round me and drew me close to him. I remember our little conversation as though it had occurred this morning!

'Look here, Jacko!' he said. 'You mustn't mind things so much. Why, I thought you were going to blub! It was only a bit of fun.'

I hated his touch, the pressure of his fingers against my neck. However, I pretended not to care. 'I didn't mind,' I said, 'only I thought it was a silly sort of thing to do.'

'Yes, you did mind. You know you did. You mustn't mind anything. I don't. If chaps see you mind they'll only do it all the more.'

'I don't see why I can't be left alone,' I said.

'So, you will be if you don't care. I was only ragging. I am awfully fond of you, you know. I am really.'

'That's all right,' I said sheepishly. Then he ran off laughing, without a care in the world.

Even then I was writing. The only thing I wanted to be in the world was a writer. Oddly enough Tunstall had an artistic side to him. His father was, I should imagine, a ne'er-do-well. He betted on horses and was always involved in wild-cat schemes to make money. They lived in a little house outside the town, overlooking the sea. His mother was a gentle-faced woman who had, I expect, a pretty hard life. Tunstall could draw like anything. He was always amusing the boys by drawing things for them and often the drawings were bawdy. They seemed to us miraculously clever, although even then I thought there was a certain cheapness and commonness in them. But he showed me one day some water-colours of the sea and coast that seemed to me lovely. It was on that day that most unfortunately, I told him about my writing, and under pressure I showed him one or two things.

He professed to like them greatly—especially one, a rather fantastic sort of fairy-story as I remember it. But he did say he wished that they had been a bit more 'spicy.' 'Later on, when you're selling things to the papers, put in bits about girls' legs and that sort of thing. That's what sells. After all, it is what men are always thinking of—"a bit of skirt."'

I remember the phrase 'a bit of skirt' with a very especial horror—it seemed the lowest, most common denominator to which the world could possibly be put.

I suspected then that I had been a fool to show him my writing—very soon I discovered the kind of fool that I had been! Soon everybody was teasing me 'to show my writing.' But I found that I had no need to do so, for Tunstall had informed them fully of the nature of it and especially of the fairy-story, which contained a character called King Dodderer. This became my nickname. How I hated him then! I did have at least the pluck of facing him with it. Trembling with rage I charged him with betraying my confidence.

'You swore you wouldn't tell anybody'—feeling almost a frenzy at the sight of his round cheeks, his rather coarse but thick dark hair and eyebrows, his rounded but strong and sturdy body. Our conversation was something like this:

'I didn't know you'd mind. Honest, Jacko, I didn't.'

'Of course, you knew I'd mind.'

'Honest, I didn't. And why should you? I've told everybody they're awfully good.'

'You haven't. You've made everybody laugh at them.'

'Oh, they tease a bit! What does it matter? You *are* a funny chap. You should be like me, bold as brass and not giving a damn for anybody.'

'Before I'd be like you I'd drown myself,' I answered hotly.

Then he put his hand on my arm, holding it tightly. It was a way that he had. He would stand quite close to me, holding my arm, looking into my face with his bright, bold, sparkling eyes, and I felt as though he absorbed me, took me right inside himself, inside his hateful self, and kept me there a prisoner.

'You know, Jacko, I *do* like you, although you're such a goup. I think you really like me too, although you're a bit afraid of me. I like that as well.'

'I hate you! I hate you!' I cried, breaking away from him.

Then, of course, we grew older. We both left the school when we were sixteen, I to join my father at the shop, he to go into some sort of business in London.

There are other things I remember about the two of us at that school. There was one other thing I never forgave him for. At last I made a friend, the only friend I did make at that place. He was a boy called Marillier, a tall handsome boy, popular with everyone. For some reason or other he took a great fancy to me. I was astonished when I found it was so. He was clever and read books. His great ambition was that one day he should be a publisher. 'Then I shall publish your books and we'll both make a lot of money.' He was a really charming boy, sensitive and understanding, and, after a while, I poured out my heart to him. He seemed to understand all my reserve and silence and reticence. We went for long walks along the cliffs and bathed in the coves. He made me very happy. I worshipped him and would have done anything for him. Strangely enough Tunstall was jealous of this friendship.

'You like him more than you do me, don't you?'

'Of course, I do,' I answered. 'I don't like you a little bit. I never have.'

'Oh yes you do,' he answered. 'I mean more to you than Marillier does. You can't get away from me. You think you can, but you can't.'

Then Marillier began to be a little less intimate with me. He wasn't as frank and easy with me. I taxed him with it and he denied it, but I knew it was true. I was easily hurt and brooded over things. I was sure that Tunstall had said something to Marillier about me. I taxed him with *that* and we had a quarrel. All our intimacy was spoilt. Perhaps if I had been another kind of person I would have broken down the barrier between us, but I was too shy, and our friendship was ruined.

Tunstall said one day:

'You don't see as much of Marillier as you did, Jacko.'

'You've put him against me.'

'Well, what if I have? I'm the only friend you're going to have here.'

'I'm not your friend! I'm not your friend!'

But he only laughed and teased me with his smile, as though he knew everything about me and could make me do as he wished. Other little things I can remember.

There was some sort of an examination and I helped Tunstall with his paper. This was afterwards discovered and we were both punished, but Tunstall, because he was a favourite, was let off lightly, and I, because none of the masters, save only Oxley, liked me, was severely handled.

I brooded long over this unfairness.

There was a master called Harrison, a big, fat, rosy man, rather an example physically of what Tunstall might be when he became a man. Their resemblance was, I think, more than physical. Their natures were of the same kind.

Harrison disliked me very much, and it happened that for a whole year Tunstall and I were both in his form. He seemed to understand the relationship of Tunstall and myself and fostered its disagreeableness in every way. He had a complete understanding with Tunstall and their eyes would meet and they would smile.

Harrison had a trick of jingling his keys and money in his trouser-pocket which for some reason or other disgusted me. The backs of his hands were covered with dark black hairs, and sometimes, when the weather was warm, he would take off his coat and turn up his shirt-sleeves. His thick strong arms were covered with hair, and this also revolted me.

I was, for the latter part of that year, at the top of the form and the cleverest boy in it, but he would catch me out in a fault whenever he could and would summon me in front of him, before the class. Then he would hold my arm as Tunstall sometimes did and stare at me, smiling contemptuously. I knew that Tunstall, behind my back, was watching with delight, and I felt as though I was held, a prisoner, between these two and that they were, in concert, shaming me.

Harrison had affairs with girls in the town, and at last was involved in some scandal and was dismissed from the school, but I think that he continued to see Tunstall.

During most of these school years the Great War of 1914-18 was, of course, raging and, although we boys had little actually to do with it, I don't doubt but that it affected all our nerves and that the weak nutrition of the last years of the War was bad for our health.

In 1919 both Tunstall and I left.

From 1919 until March 1929 Tunstall was in London, or in any case did not return to Seaborne. His mother and father died. Their little house by the sea was sold. It seemed that no fragment or memory of them remained.

I worked in the antique shop and, during those years, the boom years that followed the War, we did sufficiently well. In 1924 my first novel, *The Sandy Tree,* was published. I will not now, when my hopes have been so sadly disappointed, say very much of my almost delirious excitement at that time. The shore of the world is scattered with the bones of disappointed artists. I had written several novels before *The Sandy Tree* and sent them to various publishers. They were refused and I destroyed them. But on that morning when I received the letter saying that *The Sandy Tree* had been accepted I knew such joy that I was, for a while, insane. I realised on that morning that with a little luck I might be encouraged to be an entirely different human being—genial, friendly, communicative. My mother and father were almost as wildly delighted and all our friends and acquaintances were told of the event. I corrected my proofs as though they were the very blood of my body. As the day of publication approached I could scarcely sleep and ate almost nothing. Then my six presentation copies arrived in their dark-blue covers and I gave the first one that I handled to my father and mother. They both thought the book wonderful and looked at me with new eyes. Then came the day of publication. Weeks followed. Nothing happened at all. There were some reviews, none very rapturous, one or two advertisements. Some jocular remarks were made by our acquaintances. It was altogether too queer and unusual a book for their understanding. After a month the book was as though it had never been. I told myself that this always happened to a first novel of any peculiar merit. I told myself that I was so unusual that it would take time for me to be discovered by the people who really understood me.

But in my heart, I had been dealt a dreadful blow. All my life long I had looked forward to the day when I would be an author before the world. I consoled myself, at moments of bitter loneliness or disappointment, with this self-prophecy of my future glory. Now I had tried and I had failed.

In 1926 my father died. He was ill for a week from some sort of fever and then quite suddenly one evening passed away. On the last day of his life he spoke to me in a very touching manner.

He lay there seeming to me to be cleansed of all his grossness by approaching death. His eyes were dim but of a great kindness and even tenderness. I sat beside his bed and suddenly tears began to fall. I loved him for the first time and learned all that I had missed. But he himself was gay and even jocular. He had always been a merry man.

'All our lives together, John, I've loved you and you've not loved me. You've wanted to get away from me. Something in me has shocked you. But I've understood that, for I've always seemed to be both myself and yourself—the rake and the puritan bound into one body. I've not been physically faithful to your mother and she has known it and forgiven me. But I have loved her dearly all through life. Don't be too shocked at things, John. Men are partly animals, you know, and the animal in man isn't as evil as the devil in man—the devil's weapons are meanness, treachery, betrayal of heart, coldness, uncharitableness, not fornication and all lasciviousness. Remember not to judge or you may yourself be judged. It was the man whose house was swept and cleaned that took in the seven new devils.'

That was the way my father talked, in a kind of scriptural style. He pressed my hand, and that night about ten he coughed and cried out and died.

I took on the business.

★★★★★★

I should say something here about Seaborne itself, for I loved it so much until a certain evening and after that came most bitterly to hate it as, afterwards, I will write down. In Elizabeth's day it had been quite a flourishing seaport with a bustling trade. It was well situated between the hills and having in front of it a natural harbour with a strong breakwater. This was needed, for the houses of the little town went to the water's edge and, during three-quarters of the year, the storms could be terrific.

The Upper Town was like any other seaside resort in Glebeshire, with a High Street, a Methodist chapel, a tourist hotel, 'The Granby', a Smith's bookshop with its messenger-boy sign, a hosier's, a grocer's, a china-ware and our own antique shop.

Above the Upper Town, straggling up the hill, were decent villas with pleasant gardens. All this was conventional, but the Lower Town was very unconventional. It reminded one of Polchester *in piccolo,* for Polchester's Seatown on the Pol was at one time—and not so very long ago—as wild and neglected as any place you could find in England.

Seaborne's Lower Town wasn't wild and neglected. It was simply deserted. It had fallen into a still and gloomy sea-green, slimy decay. Any sea traffic there was had moved to the New Harbour, that also boasted a new pier with a hall and a cinema.

So, the Lower Town harbour had surrendered to history. The houses that abutted on the sea had still some remnants of Elizabethan architecture, and there were proposals once or twice a year that something should be done with this part of the town. 'The Green Parrot,' a very low sort of pub, hanging right over the water, and with one foot on the old deserted grass-grown landing-stage, was in reality a fine little building with the remnants of an Elizabethan staircase and spyhole. 'The Green Parrot' had in fact a long and exciting history had anyone taken the trouble to delve into it.

I little thought, at the time of my father's death, that I was, in my own destined moment, to add to that history. Possessing the twisted and restless imagination of a romantic novelist, the Lower Town appealed greatly to my taste and fancy. I liked especially on an early spring or midsummer evening to wander quite alone under the shadows of the warped and tumbled houses, looking upward into a sky faintly green with the piercing silver of a new-born star, and then down, beyond the rotting wood iridescent with slime, into the water that heaved as though it were asleep and reflected, a little out of focus, the glass of windows, the tufts of greenery between the window-joints, the pushing eaves, the drunken chimneys, and, behind them all, the line of quiet hill like a smudged drawing, grey and still. That is how it was. Green and grey, still and crooked, waiting, sleepily speculative, on the edge of the Atlantic.

On these evenings there were few passers-by. Even 'The Green Parrot' was not greatly patronised. In the daytime tourists visited the Lower Town and found it 'picturesque.' They bought postcards of it. But on my evenings, I was a solitary, and loved to be so.

4

I have now reached the point of my marriage. I must say here, for I wish to be completely frank and honest in everything, that my wife was the first woman with whom I had intercourse. I knew no woman of any sort or kind before I knew her. I was twenty-five years of age when I married her. I had, of course, my temptations as every man must have, but I put them always resolutely behind me. I wished to keep myself for the woman I loved.

I think I should say in this place that prayer helped me very much in my struggle against temptation. I was not, I suppose, a very religious young man. I went to church on Sunday to please my dear mother, but the prayers and hymns in the Church of England service seemed to me very empty and hollow. But in my own private prayers I did undoubtedly find strength and assistance. George Meredith has said: 'Who rises from his knees a better man, his prayer is answered.' I felt a contact which may indeed have been but wish-fulfilment. It had nevertheless its actual concrete effect.

I had fancied myself once or twice in love and always, I can see now, with the same type of woman. We have all of us, I fancy, a type physically of especial attraction to us, but in my own case it must be a woman retiring, virginal, modest, of the kind that Burne-Jones once wonderfully painted. With this character I liked a woman to be also slender, with a face like the heroine of Browning's great poem.

I would lie sleepless, imagining her to myself, her noble brow, her sweet mouth so formed with smiling kindly tenderness, her white delicate hands, her slender virginal waist.

Unhappily, girls answering to this physical appearance had, I was sorry to discover, characters little in common with it, and I began cynically to wonder whether the more virginal the face the looser the character.

One misadventure I had of this kind is too shocking to mention, and I shrank yet further within myself.

Then one evening I was taking a solitary walk in Lower Town when I saw a female figure standing on the decrepit landing-stage looking down into the water. It was a grey misty evening and a very slight rain was falling.

I fancied for the moment that there was something desperate in her poise, and that even it might be that she would throw herself into the sea. So, I approached her, but, on standing beside her, found that she was entirely composed and controlled. She was wearing a grey cloak and bonnet and, when she raised her face to mine, I knew at once that the love of my life had, in an instant of fiery ecstasy, been created. Her face was, for me, the loveliest I have ever seen or ever shall see. It was the face of my dreams, the features exquisitely formed, and the expression that of one of the Burne-Jones angels.

She did not seem in the least afraid of me, nor did she move away. She even smiled and said that she thought it would soon rain heavily. I have asked her since whether she was not afraid to speak to a strange young man in such a lonely place, but she said that I looked such a very innocent young man, and that in any case she was well able to look after herself.

So, we talked for a little. I was trembling with anxiety lest she should move away and I lose her for ever. She has told me since that she knew from that very first moment that I was in love with her.

She showed, however, no intention of moving away, and told me that she was in Seaborne for a holiday, that she had a job as a stenographer in London. I ventured to ask her, breathlessly, whether she were married.

She said no, that she was an orphan, and lived with a sister in Chelsea. She also told me that she disliked her present employer and hoped to find some other job. She was taking her holiday alone, which she greatly preferred.

I told her something about myself, that I had an antique shop in the High Street, that my mother was still alive, and that I had published a novel. She seemed to be greatly interested when I told her about the antique shop. She said that it was her ambition to own a little business and that she was sure that she could make a good thing of it. I ventured, my heart beating in my throat, to say that she did not look like a business woman but something very much better. She smiled at that and even laughed.

Then, by the mercy of Providence, as it seemed to me, it began to rain heavily. I had an umbrella and she had not. I suggested that I should guard her under my umbrella as far as her door.

After I left her there I could not sleep. A totally new experience had come into my life. I told myself that, when I saw her again, the spell might be broken. But of course, it was not. It was rather intensified. I called to see her on some pretext. She came and had tea with my mother and was very charming to her. She was charming to everybody with a quiet virginal tranquillity. Her interest in my antique shop, however, was more than virginal. She handled the articles—the brass, the china, the water-colours, the furniture—with an eagerness that surprised me.

Laughing, she said one day that she would stay and help me, and she remained all the afternoon. She sold a number of things and charmed the customers. I can see her now, standing there in her dove-grey costume with rose-coloured cuffs and collar. One voluble American lady liked her so much that she was ready to buy anything from her.

'I haven't enjoyed an afternoon so much,' Eve (that was her

name—Eve Paling) said, 'for years and years.' Her pale cheeks were flushed and she was to me so beautiful, standing there with a cup with yellow flowers marked on it, that I could have fallen on my knees and worshipped her.

The night before she returned to London I asked her to marry me. She showed no surprise. She must have known from the very first that I loved her. She neither accepted nor refused me. How often afterwards was I to recall the words that she said then!

'I don't know, John.' She let her hand lie very quietly and passively in mine. 'I like you very much. I'm sure I could be happy with you. And I should enjoy immensely helping you to run the shop. All that is tempting to me. But is it fair—fair to you, I mean?'

'Fair to me!' I cried. 'Fair! Why, if you marry me you'll be doing me the greatest, most wonderful—'

'Yes, I know. So, you think now. But, you see, I'm not in love with you. I know what it is, being in love. The kind of man for me physically is someone big and strong, a little violent perhaps. The kind of man,' she added, laughing, 'you read about in cheap novels, the cave-man. Now you're not a bit the cave-man, John. You'll give in to me and let me have my way. Even physically you're altogether too thin and too pale. You need fattening up.'

I had already made the discovery that she often said things that did not seem to belong to her virginal, other-worldly appearance. She had shown herself very practical indeed about the shop and had said things once or twice about men that were not virginal at all.

'If you marry me,' I said, 'I'll get so fat from content that you won't know me.'

But she shook her head and looked at me anxiously.

'We've only known one another a fortnight. We don't really know one another at all. You're in love with me now, and later on, when you've got over that part of it, you may not like me. I'm not dreamy and imaginative as you are, John. I see only what is directly in front of me and what I see is very tempting, for I like you and admire you, I hate my present job and want to get out of it. And I think that to-gether we could make a fine thing of the shop.'

I did go down on my knees then and laid my head on her lap. Then I looked up into her face and implored her—oh, how I implored her!—to take pity on me. I did not mind that she did not love me. That she liked me was enough. I would serve her, work for her . . .

'Yes,' she interrupted, 'that is just what I am afraid of. I want a man to master me, not to be my slave!'

Yes, I must always remember how frank and honest she was. All that has happened since has been my fault, not hers. She is in no way to blame—or only very little. She said that she would write to me.

A week later I received a letter saying that she would marry me. Oh, then I went mad with joy! I kissed my old mother again and again. I walked about the town like a madman; I went into Lower Town and stood on the very spot where I had first seen her. I remember that it was a sunny windy morning and that the ocean was covered with gleaming, glittering white-caps and that at my feet against the broken landing-stage the waves broke and splashed and the sun made their foam iridescent.

We were married on April 5th, 1928. We went for our brief honeymoon into Cornwall. We slept the first night at Penzance. I would have made a clumsy wooer but for her quiet, humorous command of me. She slept into the full sun of the morning with deep surrender, while I lay awake, thinking over and over again of my wonderful good fortune, but haunted by an odd little half-formed wish that she had not been quite so well-assured, so ready for my immature, inexperienced love-making.

5

That marriage is a strange business I suppose every married man and woman will in their hearts admit. Even the happiest must realise that incomprehensible mixture of intimacy and non-intimacy so that at one moment your partner seems a piece of yourself and at another it is as though you had never seen him or her before.

So, at least, it was with us, or with myself, I had better more truthfully say. My passionate desire for her remained because she never fully responded to it. This side of our married relationship she treated with a motherly irony, permitting my indulgence, as a mother gives a railway train to her little son. 'If you really feel like this,' she seemed to say, 'the least I can do is to grant you some pleasure. It doesn't hurt me and you like it—so why not?'

I realised, I suppose, from the beginning that I was not, as she had frankly told me, her type. And that was neither her fault nor mine. But I was kept for ever on the edge of unsatisfied desire—so near and yet so far! And I would lie beside her at night, while she slept so calmly, longing, praying, that one day she would of her own accord turn to me and show me that she loved me!

In all other aspects our marriage was for a long time most happy.

My mother and Eve fortunately liked one another from the start and achieved an underground understanding: it was almost an alliance against myself—a sort of intimation that they were both fond of me, but that I was a poor fish really.

I did not resent this. I was of the type of man who worships one or two women to idolatry. Eve might do anything to me, say anything to me, think anything of me that she pleased. I did not mind how much she ill-treated me (which she never did). There was something masochistic in me with regard to her. And so, my old mother very quickly took something of Eve's tone to me. I had always been a devoted son, but now, when she saw that I was on my knees to my wife, she thought that it would be amusing if I were on my knees to her too. She had lost now the use of her legs, and she would sit in her chair, a lace cap that with old-fashioned fancy she wore, on her head, a faint moustache that was often slightly moist, and her dark restless eyes regarding me with love and tyranny. Her hands were still lovely and delicate, her little body taut and straight, and when I saw the two women, the old lady in her chair, and Eve, with always that suggestion of the Quaker in her dress, her beautifully proportioned body that had been so often in my arms but that never truly yielded to me, then I would tremble, and fire would run in my veins, and I would be happy and miserable both at the same time.

To speak of more practical matters, it was at once clear that Eve had a genius for business. She was better than my father had ever been. She had a real love, too, for the things that she handled and, although when she first met me she knew nothing about antiques, by reading books and studying the things that came our way, she soon was far ahead of me in knowledge.

She quickly became a well-known figure at local sales. She specialized in Victorian furniture, china—so many things that we had all for so long thought hideous. And she had an especial liking for Pre-Raphaelite drawings and paintings. She found water-colours by J. M. Strudwick and Arthur Hughes, and Frederick Sandys and Matthew Lawless, for almost nothing at all.

She said that there would be one day a great revival in these artists, and I can see that already her prophecy is beginning to come true. She would say, laughingly, that she was herself a Pre-Raphaelite, and that the old part of Seaborne was Pre-Raphaelite. Sometimes on a day when the sea gleamed in purple and green, and the old decrepit buildings were coloured by the light in sharp, bright detail, I could see what she meant.

But it was on the business side that she was wonderful. She was marvellous with customers, studying their characters, charming to one, sharp with another, leading them on from one thing higher and higher, until they purchased far beyond their original intention, and all so quietly and with so much grace and friendliness, that they would return to our shop again and again, simply for the pleasure of seeing her.

This all meant that I left the shop more and more to her and devoted myself, with an obsession, to my writing. The novel upon which I was working during the first year of our marriage, *The Gridiron,* became an obsession to me. The theme, very briefly, was this: A wife is tortured with love for her husband, who does not care for her, and is persistently unfaithful to her. She knows in the depths of her far-seeing soul that he will one day hate her so deeply that he will murder her. She is fascinated by the thought that he will murder her and is like a rabbit before a snake. She does not attempt to leave him. Ultimately, he does murder her, and is then tortured on the gridiron—not of his conscience, for he suffers from no regrets or self-reproaches—of his new wife's hatred of himself. He adores her, she hates him. He commits suicide.

This grim story seemed neither grim nor true to Eve, with whom I discussed it. She thought it simply silly. She had a brave and practical mind, was afraid of no one and nothing.

'Women don't just wait to be murdered, however idiotic they are,' she said.

'You talk,' I answered, 'as though I had been writing about you. I've chosen someone exactly opposite—weak, yielding, gentle, loving.'

I hoped that this last word would provoke her into protesting that she *did* love me, but she paid no attention to it, only went on:

'Besides, John, you're the last man in the world to write about the feelings of a murderer; you who wouldn't hurt a fly.'

'Oh, I don't know,' I remember protesting. 'If I get an idea into my head, I can be very obstinate.'

'What's obstinacy got to do with murder?' she asked.

'A great deal. Don't you remember the other day, when Mr. Fortescue, of Four Trees, had the Burne-Jones drawing for "The Forge of Cupid" that you wanted? How, for several days, before he gave in, you could think of nothing else, could scarcely sleep?'

'Ah, that was different! What has a Burne-Jones drawing got to do with murder?'

I remember looking at her and thinking that, in some ways, she was a very stupid woman. It was imagination that she lacked, and in that there was a deep division between us.

'Both are lusts,' I answered. 'Lust of hate. Lust of possession.'

And I remember that she looked at me a little contemptuously, saying, 'Lust! What an odd word for *you* to use, John. You know nothing about lust—and you couldn't hate anybody for ten minutes together.'

Oh, couldn't I? I thought of telling her about Tunstall. But I did not. How strangely little, even after daily and nightly intimacies, two human beings know one another!

I was obsessed by *The Gridiron*. Poor *Gridiron* that nobody knows, nobody cares for. But how real both that man and that woman were to me! How thoroughly I understood their hates and their fears! It seemed to me that they were both part of me, both murderer and murderee!

I had been long fascinated by the life, personality and works of George Gissing; Morley Roberts's life-novel about him, writings on him by H. G. Wells, who had been very generously his friend; novels like *New Grub Street, The Odd Women, A Life's Morning* (in spite of its false ending), and then his momentary escape into his longed-for world of rest and light—*By the Ionian Sea, Henry Ryecroft*—all this touched me deeply. He seemed like a brother of mine. I felt that if I had known him I could have comforted him, brought him perhaps to Seaborne and cared for him. The grey dreariness of his novels was akin to me: his obsession with women I understood. I loved the man and greatly admired his art, which seemed to me a unique thing. I tried to persuade Eve to read *Demos* and *The Odd Women*, but she could not endure these books.

She enjoyed romantic novels. She wanted a happy ending. She repeated the formula as though no one had ever uttered it before.

'There's enough in life that's depressing and difficult, without books being depressing too.'

Then came the month of March 1929—a month that I am never likely to forget, however long I live.

Eve was about to give birth to our first child. She was as sensible about this as she was about everything else. She did not especially wish for a child—she had not, I think, very much of the maternal in her—but if there must be one she would do her best by it.

I was meanwhile tortured. I had never loved her so passionately. The mother of my child! The mother of my child! Our child! I imagined, of course, every kind of disaster! She looked as virginal, as slender of body as she had done on the day of our first meeting. It seemed to me an awful ordeal through which she must pass. I tried to conceal my terror, for both she and my mother would despise me for it.

The day approached. On March 10th the pains began. About three in the afternoon I walked down to the Lower Town and strode up and down the old landing-stage. Looking up from the grey-cotton waters of the sea I saw, standing close beside me, James Oliphant Tunstall.

★★★★★★

Yes, it was Tunstall.

It wasn't true that I had ever forgotten him, but now, when I saw him, it was as though he had never left me. And with that sense of his accompanying me came a sudden fear that was almost a sickness.

I stood 'rooted to the spot' as cheap novelists say. Yes, but it's a good phrase all the same. I *was* rooted, staring, terrified. Of what? Of whom?

You must remember that I was in a state of nervous tension on that afternoon, expecting the birth of my child at any moment, thinking of my adored, my beloved, and her approaching torture.

Tunstall stood grinning. Then he held out his hand.

'Well, if it isn't Jacko!'

I shook his hand, which was soft and plump. I saw that he wore on the little finger of his right hand a green scarab set in gold.

He was looking very prosperous, wearing dark red-brown tweeds and a dark-red tie, his face ruddy brown, thick-set, inclined to be stout and, although he was exactly my own height, looking shorter than I because of my slimness. His thick eyebrows stood out from his ruddy face, and there, just as they had always been, were his cheeky laughing eyes and lascivious lips. He seemed to swallow me up, in the old horrible way, as I looked at him.

'Well, if it isn't Jacko!'

'Hallo, Tunstall! What are you doing here?'

'Tunstall be damned! It's your old friend Jimmie come back to you again!' Exactly as in the old way he was close to me, his thigh pressed against mine, his hand on my arm. How I hated that contact! But I couldn't move. I waited until he released me and leant back against the railing that they had put up on the old pier to prevent people from falling into the water.

He leaned back, his hands pressed down on the green metal, grinning at me.

'How are you, Tunstall? Come on a visit?'

'Now Tunstall be blowed. I'm Jimmie to you and always will be.'

'Jimmie, then.'

'That's better. A visit, Jacko? No, my dear boy. I'm here for keeps.'

My heart contracted. I could feel the palms of my hands go damp.

'Yes,' he went on. 'We shall see plenty of one another. I always said you couldn't ever escape me and you shan't. Now confess—haven't you thought of me sometimes?'

'No. I can't say that I have.' (How vivid, how horribly, horribly vivid is this conversation to me now!)

'O, come now. That isn't true. You've thought of me often. You know you have. And *I've* thought of you. You were the boy I was fondest of at school, you know.'

'Well, I wasn't fond of you,' I said, making at last a movement. 'And now I must be getting on—'

'Wait, wait,' he cried, his eyes watching me mockingly. 'We've been apart so long and you want to leave me? What have you been doing with yourself all this time? As a matter of fact, I know. I've been down here three days and you were the first person I asked about. Your father's dead and you run the shop. Or rather your wife does. A very nice practical woman I'm told. I'm keen to meet her. And you've published a novel. You see, I know all about you. As a matter of fact, I bought the book. It wasn't my sort of novel—too highbrow altogether—but there was a lot of me in it.'

'There wasn't any of you in it,' I answered indignantly.

'Oh yes, there was! Don't you think you can write a book without *my* being in it.'

All this time he had never taken his eyes off my face and he seemed to get a great deal of pleasure and amusement out of staring at me.

Then he said:

'Don't you want to know what's been happening to me all this time?'

'I don't particularly care.'

'That *is* a rude thing to say. All the same I'll tell you. I'm quite a successful painter. Hadn't you heard? Especially with portraits. I paint people as they'd like to be. That's the thing. That's what you ought to do. What's the use of writing these books that nobody wants to read? Simply wasting your time. I've made quite a bit of money, and, like a wise man, I married a woman with money.

'So, I've come down here and taken a house—Sandy View—at the end of Chessington Street. There I'm going to be—half the year anyway. And the sooner you and your wife come to see us the better I'll be pleased.'

I noticed then for the first time that he had probably been drinking too much. Not that he was drunk. Certainly not. He was completely in command of his faculties, but there was a slight exalted shining in his eyes, a faint breath emanating from him, a suggested, rather than positive, uncertainty about his body.

Now I have always had, foolishly I am sure, a terror of drunkenness. I am myself a teetotaller, not from any virtuous or health reasons but simply because I loathe spirits and don't really care very much for wine. I am, I must repeat, really terrified of anyone whom drink has deprived of his senses. I have been on occasions in company with men so drunk that they knew neither what they were doing nor saying, and these flushed incoherent creatures reeling and tumbling, clutching at one's body, slobbering in one's face—how I have loathed them, run a mile to avoid them! Tunstall was not, of course, *drunk*, but there was the spirit of drunken recklessness about him. I felt it and trembled.

Meanwhile I must get away. Even now my child might be born. But I had one thing to say.

'Look here, Tunstall.'

'Jimmie!'

'Well, Jimmie then. I think we had better be quite clear from the start. If you are going to live here part of the year as you say, I don't want there to be any misunderstanding. I should much prefer not to visit at your house and that you should not visit at mine. I didn't like you when we were boys. I used to tell you but you wouldn't believe me. Too conceited, I suppose. We had nothing in common then. We have nothing in common now.' (I am repeating the words as I write them down. 'We have nothing in common . . .' Oh God! to whom, to what am I saying them?) 'Apart from the way I feel about you,' I went on, 'we are in different spheres. My wife and I keep a little shop. You are a successful painter with a fine house. You have money. We haven't. We couldn't possibly keep up with your scale of living. So goodbye. Keep to your world. We'll keep to ours.'

I held out my hand. He took, held it, and drew me a little towards him. I tried to draw my hand away. I could not. My whole body trembled. Now that I was close to him I smelt his breath, hot and whisky-tainted, quite distinctly.

'No, Jacko,' he said, laughing. 'It isn't as easy as that—not nearly as easy. I have you in my hand just as I had when we were at school. You say that you don't like me and never did. That may be. I'm the other side of yourself, Jacko, the side you're not very proud of. Stevenson wrote a story about that once. But this isn't Jekyll and Hyde. That was just a story. This is *real*, Jacko—a real alliance. We're like the Siamese twins and always were.'

He was suddenly serious, patted me on the back, lounged lazily away from me.

'Forget my nonsense, Jacko. I was never able to help teasing you, you know. But to pretend that we won't see one another! *What* a hope! Why, as I've told you, you were the first person I asked about when I came back. And you'll like my wife. She's good, like you, and she's fond of me just as you are. I've a sort of idea your wife will like *me*—even if you don't. And you must see my pictures. I'll paint your portrait. There's an idea! I'll take weeks over it and make a good one. So-long, Jacko—see you soon!'

He turned his back on me and walked out to the edge of the landing-stage.

★★★★★★

I found my wife in labour. Doctor Wellard, an untidy giant of a man, but a good doctor, said she would do all right. I behaved in the traditional stage-and-novel father manner, pacing the little sitting-room, listening, going to the door, digging my fingers into the palms of my hands, sweating at the brow.

At seven-thirty exactly Wellard opened the door and told me that I was the father of a son and that mother and child were doing grandly. My son! Ah! How I had prayed for a son! Perhaps for the first time in my life I was really proud of myself. Later I went up to visit Eve. There she was lying, exhausted, looking more virginal than ever, and as comfortably unagitated as though nothing had happened. How I adored, how I worshipped her! Now not only my beloved wife but also the mother of my son.

Her voice was weak but yet contained that tinge of irony that was always there when she spoke to me.

'Poor John! Have you been anxious? It wasn't bad—I had chloroform. Aren't you proud of yourself?'

'I'm proud of *you*,' I said.

'I don't know. Is it anything to be proud of—to bring a son into a world like this? Now go away. I'm sleepy.'

Before I went to my bed I saw my son. He was hideous, of course, but my heart went out to him. I had now three persons in the world to love: my mother, my wife, my son. It was enough. If they were happy and cared for me I asked for nothing more.

But that night, in my dreams, Tunstall was standing beside me. He stretched out his hand and held my arm.

6

I had better now, I think, jump nine years, for I have much to tell and little time to tell it. The sequence of events that led to my present horrible position began, I think, with a party given by the Tunstalls towards the end of January 1938, a party attended by my wife and myself.

What shall I say here about those nine years? There is so much to say and yet so little. On the outside things were little changed in my life and Eve's. During these years I published two novels, *The Gridiron* in 1930, and *The Gossip-monger* in 1936.

The Gridiron, into which I put so much good work—a novel, I am still convinced, with something unique in it, something that has never been done before and will never be done again—appeared and was dead as soon as born. And yet not quite so! For it roused the interest of certain critics, and Rose, the famous novelist, wrote me an enthusiastic letter concerning it. Now I consider Rose's novels very poor indeed—old-fashioned, romantic, platitudinous—but he *is* a very well-known writer and when he reviews a novel he helps, undoubtedly, its popularity. I have often enough inveighed against the practice of one novelist reviewing another novelist and have especially criticized Rose in this connection, but after he had said some fine quotable words about *The Gridiron* in *The Message* I felt rather differently about him. His letter to me was kind and enthusiastic, if patronizing, and when I next saw the picture of his high and shining forehead in a newspaper I felt, I must confess, quite friendly towards it.

It was not, however, until 1936 that I published my third novel, *The Gossip-monger,* and this had a considerable success. I fear that on this occasion I compromised. Why go on for ever writing novels that no one wanted to read? I compromised, as Gissing and many another has been forced to compromise. There was in *The Gossip-monger* a certain dry humour and irony and it happened that the public fancied in one of the figures of my story a caricature of Rose himself. This helped its sale, and Rose was very magnanimous, alluding, humorously, in his review to the caricature as though he had enjoyed it; as a matter of fact, I heard afterwards from a friend of his that it hurt him very much. It was Rose's great ambition in life, I think, to be considered a noble character without being thought at the same time a prig—no easy ambition.

In any case I made some money from *The Gossip-monger* and my hopes were high. My friends and neighbours in Seaborne when they saw my photograph in *The Modern World* began to take me more seriously and even ordered my book from the library.

Against this success must be set the fact that, during these years, I had withdrawn more and more into myself.

Before my marriage the shop had been an easy way for me to keep in touch with my fellow human beings. All day I was talking to this person or that; often I must visit a house or a sale, and although I was never a character to whom anyone took a very great liking, yet I had my friends and acquaintances. But after my marriage Eve's great business efficiency made my presence in the shop a superfluity and I visited it less and less. This I found Eve preferred, for she was cleverer at bargains than I and liked best to clinch them in her own way.

After my boy Archie's birth, she had only two interests in the world—her shop and her son. She continued her kindly tolerance and marital sufferance to myself, but I knew that I counted nothing in her life. My mother had died a year after Archie's birth. I wish, neither now nor later, to compel any pity, if an eye should fall on this, from any reader. But I suffered, after my mother's death, from a desperate loneliness. The boy, delicate, shy, feminine in his sensitiveness, loved only his mother. His mother loved only him. I, most unfortunately, adored them both. No new situation in this world, but a hard and testing one, especially for a man who could not express himself easily and was always frightened of a rebuff.

My shyness to the outside world was greatly increased by the presence of Tunstall in the town. He immediately, of course, made his mark there. It was known from London that he had an assured position there as a portrait-painter. He was well-off and enjoyed entertaining. He was the friend of everyone, had no social exclusiveness and apparently no pride.

After a time, certain stories were current as to his character. He was certainly no strict moralist, but people in general did not mind that so long as he had money and spent it freely.

As a matter of fact, he was, during these nine years, away from

Seaborne a great deal. His career as a portrait-painter became for a year or two quite spectacular. He painted some fashionable ladies, an actor or two, and actually Rose himself, whose picture by Tunstall, bright, shiny, gravely complacent, was in the Academy of 1936.

That, I fancy, was Tunstall's peak year. His popularity began to decline. Why? He lost his head a little, I should imagine. Went to late parties too often, drank perhaps too much, was too familiar with some of his grand ladies.

At any rate he appeared again towards the end of '37 and informed the town that he was 'fed up' with London, that he had made enough money for the rest of his days and that he would develop down here his talent for landscape painting.

I heard all this from Basil Cheeseman, a friend of his, and about Cheeseman, known to myself and some others as 'The Rat', I must say a word or two. Physically he resembled a rat, for he was a little man with very prominent white sharp upper teeth. He had reddish-brown hair and restless whisky-coloured eyes. When he smiled his teeth jutted out over his lower lip.

He was, and is, an evil little man; a journalist by profession who had settled down in a ramshackle cottage near Seaborne and there indulged in shabby orgies with girls from London or visitors to the resort. He made a living by picking up paragraphs and sending them to London and the provincial papers. He had, and has, as malicious and dirty-minded a soul as exists in the world today. He was the very man for Tunstall. He was more evil, I don't doubt, than Tunstall and yet I did not hate him half as much. He had no power over me. I thought of him possibly as a kind of emanation from Tunstall. When Tunstall couldn't come to me himself he sent the Rat instead, and I can see him now with a faint shiny stubble on his cheeks, his projecting teeth and false grin, his restless cat-like eyes. 'He's come back and he's going to stay,' the Rat said, eyeing me curiously. His malicious curiosity knew no limit. He had long ago discovered my hatred and fear of Tunstall, but what was Tunstall's hold over me? I did not look as though I had any vices. And, farther than that, why did Tunstall bother about me at all? What was my attraction for Tunstall?

He never discovered the answer to these questions, and I think at last he decided that the solution was connected with my wife.

And now I must try to explain one of the driving decisive elements in this case—Eve, my wife, from the very first moment, liked Tunstall. At least she did not dislike him. I must say here at once that no one could dislike Leila Tunstall, Tunstall's wife. This was a little round pale-faced woman whose face was almost deformed.

It was *not* deformed, although the face *was* definitely twisted, and yet where the twist was you could never decide. She was as plain as she could be but most terribly nice. Tunstall had married her for her money, of course, and he took everything she gave him for granted, patronized her, laughed at her. She accepted it all with a smile, very quietly.

You would call her, perhaps, a saint—the only one I have ever known. But not at all a prig. Nothing shocked her. She had a strong sense of humour. She liked to mother everyone. She was a very fine woman.

Oddly enough Eve liked Tunstall more than Mrs. Tunstall. 'Of course, she's a good woman,' she said. 'When you're as plain as that it's all that's left you.' Then she added quickly, 'That's cattishness. I'm jealous because she's so much better than me.'

She argued with me on the other side.

'I just can't see what you've got against Jimmie Tunstall.'

'He's foul-minded and foul-living. He's false and treacherous. Vain as a monkey. Greedy.'

'Oh, John, that's jealousy!'

'Jealousy! If I were him I'd shoot myself.'

'He likes you most awfully anyway.'

'He doesn't. He despises me. He likes teasing me, frightening me.'

'Frightening you? What have you got to be frightened of?'

'I don't know. I've always been frightened of him since we were kids.'

Nevertheless, during these nine years we did not see so very much of one another. His success kept him in London. Then he and Leila went for a year on a trip round the world. When he *did* come to Seaborne he was busy with his painting. To my great relief he seemed for a long time to have forgotten all about me. But can you escape anything that is your destiny? I think not.

That was one of the 'turning' moments of my life when Cheeseman told me that Tunstall had come back and was going to stay. I knew it. My throat contracted.

'Things have been going a bit wrong, I fancy,' Cheeseman said with satisfaction. 'He's a bit ratty. Been drinking more than's good for him. Leila's a bit worried. By the way, he said something about you this afternoon.'

'What did he say?' I asked, my heart hammering.

'Oh, only—how's Jacko?'

7

Shortly after this there came an invitation to a Tunstall party: 'Dancing. Bridge.'

'What fun!' Eve said.

'You go. You can go with Jessie Parrott. She's sure to be asked.'

Jessie Parrott was a twittering spinsterly gossip with grey hair in ironclad waves, a mole on her chin, and little nervous movements of her head like a thrush on an early-morning lawn.

'I won't go if you don't.'

'I'm not going.'

Eve was never angry. But she could look at me with contempt.

'Why ever not?'

'I detest Tunstall. That being so, I won't accept his hospitality.'

But I met him on the high road leading to Shining Cliff. He was at his best, healthy, buoyant and sober, his green scarab ring shining in the sun. He had with him his fox-terrier Scandal. Scandal was a lively merry dog, little more than a puppy, who sprang about as though his thin rough legs belonged to a toy dog.

And wasn't Tunstall glad to see me! I thought for a moment that he would kiss me. He held me with both arms and once again I had that curious sensation that he was drawing me into himself. His breast opened. I was drawn in like a stream of air. The breast closed. I was a prisoner.

The dog jumped up on me, greeting me.

'Down, Scandal, down! The dog is as fond of you as I am, you see. Of course, you're coming to the party.'

'No. I'm not.'

'Certainly, you are.' He stood directly in front of me, his broad thick-set body impeding my path. We were exactly of a height, but I was a pale shadow, cast by the misted sun, of his health, self-confidence and vigour.

'Why aren't you coming?'

'Simply because I don't want to.'

'That's very rude. I haven't seen much of you lately. I'm going to from now on. Plenty.'

I forced myself to speak up.

'Please leave me alone. It's a small profitless thing the amusement you get out of me. We have nothing in common, nothing at all, we never have had. It's just a whim of yours. You know I've always disliked you. You've pretended I don't, but you know in your heart that I do. And you hate and despise me.'

I felt as though this were the last appeal of my life that I was making to him—absurd really, here, on this sunny day with the silver slab of Shining Cliff gleaming not far off and the fox-terrier springing about near to us.

He looked at me, his eyes, now a little bloodshot, staring under the black beetling eyebrows. I could see the faint purple veins in his cheeks, the short black hairs thick in his nostrils.

'That's all right,' he said. 'You can hate me as much as you like. Love's akin to hate, you know, Jacko!' He laughed like anything at that, shaking all over. 'Of course, you're coming to the party.'

And of course, I went. Eve and Jessie Parrott and I.

★★★★★★

The Tunstall house was large and glittering. To my taste it was vulgar. In the drawing-room was a portrait of Tunstall himself painted by Walter Eckersley, R.A. It was a regular Eckersley masterpiece, exactly like a coloured photograph. The rooms were bare in the modern manner and yet colours clashed. There was a billiard-room, very elegant, a huge radio-gramophone, a little bar downstairs—and Tunstall was proud of showing us his own private bathroom, a steel and marble affair with dumb-bells and a marvellous shower gleaming with taps.

On the party-occasion we met first round the little bar behind which was a bare floor for dancing. There were some thirty people, I suppose. Eve was, in my opinion, by a great way the most beautiful woman there, in a dress of pale grey, her face nunlike, of a remote and lovely chastity.

I was afraid from the moment I entered that house that night. I had been living more and more by myself. I had had a little quarrel that afternoon with Eve about the boy, Archie, and this had upset me very much. She had said that it was time that he went to school. I had a horror of school for him. I had suffered at school so much myself, and Archie was a sensitive, shy boy, more like a girl in some things than a boy.

'That,' said Eve, 'is just why school will be so good for him. That's what he needs.'

When she was determined on something like this she could look hard and ruthless.

'You've no heart,' I said.

'I love that boy more than anything on earth.'

'Yes, more than me.'

'Oh, John!' She burst out laughing. 'Don't be so silly! You're like a girl yourself sometimes!'

But I was terrified at the thought of Archie at school. He would suffer as I had suffered. So I was upset when I went to the Tunstalls' and when I am upset it is as though all eyes are upon me, mocking me. I detest this self-consciousness, but if you *are* self-conscious what are you to do about it?

Then, as soon as I was downstairs by the bar, Tunstall made for me. It was as though I were the only guest that mattered. Now my ideal at a party (if I *must* be present) is to sit in a corner, quite unnoticed, and observe other people. How wonderful to be an invisible physical presence!

I had hoped on this occasion to find a corner and be happily undisturbed until Eve had had enough of it and was ready to go home. How dreadfully otherwise was my fate!

We went, as ordered by a stiff and shining parlour-maid, to the downstairs bar and dancing-room. There everybody was, but as we entered Tunstall seemed to detect us before we were announced. He came forward eagerly, greeted Eve and turned at once to me. 'Dear old Jacko!' he cried, in a voice that rang through the room, put his hand on my arm and led me forward.

Ah, but he was mocking me! Didn't I know it, and didn't everyone else know it?

It seemed to me that I was faced with a circle of jeering faces. I don't suppose for a moment that that was so. Although I had no warm friends in Seaborne, people on the whole respected me. I was Seaborne's only author and my photograph had been in the London papers. 'A dull dog. How he manages to write those books I can't think,' would be the verdict.

I am sure that they did not look on me with mockery, but it was part of the fate that now had me in charge that I should fancy their hostility, that it should be almost as though I were back at school again, back at the baths with my enemies uncovering my nakedness.

So, I was at my worst, sulky and uncourteous when Tunstall led me up to the little bar and insisted on my drinking. I refused, of course, a cocktail.

He looked at me humorously and addressed the laughing crowd.

'You'd never think, would you,' he said, 'that Jacko is my best friend? He has all the virtues, I all the vices. He is a very serious highbrow author. I'm a common cheap painter.' (His hand was round my neck.) 'All the same, the best friendships are between opposites.' (He was a little drunk already. I could smell his breath.) 'We've been friends all our lives, haven't we, Jacko? And will be friends to the end. Aye, and beyond the end, too. Into Eternity. I drink to you, Jacko, and will forgive you for once for drinking my health in tomato juice.'

I look back now to that party and, in the light of later events, feel that it was a kind of phantasmagoria with everyone a little out of drawing, larger than life-size. I've noticed, too (many others have noticed the same), that in any gathering of human beings you can, with a very little exercise of the imagination, see people as animals—the wolf, the fox, the snake, the rabbit, the horse, the parrot, the faithful dog. I had a sense that they were pressing in upon me and soon would begin to bark, to whistle, to snarl.

To one person at least my discomfiture was apparent, for little Leila Tunstall arrived, detached me from the others, led me to two chairs in the corner of the room.

'Don't you worry about me,' I said, more comfortable at once. 'This is what I like—to sit in a corner and not be noticed.'

'It was too bad of Jim,' she said. 'He's so fond of you, but he doesn't seem to understand you a bit. Then he likes teasing people.'

She gave me a sudden quick look: 'You know—you mustn't think me rude—you're *very* like a brother of mine in the East. In looks, voice—it's astonishing!'

But I was thinking of Tunstall.

'He likes teasing *me*, you mean,' I answered. 'And I don't take teasing well. I get self-conscious and stupid. What I'd *like* would be to sit here and watch people all the evening and not speak to anyone. That's dreadfully unsociable, isn't it?'

She was watching her husband. I could see that she was worried.

'Jim thinks such a lot of you,' she said. 'I believe you could have some influence over him. He wants a friend just now. He's disappointed with the way things have been going, and then he drinks too much and—' She stopped, feeling perhaps that she was disloyal.

'I wouldn't say all this except to a real friend of his.'

I wanted to say that I wasn't a real friend, that I hated him and always had done. But of course, I couldn't say that to her, especially when she was so kind and gentle.

It was then that I noticed someone I had never seen before. A woman. She was very handsome, bigly built, a blonde, holding herself superbly, dressed rather nakedly. She had daring laughing eyes, and plainly defied the world.

'Who is that?' I asked.

I saw at once that Leila disliked her. Leila's face had that deformed look now—somewhere a little twisted—was it the mouth, the cheek? When she looked like this you were sorry for her and loved her. You knew she would have been very unhappy had she not been too courageous to allow unhappiness.

'Oh, that? That's Bella Scorfield.'

'And *who* is Bella Scorfield?'

'Ah, no. You wouldn't have realised her yet. She and her mother have come to live here. They have taken a little house—Middlewood—not far from Shining Cliff. A desolate, lonely place *I'd* think it, and Mrs. Scorfield is a permanent invalid. Jim insisted on my paying a call—a strange woman—looks like a corpse—lies in bed all day working at chess problems and reading mathematics. Or so Bella told me. Bella doesn't seem to mind. She has a car of her own. She's—what shall I say?—a bit of a rip. She told me the other day—she likes to confide in me, I can't think why—that she had only a few years to have a good time in and she'd make the most of it. So I asked her why she had chosen this dull little place and a house miles from anywhere. She gave me a queer look and said that you could often have a better time in a dull little place.'

'You don't like her,' I said.

'No, frankly, I don't.'

'I hate her at sight,' I said.

To that Leila replied:

'What a funny man you are! To look at you one would think you were as quiet as a mouse. But when one gets to know you a little one finds you are full of intense feelings—about people especially.'

'I'd say exactly the same about you.'

She flushed a little, then answered very quietly: 'There *are* some things about which one feels intensely, of course.'

I wasn't permitted to keep my quiet corner for long. Tunstall was soon very merry. It would be untrue to say that he was drunk; he was flushed and noisy and reckless. It became, in fact, very soon a noisy party. Tunstall had that effect on people; he shook them out of their caution, and especially if there were drinks there to assist him.

And I that evening was his continuous butt. Why, *why* did I not have the wisdom to slip away and go home? Again, and again I was tempted to do so, but I did not wish to abandon Eve (she would not have cared, perhaps, if I had). I loved her that night, it seemed to me, as I had never loved her before. How her unattainability stirred my blood! Ah, could I but have been assured that when I touched her arm with my hand she would turn round and, seeing that it was I, would look at me with surprised love. I have caught that look between man and wife, and oh, have I not envied them!

She would not have cared had I gone—and yet I stayed. They danced. We went upstairs to supper, and it seemed that Tunstall could not let me alone. 'Where's Jacko?' he would cry. 'Jacko! Jacko! Where's Jacko?'

'Your master wants you,' some woman, laughing, said to me. How humiliated I was! How desperately I hated his going with me upstairs, his hand on my arm!

We were pressed about with people, and yet at one moment I had a strong impulse to push him on his soft stomach with my sharp elbow and so send him reeling backwards, losing his balance with a cry, tumbling down those sharp-edged wooden stairs, breaking his fat neck perhaps. . . . At that my heart seemed to stop. It appeared to me that I looked out from the very soul of Tunstall himself and saw that fallen, twisted body and the crowd with faces like cambric masks and sharp clown noses, peering at it. I had indeed stopped. He pushed me up the stairs, his hand pressing the small of my back.

'Come on, Jacko! Don't you want your feed? There's ginger-beer, you know—plenty of ginger-beer!'

They did the thing very well. We all sat down to supper at a long table, lit with candles. He sat me down between himself and Miss Scorfield. His knee pressed against mine. Once he laid his hot sweating hand on the back of mine. He leant across me and talked of me to Miss Scorfield almost as though I were not there. He seemed to me to be already on excellent terms with her. I did not look at her, but, in my senses, I was conscious of her half-bare bosom, her naked back, some rose-scented perfume, the heat of her body, the abandonment of her soul.

'You've got to be friends with Jacko, Bella, or you won't be friends with me. He's my better half, always has been since we were at school together.'

'It wouldn't be difficult to be *your* better half, Jimmie.'

'Ah, that's what *you* think! It's more than you'll ever be, Bella, old girl.'

This seemed to them a tremendous joke, and they laughed like anything, he with his hand on my shoulder, his crimson flushed face staring straight into her body. It was almost as though he possessed her in front of my eyes.

After supper we danced, played bridge, gossiped. The silly Parrott girl insisted on staying beside me. Didn't I think Jim Tunstall really *awful*? He couldn't leave a woman alone. How his poor wife was humiliated! And his drinking. Of course, if he went on like that his painting would soon go to pieces. In fact, she had heard that in London . . .

I put an end to this, saying that we had just enjoyed a jolly good supper at his hands, and that it wasn't in the best of taste to slander him. She gave me a viperish look.

'You know what you are, John Talbot. You're a hypocritical prig. You know that you hate Jim Tunstall like poison and always have. You wouldn't be past murdering him if you could get away with it safely. He's been laughing at you all your life, and if there's one thing you can't stand, it's being laughed at. And I'll tell you another thing. Watch Eve and your dear host you're so keen on defending. I wouldn't put it past the two of them.'

With which she walked away, pleased at having disturbed me. As indeed she had, for, at that very moment, looking across to a window-seat near the piano, I saw Eve and Tunstall close together; Tunstall was talking eagerly. Once he put out his hand and touched hers. Eve sat, quiet, beautifully composed, but quite suddenly, as I was staring at them, she laughed, looking up into his face. She gave him a smile—of impudence, daring, adventurous excitement—how should I describe it? The importance of it was in the fact that she had never, in all our married life together, given me such a smile.

You know how in a second of time you can change from good health to ill. You are perfectly well, buried in gardening or letter-writing or reading. You are comfortably settled in the rational normal world. An instant, and we've changed all that! You are trembling, shivering, heated, sick. So, it is, I found then, with jealousy. When I saw the smile that Eve gave to Tunstall I became, in that moment, a jealous lunatic.

I showed my lunacy during the walk home. When one is in love and the other feels friendship but not love, one plays, whatever happens, a losing game. There is no safe time for protests, appeals, tears.

The other is securely armoured with indifference.

I behaved like a fool on that homeward walk. Like all jealous people, I knew, at the very moment, the fool that I was! 'Say nothing. Be gay, indifferent. Pretend not to care.' That was wisdom. But I loved her too dearly, and jealousy is a cataract that rushes one's boat over the swirling falls.

I abused her for flirting with Tunstall. I said that he was a man with a monstrous reputation. I said that she had disgraced myself and our child by behaving so before the Seaborne gossips.

Then she was really angry. For the first time in our lives together she was really angry. Her voice had a hard edge to it that I had never heard before. She said some bitter things, things I don't doubt that she had long been treasuring in her heart but had been too kindly-natured to declare.

She said that I was becoming a useless, stupid old maid. She, like the Parrott, called me a prig, and said that all the world thought me one. What kind of life was it for her, did I think, to live with someone who shut himself off from everyone and wasted his life in writing books that no one wanted? I resented, she said, that anyone should have any fun. I was against all human feeling, no one must flirt, or drink, or dance. She liked Tunstall. I was absurdly unfair to him and in reality, was jealous of him because he was everything that I was not—gay, popular, a real man.

I broke in then to cry that I hated him, I hated him, I hated him! He was bad, worthless, false to his wife and everyone else. If she, my wife, could like such a man, then she was no wife for me.

She answered, with a dreadful gravity that struck terror into my heart, that perhaps that was true. Our marriage had been a mistake. She had done all she could. The shop would have closed had it not been for her. Yes. We were not suited to one another. She saw that clearly now.

At that I was abject. I said that she was right to despise me, that I *was* a prig. I begged her to understand (oh, the miserable self-humiliation of jealousy!) that I loved her so terribly that nothing and nobody mattered to me beside her. I was jealous, yes. I could not bear to see Tunstall touch her hand, to see her smile into his face. Ah, if she would only love me a little—just a little. How I prayed for it, longed for it! I would try to improve, to see more people, to help her in the shop. I would do this, do that. If only she would forgive me for my stupid jealousy there was nothing I would not do. But she would not, just then, forgive me. She was cold in my arms that night, not kind as she often was. Alas, I wept. But my tears did not move her. I could feel that she thought of me, just then, with repulsion.

Next morning, she was kind again.

★★★★★★

Everyone knows what obsessions are. They ride you like demons. They dig their talons into your heart. They accompany you, like slithery fat familiars, in all your daily and nightly doings.

From the night of Tunstall's party, I was thus ridden. I saw two things. I saw Tunstall falling backwards down the wooden stairs on to the floor of the room where the dancing was—and I saw my wife laughing up into his eyes.

Then followed the episode of the bathe. These were the early days of summer, the beginning of June. To the right of Shining Cliff there was a little beach, Bateman's Cove. At certain tides it was excellent for bathing, having a hard saffron-coloured sand and a steep shelving descent so that you need not wade ignominiously before swimming. Because the path down to it was long, steep and winding, it was less popular than certain more accessible beaches. All the more reason for my pleasure in it!

One late afternoon I went there alone to bathe. It was an exquisite day of soft milky tenderness, the air warm as a gentle embrace, little movement, the blue glassy water broken quite suddenly with the baby energy of a white-crested wave.

I was quite alone on the beach. I was half-undressed when I looked up and saw Tunstall standing there watching me. Hugging now my obsession as I did, it did not seem to me at all odd that he should be with me, for he was *always* with me. I could hardly tell whether he were real or wraith. But he was real enough. He had his bathing-towel under his arm.

'I saw you from above, Jacko. I was going to bathe on Anstey, but when I saw you all alone down there I wanted to join you so badly that I bothered with all that tiresome path. Now isn't *that* devotion?'

I looked at him almost with friendliness. He had been for some weeks now the constant companion of my mind.

'Well, what have you been doing with yourself? I haven't seen you for nearly a week.'

'"The trivial round, the common task".'

'Don't you talk just like a book? How's your most delightful wife?'

'Very well, thank you.'

'Now, there's a woman! Aren't you lucky? We've made fast friends. I hope you don't mind?'

'No. Why should I?'

'Well, if *you* dislike me, Jacko, she doesn't. You like *my* wife and I like *yours*. Isn't that lucky?'

He had thrown off his clothes and stood now in bathing-trunks. His body was a white fat. His breasts were heavy. There was thick hair on his chest and even on his shoulders. On the right arm, high up, there was tattooed a mermaid. I was slim beside him, and this was the more emphasized because we were of exactly the same height. I had fancied that I was growing a little stout, but now, looking at him, I was reassured. His red face and hands were in startling contrast with his pale body. In fact, for a moment we stared at one another.

'Do you remember,' he said slowly, 'when we were kids, and I pulled your shirt over your head?'

'Yes. I remember.'

'You minded like anything. You know,' he went on, curling his toes into the warm sand, 'it has always given me a kind of kick when you mind things. Why is that, do you suppose?'

'I've no idea.'

'I get a sort of pleasure in seeing you wince. It's like—it's like—pulling your own hair to hurt yourself.'

I tore myself away from him almost desperately. Nothing so curious as the way he held me! I ran down into the sea. He quickly followed me. He was a good swimmer and so was I. The water was indeed lovely, the advancing afternoon perfection, but all my pleasure was spoilt, I wanted to be out and dressed, and away as soon as possible. When I came out, he came out too.

As he was dressing himself, he said: 'You didn't stay in long.'

'No, I didn't.'

'That was because you wanted to get away from me.'

'Yes.'

'Well, you can't. I shall walk along with you to the bus.'

I said nothing. We dressed in silence. We walked up the path in single file.

At the top he said:

'Dear old Jacko. You'd do me a hurt if you could, wouldn't you?'

I didn't reply.

'And I'd do you one. But that's because I like you so much.'

He suddenly began to chatter. He talked all the way to the bus,

214

about himself, his painting, his jolly life. One thing he said:

'You remember Bella? You sat next to her at supper?'

'Yes.'

'Fine woman, wasn't she?'

'I suppose some men would think so.'

'You bet they do. I'll tell you about her some time—all about her and me.'

'I haven't the least desire to hear.'

'No. That's why I shall enjoy telling you.'

Looking back now I can see that it was after this episode of the bathe that I moved into a new world. I was not only obsessed, but I was obsessed with an idea—and as yet I was not certain of my idea. You know how it is when you wake of a morning and are instantly conscious that there is something overhanging your mind. For a second of time you do not know what this thing may be, then it leaps at you—pleasure or pain, terror or anticipation. It was now as though this second of uncertainty was prolonged.

Something was there, waiting to dominate me. I was not sure yet what it was.

About a fortnight after the bathe Tunstall caught me again. This time down in the Lower Town, outside the pub, from whose stomach proceeded the squeak of an amateur and very discordant jazz band.

Tunstall came out of the pub as I turned homewards. He put his hand through my arm and walked with me. He was a little drunk, and greatly excited.

'Dearest Jacko, do you know the time?'

'Yes. It's nine-thirty almost exactly.'

(Of this dialogue I, to my shame and despair, remember every syllable—far, far more than I shall ever wish to record on paper.)

'Good. Splendid. In an hour and a half's time I shall be in the arms of my beloved. Come. We'll take this way by the sea. It's longer, but I want to fill in time.'

I had not replied.

'Why don't you ask the name of my beloved? I have no secrets from *you,* Jacko. Bella. Bella. Bella. You remember Bella, don't you? The loveliest woman in England. I am going to Bella.'

'I thought she lived with her mother.'

'So, she does.'

'Well—does her mother approve?'

'Her mother doesn't know anything about it. Her mother, fortunately, takes sleeping-draughts. See, Jacko, I'll tell you all about it—the minutest details. You are my other half, my better half, my pure, austere, celibate half. I shall be delighted to stir my better half's virginity.'

He went on with all the excited eagerness of a semi-drunk man.

'I know I'm a little drunk, old Jacko, but that doesn't impair my potency, old man. As I'll be proving just two hours from now!' He pulled me a little closer to his side. The sea below us was purring like a cat.

'This is the way of it, old chap. I can see her window from Shining Cliff, and if the old lady is well away, then Bella puts a light in the window. We meet once a week—not more. I like my wife, although you mayn't think it. She's a good sort—she is really. I don't want her to suspect anything. Besides, neither Bella nor I want people to talk. I've a reputation to keep up.'

'Not much of one,' I said.

'Ah, that's all you know! Anyway, once a week is our rule. Just enough to keep the excitement going. So, we settle the evening and at the appointed time I'm out on Shining Cliff. If the light is on I advance. The house is all by itself. No road near it. Only a little path. I get in through a window, take my boots off, go up the stairs in my stockinged feet. Her bedroom door's ajar. In I go, switch on the light. There she is in bed, sitting up waiting for me. Oh, boy! Isn't that a moment! But we don't exchange a word, we just grin at one another. Then I fling my clothes off and, when they're all on the floor, then we just stare at one another. After that, in a jiffy I'm in bed.'

I began to tremble all over. I felt nausea.

'Let me go, Tunstall! Let me go!'

'No, you don't.' He holds me still with his hand. Once again, I am absorbed inside him. I pass between his ribs. I am lodged close to the beating of his heart.

Then he begins to tell me everything, detail after detail. I whisper: 'Let me go, Tunstall. For God's sake let me go!'

At last he lets me go.

8

I am never likely to forget the smallest detail of that afternoon, August 13th—the half-hour that swung me into the heart of my decision.

It was about four o'clock of a hot oppressive August day. From early morning the sun had been burning sulkily behind heavy clouds.

There had been a sniff of sulphur in the air. Dust over the garden where the flowers hung their heads. The sea rolled in heavily as an assistant politely unrolls bales of dark oilskin. We sat in our room, all three of us. Eve was at the table, examining some catalogues. She was considering certain drawings by minor Pre-Raphaelites offered therein. She sat, her thin elbows supporting her sharp, pale chin. Her dress was of grey, with an almost Elizabethan ruffle of rose-colour about her neck.

Archie was sitting in the window, turning over the pages of a magazine, looking out between the clearing of roofs to the sea. The veiled and darkened sun fell on his hair, which was the lightest gold in colour. His face was so pale and delicate, his body so slight, that I could never look at him without a pang of anxiety, but if I ever approached him with any kind of solicitude he always repulsed me. 'Oh, I'm all *right,* father!' He loved his mother, not me—or so I thought then—and I longed, how I longed, to take him in my arms and strain him to my breast and cover his pale shell-like face with kisses.

There was no human being in all the world to whom I could demonstrate affection without reproach.

Eve had in front of her a large print of J. M. Strudwick's, *The Ramparts of God's House.* She suddenly turned round to me, the narrow gold ring flashing on her finger.

'Too many angels,' she said. 'And they all have the same faces. How dark the room is! There must be thunder near.'

And so, it was. Archie was himself a Pre-Raphaelite figure, seated in the window in that deep plum-coloured air that Burne-Jones so often affected. Details stood out most clearly in that oppressive air, the shining brass of the fire-irons, the rose-colour about Eve's throat, the bright yellow of some roses in a bowl, the dim gilt binding of some books on a shelf.

I was reading Gissing's *Nether World,* that most gloomy and hopeless of all stories, but behind the façade of the book were staring figures of the poisoned world that Tunstall had created in my imagination. Yes, he had created them, and with my loathing of them and their actions went a weak inability to dismiss them. Tunstall himself, straddle-legged, mocking, laughed at me while behind him another Tunstall crept up the stairs on his stockinged feet, while behind him yet another stood, while she watched him from the sheets and he pulled his shirt over his head. . . .

The dark oppressive air, the very faint rumblings of thunder like the warning of a muffled drum, the sense that my wife and son cared nothing for me, the longing to rise and lay the back of my hand against Archie's cheek, the knowledge that if I did so he would quietly move his head while his blue eyes regarded me with a little contempt; all this with the added knowledge that everyone thought me a failure and that indeed I *was* one, and added to this again the uncertain, unhappy state of the world, with Hitler, like the brooding Mephistopheles on the Brocken, planning cold ruin and bitter destruction—with all this I was unhappy on that afternoon, beyond, it seemed, any possible alleviation.

The door opened and Tunstall came in. He had never come to our house uninvited before. He went quickly, beaming, forward to my wife, his hand outstretched.

'There's a terrible storm coming. I'm dying for a cup of tea. I have no other apology.'

He was at his most charming; quite sober, most respectful, serious-minded. The flushed purple undertone was gone from his cheeks; his hair was newly cut and sleek above his brown stout neck. He was wearing a heather-brown light coat and a dark tie, and dark purple corduroy trousers—full of colour, animation, sober restrained impudence.

Do you think that from my corner I did not watch every detail of him, feel the reverberation of his voice against my breast-bone, know that even while he was turning to Eve his broad back was full of eyes that mocked me? And he stood in his bare legs pulling his shirt over his head. . . .

But someone else was observing him, too. That was Archie, who had never seen him closely before, had never seen purple corduroy trousers, had never heard so merry, confident, cheeky a voice.

Tunstall had sat down, his legs spread, and was chatting away to Eve.

'What! The Pre-Raphaelites! You don't really admire them, do you, with all their preaching and the rest of it?'

'It isn't their preaching—it's their colour,' Eve said.

'Oh, their colour!' Tunstall answered scornfully. 'Anyone can make an effect with colour. Now, I—' Then he stopped, laughing, for she was looking at him in the mocking way that she had. 'No. I'm not going to boast. You're too sharp for me.'

'Why, what do you mean?' Eve cried.

'You think I'm terribly conceited, don't you? Well, I'm not really.

I'll even go as far as to say I might have been a much *better* painter. Oh, yes, I might, and you know it. I've let myself go a bit, and I must pull up. You might help me.'

'You've got the best wife in the world. You don't need anyone else.'

As she said this her hand came down softly on the table, and her wedding-ring clicked against the board. The little sound, I don't know why, inflamed me with jealousy. Their hands were not touching.

'Ah, Leila!' he said softly. 'Yes. She's a good woman.'

Eve got up and began to fetch and arrange the tea. I felt that she avoided my eyes. I thought that her cheek was a little flushed and that her voice was raised.

For once Tunstall did not chaff me, scarcely spoke to me. He was grave and serious. He began to drink his tea, when his eyes settled on Archie. Archie had been staring at him, and especially at his broad thigh stretched out in the purple corduroy trousers.

'What are your trousers made of?' Archie suddenly said.

Eve reproached him.

'Hush, Archie—that's rude.'

But Tunstall was delighted.

'Nonsense. He isn't rude. Here. Come and see what the trousers are made of.'

Archie came over to him shyly, and Tunstall drew him in until he was standing between his legs.

'Here, pinch them!' Tunstall said, laughing. Archie did so. 'I say, what a grand-looking boy! What do you want to be, Archie!'

'Oh, I don't know,' Archie said, with obvious admiration.

'Ever tried your hand at drawing or painting?'

'I have a little.'

'Like it, do you?'

'I do rather.'

'Having drawing lessons?'

'No. Father thinks it a waste of time.'

'Oh, he does, does he? Well, I tell you what. *I'll* give you some drawing lessons. Would you like that?'

'Oh, rather!'

'Right! You shall come over to me. We'll have a grand time. Got any drawings to show me?'

But I interrupted here. The rain was now slashing the windows. It was dark. I switched on the light and in the sudden illumination I stood facing the three of them. My voice shook. I wanted to steady it, but I could not.

'I'm awfully sorry,' I said, 'but I'm afraid not, Tunstall. Archie's got his own work to do and—'

But Tunstall broke into a shout of laughter. He threw his head back and laughed and laughed.

'Oh, dear, I'm most awfully sorry! Oh, Jacko! you'll be the death of me yet. Suddenly switching the light up and standing there like the Commander's ghost. Why, we'd forgotten all about you. I'm awfully sorry. It's very rude to laugh. If only you could see yourself!'

Eve was smiling. Archie, nervous, half frightened, half angry, put his hand on Tunstall's arm as though for protection.

It was with that movement that I suddenly saw. It was a blinding light of illumination, so that I turned round for an instant and stared at the wall. I knew what it was that had, for a long time now, been hanging at the back of my mind, just out of my consciousness.

I turned back and stared at Tunstall. He was like a new man whom I had never seen before. Everything about him was different, and my feelings towards him were different. He had a kind of consecrated air. It was as though I had had sudden secret information that he was suffering from a fatal disease. It did not matter anymore what he said or did, how he behaved. I was not jealous, nor angry. I was at peace with myself, as one is when at last one yields to a temptation against which one has long been struggling. Above all, I felt now a strong bond between himself and myself.

★★★★★★

On the afternoon of the second day following his visit to us, I was standing outside Smith's bookshop. It was August 15th, and very warm. The High Street was thronged with holiday-makers. The sun sparkled in splinters of light as though someone were placing and replacing a screen. Motors hummed like drunken bees. There was a great sense of movement and bustle. Tunstall appeared. He was hurrying into Smith's, his eyes a little bloodshot, his soft hat pushed back from his forehead, on which there were beads of perspiration.

He saw me and grinned his wicked schoolboy grin.

'Hullo, Jacko.'

'Hullo.' I smiled. I was glad to see him.

'You look as though you were pleased to see me.'

'I am.'

'Well, I never! That's a change, isn't it? I say—are you waiting for someone? I believe you've got an assignation. Oh, my naughty Jacko!'

'No. I wasn't waiting for anyone.'

'Talking of assignations.' He dropped his voice, gripped my arm and pushed his face so close to mine that I could smell the perspiration on his forehead. 'Next Thursday's the night. Yes. Rain or shine. Nice for you, Jacko.' He chuckled. 'You can picture us. Every word. Every movement. Eleven prompt I'm at Shining Cliff. Eleven-fifteen creeping up the stairs. And eleven-thirty. Oh, boy! Eleven-thirty! Nice for you, Jacko. You can enjoy it all by proxy.'

'Perhaps I'll be there one night, hiding behind the curtain.'

I could see that he was surprised at my jocularity.

'You're growing up, Jacko,' he said. 'You're certainly growing up.'

On the evening of the following Thursday I said to Eve, as we were finishing supper:

'I'm going to the pictures. Last house.'

'What's on?'

'*David Copperfield*. A revival. I liked it so much when it first came out, I've always wanted to see it again. It comes on for the last time at nine o'clock.'

I had for a moment a really choking fear that she would suggest going with me. She seemed to hesitate. But she didn't enjoy pictures.

'All right. I'm going to bed early. Come in and see me when you come back. I shall be reading.'

I went out, the collar of my waterproof turned up. It was raining— a kind of warm, misty rain. There was also a moon. This at times broke through the gusty clouds and illuminated the world with a wet, oily phantasmagoria. It was stuffy and close.

I got to the 'Regal' cinema at a quarter to nine. Inside the foyer, Bob Steele, the proprietor, was standing, with the faded carnation in his button-hole, the ill-fitting dinner-jacket (he buttoned it across the stomach, a large one), his curly black hair and his rather foxy smile. It was his business to be agreeable, and agreeable he was, especially, I believe, to little girls.

'Hullo, Talbot! How's yourself?'

'All right, thanks.'

'Rotten night.'

'Good for your business, though.'

'Yes. Mustn't complain. Remarkable how they're turning up to this, although it's an old picture.'

I went to the little glass window and paid for a one-and-sixpenny ticket. Then, with a nod at Steele (he would remember me all right),

I went in.

I found an outside seat. I watched the News Reel, and a 'Mickey Mouse.' Then *Copperfield* began. I sat through part of this and then I slipped across the passage and out of the side door, raising the iron bar very silently. I was in the side street—Couper Street. There was no one about and the rain was coming down more heavily.

I reached Shining Cliff at ten-twenty exactly. The rain had stopped, and the pale moonlight was like dust on the cliff top. I went to the edge and looked down. The drop was sheer and terrific. The tide would soon be full, and already waves were licking the boulders far below. For half an hour I sheltered behind a broken wall, for the rain came on again, and it was very dark.

Two minutes after eleven o'clock had struck from Climstock Church, I heard someone approaching. I stood up. I saw someone of Tunstall's build come to the cliff and pause. There was a faint light now, the white dusky shadow thrown before the moon emerges. I saw that he stared, and I knew for what he was looking.

I came forward to meet him. He *was* astonished!

'Why, Jacko—whatever—'

'Quite a coincidence,' I answered. 'I've been on a job for Eve—seeing the doctor in Climstock. He's the man we always have—Wellard. An awfully good doctor.' Then I added, laughing: 'Why, of course—it's Thursday! I had quite forgotten.'

I could see that he was impatient. 'Yes, it is. There's the light, though.' I could see, with him, between the trees a faint flicker like an unsteady star.

'I must be getting. Mustn't be wasting a lady's time.'

'Wait a second.' For the first time in all our two lives together I took his arm. *I* took *his* arm!

'Wait. It isn't quite true what I said. There was something rather important I wanted to tell you. Something serious.'

'Serious! Well, what about tomorrow, old boy? Really, I'm late as it is.'

I had been leading him gently forward. We were on the cliff edge. I put my arm round his broad back.

'I say, Jacko!' He turned his head to mine. I urged him ever so slightly in front of me.

'But it *is* serious. It is to do with your Bella. I heard this afternoon—'

Then with my knee I shoved him forward, using all the force in my body. At the same moment I threw him out with my arms.

I could see, in the dim light, that he clutched the air with his hands; he gave a great cry, and he fell. The sea was roaring. I knew that the tide, far down below, was deep up against the rocks. Except for the sea-noise there was no sound. The thin rain stealthily stroked my cheek.

I sat down on a wet rock and waggled the little finger of my right hand—for the jolt of his flying body had strained it ever so slightly.

9

I sat there for a considerable time waggling my finger and feeling, with a pleasant kind of sleepiness, the soft thin rain upon my face. It was so very still and quiet. Nobody was about. The only sound was the distant rhythm of the sea and the gentle hiss of the rain.

Then sharply I reflected that if my wife supposed that I was visiting the cinema she would be wondering that I should be so late. I hurried home. I felt happy and on excellent terms with myself. When I let myself into the house I found everything dark. Eve had gone to bed. But I had only just struck a match when I heard her voice from above the stairs.

'John, is that you?'

'Yes, dear, I'm coming.'

I took off my boots and left them in the kitchen. As I did so I noticed my finger again. I had certainly given it a twist.

I came into the bedroom. She was sitting up in bed and at sight of her my only desire was to take her in my arms. I would, too! I was not going to be denied this night of all nights.

'Why, John, where have you been? You can't have been at the cinema all this time?'

I took off my coat and waistcoat. There was a tear in the lining of the waistcoat.

'Indeed, I have, dear. Look! This lining's torn. I wish you'd sew it for me.'

'But it's ever so late.'

'Not really, dear.'

I sat down on the edge of the bed, slipping off my trousers. The ends were very wet and this I didn't wish her to notice.

'It's a long picture, *Copperfield*. Little Bartholomew and Rathbone as Murdstone were as good as ever. Pity they had to get an American for Micawber. The first half of the picture is much the best.'

I put on my pyjamas and went into the bathroom to brush my teeth. When I came back I saw that she was looking at me curiously.

'The cinema seems to have done you good. I've never seen you look so pleased with yourself.'

I turned out the light and got into bed.

'I don't know why it is,' she said, yawning. 'I'm as tired as anything.'

'Now look here, Eve,' I said, with a courage and energy that surprised me. 'Tonight you're going to do what *I* want, whether you like it or no.'

When I woke in the morning I felt a wonderful lightness and relief. Eve was already up. The sun was streaming in at the window. I had had one of those delicious sleeps that are the result of complete physical and spiritual satisfaction. I lay back on the pillow, my head on my hands and dodging a little to avoid the brilliant sunshine. For a little while I could think of nothing but my well-being. Then I remembered. Tunstall was gone for ever and ever and ever.

It was then that I felt the first little prick of anxiety. Suppose that his body had caught in some projecting part of the cliff? Suppose that he had lain on some ledge, bruised and battered, but gradually coming to himself, would recover enough to climb back and find his way home? For a moment my heart contracted and twisted. But I was at once reassured. The cliff fell sheer to the sea and Tunstall's body had been thrown outwards. I smiled to myself as I turned on my side. I had not the slightest feeling of compunction or regret. Tunstall was a bad man. He was no good to anyone. He was beginning to seduce my wife and my son. I had to protect my family. But, behind these reasonings and very much more important than any of them, was the certainty that I would not be bothered with him anymore. He was gone from my life. I could hear him saying: 'We're like the Siamese twins, Jacko, and always were.'

Well, we weren't. I had settled that once and for ever. No more bother from Tunstall.

When I went down to breakfast Archie was having his. I was as hungry as though I were eating Tunstall's breakfast as well as my own. Eve noticed it.

'Why, John, what's happened to you? I must say you're looking wonderfully well.'

Archie had something to say:

'Daddy, when's that nice man with the purple trousers coming again?'

'Soon, I expect.'

'I liked him. Do you think he'll really teach me to draw?'

'I expect so. He's a fine artist.'

Eve, filling my cup with coffee, let her hand rest for a moment on my shoulder and said: 'That's right, John. I thought it wasn't kind of you the other day to refuse him as you did.'

'I was feeling out of sorts.'

'The cinema seems to have done you a world of good. You're a different man today.'

Archie went on: 'Will I go to his house, Daddy?'

'I daresay that you will.'

'Oo-oo! How lovely! He's awfully strong, isn't he, Daddy?'

'Not so strong as he used to be, got a bit flabby.'

'But he's stronger than you, isn't he?'

I smiled as I helped myself to a second poached egg. Then I got up to cut myself some ham. As I passed Archie's chair I rested my hand lovingly on his shoulder. I felt the bones wriggle a little.

'I don't know that he *is* stronger. I mayn't *look* much, you know, but I keep fit. That's what you must do, Archie. Make your body stronger.'

'He's a wonderful painter, isn't he, Daddy? He's made lots and lots of money, hasn't he, painting pictures?'

'Yes, he's made a lot of money.'

I was cutting the ham with a delicacy and adroitness quite new to me.

'Much more money than you've made writing books, Daddy?'

'Oh, much more.' I turned round, smiling at him. 'Say your grace, Archie, before you leave the table.'

Archie said his grace.

'When can I go to the painter's house?'

'Soon.'

'Can I go today?'

'No, not today.'

'Oh, why not?'

But his questions were interrupted by Eve entering and saying: 'See who's here!'

It was Leila Tunstall. Her face was pale and her coat and hat a little dishevelled, the hat crooked, the coat, a rather ugly sealskin, too high on one shoulder. (I remember the tiniest details of this conversation— yes, I remember the slime of marmalade on Archie's plate and the shadow on his pale thin face raised to Leila's.)

'Why, Mrs. Tunstall!' I said. I remember that as I looked at her I realised how very, very much I liked her and wished that I did not.

She sat down at the breakfast-table.

'Yes, I know. This is a terrible time to call. But you must forgive me. The fact is I'm very anxious.'

Eve said, 'Have some coffee.'

'Yes, I think I will. Thank you so much. The fact is that Jimmie left the house after dinner last night and hasn't been back since.'

'Not been back?' I cried—and the odd thing was that half of me was really amazed that he *hadn't* been back! That cry was quite genuine.

'No, you see . . .' She hesitated. 'I'm sure I can speak safely to both of you—' She paused, looking at Archie.

'Archie,' Eve said softly, 'go upstairs, dear, and start your lessons. I'll be up very soon.'

'Yes, Mother.' He went.

'The fact is—Jimmie has been drinking too much lately. Oh, it isn't a secret. Everyone knows it. That's what makes me anxious.'

'Was he quite happy when he went out?' I asked.

'Oh, most. He was especially gay and he hadn't been drinking then, I know. He only had water at dinner. He laughed and asked me whether I didn't think he was a reformed character. He said I wasn't to stay up. He was going to see a friend. That horrible Mr. Cheeseman, I expect.' She added quickly, smiling a little: 'Forgive me, I suppose I oughtn't to say that. But I can't abide him.'

She looked at me quite urgently and asked: 'Were you out by any chance, Mr. Talbot, last night?'

'Yes,' I said, 'I went to the cinema.'

'Because it was wet—a kind of misty rain. I'm worried because I think he might have drunk a little with Mr. Cheeseman or some of them at "The Green Parrot."'

'"The Green Parrot"?'

'Yes, you must know it. In the Lower Town. That's where they go often, I believe. Oh, I hate that Mr. Cheeseman! He's responsible for so much. I hate him! I hate him!' She beat her little hands together. I longed to help her in her distress.

'He'd be all right, though,' I said.

'No, he wouldn't. Not if he was drinking with them and they came out having drunk too much. It's dark there and it would be slippery—'

'Have you asked Cheeseman?'

'Of course, I have. That's the first thing I did—on the telephone. He says he never saw Jimmie last night at all. But I never believe a word he says. But it was he who suggested I should come along and see you.'

'Us?'

'Yes. He said, "Ask the Talbots; they might know."'

'What a funny thing! Why should *we* know?'

She smiled rather wanly. 'Mr. Cheeseman always says that Jimmie is fonder of you than of anyone else.'

'Oh, but that isn't true!'

'Well, I don't know—'

Eve hadn't said a word all this time. Now, very quietly, she spoke. 'I'm terribly sorry about all this, Mrs. Tunstall. But we know nothing, I'm afraid. I went to bed and John went to the cinema.'

Leila looked at her. Her eyes were filled with tears.

'I'm silly. . . . It really *is* stupid, but I'm very fond of Jimmie. I know he isn't all that he should be. Perhaps that's why I'm fond of him. But there it is. We all have our vices and Jimmie's mine. . . .'

Eve went over, bent down and kissed her. 'Forgive me. I couldn't help it. I like Jimmie too, you know.'

I looked at those two women, so good, so fine, and both of them attached to that dirty scoundrel. Attached! Oh, no, that was surely too strong a word for Eve. But I did not know. What secrets were behind that good, sweet face? I realised two things. First, that my relationship to Eve had in some subtle way changed since last night, and secondly, that it did not matter anymore whether she was 'attached' to Tunstall or no. At that thought my heart began suddenly to pound in my breast. I felt a kind of mastery over those two women because they didn't know what *I* did.

Eve sat down beside Leila and they held hands. Leila was looking at us as though she wondered whether she dared go further. She moistened her lips with her little, very bright red tongue.

'There *is* another thing. . . . I didn't mean to say anything about it, but you're both such friends now. Only never let Jimmie have the slightest idea that I spoke of it—you promise?'

We both promised—I well knowing that my promise would be kept!

'You know Bella Scorfield? Of course, you do. You've met her at our place. There's been some talk about her and Jimmie. You've heard it, I'm sure. . . . It's justified!' Her eyes flashed. 'No use pretending. Jimmie can't be faithful to one woman and I understand that in a kind of way. But whether I understand it or not I have had to put up with it for a long time. He's having an affair with Bella Scorfield.'

'Oh, I'm so sorry,' Eve broke in.

'My dear, don't be sorry. These affairs never last. And I always think the wife's a bit to blame, don't you? Not that I like Bella Scorfield. It wouldn't be natural if I did, would it? In any case I think, I'm *sure,* that it was to Bella he went last night.'

'Why are you sure?' Eve asked.

'He's always especially jolly before he goes. I made up the story about his going to "The Green Parrot" and drinking. I'm quite sure he didn't, because at dinner he was altogether teetotal. He always is before he goes to see her. It's a certain sign.'

A little shiver seized her body, a trembling beyond her control, and I realised that this thing had, for a long time, caused her great suffering. She was revealing her soul to us.

'But,' Eve cried, 'if he was perfectly sober he couldn't . . .' She pulled herself up.

'All right, Eve, dear. May I call you Eve? I know that Jimmie does. You aren't hurting me, I'm really too used to it to be hurt. Besides, as I've said, I regard it as partly my own fault. But that *is* the point. He was quite sober when he went out and if he went to her he would go by Shining Cliff, but he'd take the inner path. He wouldn't be in any danger; however slippery it was.'

'Have you asked Miss Scorfield?'

'Yes, of course. She was the first person I telephoned. And then I was more than ever sure. I could tell that she was herself seriously worried. You could tell from the sound of her voice. She *had* been expecting him. She was distressed. She had been sitting up, I wouldn't wonder, most of the night, waiting for him.' There was a vindictive snap in Leila's voice.

Yes, I thought, she *was* sitting up, sitting up in bed, waiting for the sound of his stockinged feet. It was for the moment as though I had been he, climbing up those stairs in *my* stockinged feet.

'What did she say on the telephone?'

'Oh, not very much. I couldn't charge her, of course, with waiting for him. All I could say was that we were worried because he had been away all night and I was asking one or two of his friends whether he had said anything. She begged me to ask him to telephone to her as soon as he came in. I will, too!'

She got up. . . .

'Please, please . . . I know that you are our friends, mine and Jimmie's. *Please* don't say a word about Bella Scorfield. Even if they all know, I don't want him to think that *I* do.'

'Of course not,' Eve said.

She turned to me. I knew that I must say something. I wanted to comfort, to console her.

'I'm quite sure it will be all right, Mrs. Tunstall.'

'Thank you, Mr. Talbot. I'm sure that I'm making an absurd fuss. I'm going home now, and I know that I shall find him there, although what he *can* have been doing . . .'

She smiled bravely at both of us and went away.

'Well, of all the odd things!' Eve said.

'I don't see that it's odd,' I answered. 'Tunstall had other female friends besides Miss Scorfield. He—'

'Had?' Eve interrupted me. 'You speak as though something really had happened to Jimmie.'

'I hate your calling him Jimmie.'

'Why not? He's called me Eve from the very beginning.' She came close up to me, looked me full in the face: 'Why *do* you hate him so, John?'

I answered her quietly, 'I don't think I do. You can see him as much as you like. I'll never be jealous.'

I took her round the waist and kissed her on the mouth. She didn't resist, but when I had finished she looked at me with puzzled eyes. But I didn't care. I remember that I sat in my room that morning swimming in self-satisfaction. This was the small room where I always did my writing. It had very little in it. I believed that a writer should have nothing to distract him when he worked. There was a white bookcase, a plain deal table, photographs of my wife and son, and a drawing that I had stolen from the shop, the study for Burne-Jones's 'Nimuë beguiling Merlin'—afterwards included in his posthumously published *Flower Book*. There was something in the twisted branches of the Witches' Tree and the heavy figure of the old Merlin that greatly pleased me.

I had come up to work on my new novel. It is called *Mr. Porter's Door*. It will certainly never be finished now. I sat there, my hands folded, and looked through the opposite window to the cleft between the roofs which revealed the sea, plum-gold, and the sky blown like a field of corn above it.

I adored this fragment of sea. It was near but not too near. It could not harm me however wild it became; it could not lash my cheek with ice-cold revengeful spray. But its beauty was never-ending. I was thinking of it now, as I rested my elbows on the table and my chin on my knuckles. I was thinking of it with gratitude: it had received Tunstall's body and had dealt with Tunstall's body. I had every reason to be grateful.

It was strange perhaps that now, on the morning after, I should feel no kind of remorse. For after all I am a gentle-natured friendly man at heart. (I *am*! I *am*! Say what you will, I am! I am! I am!)

It was far from remorse that I felt as I turned my plain wedding-ring round and round on my finger and saw the glint of the gold in the sun. Instead of remorse, I felt an exultant, bursting pride! They had despised me, had they?—all of them despised me? 'Oh, John's no good,' they'd say. 'Even his books aren't any good! Even his books.' But now I'd done more than they had ever done. They had none of them thrown a man, twice their size, over a cliff, so that he was drowned! They wouldn't dare! I thought of Bob Steele of the cinema, and Cheeseman and Jessie Parrott and many another. They had all sneered at me for years. They wouldn't sneer now if they knew.

I thought of Bella Scorfield. That had excited me greatly when Leila Tunstall had spoken of her waiting for him. She, Leila, didn't know *how* she waited for him, how she sat up, straining her ears for the sound of the softly-closing door and the thin tread of the stockinged feet. For her bedroom door would be ajar and all I needed to do was to take two steps inside the room and stand there, grinning, while I threw my coat and waistcoat . . .

I? What was I thinking? I remember that I stopped, pushed my ring down into my finger and straightened my back, listening. I? The fact was that Tunstall had told me his story with so beastly a vividness that I could almost fancy that I had been there. He had forced my imagination to such a pitch that I could almost see the furniture, the wardrobe on the left, the dressing-table with its pink lace covering. . . . How did I know that it was pink? Tunstall had told me—and in any case it *would* be pink.

Bella Scorfield's bedroom. Yes, she must have sat up all night waiting for him. She must have been very sure of him; he had never failed her. By his own eagerness as shown to me he would not be late by a minute!

I walked about the room. I was smiling. I might be a poor little devil who had been, until now, a failure. But why was that? Largely because I had, since I was a small boy, suffered from this monstrous incubus, Jimmie Tunstall. Jimmie Tunstall. I had never for a single moment been free of him. I could see now that although I had pretended to mock at his 'Siamese twins' and the rest of it I *had* been conscious of a bond, and that although I had said again and again that I was free I had known in my heart that that was not really so!

But now I was free! At last, at last I was free! I stood at the window looking out to the golden fleeces of the sky that fell now, in an embracing loom of colour, over the pale hyacinth blue of the sea. My heart was glad. I gave the kind sea my blessing.

It is at this point that I wish in my recollection to be severely accurate. I am trying—no man ever tried harder—to tell the truth and only the truth. Everything depends, for my own peace of mind, on my integrity.

I was standing looking out to the sea. Leila Tunstall came to my mind. I saw her anxious disturbed face, twisted a little—just that suggestion of malformity in the thickening of the skin over the right lip—or was it the tightening of the muscles above the right eye?—As I saw her face and heard her voice I realised that she was an absolutely good woman—almost the only absolutely good human being I had ever known, and with a little sigh, a slight flutter of the heart, I realised how deeply I needed her in my life. I was not in the least in love with her but I liked her so very, very much. Liked her and admired and needed her. I needed her especially now, for, let me be self-satisfied as I might, I did now carry a burden and would always carry one— a strange burden, half of pride and half—was I beginning to realise it?—of apprehension. I did not consider that I had done Leila Tunstall any harm. She had loved Tunstall, but only because she had not known him. He would have sunk lower and ever lower. Drink, lechery, at last becoming a sot of an old man loathed and despised by everyone. I had done Leila a kindness, and although she would never know it *my* knowledge of what I had done bound us together and would always bind us. It was then—exactly then, as I watched a thin dark shadow like a fish's fin drop over the sea—that I fancied that I heard a laugh in the room behind me.

I did not turn round. My heart gave a jump and a skip, for the laugh had been a man's laugh—it even reminded me of Tunstall's sneering confidential chuckle.

I did not turn round. I disciplined myself. It was as though I spoke aloud: 'You must remember that from now on it will be very natural for you to imagine that you hear sounds or see suspicious things. You must be especially sceptical about what you fancy you *see*. Why, already this morning you imagined that Eve was looking at you in some peculiar way. Of course, she was not. You must remember that. You have some knowledge now that nobody else has got and that nobody else must have. Remember that the only real enemy you had in the whole world is gone.'

It was at that point that again I fancied I heard the laugh. I stood there, my whole body strung up, my heart stiffened.

'Who's there?' my heart seemed to whisper.

'Turn round and see,' something seemed to answer.

At last—and it was as though my body acted against its will—I did turn round. There was, of course, nobody there. The room was quite empty. The sun that had been shining over the sea was filmed now and so the room also was less bright—it was dimmed as though a thin mist pervaded it. But there was nobody there. Of course, there was nobody there.

I sat down to my table and began to concentrate on my work. In this novel of *Mr. Porter* I was trying to draw the full-length character, personality of a really wicked man.

I can see now that I had Tunstall for my sitter, although I would violently have denied it had I been accused. Mr. Porter had the physical properties of Cheeseman, the Rat, but he was laughing, speaking, moving like Tunstall.

I remember that I looked at the page of manuscript, half scribbled on, and felt a sort of disgust for it. What a second-hand thing was this writing of stories when, with your own strong fingers, you could push a big heavy man into the sea! There was a sensuous pleasure in the recollection of that moment when that body had yielded, falling backwards. There had been the cry, the pounding of the waves below. . . . My blood thickened as it does when in recollection one recovers the detail of some past sensuality.

Then, for the second time, I was sure that someone was in the room with me and, for the second time, I refused to turn round. But now I was expecting a touch on my shoulder. Crazy, as I was telling myself, to expect a touch on the shoulder when you know that there is no one there. But so, it was. My shoulders were bent a little waiting for the touch. I straightened myself. I turned round.

Archie was there, bringing me the cup of coffee that I always have in the middle of the morning when I am working. He looked at me with that half-nervous, half-doubting look that always exasperated me. I hated that the boy should be afraid of me. 'Come along. What's the matter?'

'Nothing,' Archie said, putting the cup down very gingerly on the table.

'Don't look at me as though I'd eat you.'

'I'm not, Daddy.'

'Come here.' I smiled. I drew him in between my knees. I remembered how readily he had gone to Tunstall. I drew his slight, slender body close to mine.

'Well, have we been working hard this morning?'

'Yes, Daddy.'

'What have we been doing?'

'History, Daddy. Mary Queen of Scots.'

Then he added, looking at me with wide-open eyes: 'I hate her.'

'Hate her. Why?'

'Because she killed people.'

'They were cruel to her. Her husband was a bad man.'

'I don't care how bad he was.' I felt his body slipping away from mine, eager to go.

I gave him what was almost a push. 'All right. Run along. Daddy's working.'

He ran eagerly away.

On the following morning at the top of the road that leads down to the Lower Town, I came quite suddenly upon Bella Scorfield. There are, at this spot, some villas with neat gardens and compact little garages. It was a sunny morning with a light breeze. The leaves of the elms were shivering with delicate pleasure. There was no one about, but I could hear the engine of some invisible car like a dynamo at the heart of the world. 'While I go on,' it seemed to say, 'everything is all right. But let me stop—'

We almost ran into one another.

'Oh, Mr. Talbot!' she said.

'Good morning, Miss Scorfield.'

'I wanted to see you. That is—' She looked about her in a distracted kind of way. I could see that she was greatly disturbed. A strong scent of crushed violets came from her in the breeze—(I would repeat here that no detail in my story, however small, is insignificant).

'There is no news of Mr. Tunstall?'

'I believe, none.'

She looked at me searchingly.

'Walk with me a little. This way, where there are no houses. Do you mind? I am in great trouble.'

'I am most awfully sorry—'

'No. No. I'll tell you the truth. You are, strangely enough, the only person I can tell it to.'

'I don't understand—'

'Of course, you do. You know as well as I do that it was to me he was coming the night before last.'

'Really, Miss Scorfield—'

She turned on me indignantly.

'Oh, don't pretend! It's too serious. Jimmie has told me often that you know all about us. I'm afraid he's amused me sometimes by the way he's shocked you. But that doesn't matter now. Tell me, Mr. Talbot—' She put her hand on my arm, looking up into my face. 'What has happened to him? Where has he gone to?'

'I assure you, Miss Scorfield,' I answered, looking at her very steadily, 'I don't know a thing.'

'Oh, but you must! He told you everything.'

'Indeed, he did not!'

'Yes, yes. He has the strangest relations with you. He often talked about it. He says that you are inseparables, that even when you aren't together you are together. Oh, I know that it sounds nonsense, but he really believes it.'

'If you want to know the truth, Miss Scorfield, he despises and patronizes me and I dislike him. I dislike him very much. I always have.'

'Yes. That's on the surface. But I'm sure it isn't so underneath. I know him too well.'

'We are opposite in everything,' I said.

'Yes, that's why you attract one another. But we're wasting time. Where is he, Mr. Talbot? Where is he? What has happened?'

'I don't know, Miss Scorfield. I really don't. I didn't see him that evening. I was at the cinema—at a revival of *David Copperfield*.'

She went on impatiently, her breath catching her words. 'No. No. I'm sure you didn't see him. Leila Tunstall says that he left the house, said goodbye to her, told her not to wait up. He was coming to me. Well, what happened after that? *What* happened?'

'I'm afraid I don't know any more—'

'No, but guess, man! Guess! Have some ideas! He was sober, because he always is when he is coming to me. It was wet, a sort of misty rain. But he wouldn't slip or fall into the sea or anything. I *know* he wouldn't. When he's sober he can look after himself perfectly. The funny thing is—at one moment I thought I heard him cry out. Of course, I didn't. It was only imagination, but I sat up in bed listening—'

(Yes, I could see her—I knew just how she would do that!) I saw that she wanted me to say something, so I replied quietly:

'He may have gone somewhere else. He did deceive people, you know. He may have deceived you.'

I took great pleasure in saying this, for certainly I hated her. She was part of him. Against my will I knew much more about her and her horridness than I ought to know. I hated her and her violet scent and everything about her.

'That's why I wanted to speak to you,' she cried. 'Is there someone else? Did he ever tell you there was someone else? He has always sworn there wasn't, but then he is an awful liar. I know that well enough. Perhaps he's gone off to someone else. That's what's torturing me.'

I was suddenly sorry for her, although I hated her. You can be sorry for people you hate. She looked miserable, forlorn, lost.

'I don't think there is anyone else. He'd have told me,' I added. 'Shall I tell you what I think?' (For I wanted to console her.)

'Oh, do, do! Please do!'

'I think he set off meaning to go to you. Then, seeing it was early, went in somewhere for a drink, drank too much and did go off with someone—just anyone. And he's staying away for a bit. Too ashamed to come back at once. He'll turn up suddenly with a story.'

I could see the relief, the flaming, wonderful relief, that I gave her.

'Oh, do you think so? I believe you're right. It's the only explanation, isn't it?'

'The only one,' I assured her, solemnly. 'Meanwhile, Miss Scorfield, if I may say something—'

'Please do.'

'Don't show other people that you care. It's much wiser not. They might talk.'

'Yes, you're right. How right you are! Thanks ever so much.'

She smiled and walked quickly away.

It was at that moment, just as I watched her disappearing round a bend of the road, that I thought I heard Tunstall's chuckle close behind me.

Very clearly, I remember how I stood, stiffly, without moving, and listening. I can see as though it were now before me that quiet country road, the houses neat, tidy, like toy houses, bright and shining, and each house with its gay-tinted toy garden in front of it. There was not a single soul in the road and the only sound was the distant hush-hush of the sea and the delicate shivering of the trees.

I turned round. There was no one there. I had known of course that there would not be.

Then I spoke to myself something like this: 'You must accept for the moment as part of the condition of things these hallucinations. You must not be surprised at them nor distressed at them. You have done something that you wanted to do and that you are pleased to have done, but naturally such an act must have its mental consequences. Further than that, you were under this man's influence since you were a small boy. You hated him: you detested, and still detest, everything that he did, thought, and was. You were always thinking of his voice, his laugh, his physical body. Naturally you will still be thinking of these things and for a long while to come. You must not mind this. He is dead. You know that he is dead and that nothing can ever bring him back. Even if you fancied that you saw him with your eyes, it would be sheer hallucination, for you know that the dead do not return. Remember the old proverb—*dead men tell no tales*. You must face this and master it. If you do not, you will be disturbed.'

I looked resolutely about me. There was no one at all in sight. I went home.

I discovered, however, that facing the possibility of hallucinations made me conscious of them. That night as I lay beside my wife, who was quietly sleeping, I even encouraged them.

'Now, Tunstall,' I said almost aloud, 'come out and let me see you.'

We always slept with our blinds up and our windows open. We liked the fresh air and the reassuring murmur of the sea. On this night there was a shadowed, creamy moonlight. Lying on my side I stared into the room. 'Come on, Tunstall,' I said. 'Let me see you.' I imagined him as he would be or as I had last in full light seen him. He was wearing purple corduroys and was fresh and strong and confident. 'Hullo, Jacko,' he said, 'I can come now whenever you want me.'

But he was not there, of course. However hard I might stare, he was not there. His voice was there rather than his body. I even spoke to him aloud. 'You're not there really, Tunstall,' I said. 'You can't come back, you know, however hard you try.'

But I woke Eve, which was very stupid of me.

'Who's there?' she said.

And I did another silly thing, for I pretended to be asleep.

She jogged my shoulder. I pretended to wake with a start.

'What is it?' I asked.

'You were talking to somebody.'

'In my sleep, I suppose. What a thing to wake me for!'

'No. It wasn't in your sleep. You weren't asleep.'

'I ought to know whether I was asleep or not,' I said angrily.

'You said: "You can't come back, Tunstall, however hard you try."'

'Did I? As a matter of fact, I was dreaming of Tunstall. I suppose it's because everyone's been talking about him all day.'

She said: 'I'm sure you weren't asleep. I know when you're talking in your sleep.' With a little yawn she added: 'What do you think *has* happened to him?'

'I haven't the least idea,' I said, and turned over on my other side.

On Monday morning I was in the shop alone. Eve had some shopping that she must do and I was in charge. I liked the shop. When I had worked with my father every item had been of personal interest and importance to me. Now as I moved about arranging things, dusting a little, moving furniture to its better advantage, I wondered whether in my absorption in my own work I had not allowed Eve to take everything over too completely. I felt a new energy in myself. I had a talent for these things, not Eve's business talent, but a taste that was all my own. I picked up a Waterford glass and held it against the light and thrilled at its solid independent beauty. My fingers lay about it with love and appreciation.

The bell on the shop door tinkled. Someone entered. It was, I saw to my disgust, Basil Cheeseman.

I have already said something about Cheeseman before, but I must now speak of him with more particularity, for it is at this point that he comes into my story. I loathed him, but with no obsession about him because he had no power over me.

Physically he looked what people called him—the Rat. His body was small and delicately, even effeminately, made. His face was pale and his hair a reddish brown. On the back of his hands there were reddish-brown hairs, and he had a little reddish-brown moustache. His eyes were mean and pale. He was as false as hell. He was all smiles and urbanity, a most friendly soul. But while he smiled his little eyes darted about taking in everything that might be useful.

He smoked for ever a pipe and, while he rammed the tobacco down into it, he would look at you with the eye of an adder over the top of it. He loved to tempt you into unguarded talk, and months after would say: 'You're a one to charge me with spreading stories. All your friends know the things *you* say! Remember what you said to me that day in your shop about—?'

But his profession, beyond that of journalism, was quiet, genteel blackmailing. I don't know how many of the more important people in our town were terrified of him. There was our vicar, Mr. Thomas, for one. A fat, white, oozy, kindly man with not a grain of vice in him. But he did like his choir-boys and his Boy Scouts, although most innocently. Cheeseman had the whip-hand of him. There was old Miss Chamberlain, a rich virgin with a figure like a battle-horse. A good-natured, generous soul with a liking for young men, shop-assistants, public-house young men, *any* young man who wasn't of her class.

Here again I am certain that there was nothing more than amiable, generous good-nature, but the filthy Cheeseman had a horrible hold over her all the same.

Then there was fat, greasy Bob Steele of the cinema, already mentioned by me. The less said about *his* morals the better, and Cheeseman held him in a steel trap.

Cheeseman was not only no fool: he was really clever about some things: quite an authority on gardening, for example. He worked in his garden all hours and loved it.

He was sitting now on a nice eighteenth-century chair, sitting forward, his little body held together as though he were about to spring. His russet hair had a strange glowing quality against the pallor of his skin. His eyes were everywhere. He saw me treasuring the Waterford glass. 'You like beautiful things, don't you, Talbot?' (He had tried once to call me Jacko and I very quickly stopped it.) He was smiling in a would-be friendly fashion and his prominent white teeth stuck out over his thin lower lip.

'Yes, I do.'

'Of course. One can tell that from your books. But now, for instance, what is there about that piece of glass you're holding so carefully? To me it's just a piece of old glass.'

'It would be,' I answered scornfully. Shy though I was by nature, I never attempted to disguise my contempt for him. 'It's of no use explaining to you if you can't feel it.'

'No,' he said, still smiling, 'I suppose it isn't. Flowers, now. A really

238

fine rose—there's a lovely thing. And it doesn't stay alive so long that it bores you. Now all that old furniture, those cabinets and tables, I call that junk.'

'Do you call *that* junk?' I said, standing beside a little inlaid escritoire. 'Can't you *see* its delicacy, the loveliness of its lines, the richness of its colour?'

'Yes,' he said, 'and when you sit down to try and write on it, it wobbles and there's no room for your elbows. I call it silly.'

'I'm sure you do,' I said.

'Never mind,' he said quietly. 'We all have our own tastes—and very peculiar some people's are.'

He added in the same casual tone: 'You know Tunstall's body has been found?'

His flickering whisky-coloured eyes were on me. My heart stopped a beat. I put down the piece of Waterford glass carefully on the table. I decided that it would be quite natural for me to be interested and even astonished.

'No!' I cried. 'Where?'

'On Rotherston Beach—five miles away.'

'Well, I'm damned!'

'Not a shred of clothing on it. The body badly knocked about but the face scarcely damaged.'

'When was it found?'

'Yesterday evening by some fishermen. Leila Tunstall went at once to identify it.'

'That settles *that!*' I said almost to myself.

'Poor Jimmie!' Cheeseman went on. 'I was fond of him and he was fond of me.'

There was a pause. I was wiping some plates with a duster.

'You hated him, didn't you?'

'Yes, I did.'

'And yet he was fond of you.'

'Oh, no, he wasn't. He pretended to be because it amused him.'

'Maybe.' He leaned forward a little.

'What is odd to me is how it happened. He was going to see Bella Scorfield. Everyone knows that.'

'Perhaps he wasn't,' I answered.

'How do you mean?'

'He may have lied to Miss Scorfield. He may have had some other girl as well.'

239

'Did he tell you so?'

'Why should he tell *me?*'

'I believe that he told you a sight more than he told most people.'

'Well, he didn't. He never told me anything.'

'Come on, Talbot. You know something. Let me in on it. I swear I won't tell a soul.'

I smiled. 'You're good at that, Cheeseman.'

He laughed. 'All right, you've won. But this time I mean it. What makes you think he had another girl?'

'I tell you I know nothing—nothing at all. But Tunstall was a rotter in every possible way—false to his wife, to Miss Scorfield, to anybody, everybody. He probably had heaps of women—a different one for every night of the week.'

Cheeseman sat back, drawing his two thin legs together like the closing of scissors. He patted down the tobacco in his pipe, looking at me over the top of it.

'As a matter of fact, he hadn't. I'm quite sure he hadn't. He was in love with Bella Scorfield. It was physical, of course, but that seems all kinds of other things as well while it's on.'

'You're quite a philosopher, Cheeseman,' I said. 'And now is there anything else I can do for you? I'm sorry, but I'm busy.' He got up, came close to me, knocked his pipe on the heel of his shoe.

'Yes, there *is* something. Tell me—it isn't cheek, I really want to know. What were *you* doing that evening—the evening he disappeared?'

'I think it *is* cheek,' I answered. 'Why do you want to know? What have I got to do with it?'

'I'll tell you why. Don't be angry with me. My idea, Talbot, is that you and I together can solve this mystery. I'll go further than that and say that I don't think anyone can solve it *without* you.'

'Why?'

'Because you were closer to Tunstall than anyone was. You say you hated him and he despised you. But there can be a relationship between people much deeper than hate and scorn and love. So deep that those feelings and emotions simply don't count—a relationship where two people belong to one another, have always belonged to one another, *will* always belong to one another—'

'You don't believe in that nonsense, Cheeseman?'

'Certainly, I do. I've seen it several times. But I've never seen it as I have with you two. Now I was a friend of his. He really liked me—'

'He didn't!' I broke out. 'He loathed the very sight of you!'

The moment I had said those words it seemed to me as though someone else had spoken. I looked blankly about the room. How did I know that Tunstall disliked Cheeseman? I had always, in fact, thought exactly the opposite. Until this very moment of speaking I had thought that Tunstall liked Cheeseman. What—or who?—had made me cry out those words? For it had been a cry as though from the very heart—so deep-felt, so sincere that Cheeseman himself was affronted with the sincerity.

'It's a damned lie,' he said. 'Jimmie and I were the best of pals. He showed it in a thousand ways. He said often: "Basil—if I can't trust you, old man, I can't trust anyone."' Then, more suspiciously, his white teeth shining Carker-like at me, he said:

'How do you know, anyway? Did he ever tell you he disliked me?'

'Never.' I was suddenly weary. All the virtue had gone out of me.

'What made you say that, then?'

'I don't know. Perhaps I had no right to.'

He gave me a vicious look.

'You'd better be careful what you go about saying—' His hand was on the door. 'Oh, and you haven't told me. Where *were* you that evening?'

'I went to the pictures—*David Copperfield.*'

'Oh, did you?'

'Yes, if you don't believe me, ask Bob Steele. He saw me go in.'

'Yes, and did he see you go out?'

'Really, Cheeseman—one would think that you imagine I pushed Tunstall into the sea with my own strong arms—'

He came back towards me.

'No, I know you didn't do that. You haven't the physical pluck. The point is that you know more about Tunstall's death than anyone alive. You know more about Tunstall in every way. For instance—' He came quite close to me. 'You were perfectly right. Tunstall didn't like me. We were useful to one another. But he didn't like me. But no one knew that except Tunstall and me. How did *you* know?'

But I didn't answer.

Eve came in. And as Eve came in Cheeseman went out. And so, as I see it now, this first period after Tunstall's death was almost closed— closed except for one visit. The visitor was Leila Tunstall. The time was the middle morning. Eve was upstairs giving Archie his lessons: I was seated in the window of our dining-room reading a selection from the poems of Thomas Hardy, for which I have a great affection.

I remember the poem that I was reading—*The Dark-Eyed Gentleman*. The bell rang. I went, and there was Leila looking pale and young in her mourning. As I brought her into our sunlit little room I thought her almost beautiful, for the slight deformity seemed to have been smoothed away. She began oddly:

'May I call you John?'

'Of course.'

'And you must call me Leila. I think Jimmie would like it.'

I felt a movement of revulsion. Was she going to be now the sweet, idolising-the-departed widow? I did indeed hope not.

I need not have feared. She went on:

'I hope you won't think that sentimental.'

'Of course not.'

'The fact is, Jimmie had very few real friends. I want them to be mine. Even that isn't sentimental. For the truth is that I was, and am, deeply in love with Jimmie. I don't think him any more than I did, good and fine and noble. On the contrary, he was false and greedy and lecherous. But I don't see that that has anything to do with loving him, do you?'

'Yes, I do,' I said. 'I can't love someone I despise.'

'Oh, can't you? Well, then, you've a lot to learn.' She laughed quite gaily. 'I despise myself for a thousand things—and yet I rather love myself. The fact is that Jimmie was Jimmie and *is* Jimmie. When I saw him at Rotherston lying there covered up and his face scarcely touched I *knew* that he had escaped somewhere. Knew it as surely as I know that I'm sitting here. Tumbling into the sea wouldn't finish Jimmie!'

She cried this out almost with pride.

I said very seriously: 'Please, Leila. I like you too much. I want you to trust me. So, you *must* believe me. I was *not* Jimmie's friend. Everyone seems to think I was. I distrusted him. It isn't too much to say I detested him. I hated the things he did and said, but it was more than that. He mocked me. He derided me. I was his butt. From our very earliest schooldays together. I must be honest with you about this.'

She put her hand for a moment on my arm. 'You're one of the most honest men I've ever known. I'm sure you *believe* that about yourself and Jimmie. I know he teased you. I know you disapproved of him. But all the same—there was something between you that goes deeper than being teased or disapproving of someone's morals. You and Jimmie had that sort of relationship.'

As she thus echoed Cheeseman's words, I could only look at her with a sort of stupid dumbness. What *was* this conspiracy to force me into union with this man? As though I hadn't, by my own act, union with him enough.

'In any case,' she went on, 'perhaps you'll feel a little about poor Jimmie now as I do. He can't do anything wrong or foolish any more. We can think of Jimmie always at his best now.'

'But he can!' I cried. 'If, as you said, drowning can't kill him, why shouldn't he be still here, doing wrong, teasing me, breaking your heart—'

'Oh, I didn't mean that!' she answered. 'He's free of his body now. All his troubles came from his body, which he didn't know how to control.'

'Perhaps not,' I answered. 'It may have been his spirit that was evil. And if so—'

She smiled on me as though she were my mother.

'It wasn't his spirit that was evil—he was a child. A naughty, mischievous, selfish, self-destroying little boy. Now he will begin to grow up.'

She held in her hand a little parcel.

'What I really came for, though, was to give you something. All his clothes—were gone. His body was badly hurt. But still on his finger, deeply embedded, was his scarab ring. You remember it, don't you? The green scarab he always wore. I want you to have it.'

I drew back. 'Oh, no! No!'

'Yes, please. I would like it and I know he would. He was very fond of it. He used to say that the colour changed according to the way he behaved. The green was very bright when he was doing wrong. That was one of his jokes.'

I stammered. 'Oh, but please—I would rather not—I—' She put the little parcel into my hand.

'Please take it. You can't be so unkind—'

I took it. She said goodbye and left me staring at it.

As though I had no free will I tried it on my finger. The gold ring was too large. I went to Bettany's and had it fitted. As though I had no free will I wore it from that time.

10

I count the giving to me of that ring by Leila Tunstall as the end of the first development in this terrible affair.

I may say that up to the moment of putting that ring on my finger in the jeweller's shop I had known neither fear nor compunction. My main feeling had been one of relief. Now the next stage begins and I pray to God (if I dare pray to Him) that everything I now write may be true and may prove the sanity of my brain and the clear accuracy of my memory.

I stood in Bettany's shop, and Mr. Bettany himself, a tall naked-faced man with wide-open staring owl's eyes, attended me.

'I think you will find, Mr. Talbot, that the ring fits you exactly.'

'Thank you, Mr. Bettany,' I said, putting it on.

'I know, of course, whose ring it was,' he said, in a soft, unctuous voice.

'Yes,' I said gravely. 'Mrs. Tunstall wished me to have it and to wear it.'

'A sad and strange business. We all thought so much of Mr. Tunstall.'

'Yes,' I said.

'Most mysterious his death was. However, there's no doubt, after the finding at the inquest, that in some way his foot slipped on that wet night and he fell over.'

'Yes,' I said again.

'Might happen to any of us, of course.'

But I could not attend to him. I was looking at the ring with a kind of stupid amaze—for I felt that I had had it on my finger before. The gold circlet had been strangely little damaged and the scarab itself not at all. The green of the scarab was astonishingly fresh and bright when you realised that the ring was two or three thousand years old. The carving on the inside of the ring was broken, as Tunstall had once shown me, and I remembered how difficult it was for him to get it off his finger. The horrid sensation that I now had was that *I* had pulled it with difficulty off my finger to show to somebody! I remember that I thought of the absurdity of this and that my thinking it was a proof that my nerves were anything but what they ought to be. But more than that.

As I looked at the thing I both hated it and was proud of it. I hated it seeing it on my finger for the first time and I was proud of it as an old treasured possession. Well, it wasn't an old treasured possession! But what a thing to do! To wear the ring of the man I had killed, to wear it flauntingly in the face of all the world. I remembered that old murder case when Ethel Le Neve had worn the jewellery of Crippen's wife a week or two after the murder. I had always thought it a curious and reckless thing to do. But Leila had herself given me this ring so that it was in a way a confirmation of my innocence. Then a great emotion of loathing the thing with its green and white squatness came over me. It was almost as though it were alive. I had to muster all my energies not to tear it off and throw it down there on the shop floor.

Bettany was looking at me, so I thanked him and paid him and went away. By this time, I was altogether accustomed to my hallucination of Tunstall's continual presence. I took it that this was probably the experience of most murderers during the weeks immediately following the deed. But now, walking home through the rain from Bettany's, I was aware of this new sense of fear. It was perhaps the rain. I had noticed already that I was more uncomfortable when it was raining than when it was fine, especially if the rain was thin and misty. I talked to myself *inside* myself. I had fallen into the habit of doing this and my anxiety was lest I should sometimes speak aloud.

'You know that this is all nonsense. Tunstall is dead and no one in the world has the slightest suspicion of you. Even Cheeseman is sure that you have nothing to do with it. Clear your brain of all supposition. Think only of facts. There is nothing to be afraid of—nothing whatever. The fact that you feel obliged to wear this ring is simply because you wish to please Leila Tunstall, whom you like. After a while you can put it away. She will not notice that you are not wearing it.'

But there was something stranger still. I was not *sure* that I had killed Tunstall.

When I write that, it looks like complete nonsense. Of course, I *knew* that I had killed Tunstall. I knew that I had pushed Tunstall over the cliff and that his body had been found, there had been an inquest and the body had been buried. The proof that I had killed Tunstall was in this scarab ring that I was wearing.

Nevertheless, beneath these undoubted facts was another layer of consciousness, the consciousness that I had *not* killed him and that he was still alive. I was, indeed, now entering into that world known to many perfectly sane and normal people, that world in which material facts are no more facts than non-material facts. I could, for instance, finger my ring and know that it was a fact: I could also *think* about Tunstall and feel that he was not dead.

People live in one's imagination. If they continue to live there after their physical death, then in a sense they are not dead. But I must write more of this later.

I was also now deeply concerned with three women—my wife, Leila Tunstall, and Bella Scorfield.

My wife's attitude to me had changed. I could see, although she at present said nothing, that she was greatly puzzled by me. Puzzled rather than suspicious.

She seemed physically closer. I had seen myself that I was now more masterful with her—a thing that I had always wanted to be— and that she liked this. I was altogether more masterful at home. I had taken a strange and quite unreasoning dislike to her telling me that this morning, or this afternoon, I would not be needed in the shop.

'You can keep away, John,' she used to say. 'I shan't need you.'

And now I would say:

'Who does the shop belong to? You or me or both of us?'

'Both of us, of course.'

'Well, then—we'll both run it.'

'But what about your writing?'

'That's my business.'

She was always good-tempered. She would look at me, smiling and puzzled.

'I'm glad to see you're putting on flesh, John.'

I looked at myself in the glass. It was true. My cheeks were fattening out. There was sometimes a new, almost audacious look in my eyes.

Another little thing was that I was taking a new, almost excited interest in Archie's passion for drawing and painting. I sat beside him at the table, watching him and encouraging him. One day I pulled a piece of paper towards me and drew quite a little picture—some hills, a house, and some fields.

'Why, Daddy can draw!' Archie cried. I looked at my drawing rather sheepishly—the first of my life. It wasn't very good, of course. But it wasn't very bad either. Then I tried to draw Archie sitting at the table. I made something of it. It was recognisably Archie.

'Well I'm damned!' I cried and showed it to Eve.

'You don't mean to say *you* did that!'

'I did,' I said, laughing.

'But I didn't know you could draw.'

'I didn't myself. You never know what you can do till you try.'

Leila Tunstall had gone to London. Her house was up for sale. She was staying with relations in Surbiton. I found that I missed her quite absurdly. It wasn't that I was in love with her. I had no physical feeling

246

about her at all, but she seemed to me now the one really *good* human being, besides my mother, I had ever known. It was her *goodness* I wanted—near to me, so that I could realise it and feel reassured by it. I felt as though I could confess everything to her, pour everything out to her, my loneliness, unhappiness. I wanted to talk to her and say to myself: 'You have gone far from goodness. If it weren't for Leila you would doubt perhaps that there is any goodness in the world. But look at her, listen to her voice, touch her hand, and you will know that one good person in the world is enough to convince you that goodness exists.'

Yes, I missed her quite desperately.

I was aware that Bella Scorfield was very unhappy and found some strange companionship in me. I have said that I disliked her very much. So, on one side of my nature, I still did. The Puritan in me shrank violently from the sensuality in her. She couldn't help it: she was animal in all her being. Tunstall had supplied her with what she needed and now that he was gone she was unsatisfied and lonely. On the other side I began to find that her physical presence had a kind of excitement for me. It was, I suppose, because I knew so intimately of her behaviour with Tunstall.

We had tea together one afternoon at the 'Paradise,' a tea-shop in the High Street.

'It was nice of you to come,' she said.

'Why shouldn't I?'

'Because you dislike me and everything about me. But I don't care. When I am with you Jimmie seems closer to me. Perhaps it's that ring.'

'Do you mind my wearing it? I only do because Leila Tunstall asked me to.'

'No, of course I don't. I like to see it. It reminds me of so many things. And I'll tell you another thing. You may dislike me very much, but not so much as you did. Before Jimmie died you would never have dreamed of having tea with me. Now would you?'

'Perhaps not.'

'You don't like me, but you like to be with me sometimes because you want to be reminded of Jimmie.'

'But I don't want to be reminded of Jimmie.'

'Oh, yes, you do. You were so close together, you two. Why, sometimes now the way you say things makes me think of Jimmie. Almost the same intonation.'

'You imagine that.'

'No, I don't. . . . But tell me. Do you have at all the sort of feeling I have—that he isn't really dead? I can't believe he is. With all his faults, he could look after himself, and that was such a silly way to die.'

'Why, of course he's dead!' I cried out sharply. Then pulling myself in as though I were dragging back into my very entrails some lithe animal with sharp, white teeth and red hair, I said quietly, smiling: 'Aren't I wearing his ring?'

'Oh, I know! I know! . . . Of course, he's dead. Oh, I miss him! John—Oh, I beg your pardon. It slipped out—'

'That's all right,' I said carelessly.

'May I? Fine! And you must call me Bella. Funny, isn't it? At one time I wouldn't have dreamt of it, but now—Jimmie has drawn us together a little, hasn't he? Or don't you want me to say that?'

'I think he has.'

'Well, what I was going to say is that you have no idea how dread-fully I miss him! That house is horrible to me now! Oh, you don't know how horrible it is! I have to play chess with Mother. She always wins. She likes to win. A cat with a mouse, that's what she is when she plays me. She just lets me go on. She likes to make me think I'm winning. And then she pounces! But now—she looks at me over the chess-board. I'm sure now that she knows all about Jimmie and me. I didn't think so before. But now I'm sure that she knew all the time. And she's pleased that he's dead. Horribly pleased. She hasn't men-tioned his name.'

'You're imagining all this,' I said.

'Oh, no, I'm not. You can't imagine things with someone like Mother if she wants you to be sure of something. She can make any-thing definite without saying a syllable. . . . I want to get away—to London! I must! I must!'

'Well, why don't you?'

'I can't leave Mother there helpless. Besides, she never lets me have a penny of my own. Don't let anyone else know that, will you, John? I've never let anyone else know except Jimmie. He knew and was aw-fully generous. He was always giving me money.'

I had a sudden impulse.

'I'd like you to have some,' I said, 'if it would be a help—'

'Oh, no!' She was blushing a little and looked quite young. I thought that one day perhaps if she allowed me I might kiss her. 'I wouldn't think of it. It's awfully good of you, but I wouldn't take money from anyone—Only Jimmie and I—'

248

I suddenly couldn't endure her. I wanted to get away at once, at once.

I paid the girl.

'I'm sorry,' I said. 'I promised to meet someone at the shop—'

'Of course,' she said, gathering up her gloves and bag.

I come now to the first of the events that were presently to follow. I said at the beginning of my narrative that I am writing all this down to the smallest detail that I may prove to myself, beyond any possible question, that I am telling the truth, the whole truth, and nothing but the truth, as they say in the law courts. But, if there ever should be a reader of my story, I want him to realise how sane, composed, undisturbed I am while I am writing this. It is for that reason that I record so accurately many conversations and go often into minute detail. I *am* not mad! I *am* not mad! God, God, Thou knowest. Thou hast given me this trial because of what I have done and I submit. Thou hast the right. I submit! I submit!

I found that, as the weeks proceeded, I frequented the Lower Town very considerably. As I have said already, I had a great liking for it, its silence, its green undisturbed atmosphere, the lapping of the sea waters against the broken pier, and sometimes the sea storming and leaping over the old boards and thundering against the age-stout shore.

I never, until a certain evening, entered 'The Green Parrot.' I found now that I was attracted to it as I had never been in the old days. Attracted and repelled! Something told me not to pass those doors, just as in childhood something had told me not to steal a sweet or read a book that had been forbidden me.

But on one wet, dreary evening the temptation was too strong for me and I went in. 'The Green Parrot' hung, in its upper storeys, over the sea, and when you were inside the bar-room you could hear the sound of the waters quite clearly. The room was very bright and cheerful on this particular evening, but as I stood a little uncertainly by the door, I saw to my alarm that Basil Cheeseman, Bob Steele, and a young good-for-nothing called Frank Romilly were seated, drinking together, at a table. They were the very last companions I wanted just then and I would have retreated had I been able, but it was too late.

Cheeseman, lifting his pipe and waving it in the air, called out:

'Talbot! Talbot! . . . Why, who would have thought . . .'

There was a man or two leaning on the bar and talking to the barmaid—Ted Warner, the fat landlord with a round face like a turnip lantern, and a bald head that was always perspiring, looked at me with astonishment.

I went over to the table. They put a chair for me; they were all greatly surprised to see me there.

'What will you have?' Cheeseman asked. 'Now, boys, what about another? All of you. The drinks are on me.'

'I'll have a ginger ale,' I said. They all laughed. Cheeseman was half-way towards the bar. He looked back, his foxy face agrin. 'A ginger ale! Nonsense! No one has a ginger ale here, do they, Ted?'

'I'm a teetotaller, you know,' I said, with that half-ashamed, half-boasting tone that teetotallers always assume.

'All right,' Cheeseman said. 'It's your funeral—not mine.'

He said something to Ted and they both laughed; then he came back to us.

Frank Romilly was a good-looking, dissipated young fellow whose character was as weak as a spider's web. He was supposed to work in an oil business of his uncle's, but he was supposed also to live on the favours of a rich widow called Mrs. Godfrey, who owned much property some ten miles from our town. I saw at once that Cheeseman had, before my arrival, been turning the screw on both Steele and Romilly. He was in excellent spirits while they were both in the sulks.

Something urged me to continue sitting there; something else pressed me to be gone. I couldn't understand my own mood. But after I had drunk my ginger ale, which I did almost at a gulp, I felt a kind of audacity, a new, bold spirit. It was the best ginger ale I had ever drunk and had a flavour to it that was most agreeable. When I had finished Cheeseman said:

'Now for another!'

'It's on me this time!' I cried. 'As soon as you're ready, all of you—it's on me.'

Cheeseman took my glass and went to the bar with it.

'So, you're wearing Jimmy Tunstall's ring,' Romilly said. 'Poor old chap! Christ, how I miss him! Do you remember, Bob, how we used to sit at this very table and the songs he'd sing?'

'God! I should say I did,' said Steele, who was a little drunk. 'Why, old man,' he said, leaning towards me and laying his podgy fingers on my arm, 'it was that very night you came into my cinema—*David Copperfield*—do you remember? 'Strewth, it was that very same night ... poor old Jimmie—the best sport, the best ...'

But Cheeseman had returned to the table with my drink, and the effect that he had on his two friends was truly remarkable. It was clear that he had been telling them of something unpleasant.

I drank half of my glass with one impulse: then I put the glass down on the table with a shudder. Cheeseman this time had given me a whisky and soda. I had all my life loathed the smell of whisky, and once, given a very small amount as a medicine, had been sick from it. The very thought of whisky made me ill. Now when I had drunk unsuspiciously half a glass of it I was revolted as though I had committed an obscene act. At the same time, I was familiar with it. It seemed to me that there was nothing strange in it and that I loved it while I hated it. And yet I was trembling with rage at Cheeseman. It was all I could do not to throw the glass in his face.

He was watching me, grinning at me over the top of his pipe.

'That was whisky,' I said.

'As a matter of fact, it was.'

'What right had you . . .? You know I loathe the filthy stuff.'

'You can't loathe it, old boy, if you've never tasted it.'

The other men laughed.

'Now come—confess—it wasn't so bad.'

I got on to my feet. I was about to tell him what I thought of him and go when I did an incredible thing. I drank the rest of the whisky. It wasn't I. Oh, I swear that it wasn't I who acted thus—an action that was to be one of the landmarks in my story. I hadn't known that I had drunk it until I realised that I was standing there stupidly looking at the empty glass.

How they laughed, all three of them! There was I, furious in the very act of saying that I hated the stuff, and I drank it. My body was warm, the room glowed in the light of the fire. I could see Ted smiling at me across the floor.

'No,' cried Steele, clapping me on the haunches. 'It wasn't so bad, old man, was it? And there's plenty more where that came from.'

I remembered that the drinks were to be on me. I sat down. 'What are you all having?' I said.

After that a great friendliness seemed to spring up between us. I felt as though I had known young Romilly most intimately although, in actual fact, I had with him a very slight acquaintance. I had always disapproved of him and said so.

After a little time, he alluded to this: he had drunk freely by now and his eyes shone brightly, his lips were wet, and he smiled at me as though he loved me. 'It's a funny thing, Talbot, but either I'm changed or you are. I've often thought I'd like to know you better, but you've always been so damned stand-offish. "Who does he think he is?" I used to say, meaning you and no offence meant. And they'd tell me you didn't like me a bit and used to warn the girls off me. Not that that had any effect, you know!' He threw his handsome head back and laughed like anything. 'But now you're a regular fellow. I'll swear he is. Isn't he, Bob? And I'm damned glad we're friends. Always wanted to be friends and now we *are* friends! It's as though your wearing old Jimmie's ring has sort of brought us together. Let's shake hands on it!'

His hand was damp and strong and warm.

I noticed at the same time that something came from under the table. It was Tunstall's fox-terrier, Scandal, the dog that had been down with us on the beach that day. When Tunstall had been there the dog, who had been devoted to him, never paid any attention to anyone else.

He now came from under the table and sat there on his haunches looking at us with large, mournful eyes.

'Why, that's Tunstall's dog?' I said.

'Yes,' Cheeseman said, 'I've taken him over. Here, Scandal, old boy. Come along, old boy.' But the dog didn't move. He stared at Cheeseman with the same intense melancholy. A shiver ran down his spine. Suddenly he lifted up his head and howled.

I cannot possibly describe the effect that that dog's howl had on the warm and brightly-lit bar. It was like what an unexpected gunshot would be in a cathedral!

We all cried out at once: 'Oh, drown the bastard!'—'What the hell—'—'We can't have that here, Mr. Cheeseman!' After the rest I said: 'What's the matter, old boy?' At once he turned his head to me. He looked at me as though he would stare my face away. Then, very slowly, he came towards me. It was almost as though he crawled. We all watched in silence. He came. He sniffed at my trousers. He sniffed again and again. He raised his head and stared again. Then with a sigh he lay down and stayed stretched out, his handsome head with its short, stiff white curls resting on his paws.

'He seems to know you,' Cheeseman said.

'He's seen me when I've been with Tunstall.'

'I can't say he's been much fun since I've had him,' Cheeseman said. 'Misses his master all the time. And Jimmie didn't treat him over well, either.'

'Treat 'em rough. Treat 'em rough,' Romilly said. 'Women and dogs. Treat 'em rough.'

'Well, Jimmie certainly did.'

'Jimmie! Jimmie!' Bob Steele suddenly broke out in his thick, mumbling voice. 'Why has it always got to be Jimmie? I hated the man personally. Oh, I know he seemed jolly enough, but he wasn't jolly really—not by a long chalk. He is dead and there's no one very sorry if you ask me. Yet here we are, always talking about him as though he were still alive. You'd think he was sitting at the very table with us by the way you go on.'

I looked at Steele with a grim determination.

'So that's how you feel, is it?' I said to him, and I could see at once how greatly surprised he was both by my look and my voice. 'Well, that's pretty ungrateful and you know that it is. Many's the time he's helped you out of a nasty scrape. What about that time in Nottingham and the girl—?'

He broke in. 'By God, Talbot, who told you about that? He can't have done. And yet nobody else knew. But you keep your mouth shut, do you hear? How did you know? He can't have told you—'

'Never mind how I know,' I answered. 'I'm blasted well disgusted with you, Steele, you ungrateful bastard—'

And those are the last words that I clearly and definitely remember. I had never drunk whisky before. I had never sworn before. Whether they were connected I cannot say.

All I can remember is that I went on drinking and while I was drinking I began to disintegrate. I disintegrated before my own eyes. I had always been sure that I had a personality and had suspected that I had a soul to be saved, but now I fell apart—a leg there, ribs and intestines here, blood and muscles and nerves—all tumbling into a golden haze that seemed to emanate from the taproom fire. And if I had no body, what was there to assure me that I had a soul? Why should I imagine that there was any such entity as John Talbot?—a bit of John Talbot, a bit of someone else—a bit of a dog, of a fox, of a bird, of a stoat. I remember that I leant across the table wagging my finger and saying something like this:

'I am nothing. You are nothing. My spittle is as good as your spittle and it is only spittle. Isn't it? Now answer me. You're afraid to. You're afraid because you must have your identity. What's your name? Romilly. Frank Romilly. That's right. Well, Frank Romilly, without your identity you're nothing—see? An empty dwelling-place and seven devils enter in. And the last state of that house shall be worse. See what I mean, Romilly? A devil *has* entered into you. It's looking out of your eyes now. I'll wash him out for you.'

And I threw the rest of my glass of whisky and soda in his face. I don't know what happened after that.

I was valiant, standing on my feet singing the indecent song 'My landlady fell down, fell down . . .' I didn't know the song. I had never sung it before. And then I crawled on the floor imitating the dog Scandal. And then Cheeseman was seeing me home through the cool night air.

I remember Cheeseman saying before we reached my door:

'I haven't heard anyone sing that song about the landlady since Tunstall sang it up at the Spider Club one night—'

I was violently sick and Cheeseman stood there and waited. Then he opened my door for me, led me in and left me.

I sat down in the dark room on the sofa. The fit of nausea had cleared my head and I was cold as though lapped in snow. I was also terrified. I called out at the top of my voice: 'Eve! Eve! Eve!' A moment later her step was on the stairs, she had switched on the electric light, and in her primrose-coloured dressing-gown, her hair bound virginally with a silk handkerchief, she stood looking at me.

'John!' Then she added, half-way towards me: 'You're drunk!'

'I am.' I was too wretched to care. But I was frightened. 'There's someone in the room.'

She paid no attention to that. She came over to me and sat on the sofa beside me. I put my head against her breast.

'I'm ashamed. . . . It's never happened before. . . . You know it hasn't. . . . Be kind. I need you so.'

But she was not at all angry, only business-like.

'I should hope it hasn't. I'm completely astonished. Now come upstairs. I'll help you to undress.'

She assisted me upstairs. She helped me to undress. When we were in bed she tucked me up and then lay at some distance from me. I longed that she should take me in her arms, but I was ashamed and I realised that I stank of whisky.

'My head aches,' I murmured.

'Here, rub this on your forehead. Now you know how unpleasant the effects of drinking are, you won't do it again.'

As I lay there I realised that I was completely my old self. I was not masterful nor roguish nor obscene.

The thought of Cheeseman and his companions, the memory of my chatter, the soft warmth of Romilly's hand—these things repelled and revolted me.

'Where did you go? Who were you with?'

Eve's voice, calm, resolved, unangered, told me that I was in for a questioning. I knew well by now Eve's investigations. There was nothing in the world more definite and relentless. My head throbbed, my body shivered. I was afraid, I knew not why. I stretched out my cold hand and took hers. She let my hand lie in hers, but I knew that she was scarcely aware that it lay there. When she was determined to satisfy some curiosity, she could be ravished and not know her ravisher.

'Where did you go?' she repeated. 'And why? It's so unlike you.'

I lifted my hand and laid it under her breast, but so unconscious was that breast of any contact that I took my hand away again.

'I'm frightened,' I said, and drew closer to her.

'Poor John! What are you frightened of?'

I lay close against her warm, strong side and could feel the calm beating of her heart.

'I'll tell you,' I said. 'I was in the Lower Town. I pushed open the door of "The Green Parrot" because it was wet and went in. Cheeseman and Bob Steele and Frank Romilly were there.'

'The worst—' murmured Eve.

'Yes, of course, I know. I've always hated them, especially Cheeseman. But something made me. I sat down with them. I had a ginger ale. I think now that Cheeseman must have put something to it, for it was strong, better than any ginger ale I ever . . .' I broke off. 'Eve,' I said pitifully, 'put your arms round me. I'm so miserable. My head is awful.'

'Yes. All right.' She put her soft arms around me. I buried my face in her nightdress then timidly raised my head and kissed her soft, warm, enchanting cheek.

'I know,' I murmured. 'The whisky . . . it's hateful. . . .'

But she wasn't caring for what I did. She said quickly, in the clear, sharp tone of one who is thinking of nothing but the answer to a question: 'Yes, yes. He put something into the ginger ale. Gin, I suppose. What happened then?'

'I drank it. I liked it. Cheeseman asked me whether I wanted another. I said yes. Then the dog howled.'

'What dog?'

'Tunstall's dog. That nice fox-terrier with the rough curly head. They call him Scandal.'

'Why did he howl?'

'I don't know. But it was awful there, quite suddenly, when everything was so cheerful.'

'What happened then?'

'I spoke to him and he came over and sniffed my trousers. Then he lay down.'

'Well, never mind the dog. What happened then?'

'Cheeseman brought me another drink. I drank half of it before I realised it was whisky. I was furious and began to curse Cheeseman, but while I was cursing him I drank the rest of it. Oh, Eve, that was the awful part! I've always hated whisky. You know I have. Even the smell of whisky makes me sick. You know it does. But now I drank it and liked it.'

'Well, that's nothing. Lots of people have thought they hated whisky and found they didn't when they tried it.'

'But, Eve, Eve . . . the dreadful thing . . . the dreadful thing . . . I'd drunk it before and liked it. I knew I had. I'd drunk it before. . . .'

My whole body was trembling so that she was aware of it.

'You haven't drunk it before. You've often told me. But that's nothing. I've never drunk port, but I know just what it tastes like. Why, you're trembling! Poor old John! This will teach you not to get drunk again.'

I remember it struck me as strange that my virginal Eve should feel little disgust at my condition, should take it indeed as an often-experienced commonplace. How was it, I dimly thought? Had she known drunk men before? But this foolish question was at once forgotten in my surprise at the urgent curiosity in her voice.

'I want to know, John—I've been wanting to know for a long time. What's changed you so completely in these last weeks?'

'These last weeks?'

'Yes—since Jimmie Tunstall fell into the sea.'

'I don't know of any change.'

'Of course, there is!' She gave me a little shake with her firm hand. 'I've lived with you for years so I ought to know. Sometimes you're as you've always been, but sometimes—' She leaned towards me. 'Are you listening? You haven't gone to sleep?'

'No, of course I haven't.'

'Sometimes you've been another man altogether. Bossy. Ordering me about. To tell the truth, I've rather liked it. With Archie, too, you're quite different. He's beginning to look up to you. And your drawing suddenly. And now getting drunk. . . .'

My terror had returned, dreadfully, remorselessly.

'Let me alone,' I murmured. 'I want to sleep. This headache—' She was leaning right over me now. She caught my shoulder with her hand.

'I want to know. I *must* know. What's happened? You have some information that has changed you—something about Jimmie Tunstall's death—something that pleases you, puts you above yourself—'

'I don't know anything.'

'Yes, you do, John. And I'll tell you what it is. You had a quarrel that night. You struggled and he fell over—something like that . . .'

'I didn't—I never saw him—I was at the cinema.'

I pulled myself away from her hand.

'So, you say. But, John, I know better. When you came in that night the ends of your trousers were wet. You'd been walking in grass.'

'Of course, I hadn't. You can't walk in grass in a cinema.'

'But you weren't *in* the cinema. Or if you were, you soon came out again. I've noticed often since how you kept telling people you went to the cinema, when they hadn't asked you. Guilty conscience.'

I sat up. I put my hands to my head.

'And more than that. How about that night when you talked, pretended you had been asleep? You were no more asleep than I was, and you were talking out aloud to Jimmie, just as though he were in the room.'

I cried out: 'Stop it, Eve, stop it! I can't bear it!'

'I've got to know—I've got to know.'

I turned round. I felt for her hand and caught it.

'There isn't anything to know—at least it's all imagination. You're right this far. Since Tunstall's death I've had a ridiculous obsession that he isn't really dead. I don't know how he died. That night I *was* at the cinema and I came back through Cottar's Lane—that's where I got my trousers wet. How he died, where he died, I haven't the least idea. But I suppose I hated him so much that he's obsessed me—is obsessing me now. Tonight I began to drink because he seemed to be there in that pub. Perhaps it's true what he used to say to me—that death wouldn't separate us. Eve, I'm frightened. I'm terribly frightened. Be kind to me. Be kind—'

I clung to her, kneeling on the bed, my cheek close to hers. I put my hand up and stroked her hair.

With an immense good-nature she kissed me, then laid me back in the bed as she would a child.

'Now you're the old John, the John I married—always imagining things. Of course, Jimmie Tunstall's dead. And a good riddance I daresay, although I couldn't help a kind of feeling—Now go to sleep—all right, I'll kiss you. Is that better? Now, John—be good, go to sleep. There's nothing to be frightened of.'

She left me, turned on her side and was soon asleep.

But I lay there, agonizing. For I was empty, empty as a cleaned-out bin. I was little John Talbot, just as I used to be. But John Talbot who had been ravished, assaulted, invaded, possessed. Something—someone?—had been within me that night. Yes—had dwelt within me and been master of me.

I strained my ears into the dark. The rain lashed the half-raised window-pane and the sea roared and sulked, and sulked and roared.

In my terror as I lay, my heart beating thickly as though it were twisting a muffler round my neck, I waited, wondering whether that something would invade me again. In the dark room it seemed to be waiting, making no sound, its eyes not moving, watching, on the alert. . . . When would it cross the intervening space? Would I suddenly be aware of its naked entry, the thick limbs pushing between my ribs, the brain within my brain, directing, commanding, the wicked will, the lascivious mind . . .

To the falling mutter of the sea I fell asleep.

11

In the spring I went up to London. I had to see Leila Tunstall.

I went to see her as I might go to a physician. Looking back, I can see now that this journey to London was my first actual admission to myself that I was ill. I said quite simply to Eve: 'My nerves are in bits. I know of a doctor in London. Charles Hopping told me about him. He's grand about nerves.'

But she answered quite directly: 'You're going to see Leila Tunstall.'

'I shall call on her probably,' I said.

'Are you in love with her?' Eve asked.

'Of course not.'

'Because I shan't be in the least bit jealous if you are.'

'Of course not. You're the only woman I've ever been in love with—or ever shall be.'

'Well—are you afraid of her, then?'

'Afraid of her?'

'Yes—does she know something that no one else knows?'

'There's nothing to know.'

I realised then that Eve was eaten up, obsessed, devoured by curiosity. Nothing now mattered to her beside the correct answer to this question: 'What connection had I had with Jimmie Tunstall's death?'

His death had wrought some deep change in me. What was it that had occurred?

That last night before I went up to London I behaved to her like the cave-man of the popular novel. She enjoyed it. She responded as she had never responded to me before. For five happy minutes I cheated myself into believing that, after all, she loved me.

When I arrived in London it was a late spring evening, very lovely and delicate with a glistening light on the fresh trees and the pearl-grey stone of the buildings like pigeons' wings. When I had been half an hour in my hotel, however, I realised the apprehension everywhere.

A short while before, in March, Hitler had occupied Prague. Now, what would his next move be? I cared nothing for politics. I was an artist. But I had for years past hated the Nazis almost with hysteria. This evening, as I sat at a little table by myself and listened to an elderly man and woman expressing their horror of the Gestapo, I found myself, to my surprise, almost condoning Hitler in my mind. The two old people were discussing the news. On the day preceding (April 26th, I see by my diary, was the date) Conscription had been announced, and there had been Simon's new Budget, with its heavy tax on motorcars, raising surtax and so on.

The two old people were saying that it was all Hitler's fault and what a devil he was and when was anyone going to have the courage to put a stop to his bloody deeds? They were very fierce-minded, and I remember that the lady's white-haired head had a perpetual tremble and the old gentleman had large brown warts across the backs of his hands. Only a little while ago how cordially would I have agreed with him. Now, as I studied sceptically my *vol-au-vent* (for this was not an expensive hotel), the thought shot hotly through my body: 'Why shouldn't Hitler do his best for his country? It's quite true Germany must have expansion. Everyone denies it her. Hitler is a great man.' And the chicken nearly choked me. I put down my knife and fork. I stared across the hideously decorated room. What had happened to me? This could not be I who was exonerating that band of cruel sadistic toughs? And if not I, who was it?

I could eat no more. I went out and walked the Bloomsbury streets. There were few lights. Only little red patches of colour and the dim swift opalescence from some passing taxi. . . . But in the sky, there was a violet glow and a sweet soft air, an almost sacred silence. The British Museum was lumped against the sky, nonchalantly, as though it knew that all the relics of past time held within it made time timeless. But did they? I looked up at the sky, pierced with the sparkle of the stars and with the honeyed star-dust of countless worlds. From that same violet sky one bomb might one day fall, and where would the mummies be then?

A shiver of apprehension shook me and I realised, as I had never done before, that this world had lost, for the first time in history, all its security.

Then, on the opposite side of the street, I thought that I saw a sturdy, thick figure standing in front of the Museum gates. I thought I heard a chuckle and stayed breath-suspended, expecting to hear: 'Hullo, Jacko . . .'

I crossed the street, determined that this time I would challenge him. But of course, there was no one there.

I had Leila's address—15 Effingham Road, Surbiton. I wrote to her and she invited me to tea. It was a grey, cold day, with little promise of summer in it, when I caught my train at Waterloo and handed myself over to Suburbia.

I was in a curious state of eager anticipation—as though I had persuaded myself that an hour with Leila would set right all my troubles. I was going to be completely honest with her, and yet I was not going to be honest with her at all—for of course I would not tell her that I had killed her husband. What I *would* tell her was of my own unhappiness, and I felt that she would lay her hand on my forehead and heal me. I did not ask myself, as I should have done—How could she heal me when I held back the truth from her?

One thing I learnt during this short journey to Surbiton. There was a short, stout, red-faced, elegantly-dressed man, with a carnation in his buttonhole, sitting on the left side of the window. Suddenly his voice snapped at me: 'Are you looking for someone, sir? If not, would you mind closing the window? Damned cold day.'

Then I realised, as I had not until then done, that as the train started I had leaned out of the window, peering up the platform as though looking for someone, and that even when the train had left the station I was still staring up the line. I withdrew into the carriage, apologizing to the gentleman, murmuring something. As I sat in my corner I felt that my face had a furtive look and that my companion looked at me with suspicion.

I realised that I was now doing things without consciousness of them. This frightened me.

I walked from the station to Effingham Road. Rain was threatening and a little chill wind blew fragments of paper about my feet. It was indeed little like summer and I was glad to find a fire in the sitting-room where the maid left me while she went to summon Leila. The room's walls were thickly covered with very bad water-colours, painted, I saw from the signature, by Leila's brother-in-law. Leila was staying with her sister. The piano had an old-fashioned air, because, I suppose, the music of Noel Coward's *Bitter Sweet* was open upon it.

There was a clock with a furtive tickling noise and a bird that rustled in a cage by the window. All these things made me feel that I should not get on very well with Leila's sister, so I was glad when Leila came in and said:

'Joan and Forrester have gone to the pictures. Wasn't it tactful of them?'

While the maid brought the tea and for some time after, we talked very conventionally. She was wearing black and it suited her. Her face seemed a little more crooked than it had been, but her eyes were as kind, as tender, as understanding as I had always so gratefully known them. Quite suddenly she said:

'John, what's the matter?'

'The matter?' I asked.

'Yes, you look a sick man.'

'I'm not awfully well. I thought it was time I took some kind of holiday. But never mind me. Tell me about yourself.'

'Oh, I'm all right! It takes some getting used to, you know—being a widow. If I didn't feel that Jimmie was still around I'd be very lonely.'

'Do you like your sister and brother-in-law?'

'Very much. Forrester paints in his spare time, as you can see from this room.' She laughed. 'How Jimmie hated his painting! We stayed here once and I'm afraid they didn't get on at all.'

'No, I know they didn't.'

'What do you mean?'

I pulled myself up. 'What a silly thing to say! Of course, I didn't know. How much longer are you going to stay here?'

She sighed. 'To tell you the truth, John, I don't know quite what I am going to do. This isn't like one's own home, of course, and although they are awfully good they don't, naturally, want me here for ever. The fact is—well, I am not very well off nowadays. Jimmie left nothing but debts, I'm afraid. I have a little bit of my own. I like London and I expect I shall take a small flat somewhere.'

There was a silence. Then she said:

'How's Eve? And the boy?'

'They're very well. But I don't want Archie to go to school and Eve does.'

'Isn't it better for a boy to go to school?'

'I was so miserable there myself and Archie's very like me in some ways—sensitive, you know, and shy.'

'If you found the right school—'

'He'd have to go to the local place, where I was. We haven't much money to spare.'

'How's your book getting on?'

'Not very well, I'm afraid. I haven't done much at it lately.'

She leaned forward and laid her hand on mine.

'John—what's the matter? Tell me.'

Then I broke down and did what I hadn't done for a long time—I began to cry.

She was deeply moved but with her great tact and understanding she did nothing to disturb me, only held my hand in her soft small one and waited.

At last I began to talk. I said that I was unhappy, frightened, that I didn't know what was happening to me. I could not get Jimmie out of my mind.

'You must not care what I say. Think that I am not right in my head. For that's the truth. My nerves are all in pieces. I know that Jimmie is dead and yet I feel that he is not. He is always near me. Sometimes I even think he is inside me. Oh! keep him away! Keep him away!'

At that I fell on my knees at her feet and laid my head against her dress. I held to her as though she were my only anchor. My body shook. Then I felt ashamed of myself. I got up and sat down.

'I don't know why I should behave like this to you. We know one another very little, but I sometimes think you are the only good person I have ever met. I'm in this trouble because of my own sins. . . . I feel as though he—Jimmie—your husband were pursuing me. . . . I have this obsession. Show me, for God's sake, that that is all it is.'

'For God's sake?' she asked.

'Yes. You believe in God, don't you?'

'Yes. I do.'

'Pray to Him for me. Ask Him to help me. I don't believe enough. I can't believe enough. Soon—if this power gets more hold of me it will be too late. Pray now. Pray now.'

Leila answered: 'I do pray for you. I have for a long while. I knew that you wanted me to. I pray for you and Jimmie together.'

'No. No. No . . . you mustn't. I hated him. I hate him still.'

'So, you think,' she said. 'But he needed my prayers just as you do now. He was obsessed with evil too—he wanted to be rid of it but couldn't.'

'No, he didn't,' I interrupted fiercely. 'He liked to be evil. He was evil. He is evil still.'

'He was possessed by a devil. I used to tell him so. "That's your devil, Jimmie," I'd say—"not you."'

'He was possessed by one so long that he became one.' I didn't care how much I hurt her. Something inside me was crying out against something else inside me: 'So you believe in evil?' I asked her. 'A real power of evil in the world, always fighting good. A constant battle. A fight.'

'Of course, I do,' she answered. 'Nothing else explains life. If there weren't a fight there'd be no progress. If there weren't evil—strong, active, clever evil—there'd be nothing for good to put its teeth into. God has done us the great honour of giving us our own free will. We have to fight our battle ourselves. But He has given us things to aid us—the love and companionship of Jesus Christ, for one thing—' She stopped with a little laugh. 'Now I'm preaching. But you asked me, didn't you?'

'Is it only my imagination that I think Jimmie is still alive?'

'I don't know what death is,' she said. 'If someone lives on in our minds and hearts, then for us anyway he isn't dead. More than that, I don't know.'

'Does Jimmie live on like that with you?'

'Yes. He does.'

'Then for both of us he is still alive. But for me he is evil—for you he is good.'

She paused for a long time before she answered:

'I wouldn't say this to anyone but you, John. I feel he *is,* at this moment, evil. I have prayed and prayed to see him released from evil, but I can't. I think that at this time he is in the control of an evil spirit. If I have been conscious of any contact with him, it is an evil contact.'

There was a dreadful silence in the room, made more menacing by the rustle of the bird in the cage.

'I must tell you something else,' she added. 'When you are near me, John, I feel that he is near me, too.'

I did not answer her. My throat was as dry as sand.

She took my hand and held it tightly.

'You must think of certain things, John. One, that many—indeed most—wise, sensible, intelligent people would think these ideas nonsense. They would say, perhaps quite rightly, that our nerves have been shaken, that we are imagining absurdities. Secondly, that we are together in this, friends, and that whenever you want me I am there for you. And thirdly, that I, at least, believe in God and the love of Jesus Christ, and that the power of good is infinitely stronger than the power of evil. I think that just now the powers of evil are threatening not only us but the whole world, and that however successful they may seem to be for a time, they cannot win in the end. We must take a long view, the longest God allows us to have.'

We sat there, side by side in that dreadful cold silence.

'Think of me, John,' she said, 'whenever you begin to imagine anything bad. And don't run away from anything. Anything that is real to you *is* real to you, however absurd it may seem to anyone else. Face it. Face it. Even though you thought that Jimmie was in this very room, face him. Ideas are as real as facts, more real often. You can only get rid of them by facing them.'

At that moment, as I now so desperately remember, the door opened. I don't know what, or whom, we expected to see, but in actual truth a mild little inoffensive man stood there, a little man in a rather shabby suit. He gave us a look and a smile, and said: 'Oh, I say— I'm sorry,' and before we could do or say anything he was gone, very softly closing the door behind him. Leila laughed.

'That was Richard. So, like him, appearing and vanishing like that.'

'Richard?' I asked.

'Yes. My brother. You had forgotten I had one, hadn't you? He's been in China for years in a tea business. Now they've moved him to London. He's a darling. He's the human being with most goodness I've ever known.'

'He reminds me of someone,' I said.

'Well, if it wasn't too silly,' she answered, laughing, 'I'd say he reminds you of yourself. I'm sure I've mentioned it before. Don't you see the resemblance? At any rate to you as you were a few months ago. For you've fattened out, you know. Your cheeks are plumper. But I'll never forget the day I first saw you—the day Jimmie first brought you to the house. The physical resemblance was extraordinary. I positively thought it was Richard standing there. That's why I think I liked you from the very beginning.'

My apprehension was gone. The room seemed normal and happy. I kissed Leila on the forehead.

'I've got what I came here for,' I said. 'I've been letting myself get foolish. I needed a change. That's what it was. Will you have dinner with me one night before I go?'

She promised that she would.

PART 2

NARRATIVE 1

1

I come now to an episode that seems to me, when I consider my past life, quite incredible, and is for me, in all my saner moments, of a peculiar horror. But I wish here to state the truth and omit nothing save the grosser aspects of the incident.

During this stay in London I found that the evenings and nights fascinated me. My little hotel in Bloomsbury was, in any case, not appetizing in the evening and theatres and cinemas seemed difficult. I asked a man at the hotel about the theatres.

'There's a very good piece at the Grand,' he said. 'I saw it last week. I *did* enjoy it.'

'What sort of a piece?' I asked.

He scratched his head. 'I don't remember anything much about it, but it was excellent.'

So even the theatres were veiled in mystery!

However, I was quite happy. I would take an omnibus down to Leicester Square and then walk up Piccadilly. As I have said, I had begun to be uncertain of my own identity. Was there really anyone called John Ozias Talbot? And if there was not, then none of this crowd that passed so dimly to and fro was an entity either. We were all fragments of fragment hanging like the wings of flies to a dead cinder! And yet how alive these ghostly figures seemed! How they laughed and jested as they passed me, making love, discussing food, gossiping about this shadow and that. But I did not feel lonely. I had the obsession that Tunstall now followed me everywhere and sometimes so closely that he and I were one. At other times my brain was completely clear. I knew, as I know now, that I was John Talbot, a separate independent soul, and that the shock following on what I had done had penetrated me as an illness. That this was all imagination about Tunstall and that I must conquer it with my strong, assured common sense.

Nevertheless, walking along these shadowy streets among these dim figures, I had sometimes crazy impulses. Once just outside Lyons' Corner House I almost grabbed a stout man in a waterproof by the arm: 'Come inside and have some coffee with me. I will tell you a story. Then *you* can tell *me* whether I am not as sane as you are.'

Happily, I did not do this.

Then this very horrible thing occurred. I was walking westward along Piccadilly. I was almost opposite the Ritz Hotel. It was a wet night and two women were sheltering under a doorway. One of them said:

'Hallo, darling! Can't I speak to you?'

I walked forward a step or two. My heart was pounding in my breast. I was inflamed with desire. That is a conventional phrase, but it is how I was. Fire licked my loins. I had always felt a shuddering horror of such women. I had never understood how men could surrender themselves to such terrible company. Now, not only was I madly excited so that there was a singing in my ears and my mouth was dry, but I had been so before. This was, it seemed, an accustomed experience to me. I walked back with assurance to the women.

'Did you speak to me?' I asked. They had been chatting eagerly together, but the smaller of the two—she was a little bird-like creature with a face so painted that it resembled a mask—put her hand on my waterproof.

'Of course I did, darling. . . . Coming home with us?'

'What, with both of you?' I said, laughing, for I was bold, masterful, completely at my ease.

The other woman, tall and stout, said in a husky voice:

'You pays your money and you takes your choice.'

They both laughed. I called a taxi. The little woman gave an address in the direction of Great Portland Street. Inside the taxi I sat between them, but they paid no attention to me at all. Across my body they continued their discussion about a certain Lucy and a Mr. Board. How well I remember those names and that Mr. Board had promised to call on a certain night and Lucy had waited for him and been furious at losing an evening, for he had not come and, indeed, was never heard of again and owed Lucy quite a packet. And Lucy liked him more than a little, and still as she walked from corner to corner in Piccadilly looked for him, and things weren't too good for her, anyway, just now, as she was fined four times last week and seemed to have lost all heart in her business.

Their voices were compassionate and kindly, but I still burned with this fire: my cheeks were flaming. The hand of the smaller of the two women lay coldly in mine. She suddenly cried: 'Christ! but your hand's hot, darling!'

It seemed to me that I had ridden in this cab and heard these words many times before. I felt big and masterful. My body seemed to swell as I sat there. It would not be difficult for me to crush both women in my arms. I felt that I had often crushed women in my arms.

Then the fat woman said to the other (as though I were the un-hearing, unseeing specimen of some animal product), 'He's quite a little fellow, isn't he?'

They glanced at me, but not for more than a moment. 'I don't blame Lucy,' the big one summed up. 'I'd bloody well have done the same myself. After all, if *he* wasn't there to pay she'd a right to take it out of someone else—that's what *I* say.'

'The poor soft!' the mask-faced woman said.

The cab stopped. We all got out. It was raining hard. I paid.

Evil builds up its dour atmosphere, doesn't it? I mean the evil for which human beings are not responsible—evil like a wet dish-cloth lying of its own volition on the edge of the table, the drops falling, the pool assembling, the damp stench smoking in vapour. It was so now in this house. As we climbed the stairs my nostrils were dank with corrup-tion, and of course, from above, there came the sound of a tap dripping.

The big woman unlocked a door. We entered a sitting-room and stood there.

'Now,' the big woman said in a motherly housekeeping tone. 'We won't waste time. It's my room to the right, Molly's to the left—which do you prefer?'

The electric light showed a dusty room, heavy with chill. There was a piano. A pot with a fern. Some shabby bawdy prints in gilt frames. The prints were 'foxed' and the frames chipped.

I went into the room on the left with Molly. She undressed with lightning speed, saying not a single word. I whistled, I sang. I told her a story about Rio de Janeiro.

'How much are you giving me?' she asked.

'Five quid,' I answered jovially.

'Thank God, I shan't have to go out again—raining monkeys and coconuts.'

I was so wildly excited that my fingers fumbled with my collar-stud. This was only one of innumerable experiences. I sat on the edge of the bed and told her some stories. Aden, Marseilles, Brindisi, especially Brindisi. After that I nearly killed her. She scratched my cheek.

A vast enveloping horror and disgust chilled my poor ghost of a body. Slowly the little room that had been cloudy with a sort of exultation repeated itself to me. The cheap lace curtains, the round, black metal clock, my clothes on the floor, a cheap photograph of Velasquez' 'Rokeby Venus,' all these were symbols of my shame, my humiliation, my self-disgust.

'Tell me some more about Brindisi, strong boy,' she said. She was lying on her back staring at me. 'You know, to look at you one would never think—'

'I've never been to Brindisi,' I said in a whisper.

'What!' she said. 'You're a bloody liar! You've just been telling me—'

'I've never been to Brindisi.' A strange longing for home pervaded me. To catch Eve's glance as she looked up from the table! But how dare I even think of her? My head hung. My hands were folded on my breast. I was bitterly, bitterly cold. She regarded me with some compassion. 'You're shivering, and this room's as hot as hell. You'd better put some clothes on.'

I looked at her intently.

'I want you to understand something. That was another man who was with you just now. *He's* been to Aden and Brindisi and the rest. I haven't.'

'You're crackers,' she said. She sat up. 'I've had 'em crackers before, and I know how to act with them, see? So, don't you try—'

'I'm not trying anything,' I said, my teeth chattering. I felt the fresh blood from the scratch on my cheek. 'I'm only telling you. That wasn't me, that other man.'

'What the hell do I care who it was as long as he pays the five quid? Don't forget it, darling, will you? Maybe I'll go out again. The rain don't sound so hard—'

I dressed. I laid a five-pound note on the mantelpiece. I went away.

2

I was myself again. I was my complete, real, unalterable self. I was free. I had no thought of Tunstall, nor of his death, nor of his insistent

268

neighbourhood. I had no desire for anything but my own life and the company of my wife and son.

In the train I sat closely folded up in my corner, reading *The House with the Green Shutters,* a novel that had once exerted a great influence upon me. So, it did again now. This was the kind of novel that I wanted to write—in my own idiom, of course—but the figures of Bella Scorfield, Cheeseman, and the rest hung before me as starting-points from which my own creations should come. 'The Green Parrot' should be the background, and I saw the start of my novel with the wet, misty evening and the slap of the wave against the wooden skirting of the overhanging walls. I was myself again. I was creative again. I would abandon the novel that I had been writing and follow this new impulse. I sat there hugging my bony knees, thinking about Eve and Archie, feeling that I had been swept clean of whatever corruption had entered me. I was rid of Tunstall. Those odd obsessions had been simply the reaction from what I had done. I thought—how very strange! I have no shame at all because I killed Tunstall, but my cheeks burn if I think of Great Portland Street.

I pushed all such notions from me. I was going home. I would soon be with Eve and Archie again.

Oh, but I was happy when I entered my own home and saw my wife seated quietly reading and Archie at the table doing his homework. I caught her up and almost swung her off her feet. I kissed her again and again. She released herself, laughing:

'Here, here, John! Whatever's come over you? Glad to be home? I think you ought to be!'

Then she stood back and looked at me.

'Why, how you've altered! You're quite fat!'

'No, I'm not. I've not altered a bit.'

'Yes, you are. The shape of your face has changed. It has, really! Why, your hair's thicker! That little bald patch is almost gone! And your eyebrows! You usen't to have any! What hair-restorer have you been using? It suits you, I'll admit.'

I turned and looked in the glass. I could see no change except that my colour was high with my pleasure at being home again. My eyebrows? I put my hand up and felt one. It *was* a little thicker and I was pleased, because I had been teased about them when I was a young man. I kissed Archie and he seemed to like me, too. I spent a very happy evening with my family.

On the following afternoon, a beautiful day, I took a walk alone to think out the opening chapter of my new novel. I walked on the Common towards Shining Cliff. I had not intended to go that way; suddenly I found myself there. Birds were singing and the sea purred like a cat. At exactly the spot where I had encountered Tunstall on that wet, misty evening I encountered him again. . . .

When I say 'encountered' I want to be perfectly clear. I knew by now that you could encounter someone without seeing their physical body, that, in fact, we are all of us encountering many people every day whom with our physical eyes we do not see. I was aware now of the symptoms in the order in which they occurred. It was always the same. First there was a physical nausea similar to the suggestion of sickness that comes to you when your pipe goes suddenly bad on you. Then there was a quick, almost suffocating beating of the heart and a weakness through all the limbs. After that the certainty of the nearness.

All of us have been in a street, the room of an inn, a theatre, and are aware, with a stab of apprehension, that someone whom one greatly dislikes is drawing near. One looks quickly round to see whether there is not some avenue of escape, and if there is not time for that, one submits with the best grace one may. After that there is the fear of contact, the sickening fear that one's body may be touched in some way. But my apprehension of Tunstall was worse than this, for it was a peculiar physical fear, the sense that one's body would open and allow this horrible presence in. When I had been a boy I had thought that children emerged from the opening breasts of women. This was the same except that it was an entrance rather than an exit. I am trying to be exact in my terms, but no words can explain this dreadful, degrading, sickening fear.

Now with the sun pouring down upon me and the birds singing above me, I was rooted there, staring at nothing, my body like water. The contact grew closer. I knew that it was but nervous hallucination and yet I spoke aloud: 'Ah, leave me! For God's sake leave me! Spare me. Spare me—for pity's sake spare me!'

It is important, I think, that I should record that on this occasion I very distinctly saw a form, although I was aware, with full conscious clarity, that there was no form there. It is very easy, if you stare in front of you and then conjure up the physical presence of someone, clothed or naked, whom you know well, to fancy at last that that person is present. If you do this at a stated time in the day and repeat the effort week after week, your imagination will supply all that you need. But today my experience was rather different. I saw standing in front of me the stout body, the laughing face, the bloodshot eyes, the thick eyebrows of Tunstall, but I fancied that I also saw—some projection of myself! It was as though the spectre of Tunstall were transparent, and as through a glass I saw my own body *behind* his.

At the same time, although I did not move physically from where I stood, I felt as though my spirit commingled with something— as your breath mingles with another's when you kiss. This mingling was indescribably horrid, as though I had been unnaturally ravished. I heard the sharp metallic singing of a bird and the warm purr of the sea. Then I fainted, crumpling up on the grass.

I came to myself to find that I was lying on the grass, my face wet and my head against Cheeseman's knee. He had splashed my face with water and was forcing some brandy between my lips. The dog Scandal was roughly licking my limp hand.

I have now, when I look back on the events that followed, no doubt whatever but that Cheeseman had been following me, probably from the town. I suspect that from the moment I returned from London he had been spying on me. It was of the Rat's nature to spy, to ferret out a secret, to discover something that would lead to black-mail. The scene at 'The Green Parrot' had, I don't doubt, excited his intensest curiosity.

In any case there he was, seated on a hard, flat stone, his carroty hair shining in the sun, a pipe between his lips, and his horrid white hands, with the red hair on their backs, resting one on his knee, the other at the flask of brandy pressed to my lips.

I sat up. I looked up at his face. I hated him, yes, but it seemed to me that he had been for years my companion and that we had shared many secrets. And I knew that that was not so.

'How did you come here?' I asked him none too graciously. With some trouble I got to my feet, feeling weak, sat down on the stone.

'I happened to be passing.' He looked at me with eager, almost burning curiosity.—'I say—you did topple down! Whatever was the matter?'

'Oh, nothing. I go dizzy sometimes.' My only desire was to get away from him. I was ashamed, oh, how deeply ashamed, that he had seen me. But he would not, of course, let me go like that.

'That dog's fond of you, isn't he? Funny. He'd never look at anyone but Jimmie when he was alive. . . . But, I say, what *was* the matter?'

'The matter? With me? Why, nothing at all!'

'Oh, but there was! I was taking a stroll—lovely afternoon and all that. I've been working on my roses all the morning. They're a fair treat, you ought to see them. So, I strolled along, smoking my pipe, not thinking of anything in particular, when I saw you standing there as though you were turned into a statue, staring straight in front of you—staring like mad as though there were somebody there. Then you began to speak. I could see your lips moving. I couldn't hear what you said, of course—I didn't want to—I'm not the sort of man to spy on anybody. But you were talking as though there were somebody there. You were, really. And then quite suddenly, all in a jiffy, you throw up your hands and tumble forward on your face. I came up and you'd gone right off—you had, really. So, I pulled you over here, splashed some water from that puddle on your face and gave you a drop from this flask. You're not properly round yet. You're as white as a sheet of paper.'

'Oh, I'm all right.' How I hated him! How I wanted him to go! Well, if he wouldn't, I would. I staggered to my feet, I could just stand.

'Thanks very much, Cheeseman,' I said. 'It was just a touch of the sun! I must be getting back.'

'I'll come along with you.'

'No, don't you turn back. It's such a lovely day.'

He looked at me, grinning, his pipe clenched between his shining teeth.

'All right. If you don't want me. But do you remember my telling you a good while ago that you knew more about Jimmie Tunstall's death than anyone else alive? And so, you do! There's some mystery here. And it's about here he fell over into the sea. I'm certain of it. On his way to Bella's. And you saw him or were close by or something.'

I turned on him.

'You think you're clever, but you can't blackmail me, Cheeseman, as you do so many others.'

He sprang to his feet.

'That's a bloody, dirty lie, and you shall—'

'Come along, Cheeseman,' I said. 'You can't put that over on me. Do you remember that you tried it once over what I told you about Brindisi, and how you failed?'

He stared at me as though I were indeed crazy. . . .

'Brindisi? But you've never been to Brindisi! That was Jimmie—'

We stood looking at one another. I picked up my hat that had fallen on to the grass. Cheeseman had to hold the dog tightly to prevent his following me.

No, I had never been in Brindisi. . . . The time had come for a quiet, unsensational, common-sense examination of my situation. And behind the common-sense lurked a horror.

That night after Eve had gone up to bed I went to my little room where I worked. It was a hot summer evening. I could hear the lovely sound of the sea through the open window. I locked the door and then I stripped. There was a long old eighteenth-century mirror hanging on the right side of the window. In this I examined myself. Was I physically changed or no? I was stouter, heavier in the chest, the belly, the thighs. My face was fuller and rounder. There was nothing in that. I had always had a tendency to stoutness. Then as I looked in the mirror I had a crazy hallucination that another naked figure was behind mine, a figure of exactly my height, heavier and stouter, the features of the face coarser and bolder, the hair thicker. And as I looked they merged and became one figure.

I did not faint now. I was absorbed as though I were studying an abstract problem. I put on my vest and drawers and sat down to consider.

The fact was simply this: the crime—or whatever you care to call it—committed by me—had affected my nervous system so deeply that I was the victim of a hallucination. My hallucination was that Tunstall was possessing me. Occupying me body and soul.

It was a crazy, meaningless, monstrous obsession, but unless I could rid myself of it, I was running straight to madness.

I sat there, the perspiration on my hands and forehead and chest. I must do something to prove to myself quite definitely, once and for ever, that this *was* an obsession—something . . . something . . . something . . .

And quite suddenly, as though it were whispered into my ear, I had the solution. I had heard that very morning that Bella Scorfield and her mother had shut up their house and gone away for ten days.

At night there would be nobody there. I had never in all my life been inside the house. I would enter it, walk upstairs and visit Bella's bedroom. If my obsession were *not* an obsession, everything in that bedroom would be strange to me. If, on the other hand, the furniture and the rest were just as I expected them, then . . .

3

As soon as the idea entered my head it became a passionate desire. Day and night now I thought of nothing else.

I made the most careful enquiries. I discovered that it was an actual and positive fact that the house was empty. Some neighbour visited it occasionally to make sure that all was well. He kept the keys, but I would tell no one of my purpose. Tunstall had told me once—or had he?—at any rate I knew it as a certain fact—that the window by which he entered was easily opened if you pushed a penknife between the wood that separated the two panes. He had entered in that fashion—how did I know this?—often enough. The period for the execution of my plan was limited. They were to be away for ten days. Their departure interested the town, for Mrs. Scorfield, it seemed, had not left her bed for over a year until now. They had gone to London, apparently, about a will or some legacy.

Eve, of course, noticed my new preoccupation. The relationship between us was now very peculiar. Sexually it was ardent for the first time since our marriage. She seemed to be developing a physical love for me that she had never felt before, and as she grew more affectionate I became less so. I saw several women in the town who were attractive to me. I began to think of women continually. She watched my moods with a passionate interest. I was often very unhappy and would sit brooding in my chair and not speaking. I appeared to have lost all interest, both in the shop and my writing, but my new accomplishment of drawing fascinated me. I had a queer technical facility although I had, of course, never taken lessons. I would make, almost without knowing it, indecent drawings, and then, with shuddering horror, tear them to fragments.

When Eve realised that some preoccupation was obsessing me, she could not let me alone. She had developed now a sort of 'flirting' with me. There was a sexual impulse behind all her words. She did her best to discover my secret and one evening came very near to it.

Looking up at me and smiling provocatively she said:

'You must be fearfully bored, John, now that both your *belles* are away.'

'My *belles?* I have none.'

'Once you hadn't. *I* was your only love. Now there are others and oddly enough I like you the better for it.'

It was strange to me when I looked at her how coarse and common she could sometimes be.

'Who are my *belles*, then?'

'Bella Scorfield and Leila Tunstall, of course.'

'What nonsense! You are and always have been the only woman

I've ever looked at.'

'Nonsense! You are a regular Don Juan nowadays. Everyone is talking about it.'

There is nothing more irritating than to be told that 'everyone' is talking!

'What an absurdity! Everyone talking about me! They have better things to do.'

'They are, all the same—the change in you. Why, even, they say, you look different. They ask me what I've been feeding you on. Someone the other day said that you were quite gay with women now. I'm afraid they used to think you a very dull dog indeed—and so did I sometimes. Certainly, you've changed. I've got a lover now as well as a husband, but I don't want too many other women to discover that you've altered.'

I was drinking a mild whisky and soda.

'Perhaps it's the whisky.'

'Nothing could be milder.' I held up the glass for her to see.

'No, but it isn't always so mild. There's quite a whisky bill nowadays. Until recently you loathed the smell of it. Not that I mind a man drinking a little. It makes him more amiable.'

As she had coarsened so had I. I was drawing some other self out of her that through all our years of married life I had not known existed.

'But you must not get too fat, John. You haven't the figure to carry it.'

'Everyone says I'm putting on weight. I'm not really.'

'Of course, you are! Look at that scarab ring that used to belong to poor Jim Tunstall. It's quite embedded in your finger. You can't pull it off.'

I tried. She was right. The thing seemed to cling to my flesh, to be part of my body, and as I pulled at it the green markings were most vivid. The beetle, under the artificial light, seemed to be alive.

The time had come. I dared not leave it any longer. The evening I chose was dimmed with warm, misty rain. I did not wish to be seen by anybody—in fact I must *not* be seen. The misty rain would obscure me.

I told Eve that I was going to the cinema and I started out. It is very difficult for me to describe the mixture of fear and a kind of greedy ecstasy that was in my heart. Partly I knew that my purpose was absurd. I had never entered the house and therefore could not know what it contained. That was clear. On the other hand, a wild and exaggerated excitement urged me forward. Something in me whispered that it would be wonderful to be there again. Something else in me—the strongest of these emotions on my setting out—tried to hold me back from visiting Shining Cliff again. I was now *afraid* of Shining Cliff. I had not been. A few weeks ago, I would have visited it at any time of day or night without a tremor. But now I wished dreadfully *not* to go. As I approached the place I felt the damp sweat on my forehead. It may have been, of course, the thin rain which spider-webbed the air exactly as it had done on that other evening.

I was walking fast. I was perspiring. The beat of my heart was uncomfortable. There was no doubt but that I had grown stouter, for my body was heavy under my clothes, the clothes clinging to it and yet the body staying separate and apart as it does when it is frightened. In fact, I noticed a queer thing, which was that as I approached the Cliff more nearly, physical symptoms arose in my body that did not really belong to me. Any of us who have lived a long time have become accustomed to certain physical properties—a small bone aches in the left wrist; there is a little cough at times that is peculiarly ours; a toe on the right foot burns fierily in certain weathers. I was aware in myself now of new symptoms that were yet accustomed ones. Having been always spare, a teetotaller and a sparse feeder, my stomach had rarely troubled me. But now I was constantly aware of a sort of heartburn that comes from indigestion. My heart, too, sometimes made me breathless. My neck felt thick and congested. And I noticed on this especial evening that the scarab ring dug into my finger as though it bit me.

So, I stopped for breath at the very spot on the Cliff whence I had thrown Tunstall over. I was all alone tonight and I longed for company. I would have welcomed anybody, Cheeseman or another. The rain stroked my cheeks with greedy fingers. What a fool I was to pursue this fantasy! And who could say? I might be arrested by the local policeman for house-breaking and what an ignominious thing that would be! Nay—more than ignominious, dangerous. For once they began an enquiry as to why I should enter at night the Scorfield house, their enquiries would stretch further.

My own self, as I stood in my waterproof dismally shivering on the Cliff edge, urged me to go home. Something else in me, hot, lustful, reckless, drove me forward. I went on.

I found, to my intense relief, that I did not know the way. Then, indeed, I might have turned home, for had I not proved my case? I did not know the way. I hesitated at every turn. But as I hesitated I felt as though I were deliberately myself holding back information from myself, or as though something devilish in me was maliciously refusing to tell me what I longed to know—'*I* could tell you the way. Are you so idiotic as to fancy that *I* don't know it? I am well aware of every single step and turn, but wait . . . wait . . . I am watching to see what you will do—you poor, pitiable, frightened fool!'

Have we not all at times noticed just such scornful bullying voices within our own breasts? At one point I did almost turn home. I had left the sea-path, crossed a little wood and come to the parting of the ways. I was sure that the little rough-stoned path to the left must be the one to take, and yet my feet seemed to drive me to the other. I had to force myself to take the path to the left.

And then most abruptly I came upon the house. It squatted there in sulky, sodden silence. The thin misted rain blew in gusts across my eyes. Dark wet laurels crowded almost to the windows. The ragged drive halted before the steps of the pillared door. To the left was the lawn and I crossed over to this and looked up at the building's other side. How I hated that house with the long dead windows, the beat of the sea seeming to break against their hostile glass, the chimneys appearing to raise insulting ears to me against the dreary sky. No one was there. No one ever had been there. It was a house of kitchen-ghosts and cellar-phantoms!

'Now—do you know the place?' something seemed to whisper to me. But I did not—triumphantly I did not. I could have gone down on my knees on the sopping grass and thanked my Maker.

I was myself. I was myself, and no one else, and had never seen this beastly house before! Ah, but it would have been well for me if I had turned then and run the whole way home!

But already, as I stood on the lawn, it was as though some other quite opposite past-consciousness was approaching my brain. I walked forwards toward one of the windows, and as I walked it seemed to me that I had crossed just here a hundred times. I was near to the window. I had pressed my nose against it. Then, like a man obeying a command, I took out my pocket-knife.

I pushed up the lower pane and, bending my back, climbed into the room. It was dark with a sort of musty greenish darkness—or so I felt. The furniture stood about like watching spies, but I realised with a kind of reassurance, as though a friend had laid his hand on my shoulder, that I did not know *what the furniture was*. There were dim pictures on the wall. Opposite me was a portrait, but I could not tell from where I was whether it were male or female. I could not tell! I could not tell!

'Can you not?' a voice whispered to me. It was like a physical voice, thick and husky.—'Jacko, can you not?'

I dared not move—I felt as though with one step I should advance into some horror from which I should never again escape. And so indeed it has proved. For I am now in that horror—and I shall never again escape! Oh, God! What have I done that Thou shouldst so horribly punish me? Or if my crime is so great—and even as I write these words they mock me by their foolishness. There *is* no God but in the silly superstitions of man's heart. . . .

I did not move. I was trembling with a kind of sick disgust. I may have muttered—I cannot tell for sure—'Leave me! I am not yours. . . I am my own master. . . .'

And then I think I heard the mocking voice—'Jacko . . . Jacko . . Jacko!'

I only know for sure that wretchedly I knelt down on the floor and took off my damp boots. My fingers muddled with the wet laces.

On my stockinged feet I crept into the hall and began to climb the stairs. A clock began to strike. With agonized certainty I stayed and waited, for I *knew* that before the last stroke there would be a whirr and a grumble as of an old man coughing. I waited. It was so. I moved anxiously lest the boards of the stairs should creak.

In the passage above I moved left. I pushed at a door (I had no doubt now as to *which* door) and entered. I did not switch on the light. I knew exactly how the furniture was. The bed against the wall and on it a pink counterpane. Next to the bed a small table and a lamp with a silver-grey shade. A round tin box covered with an old print of Westminster Abbey that held biscuits. Above the bed two pictures, prints from Hogarth's 'Marriage.' Above the fireplace, two birds in Lalique. A wardrobe of dark mahogany. An easy cushioned chair coloured rose.

I switched on the light. The room was as I have said. I threw off my coat and waistcoat. Then, staring at the bed, breathing fiercely, I pulled my shirt up over my head . . .

NARRATIVE 2

1

. . . The war has lasted two months now and I caused quite a stir at Leila's tea-party yesterday afternoon by what I said. Eve was there, the

Parrott, Richard Thorne, Leila's meek-and-mild little brother (who is, so everyone says, the image of what I used to be!), and several pious ladies and gentlemen, the sort that Leila likes to have around her, and Mr. Birthwaite of St. Peter's, a stout, muscular clergyman, the sporting 'Play Football for Christ' clergyman, the kind that I detest.

Well, there we all were, in Leila's little house (she has come back to Seaborne after all), something of the cottage-bungalow variety not far from the sea. There she lives with one little maid most modestly. Her brother Richard, who was in the East so long, stays with her and pays her expenses partly, I imagine.

I think that I disliked that fellow on sight and now I positively hate him. He knows that I do and there is that sort of secret relation between us. Why do I hate him?

Well, I've become a violent domineering kind of fellow lately and I'm proud of it. How I despise that old miserable John Talbot creeping and crawling about, afraid of his wife, afraid of his son, trying to write ridiculous feeble books that no one could possibly want, afraid of a dirty story, of companionship with rough-and-ready chaps like Cheeseman and Bob Steele. Yes—nor am I afraid of Tunstall's ghost any more. I can see that I was altogether wrong when I thought so badly of Tunstall. I can see now that he was only teasing me half the time. I hate myself—or rather my old self—for pushing him over that Cliff, and that is why I think I detest Richard, Leila's brother.

It's almost as though *he* pushed Tunstall over. Physically he's just the man I used to be but, thank heaven, am no longer. Other people have noticed it. He's got no eyebrows and is pasty-faced and has a thin, poor physique. He won't touch whisky or any intoxicating liquor and is as quiet as a mouse, sitting in a corner of the room without speaking, just as I used to do.

He gave me a start the other day when he asked me whether I'd read any of Gissing's novels and whether I didn't like him. I said that I used to like them once but had grown out of them.

I added, in that rough way that I like to put on with people who are frightened of me, that I hadn't much time for reading now and that anyway Gissing seemed to me a miserable sort of writer. I liked a novel to have some meat in it. He looked surprised at that and said he'd asked me because he thought my novels showed Gissing's influence.

'My novels!' I answered, laughing. 'Don't you mention them to *me!* I'm thoroughly ashamed of them. If I had time to write now I'd put some meat into them—a bit of skirt, that's what people want in a novel.'

I felt in a sort of rage with him because somewhere deep down in me I felt ashamed of what I'd said, and I *hate* to be ashamed of myself and I'd kill anyone who made me feel so.

My fierceness frightened him and he went away without saying anything.

For one reason, anyway, I like to be with him. Looking at him reminds me of what I *used* to be. I can estimate it the more truly because we're about the same height, he and I. How I've filled out! It's astonishing. It's not only that I'm broader and thicker altogether, but you'd imagine I'd been using some restorer by the way my hair grows. On the head, my eyebrows, quite thick on my chest—everywhere that a manly man ought to have hair! I've got a chest for hair to grow on, too! *And* a bit of a stomach if the truth *must* come out.

I think it is due to the open-air life I lead. None of that skulking about in that silly shop any more. Eve manages that entirely. I play golf, I shoot, I fish. You may say it's late for a man to begin all these things, but Basil Cheeseman, Steele, and some of the others have shown me the way—yes, and to other things, too!

All in the space of less than a year, and if you ask me I'd say that it's never too late for a man to learn. Not that I'm always in good spirits. No one is! And I drink a bit too much. Then I've been developing the devil of a temper lately. There's something in me beyond my control, and when I see red I often wish I didn't. But there! We can only live once and while we live let us enjoy ourselves.

At any rate, whatever else I am, I'm not a hypocrite. What I mean I say!

It was the hypocrisy that made me so bloody mad at Leila's when they were discussing this war. Of course, down in this little place, except for the black-out we haven't felt the war yet at all. People are all saying it's a phoney war, not like a real war at all.

They were all sitting round as usual, clinking the tea-cups, nibbling little bits of bread and butter and saying all the usual things—that Hitler and Goering and the others were emissaries of the Devil, and that we were all saints and the saviours of civilization.

I listened for a bit and then I could stand it no longer. I said that what we were was a nation of hypocrites. What right had we to stop Germany from expanding if she wanted to? We had more than half the globe, anyway, and how had we got it? By plundering, thieving, bullying natives. For my part, I thought Hitler was a fine fellow. He had brought his people up from miserable subjection to be a great people again. He was clever and knew what he was about, while we were stupid and decadent. All that Hitler did was to go for what he wanted. After all, he had the strength and was using it.

'I suppose,' the parson said in that gooseberry-in-the-throat sort of voice that parsons have, 'you'd say that Might is Right—a wicked doctrine and straight from the Devil.'

'I don't know about the Devil,' I said, in that laughing boisterous voice that I enjoy using, 'but I do know that we're a nation of hypocrites and if Germany defeats us we deserve it.'

There was a shocked silence after that and only Leila said: 'You wouldn't have said that once, John.'

Now I like Leila. I have always liked her, but of late that liking has greatly increased. For one thing she is, I think, the only person in the world who really understands me. She is certainly more understanding of me than my wife.

I am not, of course, in the least in love with her. I am keeping this journal day by day, all that remains of my old writing habit, and I may say that at this actual moment of writing I am more at ease with her than with any other human being alive. The feeling that I have for her, queerly enough, is rather as though I had been married to her for many years. I have for her that sense of companionship that comes from long mutual and physical contact, and that is certainly peculiar because we have been nothing more than casual friends. There was, of course, that rather absurd scene with her in London when I was sentimental and wept. But at that time my old self, which I regard now as feminine and ridiculous, was uppermost. It would take something very remarkable to make me weep to-day.

When, however, she said that once I would not have spoken as I did I was abashed. I was angry with myself for being so and left as soon as possible.

My outspokenness about Hitler has been reported and I am aware that numbers of people in this silly little town now look on me unfavourably. Not that I give a damn! When I was meek and mild and took care to offend nobody, they said that I was a milk-sop. Now that I show some spirit and speak my mind, they say that I was better as I used to be. Well, let them say! If this town is typical of England, then I declare, and I don't care who hears me, that England is finished and done for and deserves to be beaten by the Germans, whose courage and resource and daring I cannot but admire!

I must say something now about my home affairs. The other evening, I had a quarrel with Eve and some curious things were said during it.

Eve loves me and sometimes I wish she did not. I know that if once I had written this down on paper I should have been wild with joy, about her loving me, I mean. I am sure she has nothing to complain of me as a husband, but after all, when you have been married for as long as we have, it is only natural and right that the physical part of marriage should take a secondary place. Other things are of more importance. But whereas that side of marriage is of less importance to me it seems to be all-important to Eve. The plain fact is that she is absurdly jealous and would like to make scenes every night if I allowed her to. She is for ever wanting to know where I have been; what I have done; to whom I have spoken.

The other evening after dinner, when I was happily enjoying a whisky and soda, she put her hand over the decanter.

'No, John—you've had enough for tonight.'

I could scarcely believe my ears.

'Who says?' I asked.

'I do,' she answered. I could see that she was a little frightened and I like her to be frightened.

'Oh, you do, do you?' I said.

'Yes. . . . Oh, John, do listen to me! I've been wanting to say something for weeks!'

She always looks her best when she has tears in her eyes. That excites something in me. She is like one of those old Virginal Priestesses who is suddenly human and pleading.

'Go ahead!' I said, stretching out my legs.

'There was a time,' she began, 'when I wanted you to be more dashing, more of a man, to go about more . . . but now . . .'

'Well—now?' I asked her mockingly.

'I haven't the right to speak, perhaps. You know what you're doing and I must confess that I *am* much fonder of you than I used to be. You're much more of a man—physically and in every way. But need you—don't be angry with me—drink as much as you do? Need you always be with men like Cheeseman and Bob Steele and young Romilly? Then you offend people by the way you speak to them, swearing and saying you're pro-German and things like that. I know I'm jealous. I never used to be. But then you never used to look at other women—I sometimes wished you did. Sometimes you're so angry with me and over nothing at all. I'm sure it's drinking makes you

282

lose your temper. Sometimes when you're angry you look terrible. I feel as though you weren't the old John at all, your face is so changed. Don't you think—please, please, don't be angry—that if you drank less and went back to your writing again you'd be happier, that we'd all be, you, I and Archie? I'm sure Archie loves you, but he's afraid of you, you know he is. And I'm afraid of you sometimes, too. And you're not really happy—we none of us are.'

She ended breathlessly, her eyes beseeching mine, and she put her hand on my arm.

I did what all proper husbands would do. I poured myself out another glass of whisky.

Then I said, quietly: 'Have you quite done?'

She nodded. 'Yes—we've always been honest with one another, John—said what we think.'

'Yes—well, I'm going to say what *I* think. If you don't like it you can bloody well lump it. That's coarse and vulgar, I know, but then I *am* coarse and vulgar. I wasn't once, and you didn't like it. I am now and you don't like that either.'

(It's agreeable to write dialogue again. There's something in me, some remnant of my old life, that sometimes cries out for the novel-writing again. Well, if I ever *do* write another novel it will be a bit more lusty than the earlier ones were!)

'Not that *I* care what you think. For years and years, I was your slave, wasn't I? Do you remember our coming away from a party at Tunstall's house once and your being angry with me for not liking him and threatening to leave me? As a matter of fact, you were right that evening. Tunstall wasn't such a bad sort, only I was such a damned prig that I took him too seriously. But do you remember that when you threatened to leave me I broke down and said I'd do anything to please you—crawled in fact—and how you graciously forgave me like a queen her slave? Do you remember that, Eve? You had your time, you know, and a grand time it was. But the worm *will* turn—and *when* it turns, it changes. This worm isn't a worm any longer—see? Nothing like a worm. Quite a different animal.'

I thought this a good speech and sat back in my chair, pushing my stomach out and feeling thoroughly pleased with myself. I had been drinking quite a bit. But, after all, it was Eve who astonished me, for she didn't answer anything that I had been saying, but asked, very quietly, this question:

'John, what was it you did to Jim Tunstall?'

283

I can tell you that that astonished me. All the questions and whispers about Tunstall's death had died down by now. No one had mentioned him for months. There seemed to be a sort of conspiracy *not* to mention him.

I myself hadn't thought about it, and the sense that I used to have about his being near to me, the horror, the suspense, the terror—all that had gone—yes, really gone except for some unhappy moments about which I will have something to say in a minute. The *great* change in me now is that I admire Tunstall instead of hating him. By God, I do! He seems to me now the only man who woke this place up a bit. You may say that in a small way I copy him. Basil Cheeseman says, laughing, that I *became* Jim Tunstall as soon as I put his scarab ring on my finger. 'Why, you're getting to be the spitting image of him,' he said, and we had a good laugh about it. I had an absurd and most dangerous temptation to say, 'I can't be Tunstall because I killed him'—a crazy thing to say to the Rat, who isn't to be trusted a yard. Although I like him, mind you. He is damned good company; he knows the hell of a lot about everyone in this place and *nothing* to their credit—and, by heaven, he *can* grow roses!

He said that to me about being like Tunstall yesterday when he handed me over Scandal.

'It's no use my keeping him,' he said. 'The damned dog is never happy except when he's with you. It's a funny thing. He was just the same when he was with Tunstall. He's a one-man dog, I suppose.'

As a matter of fact, Scandal was lying at my feet when I had this row with Eve. He's a ripping little dog, his hair curly like shavings and his whiskers as strong and virile as though made of wire. He looks at me with the most loving eyes and yet he's as sporting a dog as ever I've seen. He obeys me as though he were my familiar spirit. A funny thing, too, that he'll have nothing to say to Eve or Archie. He's quite polite and endures their pattings and strokings, but he's as distant from them as the parson is from me.

I'm sitting here writing and it's late, and I know that Eve is in bed unable to sleep, waiting for me to come to her. That gives me considerable satisfaction.

I must return to my quarrel, from which I have considerably wandered. I didn't answer her question at once. I should have done, but that uncomfortable and maddening consciousness I have (I shall speak of it later) of something unhappy, lonely, desolate (silly words these, and most unfit for a man to use), came up into my throat and choked my words.

At last I said: 'What *do* you mean? What did I do to Tunstall? Why, nothing, of course. Do you think I killed him?'

'No . . . not that.' I saw that she was picking her words. 'But you met him that night. I am quite certain that you did. And it was from that night that you changed, and it was from that night that I began to love you. It was from that night that we all began to be unhappy, Archie and you and I. You have changed more and more. Your face has changed, your voice, your habits—everything. You know it as well as anyone. You don't love me anymore, either.'

'Of course, I do,' I said.

'You do?' She caught me up eagerly. 'Oh, John, promise me that and I can stand anything. Promise me that you love me, even though it's in a different way. Do you—do you really?'

Everyone knows that there is nothing in the world more exasperating than to be asked again if you love someone whom in fact you love no longer.

I *like* Eve, of course. She is a fine woman, and I admire her when she is brisk and business-like and unsentimental. But love? I don't, I fancy, love anybody—unless it's my son. Yes, I love Archie and must admit that I have a damned funny way of showing it sometimes.

Anyway, I was exasperated and irritated and had been drinking, so I'm afraid I swore at her and said a lot of things I shouldn't have said.

I spoke with great bitterness and I think that I had a right to. I said that she accused me of being changed, but what about herself? Did she realise what her behaviour had been during the last months? That I couldn't go anywhere, speak to anybody, without her wanting to know all about it.

'It isn't true! It isn't true! I haven't . . . I don't . . .' she burst in. Her eyes were fixed on me, pleading, begging me, but I felt no temptation towards mercy. I had better put my foot down once and for all. Every man knows that it's a case of either the husband or the wife. I was master here now whatever I had once been, and I intended to go on being master.

I'm not a sadist (or only as much of one as any real man is), but I have noticed lately that my blood begins to rage and my heart beat thickly over quite small occasions. There *is* something in what Eve says. When I am excited or angry I *know* that my face changes. I can feel that my eyes are bloodshot and a heavy pulse beats in my temples. I like to feel this. I feel masterful and ready to beat the world.

All this about feelings! And I notice that I have repeated the word 'feel' in three adjacent sentences, which the careful John Talbot of a year ago would never have done. Not that I care. I'm not writing this for publication! I simply get rid of my superfluous energy this way. Well, I told her that I wasn't going to be spied on. I should go where I pleased and see whom I pleased. I was answerable to nobody. Did she understand that?

Yes, she said. Oh, yes, she did.

Another thing, I went on—she must understand once and for all that I wasn't a sentimental man. I might have been once, but I wasn't now. Actually, it was she who had taught me not to be by being so cold for so long and refusing my advances when I offered them. It would be better, perhaps, if we had separate rooms. She broke out at that and begged, implored me not to do that. As a matter of fact, this had been in my mind for some time and I determined to settle the question here and now. I told her that I could have a bed in my working-room very easily and that I would see about it. There was nothing to make a fuss about—we could see each other when we liked just as we had always done. I was often out late and it was much better not to disturb her.

'I lie awake—' she began.

'Well, you're not to lie awake,' I said. 'That is just what is so irritating.' It's maddening, I told her, coming back at one or two in the morning and finding her waiting for me. Besides, most modern married people had separate rooms, nowadays.

Then there was the question of Archie. How dare she say that I frightened him? The fact was that she had fussed altogether too much over Archie. She would make a regular mollycoddle of him. I was determined to stop it. It was funny to remember, I remarked, that it was she who had wanted to send Archie to school and I who had wished to keep him at home. Well, I had given in about that, hadn't I? He had gone to school, which was what she wanted, and yet she fussed over him when he was at home, making him quite unfit for being with other boys.

She replied, in a voice so low that I could scarcely catch her words, that all that she meant was that she wanted him to love me and when I was angry—

That infuriated me. If she interfered between Archie and me, I told her, she'd have to look out. She'd get something she wasn't expecting. That was something I wouldn't stand. She'd better look out! She'd better look out!

I'll admit that I was rather excited at this point and shouted a bit.

Then she began to cry. I can't stand it when women cry. It does something to me. It excites me. I got up and stood close to her. I didn't say a word. I saw the chairs and the table in a blur—

She sat there, looking up at me as though she were waiting for something. Scandal, I remember, raised his head and looked at me. I went out of the room.

I've recalled every word and every detail of this little scene because it gives me pleasure to do so.

I have now come to the time when I should write a clear and honest account of my strange affair with Bella Scorfield. Honest? If I'm not that I'm not anything. I'm not ashamed of anything I do or say or feel. Why should I be? I am so honest that I'm not going to deny that something curious goes on in my brain that I don't at all understand. Insanity is a big loose word. I know that for a long time I was afraid that I was going insane, but after that visit to the Scorfields' house when they were away, I threw over my scruples and fears altogether and became the altered man everyone says I am.

But between myself and this paper I'm not altered as completely as I would wish; I wouldn't like anyone to know that, and especially not Eve. The fact is there's something of the old man imprisoned in me still. I have quite unaccountable moods of the old, weak senti-mental idiot I used to be—moods when it is almost as though some-thing were imprisoned in me trying to get out. I crush them quickly enough, of course, and after they are ended I hate myself for indulging them. Just as in the old days I used to hate poor Jim Tunstall for stir-ring just the opposite in me. I can see now that he was trying to make a man of me. If I'd realised that earlier, we might have been friends in-stead of enemies. If he was around now we would be friends, I'm sure.

I understand, though, why it is that I dislike Leila's brother, Rich-ard, so much. He reminds me whenever I see him of what I *used* to be! He's for ever apologizing and he's so polite that it makes you sick. When I'm sarcastic with him—as I generally am—he blushes all over—exactly as I used to do.

And that's why I hate him. I don't want to be reminded a dozen times a day of the fool that I must have seemed to other people. And how I loathe that milk-and-water, down-on-your-hams, 'I won't touch you if you don't touch me' kind of attitude. He's so good and virtuous! A sort of saint! He even wears the kind of clothes I used

287

to—rather shabby blue or black. G-rrr! If he doesn't look out I'll twist his neck one day!

Now I must tell the truth—amusing and instructive to me to see it all put down on to paper—of my affair with Bella Scorfield. I confess that I'm proud of the clever fashion in which I conducted it. I was a fool about women once—but now—oh, boy!

Very soon after Jim Tunstall's death, Bella began to take an interest in me. She was lonely, I don't doubt, poor thing. Wanted *some* man's embraces, didn't matter whose!

But that isn't quite true. She loved Jim Tunstall in her own brainless, common, passionate way. Often, after a while, she said that I reminded her of him. It is true that with all my outdoor life I began to thicken out and take on a sort of tan.

She told me only last night that she couldn't ever bear skinny men and that she had always liked me and admired my brains but had hated the idea of being kissed by me because she'd feel my cheekbones.

'And now you're quite plump,' she said, pinching me just as you would a chicken in a shop. She's pleased, too, that I have hair on my chest. Any proper man ought to have, she said.

Now the odd thing is that from the moment I gave poor Tunstall that push over the Cliff, she began to be afraid of me. Basil Cheeseman had told her that I had had something to do with Tunstall's death or, at any rate, knew more than I would say. She wasn't a brainy girl but she told me that from the first I was always reminding her of Tunstall.

I didn't tell her, of course, of the night that I had entered their house. That would have sounded altogether too mad, but I did wonder at the ridiculous fuss that I made over that visit. After all, Tunstall had given me a few details of that bedroom when he had given me also details of certain other things and I had subconsciously remembered them. No, but what fascinated me was that I should go back into that house and do *exactly* what Jim Tunstall had done—repeat one of his evenings in every sort of particular. At the very suggestion of this to myself my brain would grow heated, my heart hammer in my throat. I would grow weak at the knees with desire.

So passionate became my longing for this event that I would lie beside Eve at night thinking of it, going over again and again every detail. Why did I want it so desperately? It was not only Bella, not only the sense of adventure. It was, I suppose, a hark-back to the day when Tunstall had taken me by the arm and whispered in my ear.

It was, also, something, something . . . a reminiscence? What other lives have we lived? Do we not sometimes repeat an experience that we have had in one of them? Who can tell? In any case Bella gradually fell in love with me, but never lost her fear of me. Then came a time when I knew that she was ready to do anything that I asked her. But I waited. I savoured the anticipation. I did not wish to lose a moment of it.

Then came the occasion. I asked her.

'You know that I am in love with you, Bella.'

'I like you, too, very much.' She went on: 'I've been lonely since Jim was killed.'

'Don't say "was killed,"' I said. 'Poor fellow, I've missed him a lot.'

'And you used to say you hated him! How you've changed—and it's since you've changed I've liked you so much. You often remind me of Jim. Perhaps that's why.'

We were sitting at a little table in the corner of the 'Paradise.' I can't remember what she said after that, but I explained to her exactly what I wanted. She is a girl with a full bosom and high colour and fair hair. She's what a woman ought to be, full of good, warm blood. You could see the blood mounting in her cheeks now. She said—wasn't there something nasty about it? I said, no, of course not. I said that Jim had told me so often about it. He'd understand. Perhaps he'd been watching us and giving us his blessing.

I could see that she didn't care how I made love to her as long as I did it. She had been wanting exactly that for months.

'But what will your wife say?' she asked.

'Oh, she can lump it,' I answered, looking her full in her bold eyes. I felt as though I had had her in my arms many times, but not for a long while. Of course, it wasn't so. It was only my fancy. But I was triumphant in a wild sort of way as I looked at her. We arranged all the details.

I told Basil Cheeseman about it. I'll confess that I have fallen greatly under his influence of late. There was a time, I know, when I didn't like him at all, even hated him. I seem, when I look back, to have hated him for years. I wouldn't say that I like him now. I don't think anyone could. And certainly, I don't trust him. But I don't know a better companion anywhere; he's a wonderful fellow for bawdy stories that really *are* funny; he can drink anyone under the table, and he's ready for any sort of adventure. I am not sure, though, that I can account for his influence over me. He's a great lad for ferreting out people's weaknesses and then making use of them—like Hitler. But, for some reason or other, I'm a proper mystery to him. He knew Tunstall better than anyone else did, and he keeps telling me that being with me is like being with Tunstall all over again. His favourite question is: 'How the hell did you know about Brindisi?' It seems that some while ago I said something about an adventure in Brindisi that only he and Tunstall knew. He says that I often tell him things that only he and Tunstall knew—which is, of course, nonsense.

I frighten him sometimes and I'm glad I do, for that keeps up my self-respect. He's such a miserable physical specimen with his little moustache and prominent teeth and red hair and eternal pipe. I could catch him round the throat with one hand and throttle him easily. I nearly do sometimes. He says that Tunstall, when he was drunk, used to threaten him with the same thing. 'I always told him,' he said, 'that he was born to be hanged.'

But when I told him about Bella he was for once quite shocked.

'I say, Talbot—she was Tunstall's girl, you know.'

'What the hell does that matter?'

'Oh, I don't know—but going to the same room—everything the same—'

'He shouldn't have told me so much about it,' I said, laughing.

He looked frightened—a thing he seldom does. I asked him why.

'You look—oh, hell! I don't know how you look! I tell you what it is, Talbot—your eyes have the most unpleasant sort of stare in them sometimes.'

So, just for fun, I put my hand on his shoulder. I felt him quiver all over, but he didn't say anything and he didn't move.

The evening came all right. It was three nights ago as a matter of fact. There was a thin baby moon and a clear sky. When I got to the house it was as silent as the grave. The lawn was like milk. I'm not going in for a lot of description. I leave that to my old writing days. But I could paint it, I think (I've come on a lot in my painting)—with the house so dark and still and all those beastly laurels. I hate masses of laurel close up against a house. They seem to speak of death. They are so chill and leathery and seem to have a creepy life of their own. I was anything but chill myself. I was burning all over and my hands shook. I pushed up the window, climbed into the room, took off my shoes and went up the stairs. I opened her door and there she was, sitting up in bed waiting for me. I took off my coat and waistcoat and then grinned at her. Didn't I just grin?

★★★★★★

290

Now one thing I want to make perfectly clear—I am not writing all this to justify myself. I write this down, I suppose, for my own benefit because no one but myself is ever going to read it. Why should I want to assure myself that I'm not justifying myself? Am I uneasy? To be quite honest, I suppose I am a little. Everyone in this place, except my few close friends, seems to have turned against me. I have been aware of it, of course, for some time, but it was the Parrott that gave me the full account. With her sharp little eyes and tinny rasping voice she informed me, first, that I was a pro-German by my own confession; secondly, that I kept bad company; thirdly, that I drank too much and flirted with women too much; fourthly, that I ill-treated my wife and son. She ended up: 'I used to think you a cissy, John Talbot. Now I wouldn't like to soil my lips with what I think you. You can knock me down if you like.' I didn't do that, but I told her in very coarse terms what *she* was, of her scandalmongering and backbiting, her spying curiosity as to who slept with whom. I told her that if she'd had any sexual experience herself she wouldn't be half so interested, and that she wanted a thorough good raping, but, I said, she'd have the devil of a time in finding anyone willing to rape her. Then I looked at her and laughed and she was really frightened—for the first time in her life, I should think!

However, when I was alone in my room again I was not happy—something inside me was not happy. As I sat there thinking, I felt a great misery rising within me, something apart from myself as though it were quite another personality. I began to wish that I was still as I had once been. I felt as though something within me was imprisoned and was fighting to get out. 'Let me out! Let me out!' some part of myself was urging.

We all have moods of this kind and I put this one down to that interfering old Poll Parrott, a bit of indigestion, I shouldn't wonder, and certainly to my having drunk too much lately. The trouble is nowadays that I don't know how much I'm drinking. Then I get muzzy and drink some more without knowing I'm doing it. Anyway, it's been a rotten week and I'm not happy. It's somebody's fault that I'm not, and when I find out who it is, I'll let them know it.

And this brings me to a little scene I had yesterday evening with Archie.

Archie's a nice-looking little boy but too girlish for my tastes. He is very thin and fair-coloured and sometimes looks the baby that I'm afraid he still is. The fact is that I myself must have mollycoddled him too much in the early years. And yet I used to be exasperated by him when he shrank from me. I can remember how his shoulder-blades used to shrink when I touched him. I suppose he wanted a more sporting father because I remember how immediately he took to Tunstall and his purple corduroys, and Tunstall promised to teach him to draw.

With me now he is very different at different times. He *is* a bit afraid of me, and because I love him, I like him to be, but I don't want him to be afraid of me all the time. The fact is he's a bit of a prig and doesn't like it when I swear or am drunk or show him a funny drawing I've made. He's very like I used to be, with no sense of humour.

It happened that I was in my work-room, sitting on my bed drawing a bit, when I heard him pass, so I called him in. When I saw him standing there in the doorway, with his fair hair and blue eyes, a great rush of love came into my heart and I caught him to me and kissed him. I suppose my breath stank a bit, for I felt him withdraw inside his skin and that irritated me.

However, I held him between my legs and asked him how he'd been getting on. All right, he said. He really has the complexion of a girl and blushes like a girl. His body is so thin and fragile between my arms that I could crush the breath out of him as easy as nothing.

'How are the games getting on?' I asked. He wasn't awfully good at games and didn't like them very much.

What did he like? I asked.

He liked best drawing and reading.

What did he read? I asked.

Oh, he liked Southey's *Life of Nelson* and a book about Garibaldi and the *Idylls of the King* and a *Life of Scott* who went to the Pole and *Greenmantle*. He poured out a list of titles—those are some that I remember. Holding him with my arms I gave him a lecture then, how reading was all very well but it was no use being a book-worm at his age.

'You used to read, Daddy,' he said. 'An awful lot.'

'I've seen the error of my ways,' I answered him. 'What I like is the open air—shooting, fishing, and swimming. I want you to be good at games, see?'

'I'm afraid I never shall be,' he said.

'Of course, you never will be,' I said, shaking him a little, 'if you *say* you won't be. You've got to be. That's what you're at school for.'

Then I saw that he was frightened. When he's frightened his mouth

292

trembles and I can't bear to see that. It makes me savage. So, I said:

'Have you got any of your drawings here?'

Yes, he had, and he ran off to get them. When he returned and showed them to me I was really greatly pleased. He could draw. There was no doubt at all about that. They were drawings influenced, I could see, by his mother's liking for the Pre-Raphaelites. He drew knights and horsemen riding by the sea and Lancelot in front of a tower.

'Now see what I'm drawing,' I said. I shouldn't have done it, of course. I think there's a sort of devil in me sometimes. In any case he blushed crimson and he turned his head away.

'Don't you like it?' I said, laughing and half ashamed of myself, too.

'No. No. I don't. I don't!' he cried, and ran from me, actually pushing me with his hand.

I heard him run down the passage, closing the door behind him.

At any rate, whatever anyone else thinks, Scandal adores me. He is a splendid little dog. I know, of course, that you can say about dogs that they love you because you feed them and protect them. I know, too, that they flatter you because they pay no attention to your ill-humours and forgive you any unkindness. But I think there is more than this between Scandal and myself. He knows, I am convinced, what I am thinking and why I do what I do. In any case he prefers me to anyone else and is not ashamed to be seen with me. Indeed, he will not leave my side.

Then he is so clean, so strong, and able to look after himself in any situation. He is sporting and fearless and gives no one any trouble. About how many human beings can you say this?

He was with me two afternoons ago when I had an encounter with Richard, Leila's brother.

I was walking down through the little wood above the town. There was frost in the air and a cold, remote sun, yellow as an orange. I was going down the path, swinging my stick and feeling as fit as anything. Scandal was scurrying and sniffing among the leaves. Richard was coming up the path and with a hurried 'Good afternoon' would have passed me. I was in a good humour, though, and was determined to hold him. When I saw his pale, anxious face and his nervous manner I felt a kind of disgust. What right has the man to fear me? I have never done him any harm!

'What are you cutting me for?' I asked him, laughing.

Then, driven by some impulse, I said to him what Jim Tunstall had so often said to me: 'You can't escape me, you know.'

'What do you mean?' he asked. 'I don't want to escape you.'

I stood with my legs spread, filling the path and swinging my stick a little to and fro.

'Yes, you do. Look here—I've wanted to ask you for some time— we're alone and I've got you at my mercy, so to speak. Why do you dislike me so much?'

He didn't answer. I could see his mild anxious eyes looking round to see whether he couldn't pass.

'Tell me why. Leila's one of my best friends. She doesn't dislike me. Why should you?'

'I don't know you,' he said.

'Don't you?' I laughed some more and came closer to him so that my hand almost touched his waistcoat buttons.

'You soon will. I'm determined that we shall be friends. Leila's brother? But of course, we must be friends.'

He still said nothing.

'No but tell me. Is it because of my political opinions?'

He said then, slowly, as though he had realised that there was no escape:

'It's true that I don't like you, Talbot. I like very few people, I've lived so long in the East that I'm not accustomed to English life, per- haps.'

'Well, even if you don't like me,' I said, my temper rising, 'that's no reason why you should be rude to me whenever we meet.'

'I didn't know that I was. I might ask you the same. I've seen you looking at me sometimes as though you hated me. I can't think why. I often wonder about it. Why don't you leave me alone? I'm not your sort. I can't be of the slightest interest to you.'

'Oh, aren't you?' I answered. 'That's all you know. Aren't I a novel- ist? Everyone interests me.'

He said: 'I've read your novels. You don't seem to me the man who wrote those books.'

'Oh, don't I? Well, I did write them all the same. In those days I was the sort of man you are now—always creeping about, afraid to swear or have a drink. That's why I'm interested in you, perhaps. You're like the man I used to be, and thank God am not anymore.'

But he had no spirit. If anyone had talked to me like that I'd have knocked him down.

'That's strange,' he said. 'I don't think people do change. Certain traits develop in people, of course, as they get older.' Then he said, almost defiantly: 'Would you mind letting me pass? It's cold.'

I looked at him then and wanted to knock him down. I can't abide these meek-and-mild little men who are always wanting to get out of your way. I looked at him and he stepped back.

'All right,' I said. 'I'm not going to touch you. I only asked a civil question. But if you say anything to Leila against me, I'll hear of it and I'll know what to do.'

'Of course, I shan't say anything to Leila. I never mention you to her. When I said I disliked you, it was perhaps too strong. I simply don't know you. Your affairs are no business of mine.'

'All the same,' I said fiercely, 'you listen to everything that's said about me, don't you? How I drink and womanize and ill-treat my wife and am pro-German. I bet you enjoy it all.'

How I hated him then, nervously plucking at his coat, fear in every part of him, looking at the darkening wood, expecting me to murder him then and there, I daresay.

I stood aside.

'Watch out!' I said. 'If I hear you've been telling Leila anything—'

He slipped up the path like a scurrying rabbit. Scandal came jumping up at me, pleading with me to go on with our walk. I bent down and pulled his ears and he licked my cheek. Then he barked like mad and seemed altogether wild with joy.

2

It's all very well, but I must take a pull on myself. I'm afraid of nobody and nothing. Not of the Devil himself. But I *am* afraid of something. I write down what I've written down here pretty often— that I'm drinking too much. Yes, but what good does writing it down do? Of course, I can stop it when I want to. Cheeseman says it's because I've taken to it rather late in life that I indulge. But he's the Devil at my elbow. There isn't a thing that I want to do and know I shouldn't but he encourages me.

All the same it's not drink I'm afraid of. Is it the past? He's a poor sort of creature who's afraid of his past. The past's past. The past *is* past.

But I had a look the other day at the earlier journal that I used to keep. It made me sick. I couldn't read more than a dozen pages. All that pious stuff, saying one's prayers, and then that ridiculous hatred of poor old Tunstall. Am I afraid, then, of what I did to *him?* Not on your life! No one will ever know and he teased me into it. Besides, I don't feel that Tunstall reproaches me for it. Oh, the dead *are* dead—every sensible man knows that. Tunstall's physically dead all right, but I can't feel that he's gone, altogether. And if he isn't gone, what crime have I committed? *And,* if he isn't gone, he bears me no malice. I'm quite sure of that. What am I afraid of, then? Well—imagining things—if I'm quite frank with myself. It isn't the pink mice that you see when you've got D.T's, but it's something very like it. What I keep imagining I see is either Richard Thorne or—myself. Myself as I used to be. That's crazy enough, isn't it? Oh, I know it is! I know it is! This is nonsense that I'm writing. I'll give it up, chuck the thing. But it relieves me putting things down in black and white. The truth is I'm not living the life I ought to. Heartburn simply terrible, and none of those digestive pills do me any good. My eyes are bloodshot. My hands tremble. I'm going to cut out the drink. I'll tell Cheeseman to go to hell. I'll be a bit like the chap I once was, not such a prig, of course, and I'll be damned if I give up Bella. All the same, I've got to get a hold on that temper of mine. I'll be throttling someone one of these days if I'm not careful. But the fact is it doesn't make you happy to let yourself go in every direction. I fancy that there's something in believing in God—even if you *don't* believe, so to speak. It puts you in touch with something or someone. . . .

Well, then—what is it I think I see? A thin, weak figure in a worn blue suit beseeching me with its eyes. It's the eyes that seem so real. They cut right into my gizzards. What is it that he is asking me? To let him go—to release him. Release him from what?

Now see where this is taking me! Plumb crazy! Cut out the drink, Johnny, my boy. Cut out the drink! Oh, Jacko—Isn't that what Tunstall used to call me? Just for fun I'll call it out here in this room in the laughing, teasing voice that Tunstall used—'Jacko! Jacko! Jacko!'

By God, it makes me feel queer—I seem to have caught Tunstall's very accents. A pity the old boy isn't here. He could sing out 'Jacko' as often as he pleased. And *that's* a funny thing to say about the man you murdered!

But now I must get to facts. No nonsense now. Write down things as they are.

Well, two nights ago I was with Bella. I left her about three in the morning. We were neither of us very happy. When I had finished dressing I sat on the edge of the bed and held her hand.

'You were crying in your sleep,' I said.

'Oh, no, was I? . . .' Then she added: 'Go along now, Johnny dear. It's always depressing when it's all over. At least that's how I feel.'

'That's how many people feel,' I answered. 'That's the time you ask yourself why the hell—' I stopped just in time.

But she was quick.

'Why are you so unhappy?' she asked.

'Unhappy?'

'Yes—Jimmy wasn't. He was sulky and cross sometimes. And often he was as savage as anything. But he wasn't unhappy like you are. At least—' She puckered her forehead. 'I don't know. Are *all* men unhappy when they've made love—unhappy or so damned sleepy they don't know what they are?'

I looked at her gloomily.

'I don't care what Tunstall was. Why are you always bringing *him* up?' Then I kissed her. 'We don't really love one another, Bella. I don't think I love anybody but my dog.'

'I tell you what it is, Johnny,' she said, 'you're drinking too much. You don't mind my mentioning it, do you? But you are, really.'

I suddenly caught her arm.

'Wait,' I said. 'You don't hear anybody, do you? It's like somebody crying.'

We both listened.

'It's only the clock, silly,' she said. So, I kissed her and left her.

What I am going to describe now is exactly what *seemed* to happen, but I don't say that it is at all what happened in actuality. In the old days when I fancied myself a writer I thought myself a handsome dab at what the professors call 'psychology.' That earlier journal of mine is full of the stuff and of things I fancied that I saw or heard. I remember that I even fainted on the Cliff one afternoon because of what I thought I saw. I've shaken myself out of all *that* nonsense, which makes my other fancies on this particular morning all the more peculiar. And that is why I want to be minute and exact. Because I won't deny to myself that I was frightened, and I won't allow myself to be frightened. Do you hear that, you miserable, pitiful-looking, lamb-like scarecrow? I don't believe in ghosts or shadows or anything that is dead. When you're dead, you're *dead*. Do you hear? *DEAD*.

The odd thing was that I had drunk nothing but water since lunch on the day previous. I never touch anything intoxicating before I pay Bella one of my visits because she doesn't like it. One wants to please her when one can. It's a little thing to do—yet it's damned difficult sometimes. So, it wasn't that. It wasn't liquor.

Anyway, the fact remains that when I stood outside her bedroom

297

door in my stockinged feet I didn't like it. Didn't like what? I don't know. We had both been pretty depressed, and as I stood there hesitating, I wondered how long it would last. It wasn't real love, of course, on either side. I knew what real love was because I had once loved Eve. The real thing is as unlike the sham thing as a diamond is to a piece of glass. Is that sentimental? I don't think so. Ask the roughest tough in Dartmoor Prison and he'll tell you it's true enough. The worst of the other thing—the thing that isn't love, is that if you go in for it, it's just like drink. The more you have the more you want. You want that freshness, that newness. The bloom's off as soon as you touch it. I suppose that that was why we were both sad the other morning—because we knew that once again we had been deceived. It wasn't the real thing. One more experience and we were further from the real thing than ever. Now this is the sort of thing I *used* to write and despise even thinking—so let me get to the facts.

When I had been sitting on Bella's bed I fancied that I heard someone crying. That gives you a sort of a shock in a house that is as silent as the grave, when everyone is asleep at three o'clock in the morning. And certainly, when we both listened we heard nothing. I can tell you also that there is something *very* uncomfortable when two people listen together in the middle of the night. The sudden silence filling the room you're both in thrusts on you all sorts of sounds that you didn't hear before. If I ever write novels again (which I won't) I'll write something about that.

I stood outside the door and listened and again I seemed to hear someone crying. It was very faint and it might have been the drip of a tap or the wind blowing through the wall. No, it certainly wasn't a tap and there was no wind that night. Not a breath. The crying—if it *was* crying—was a hopeless sort of whimpering. But it was not the crying of a child. There was a mature despair in it. In concert with it was the ticking of the clock on the stairs, with that drunken whirr every now and then. Because of the clock I couldn't be sure there was any other sound at all. I decided that there wasn't and I started down the stairs. I was always very careful going down, for, after all, the old woman, Bella's mother, might be awake. Bella had told me that she was sure that she knew all about Jim Tunstall, but she mightn't be greatly pleased if she knew that her daughter had taken another lover so soon after Tunstall's death.

But a stair creaked and I stopped. Against the clock and the beating of my heart (which races madly sometimes) I seemed again to hear that crying. I seemed even to hear words—'Let me go! Let me go!' but that was, of course, nonsense.

I got into the dark room, crossed without touching anything and opened the window. Outside there was a misty, moony greyness.

Here I must be exact as though I were surveying the whole scene with a painter's eyes. While I had crouched down on the room floor, putting on my shoes, I had listened with all possible intensity and had heard no sound at all save the ticking of the clock on the stairs and the mouse-like scratching of a clock in the room where I was. But when I stood on the edge of the lawn and looked about me I was frightened—once again I had that sense of moving outside myself. It is the most grisly feeling in the world, for—if you are not sure of yourself, what are you sure of? I was standing there, looking about me, as though I had never been there before. The laurels made me feel sick. In that misty pallor they looked like a mass of moving fungi advancing on the house. You could swear that they were alive and that they turned their cold, leathery leaves upward as you move your hand. As I stared at them I felt that they might close in on me and their chilly palms move up and hang about my throat and then flap like the fins of fish about my cheeks and against my eyes. I would be blinded then and dragged to my knees. They would tower above me and I would be suffocated under their bloodless, boneless touch.

I write this down to prove to myself how overwrought I was. Not a bit myself. So, it was natural, considering the state that I was in about those laurels, that I should fancy that I saw someone standing in front of a tree on the right corner of the lawn. I stared and felt sure that I was not mistaken. It was Richard Thorne standing there and looking as much like what I used to look as was possible! He was even wearing the silly bowler hat that I used to wear. The hat that Eve was always trying to persuade me to destroy, one of those bowlers with a large crown and a narrow brim. An awful thing that today I wouldn't be seen dead in!

As a matter of fact, I have seen Richard Thorne wearing a bowler—nothing as old-fashioned as I used to wear. But still—bowlers *are* old-fashioned, aren't they?

There he stood, staring at me, his hands hanging at his sides. It was, of course, only the shadows. When I moved forward on to the lawn, he was gone. Only shadows—but when I moved back to my old place near the house, there he was again!

It was time I went home. It was damp and chilly, anyway. For some reason I loathed, that night, the house and everything about it. I even hated the thought of poor Bella. I wanted to be in my own warm bed in my own cosy house. I had a sick feeling that I was never going to reach it. The distance, at that moment, between myself and my home seemed enormous.

So, I started off. But when I had reached the end of the untidy drive and started towards the Common I felt sure that someone was following me. There was gravel on the drive, and after my step there was an echo of my step. I stopped and the echo stopped, which was natural enough. I went on and then, halfway along the path, I heard that beastly crying again. By this time, I could catch the rhythmic beat of the sea and, when you hear the sea, you often hear many other sounds as well. But I stopped and looked back, my heart hammering like a drum. Oh, I may as well confess it! I was as frightened as hell. I was tempted actually to take to my feet and run! I could see no figure, but the light was so uncomfortable, like the fluorescence you see sometimes on the surface of a watery soup, and you couldn't be sure of anything. But as I looked back I seemed to catch again, through the steady beat of the sea, that thin, pitiful voice crying: 'Let me go! Let me go!'

I pulled myself together. What I had got to do was to reach home, to throw off my clothes, climb into bed and sleep, sleep, sleep. I was suddenly infinitely weary and my legs hurt like toothache.

I walked quickly and reached the Common with Shining Cliff at the end of it, poking up its wicked sharp head, razor-edged sheer to the sea.

I almost ran (but not quite) to the Cliff edge. 'Now, no nonsense,' I thought, and I formed the words (or did I?): 'Come on, you dirty coward. Face me if you've got any pluck!'

There *was* a figure there! I'll swear that there was. Alone, isolated on that misted turf, and it seemed to me that now the crying came to me most clearly, so desolate and unhappy. The figure was outlined— the bowler hat, the dark suit, the hanging hands—myself as I used to be, or Richard Thorne—not a penny to choose between them.

Of course, it wasn't so. I have said already that the whole thing was, as I saw clearly later on, a hallucination. But through my fear (for I was still afraid) a rage beat up. Here I was at the very spot where I had thrown Jim Tunstall over. Poor Jim! Why had I done that cruel thing? For I felt it now to be cruel. For the first time I was filled with rage for what I had done—or what my earlier self had done. If Jim were here now we would be friends. I would understand him now, his jokes and jollity and indifference to what people had done to him. And I knew now, with a sudden revelation, why it was that I detested Leila's brother. He reminded me, with every look and movement, yes, and whenever I thought of him, of that miserable, pious, prayer-making, murderous John Talbot I had once been. I had the fantastic notion that if I met that earlier self of mine here and now, I would catch him and hold him and squeeze his miserable, bony throat until there was no life left in it and hurl him over that cliff just as once I had hurled Tunstall. I was mad with fear and rage and violence. I cried: 'Come on, you dirty swine! Come on if you're not afraid!'

Then I heard that miserable wretched crying again—and I took to my feet and ran.

3

Since the morning that I have just described, things have changed for the worse. To hell with the lot of them!—and it gives me considerable satisfaction to write it down. If we are to have air raids over this country (and I must say there are no signs of them as yet) this wouldn't be a bad little place for them to start with. They could destroy the lot as far as I'm concerned—with the exception of Leila and one or two more—and little harm would be done.

Harm? What harm have I ever done *them?* And yet you would think by the way they cold-shoulder and avoid me that I carried cholera germs with me. I'm sure I've tried to be jolly with everyone—especially the women. All right. Be damned to the lot of them. If they don't like me jolly they can have me savage. It's true that I was drunk in 'The Queen's' the other night and made a bit of a noise, but what harm did *that* do anybody?

I understand now something of what Hitler must have felt, ill-treated and spurned and spat upon. A few concentration camps wouldn't do *this* country any harm, if you ask me.

I acknowledge that I am pretty easily irritated these days. Then I have a lot to annoy me. Wherever I go that miserable brother of Leila's is on view. I see him everywhere, always silent in a corner, watching me. One day I shall make him sorry for himself. I've told Cheeseman about him. He agrees that he's a wretched specimen. 'The sort of fellow you used to be yourself,' he said. But none of this is the real trouble. There is something in me, savage, fierce, that won't let me rest. Is it anger with myself that I killed Tunstall? I think it is in a way.

I feel it now with a kind of self-pity, almost as though I had done myself in. But how am I to explain that to anybody? They won't understand! They won't understand! Even Leila doesn't, although I think she knows more about me than anyone else. Strange the notion I have that makes me feel that we have been together for ages. She's plain enough and yet her face is comforting to me. I detest all her silly talk about God and goodness. God? I hate that superstitious nonsense—and yet I listen to her.

Which brings me to Eve. Last night I behaved badly to her. Oh, I know it! I'm sorry. But was there ever any woman so aggravating?

After Archie had gone to bed she said: 'Please, John—don't show Archie any more of those drawings.'

I said: 'What drawings?' although of course I knew.

'You think them funny, I know—and I daresay they're all right for a grown person. But he's only a little boy and—he hates it.'

That made me angry. As though I'm not as well able to look after Archie as she is!

'Who says he hates it?' I asked.

'He's very loyal to you. He wouldn't say anything. But I know he does.'

'Oh, you know he does, do you?'

I was sitting near to her. I dropped my paper and took Scandal on my lap to hide the trembling of my hands. He can't abide to be petted, but he'll let me do anything to him.

She answered at last: 'I think we'd better go away for a little, Archie and I. We're all very miserable, aren't we? Perhaps it will be better if we go away for a bit.'

'I see,' I said. 'You'll take my son away from me, will you?'

'Only for a little while. A week or two. When the Christmas holidays begin.'

'Well, you won't, do you see? I'm not going to have everyone saying I've driven my wife out of the house. They say bad enough things already. And I'm not going to let you put Archie against me. That's what you want to do, isn't it?'

'No—of course not. What terrible things you say now, John! You'd think we were enemies.'

'Well, we are enemies,' I shouted. 'If you separate me from Archie—if you do that—look out, look out, I tell you!'

I was trembling all over. I tried to pull myself together. Something inside me warned me. Something was praying me not to go too far.

But I could see from her face that she was frightened of the way that I looked. Cheeseman said to me the other day when I was angry in the High Street when someone pushed me: 'By Jove, Talbot, you looked like the Devil just then.'

I can't help my looks, can I? When a man's angry, he looks angry.

I put Scandal down and got up. She got up, too.

'Oh, John!' she said, 'I can't stand it! I can't stand it!' She began to cry. She ought to have known that that's a thing I can't endure.

I struck her. I struck her on the breast. She fell, almost on to her knees. She got up slowly and, still crying, went out of the room.

I shouldn't have done it, I know that. Something in me was very unhappy. I sat there for a long time with Scandal on my knees.

4

Since my night at Bella's and my last quarrel with Eve, things have been moving faster and faster. I feel as though I were being hurried along towards some climax. I dream horrible dreams at night. One especially seems to recur, although I may have dreamed it only once and thought about it afterwards. I am in a prison deep down in the bowels of the earth, naked, chained to a wall sweating with damp. Rats fight their way over my bare flesh. Tunstall, grinning, looks down at me through a grating—'Jacko!' he says softly. 'Jacko!' But then, suddenly, he too is in the prison naked and tied to the wall by the same chain as I. We are so close that it is almost as though our pallid and corrupting flesh mingles. He has the blue tattoo-mark on his right arm. He tries to kill me and I try to kill him. We are bound so closely together that we can hug one another, that we may crush one another. Then slowly his bare chest opens and I begin to be drawn, struggling, screaming, crying, inside. I wake trembling.

It is indeed a vicious circle, for I drink to escape my apprehension which comes from my nerves, and the drinking makes me more nervous and more nervous. I would be better if that spy and murderer Richard Thorne were not watching me at every step. For I have now the conviction that Richard Thorne has somewhere murdered a fellow human being—out in the East perhaps. He has just that skulking hang-dog look. He suspects that I have discovered his secret. Perhaps also he knows mine. But I will put a stop to his plots and his secret following of me and spying upon me. He's the kind of man that poor Jim Tunstall would have despised. He would have been for ever teasing him just as he once teased me.

And this brings me to something that happened yesterday, something of importance. Just after breakfast a letter was brought by hand. It was from Leila. She asked me whether I would come to tea that afternoon as she had something important to say to me. I sent back the message that of course I would.

So, in the afternoon, about four, across to her little house Scandal and I walked. I hesitated at first about taking Scandal with me because he always hates Leila's brother. All his hair goes up. He refuses to have anything to do with him. But I had a kind of hunch that the little pipsqueak would be out. Certainly, he would not be there if he knew I was coming, or not there for me to see. He might, of course, be hiding behind the curtains or peeping through the keyhole.

The sitting-room—light and shining, gay with chrysanthemums, Leila's touch over everything—was quite empty when Scandal and I came into it. Scandal went at once and lay down near the fire, his beautiful head, with its snow-white paper-shaving curls and his military whiskers and his bright, burning, loving, intelligent eyes, raised a little, listening to every sound—I ask you where among any human beings will you find anyone as beautiful and modest, as intelligent and unboring, as vigorous and unassuming, as loving and as unsentimental? In the firelight he shone roughly as though he were made of some precious metal. I thought to myself—if people trusted and believed in me as this dog does, how temperate and amiable I would be! Then Leila came in, still wearing black for Jim, and once again I felt as I always do when I see her, as though I had known her always, as though we shared a deep intimacy, so deep that no words need be spoken.

While the little maid brought in the tea we spoke commonplaces. She mocked me for my growing stoutness. 'Why, you'll soon be fatter than Jim was! I'm afraid Eve feeds you too well.'

At that moment my scarab ring bit into my finger. I have grown much stouter, there's no doubt of it, and the ring now is so embedded in the flesh that only if it is cut with an instrument shall I ever be able to get it off. Lately I have fancied that the growing flesh has caused it to split where the join of the gold is because on several occasions it has been exactly as though the ring were biting into my finger. I have, however, looked carefully and I can see no split. The pain is very sharp and sudden, like the bite of an animal.

I held up the finger now. 'Look, Leila,' I said, 'I'm afraid you're right. Poor Jim's scarab that you gave me is deeply embedded.'

While she talked, lightly, pouring out my tea, I could see that she

304

was examining me. We had not been alone together for a considerable time. I could see, too (for I have become very observant—suspicious perhaps), that she was shocked by what she saw. I know that I am not very well just now. My hands tremble, my complexion is pasty, I am a bit flabby. I would have been furious enough if anyone else had looked me over like that, but with Leila it is different.

As soon as the maid had left the room, she said:

'John—why are you persecuting Richard? He's never done you any harm?'

'Persecuting,' I said sulkily. 'That's a strong word—and it's nonsense.' (I translate the drift of all this into dialogue. I cannot, of course, claim the exact words.)

'Now listen to me,' she said, leaning forward and looking at me intently. She held her thin, blue-veined hand forward to protect her face from the fire. I could see the half-deformity working in her face.

Scandal had looked up and was gazing at her with great intentness. 'John Talbot, you have been making a fool of yourself for the last six months—rather in the way Jimmie used to do, only worse. I won't say what you've been doing, you know well enough without my telling you. What you do, how you choose to behave, is your own affair. But we're very old friends and I'm sorry at all this.

'When it comes to Richard, though, it's quite another thing. Now that Jimmie's dead I love him more than any other human. He's in my care. He wouldn't hurt a beetle or even a slug. You are frightening him and I won't have it. And I want to know why you're behaving as you are.'

'Frightening him?' I tried to speak scornfully. 'How am I frightening him?'

'He says you are following him, seeking him out wherever he is. If you are in a room together you stare at him, look at him insultingly. He says you stopped him in Carfax Wood the other day and were very rude to him, and he thought you were going to knock him down. He can't understand it—nor can I.'

Her voice was softer as she said urgently: 'John—John—please—tell me why you're doing this.'

I paused before I answered.

'For one thing, Leila, he's greatly exaggerated everything. He must be a pretty nervous subject if he takes alarm because I look at him or speak to him.'

'It's more than that,' she broke out warmly, 'you know it is! Besides, Dick isn't a coward. He's simply one of the finest human beings alive—warm-hearted, generous. Sometimes he's gay and sometimes not so. He's shy, of course, and retiring, but I should think he's never been frightened of anybody before. But he *is* of you. It's making him ill. Tell me, John—dear John, we've been friends for so long. Tell me at least why you dislike him.'

'Yes, I do dislike him,' I said. 'I can't bear him.'

'Why? Why?'

'For one thing because he's so like what I myself used to be—and I hate what I used to be—pious and frightened and sensitive. What I did to Jim—' I pulled myself up with a jerk.

'*What* did you do to Jim?' she said quickly.

'Oh, nothing—except that I was so silly about him. Poor old Jim— I see now that he was only good-naturedly teasing me and I *wanted* teasing. But I told everybody I hated him and ran him down—'

'No,' she said quickly. 'Wait. It wasn't a case of "poor old Jim" at all. During those last years Jim was bad. It was as though he were possessed with evil and hated it but couldn't escape it. He was dreadfully unhappy and I could do nothing for him. Oh, I know because I lived with him! He was bad—or at least something in him was.'

'Now, Leila,' I said angrily, 'don't you of all people go running Jim down. He was very fond of you, even though he did go after women a bit. I misjudged him. Everyone did.'

She was looking me through, and I stared down on to the strong curly hair of Scandal's coat.

'It's strange, John; you spoke then just as Jim used to do. He would defend himself just like that. "I'm misjudged," he would say, "Everyone's down on me. I'm not a bad fellow really." But he was—he was terrible to live with towards the end.'

'But you loved him always, didn't you?' I said eagerly.

'Yes, I loved him always.'

Something impelled me to say: 'All that nonsense about evil—you don't really believe it, do you?'

'That there's evil in the world? Of course, I do.'

'Poor old Leila! You're a thousand years behind the times. What do you mean by evil?'

She spoke then sensibly with no sensationalism, and I was compelled to listen, although it was all nonsense and anyone else but Leila I would have laughed at.

'I believe—and, more than that, I know—that there are powers of evil as well as of good. They fight together eternally and we—all human souls—share in the struggle. Indeed, it is about *us* that the battle rages. If we are weak and submit we can be possessed with evil. It can enter us and own us just as good can. God has given us complete free will. We are our own masters. Why, John,' she went on, her voice rising, 'it's never been clearer than in the present war. Hitler and Himmler and the rest of that wretched crew don't matter as individuals, but they are the strongest instruments of evil the world has seen for hundreds of years. Their doctrines are completely evil—against God, goodness, kindness, freedom, love. They believe in cruelty, atheism, slavery. And we've been so lazy and selfish and idle that we have given them the weapons they wanted.'

'Now, Leila,' I said tolerantly, 'I'm not going to start a war discussion with you. There's a lot to be said for Hitler as a matter of fact. The Germans have been villainously treated—ruined, deprived of livelihood, spat upon.'

'They needn't have been,' she said quickly. 'And anyhow I'm not hating anybody. Not even Hitler and his crew. We are fighting something much more terrible than any *men*. And we've got to win, or we lose—not only our bodies but our souls.'

I laughed. Then I got up, stood in front of the fire, stretched my arms and my legs and said: 'Never mind all that. What you say is sentimental woman's nonsense. What did you really ask me to come and see you for?'

She looked at me sadly. She said, as though to herself: 'I can do nothing . . . I see that . . . nothing at all.' Then she went on quickly: 'First to tell you, John, that you *must* leave Dick alone. If you don't, I shall protect him. We have been friends so long—I have been so fond of you—but this is closer to my heart than anything in the world. I don't know why you are doing it. Nothing that you have said explains it. What you have said about your past is true. You *are* changed—terribly. But what has Dick to do with that? He *is* like what you were. I often thought of it when he was abroad. But he is stronger than you ever were, much, much stronger.

'But' the other thing I wanted to say'—she leaned forward with her urgency until she almost touched me—'is that you are in terrible danger—terrible, dreadful danger. You are moving, John, to some awful catastrophe. Those words aren't too strong. You are possessed as Jim was possessed. It is the same evil. Dear John—I beg you, I implore you, whether you believe in God or not, to take a chance—implore Him to help you. Beg Him to make you strong enough to fight this. Throw the evil spirit out. It's not too late. But almost—almost . . .'

Her eyes were filled with tears. I had an impulse to go on my knees to her, to confess everything, to implore her to help me. And directly after that I was angry. What right had she, with all her silly chatter about God and evil and the rest of it, to talk such exaggerated stuff? Wasn't I a grown man? Didn't I know what I was doing?

'All right, Leila, if that's all you have to say.' I looked at her with contempt, for that was what she deserved. 'Come along, Scandal,' I said, and I left her.

5

Leila made a mistake in talking to me about Richard. Somehow it increased my anger against him. To think that she should be protecting him. Why shouldn't she be protecting *me?* I needed someone to look after me very much more than did Richard. And what a miserable skunk he must be to hide under his sister's petticoats! It was the kind of way in which I used to hide behind Eve in the old days. And imagine a grown mature man going to his sister and complaining because someone in the town frightened him! Frightened him! A man of mature years! It is true that I myself used to be frightened of Tunstall, but then what a shameful ass *I* was in those days! How I despise that old self of mine!

In any case, this thought that Richard was hiding behind his sister made me want to get at him and do him a mischief. I'd give it him for complaining to Leila.

He could be seen every day driving about in a little maroon-coloured Morris. He'd stop in the High Street to do some shopping. He'd draw the car up at the side of the street, then very cautiously step out and look about him and nervously put his hand to his collar. His face had an anxious peaked look and it irritated me that he had almost no eyebrows. It amused me, though, to stand near the shop door and watch him go in. 'Good morning, Richard,' I would say suddenly, and he would jump inside his collar. I would tease him just as Jim Tunstall used to tease me. I would touch his arm. 'You can't escape me, you see, Richard,' I would say, smiling.

Then a wonderful chance came to me—a real opportunity for teasing. It was a lovely, soft, gentle evening—the sky was pale white-blue with pools of light green in it. I can't describe it, but I think I could paint it.

I went down to meet Cheeseman at 'The Green Parrot.' I stopped on the rough grass-grown little jetty to look at the way in which the green and blue sky, now turning, under the influence of two glittering sparkling stars, into grey dusk, reflected its delicate shades in the gently-heaving water.

Someone came towards me. I looked—and behold, it was Richard.

'Why, Jacko!' I cried—and then, as I caught his arm, laughed because the parallel of Tunstall's stopping me on this very same spot was so close that I had actually used his old jesting name for myself. And realising that, I had an idea.

I caught his arm and felt the slender weakness of it and saw the terror—yes, real, true terror—in his eyes.

'What is it, Talbot?' he said almost hysterically. 'What are you going to do? Let me go!'

'This is a very good little place,' I said, 'for us to have a talk. I've seen you a lot of times lately, as you very well know, but there have always been people about. There is no one in sight now.'

'What do you want to speak to me about?'

'For one thing you've been complaining about me to your sister.'

'I haven't. . . . Complaining? Of course not—what should I complain about?'

I could tell that he was frightened, but I could feel also some real resistance rising up in him, a secret, unseen stiffness that came partly from his very loathing that I should touch him. Just so had I loathed that Tunstall should touch me!

'I'm not angry,' I said, smiling and almost caressing him with my touch. 'Why should I be? I don't mind whether you complain to Leila. I'm only sorry that you should dislike me so much.'

'I don't dislike you,' he said. His face stiffened. 'Why should I lie? I do dislike you intensely. I hate you even to touch me.' I knew that he was trembling.

'That's all right,' I said cheerfully. 'Come in and have a drink on it.' I jerked my finger towards 'The Green Parrot.'

'In there? . . . Oh, no! Besides, I don't drink!'

'Now don't be so unkind—one drink to show there's no ill-feeling. It will do you good, Jacko. It will indeed!'

'Jacko! That's not my name. Why do you call me that?'

The sky was white now—white with a faint green shade. The water could scarcely be seen.

'Silly of me. Someone used to call me that once. A pet name.'

'Let me go. I want to get home.'

'No—no. One drink with me. The 'Parrot's' a jolly place. You'll like it. I won't keep you.'

I had my arm round his shoulders. He hung his head as though he were ashamed. But he didn't resist. I led him. I touched for a moment his hand and it was as chill as the green sky. I took him in with me.

The room was warm and smoky. The stout landlord stood behind the bar, and Cheeseman was alone at a table. I was amused to see the Rat's look of surprise. He was smoking his pipe, of course, and he looked over the top of it, his nasty little eyes narrowing and the red hairs standing out on the back of his pale fish-scale hand. Part of me loathed and hated him, the other part of me welcomed him as an element in the jolly gross side of life—the warm, juicy, odorous mud in which everyone, sinner and saint, likes at times to wallow. Oh, yes, they do! In the secrecy of the dark forest they play their games . . . or would if they had the courage. I'm writing fine words. What I really mean is that there is the jolly friendly nuzzling hog in the best of us. Well, the Rat is a hog all right, *and* a nuzzler!

He was polite to Richard and greatly amused to see him there.

'Now—what will you have?' I asked him.

'Oh, I don't know,' he answered. 'A ginger ale if you like. I'm a teetotaller.'

'Don't tell me,' the Rat remarked. 'Out in the East all that time and a teetotaller?'

'Oh, there's a lot of nonsense talked about the East. Plenty of fellows are teetotal. As a matter of fact, I hate spirits.'

He seemed remarkably at his ease. I suddenly realised that he was afraid of me no longer and that annoyed me. I wanted him to be afraid of me.

'How's your car going, Thorne,' Cheeseman asked. 'Nice little Morris that.'

'Just like any other Morris,' Richard answered quickly. I could see that he detested Cheeseman. He finished his ginger ale and I had an idea.

'Have another,' I said, and before he could answer had gone up to the bar with his glass.

I had it filled with a strong whisky and soda. I brought it back.

'Here you are,' I said, grinning.

He picked it up, then put it on the table.

'That's whisky,' he said.

'All right, old man,' I cried jovially. 'Try it—you'll find you like it.'

He picked it up and for a moment, an exciting, stirring moment, I thought he was going to drink it. Richard drunk would be quite an experience. But it slipped from his fingers and shivered on to the floor.

'I'm so sorry,' he said. . . . 'Goodnight,' and before either of us could answer him, he was out of the door.

'Well, I'm damned!' Cheeseman said. 'Very different from the way you behaved once, Talbot. Remember?'

Quietly I vowed to myself that I owed Richard one for that. *And* he would pay!

We sat on there and quickly Cheeseman swathed me with the veil of his influence. It was like that. It wasn't at all that I was ever afraid of the man or trusted him. I certainly did not admire him. Once, when I was in love with a girl, oh, years ago, I remember walking up and down the streets of Glasgow, Bute Street and Sauchiehall Street, in a sort of mesmerised trance. One Sunday I especially remember. It was years ago—long before I married Eve. One of my very rare trips to Scotland. I was young and that soppy, contemptible kind of ass that I once was. It was a wet Sunday, but she and I, hands interlocked, walked regardless of all other human bodies, houses, vehicles. We said little, but I remember the strong, cool clutch of her fingers and her generous, kindly eyes. With Cheeseman there was disgust rather than love, but he spun something of the same kind of web around his fellows. Was it mesmeric?

There was something in those evil, hot little eyes. . . . Mind you, I like the fellow. There is no dirty thing he hasn't done, no filthy sight he hasn't seen. I admire him for his honesty and his persistence. If he's after something or somebody he will go on quietly for years tracking it down. So tonight, he caught me.

'Whatever did you bring him in here for?'

'I like him. He reminds me of my old, good, simple self.'

'You don't. You hate him.'

'Yes, I hate him. I'd like to do him an injury. I will, too. The damned cheek. He dropped that glass on purpose.'

'Of course, he did.' Cheeseman picked his protruding teeth. 'Still you never know, for all his saint-like conduct. You'd be surprised at the things that good quiet people do! I've caught them out many a time and then don't they just squirm! Your good citizen has one pet vice and no one knows of it—but if you discover it you are taking away from him the *only* fun he has. He isn't like you or me, Talbot, who have

311

our eggs in several baskets.' He chuckled. 'Don't you hate the holy men, Talbot? The bloody hypocrites!'

Something made me say, 'Perhaps they are not all hypocrites.'

'Of course, they are. There's not one righteous man anywhere.'

'I wasn't a hypocrite before I killed Tunstall.'

There was a long pause. Cheeseman leaned forward. 'Before you did—what?'

So, I had told him. I didn't care. He would have got it out of me sooner or later.

'I pushed Tunstall over Shining Cliff.'

'You didn't! . . . My God!'

No. I didn't care. And yet I felt as though I were bound to him from now on. And yet I didn't care.

The room was very deserted. There was nobody near us.

'You guessed—long ago.'

His little eyes stared into mine. 'Well—I wondered. I didn't think you had it in you—not then. Now you might. Why did you do it?'

'He teased and taunted me all my life. He was making love to my wife—or I thought so. I fancied a lot of things. It was mad, crazy. I wish I could have him back. I'd tell him how sorry I was. We'd get on like anything if he was here now.'

'I believe you would. Poor old Jim! Although he never liked me. Do you remember how you knew that, although no one ever told you? And how you've changed since that night! I suppose a thing like that *does* something to you. I've known one or two murderers . .' He paused reflectively. 'I might even be called a murderer myself. . . . Somehow, what with the last war and this one, you can't take killing anyone very seriously. And poor old Jim was going downhill fast—'

Yes—I was tied to Cheeseman for the rest of my days. Something inside me gave a sort of lurch of nausea.

'Don't go telling other people,' he said.

'What do you think?' I laughed.

'Have another whisky; I'm going to.'

'Thanks.'

I could see that he was thinking hard. It was as though, in his mind, he was going over the list of his prisoners and captives. Now he had one to add.

'How did you do it? I wouldn't have thought you had the strength—not at that time.'

'We were on the edge of the cliff—I pushed him over.'

I could see the Rat's white hands clench sadistically. The knuckles stood out like a dead animal's bleached bones.

'Yes. Did he cry out?'

'Once.'

Cheeseman drank his whisky:

'Here's how.'

6

I am writing with the tears drying on my cheeks. I am writing because I must—to rid myself a little of the sorrow and rage in my heart. Soon I will be quiet. Tomorrow I go up to London to return tit for tat. *Tit for Tat. Tit for Tat.* The revolver that I got last spring is on the table beside me. When I wangled the licence, I wondered whether I should ever use it. I don't wonder any longer. I have been crying, I who have not cried for so long. They shall be the last tears I shall ever shed—the last tears for the last friend.

Yesterday afternoon Scandal and I had our last game together. He was a regular baby for a dog as old as he was—or at any rate he would be a baby with me. He would be anything with me if I wanted him to be. I have an old leather bedroom slipper that was his especial property. People sometimes say that dogs have no imagination. Ignorant people that don't know anything about dogs. Scandal certainly had plenty. He knew that the old shoe was an old shoe, but he also knew that, when he wanted it, that old shoe was a rat, a rabbit, a cat, and then, after that, something more—all his longing for glory and adventure and romance.

When I brought it out from its drawer and showed it him, at once our two selves were drawn close together. We were one romantic longing and desire. I don't believe any more in romance or sentiment or any kind of weak, silly slop, but there was nothing silly in *our* alliance. And now he is gone—the only friend, except Leila, that I had in the world.

I was proud, too, of the disregard that he had for everyone else. He never gave Eve and Archie a thought. He was polite to them, of course. He was a proper little gentleman and had beautiful manners, but they meant nothing at all to him. Nor did anyone else anywhere.

Everyone in this damned place thinks that I'm going to perdition—or have gone there already. But Scandal didn't. He thought I was simply the most perfect creature in the world, silly little fool. If I was sharp or violent to Eve he thought it was Eve's fault and would give her a nasty look. If I had drunk a drop too much, he would grin at me as much as to say: 'Drink all you want to. We can only live once.'

How physically beautiful he was! There was never another dog to touch him! The bright strong curls on his coat seemed to promise that he would live for ever. He was utterly fearless, but he wasn't one of those dogs that just fought any dog he saw. Many dogs were not worthy of his attentions. He had a wonderful dignity although he could play like a baby if he wanted to. I can't believe that he's left me. I can't believe that I shall never hear his quick excited bark again.

After luncheon yesterday, I took Scandal with me for a walk in Carfax Wood. The high road passes on the north of the town. I was about to cross it. Scandal ran ahead of me. A maroon-coloured Morris car turned the corner and approached us. I saw the driver and was certain that it was Richard Thorne. The car caught Scandal, drove swiftly on. When I ran up to him he was already dead. I picked him up in my arms and rushed down the road, shouting I know not what.

This morning I went to Leila's house. The servant told me that she and her brother had left for London.

When this afternoon I told Eve that I was going to London, she kissed my cheek and said that she would be waiting for me when I came back.

I buried Scandal in our little garden under the rose-bush in the right-hand corner near the road.

While I have been writing this a strange urge has been strengthening in me to take revenge on this filthy crowd of human beings who have insulted and derided and tried to murder me—who have killed the only friend I had.

NARRATIVE 3

1

I frightened him all right. I certainly frightened him. I've begun to write again because it tranquillises me. What am I writing? Anything. What does it matter? Except that I'm telling the truth and the whole bloody lot will be astonished when they hear it; they think that there's only this phoney war on—this war in which no one does anything but creep about in the dark. They don't realise that there's another war on too and that's *my* war. First to deal with Mr. Richard Thorne and then settle all the others—the nasty, mangy, creeping, crawling crew.

I return to facts. Facts are tranquillising. I will report to my friendly Demon *exactly* the Facts. Is that Demon Cheeseman? For he is with

314

me. We arrived last evening at 5.30, just before the black-out; it was raining and we discovered this boarding-house standing in a puddle of water.

The taximan asked us where he should drive us and I said: 'Bloomsbury. And go on until we stop you.' But, turning the corner by the museum, I saw this boarding-house before it saw me. I knew at once that it was the very place for us. To begin with, it is painted a liverish colour like a piece of underdone beef and all its windows are ugly like old maids looking through keyholes. All the old women with sooty glass faces stared down at us as our taxi halted, and I could hear them whispering: 'Here comes the very man for us. If we watch him we'll see something.'

Yes, there were two bedrooms and everyone had meals in common amity. Mrs. Foxborne her name was, and she is dressed like the British flag in red, white and blue and has the coldest, chilliest eyes I've ever welcomed. Her hands are like claws. She has a large pink-and-white brooch with the Three Graces carved upon it.

I gave myself the best bedroom, of course. Cheeseman doesn't mind what he has. He is so deeply excited about what is going to happen that he has no thought for anything else. And he knows that it will not be for long.

All I said to him was:

'You know that Richard Thorne killed my dog.'

'Oh, did he?' he said.

'He's flown to London because he's frightened and I'm flying after him.'

'I'll fly too.'

That's all we said, but in my mind's eye I saw two big black birds feasting just outside the Leicester Square Tube in a dark and empty London on somebody's carcase. I showed him my revolver.

'I'm going to chase him first,' I said.

There's a jerry under the bed, a large tear in the carpet, a picture on the wall of Christ blessing the children. There is a clock, too, that stopped at four-thirty years and years ago. Last night before I went to bed I painted a little. It was a fanciful picture of London like a spider-web and two eyes where the spider ought to be. There is dried blood stiffening the corner of the web, and the eight-day clock ticks although the web is strangling it.

I tore it up and jumped into bed. I was very cold but my head was hot as hell. I didn't sleep very well. I lay there remembering how once, after leaving that girl in Glasgow whom I loved so much, when she didn't write I was hot and cold all day long and trembled when the post came. But at supper I had a good meal—roast beef and apple-tart. There were half a dozen of us at the table, one thin, one fat, one round, one straight, and one with a hare-lip. Who was the other? There was an empty chair. I ate because I was hungry, but as I looked at them sitting round the table and mincing their words I thought how pleasant it would be to tie them to their chairs with green window-blind cord and shoot them, slowly, quietly, one after the other. You would gag them first with their soiled table-napkins. How their eyes would stare as they realised that death was coming to them after all—real positive death that is never real until it is actually upon you. No escape for them as they stare frantically at 'The Fighting Téméraire' and 'Christ Leaving the Temple' and the beef congealing on the plate and two flies digging into the sugar-dish. Then I aim, with what a jolly, friendly smile I aim at first one then another. Their arms are bound backwards on to the sides of the chairs, so as they are hit their bodies bound forward. How delightful for the others to watch while their friends depart!

I leave one to the end. I think it should be the young man with no eyebrows. It is indecent not to have eyebrows.

And I should say to him:

'Have you ever loved a dog?'

He will be too sadly terrified to reply.

'Have you ever been thrown into the sea?'

Still no reply.

'Have you ever been mocked and taunted by all the citizens of your filthy little town?'

Then I shall fire.

2

I have bought two pairs of shoes with felt soles. I love to walk in the dark without sound. I will jump upon Richard before he can hear me coming.

I love this darkness. I adore it. I belong to it. It is what I have always wanted.

There are still many theatres open in London and the crowds move in Leicester Square, in Piccadilly Circus, in Regent Street, in thick moth-like throngs, laughing, loving, moving adroitly out of the way of one another. But these are not the places where I at present resort. I am only at the beginning of my pursuit, with my dark soft hat pulled over my eyes, my face pale if someone flashes a torch, my little revolver in my pocket, my soft, soundless tread.

Once the darkness falls I find it difficult to stay indoors. But I like first to have my evening meal with the boarders. They are afraid of myself and Cheeseman. I know their names now—Miss Lucy Bates, Mr. Henry Bates, her brother (he has the hare-lip), Mrs. Constantine, Mr. Floss, and very old Mrs. Taylor.

In the first place they dislike my silent approach. I come upon them in the passages, in the bathroom, in the sitting-room, on the stairs before they are aware of it. I am very polite and courteous, and especially so to my landlady Mrs. Foxborne. Then when they speak to me they become uneasy under my stare. Yesterday evening I walked down the stairs behind old Mrs. Taylor huddled under her shawl and looking at every step cautiously with her blind, red-rimmed eyes.

Before she took the last step, I said gently:

'Good evening, Mrs. Taylor.'

She gave a little shawl-muffled scream.

'Tell me, Mrs. Taylor, why don't you have a little dog—a Pekinese, for example?'

She held her hand on her heart. 'Oh, dear—I never heard you coming.'

'Why don't you have a little dog, Mrs. Taylor?'

'Oh, dear—I don't know.'

'I had a dog that I loved very much. It was killed by a motorcar.'

I opened, with a little bow, the door of the dining-room.

During the meal I like very much to silence the conversation. It begins very briskly and soon they are all talking gaily about the war, the black-out, the theatres, and what they have done during the day. What I enjoy is to look at them one after the other. There is something about my face that they dislike. I have a strange feeling about my face. I feel it to be a mask, a mask through which my eyes burn. Behind it what thoughts and fancies burn! It would never do if they should see my real face, for passions rage in it—passions of anger and violence because I am in this world now for one purpose only—to be revenged on just such miserable cattle as these who have spoiled my peace and attempted to destroy me.

And so, I look at first one and then another. I look at them one by one and they look at me and their eyes drop. Gradually a silence falls.

When the meal is over I put on my hat and coat and go out. If it is a dark night without moon or stars, it is as though you walked in a vast underworld where the little red lights, whether in the air or just above the ground, are like the eyes of animals. I walk, making no sound, through the streets. The darkness is doubly, trebly enfolded, layer upon layer. You can put out your hand and feel it. Suddenly you are on the edge of plunging into some abyss. You pull yourself up sharply and your heart beats at the escape of some fine danger. My gloved hand closes round the revolver in my coat pocket. I love to feel it there.

There are not many people in these streets, but what I love is to touch them suddenly, coming up upon them before they know it. I put out my gloved hand and for an instant rub their arm, or push against their back, or even touch their neck. They flash their torch perhaps and sometimes cry out. I apologise very politely, raising my hat. But I cannot help thinking how pleasant it would be to turn a neck and twist it or throw them down and stamp upon their silly meaningless faces.

But of course, those are things that I must not do.

When I am accustomed to it, the darkness has many colours— purple and dark green and opalescent grey. It moves like blown water and you can feel its waves upon your face. It contains also many odours: the acrid tang of smoke, the stifling thickness of petrol, the damp of wet towels, the thin clamminess of human breath.

The buildings, filled with invisible human beings, which they hold like prisoners, contemptuously, share gladly in the darkness. At last, after so many years, they are truly themselves and can pursue their own purpose unwatched by men. You can tell by the sounds they make— the gurgling of waterspouts, the straining of boards, the creaking of doors and windows, that they are alive and busy.

These are only the preliminaries. My great purpose here is to find Richard. And very quickly I have found him. I remembered that once Leila had said to me that Richard, when he was in London, found much pleasure and solace in the Coffee Club. When I asked her, what was the Coffee Club, she told me that it was a little place off Jermyn Street, a small club for gentlemen who had been in the East or were interested in the East. That Richard could have a meal there and talk with friendly and congenial souls.

Two days after my arrival in London, on a fine and sunny afternoon, I went along to Jermyn Street. I walked from one end of it to the other, down to St. James's Square, along King Street, up St. James's, back along Jermyn Street. 'You'll be getting it one of these days,' I thought to myself, 'you swanky, leather-smelling, school-club-tie sycophants and snobs with your nice smart little church where there are royal services for Royalty, and your rich Turkish baths with a nice blue plate on one of them to that King of Snobs, Walter Scott, and your shoe shops and your hat shops and your picture shops, and your Orleans Club where there is the best food and drink in London, and your grand St. James's Theatre where Sir George Alexander of the crooked smile and creased pants once had his famous first nights and Oscar Wilde received his grand bouquet of cabbages. Oh, all you ancient, leather-stinking, stuck-up guardsmen and harlots,' I thought to myself, 'the time is coming, and is not far distant either, when the bombs will be raining down on you and the holes where the window-panes ought to be will be hot with roaring fires. You can pile your sandbags up one on top of another! A lot of good they will do you!'

I must say these thoughts give me the greatest of pleasure, because I detest all those conceited stick-to-yourselves, we-are-the-best-people-on-earth kind of Englishmen. What a lot of good a few nice bombs will do them!

As a matter of fact, I could see, even as I walked about, how they looked down on me and took care that the hems of their garments should not touch me! I felt spasms of rage contract my fingers as I saw them sneer at me! What harm was I doing them? In fact, I spoke to one man, an elderly pompous fool with watery eyes and a white moustache. I said, 'You'll know me again, won't you, sir?' and walked on, leaving him pretty astonished. But what right had he to stare at me as though I were a criminal? I must confess that when I saw a shop-window in Jermyn Street with all the regimental ties laid out in patterns, and gloves as elegant as any dandy could wish, and silk handkerchiefs with initials embroidered on them, it was all I could do not to fire my revolver into the middle of them. They positively sneered at me, those things in that window. As I write those words down I know that they are true. Why, there was one tie of red and green and purple that spoke to me, saying: 'How is little Scandal? Ha! Ha! Nice little dog, wasn't he?'

However, to get on with my dear Richard.

At length, at the corner of St. James's Square, I asked a chauffeur standing beside his elegant car whether he had ever heard of the Coffee Club. He scratched his head and asked another chauffeur. I could see that they were laughing down their sleeve at me, the parasites, but I didn't care. At last the fellow came to me and said that he thought it was opposite the women's Turkish baths, to which he pointed up the hill—somewhere there, in any case. He was staring at me as though he didn't like my face. However, I had more important business, so I went up the street, and there, on the right-hand side, sure enough was a little brass plate, 'The Coffee Club.' I drew a deep breath of satisfaction. I agreed with Cheeseman that we should divide our time in watching. The most likely time for Richard to be there would be luncheon and he would come out, in all probability, somewhere between half-past two and three. If days passed and I didn't catch him, I should go into the Club and ask for him. All that I wanted for the moment was that he should know I was in London.

Well, two days later out he came—just as though I had summoned him. It was exactly three-fifteen of a chill, foggy afternoon. It was not at all a fog of the old pea-soup variety—I fancy that they are vanishing as a feature of London life. It was rather wispy and straggly and grey-white with a kind of thin drizzle at the heart of it. The lights were already in the shop-windows, and as the fog blew in the breeze, everything seemed to move, the buildings, the lights, the shadows of St. James's Square. I was just thinking that I would go home for the day when the door opened and out stepped Richard, almost into my arms.

'Good afternoon, Richard,' I said. For a moment he didn't recognise me, for my hat was pulled down over my forehead. Then he stepped back. After that he didn't speak and he didn't move.

'I only wanted you to know, Richard,' I said, 'that I am in London and you will be seeing me very soon again.'

3

The pursuit has begun. I am in a state of exultation. I am obeying the will of my Master who tells me what I must do.

I cannot remain still and I hate to be alone. If I am not in pursuit I am wasting my time. If I am alone I am aware of something within me that is struggling not to obey.

I remember reading somewhere in Memoirs by a contemporary that Napoleon once told the writer that he had always been compelled to make his decisions '*against the sometimes absurd and cowardly remonstrances of his weaker self*,' or words to that effect.

I often feel in Hitler's speeches that his oratory is loud and powerful not only to convince his audience, but also to silence something inside himself—something that he knows is weak and sentimental, something that would betray him altogether were he to give way to it. So, it is now with me. When I am alone in the boarding-house, especially at night in my room, I am conscious of an urge to get something free in myself. I envisage this as a prisoner whom I have subjected. Were I to listen even for a moment, I would be betrayed and by myself. I can hear sometimes a weak, pitiful voice in my ear, and sometimes I fancy, as I have done in the past, that a figure lingers beseeching in the shadows of the room. This condition is undoubtedly due to this nervous ecstasy that I now experience. The thought of settling my debt with Richard once and for all is a deep sensuous delight to me. I will revenge upon his miserable body all the miseries that I have suffered and the contempt that has been poured on me. Hallelujah! Hallelujah! Upon this town that has rejected me shall be showered hailstones of fire—huge bursting hailstones like flaming, destroying angels.

And now I must say something about my visit to Leila yesterday. I went to the little house where once I had tea with her and, pitiful fool that I was, wept at her feet. I rang the bell, asked whether Mrs. Tunstall was at home, and before the maid could answer me, brushed past her and opened the sitting-room door. She was sitting on the sofa, her feet up, reading. I stood in the doorway, like the avenger from God, and I felt my power to be so great that I could, with one hand, command this house to be ashes. I felt my eyes burn through the brick and mortar and look into eternity.

She was not afraid of me. Unlike others, she has never been afraid of me. She said:

'Oh, poor John!'

That would, in another, have been so insulting to my pride that I would have wrung their neck, but Leila has always had an influence upon me. Yes, for many, many years.

She said quickly: 'Richard isn't here.' Then she got up.

'Poor John, come and sit down. You look exhausted.'

Exhausted! When I am at the height of exultation.

I didn't move from the door. 'It doesn't matter,' I said, 'where Richard is. I shall get him when I want him.'

The sight of her kind face with its tenderness and slight deformity always moves me. I was ashamed of myself, but I said almost beseechingly:

'Richard killed my dog; Scandal was my only friend.'

She gave a real cry of sympathy. 'Oh, poor John! Is Scandal really dead?'

'Richard rode over him in his car.'

'I am sure that he did not. When did it happen?'

'The day before you left for London.'

She stood for a moment thinking. 'Richard never used the car that day.'

But this is the important thing—the words that I now spoke. I don't know why I said them.

'Richard isn't your brother,' I said. 'He is John Talbot.'

She only gazed at me. She has always been very kind to me.

'I am Jim Tunstall, your husband. Talbot tried to kill me and now I am going to kill him. That's fair, isn't it?'

I felt an immense relief. It was all so right and so just.

Leila spoke very quietly and slowly, as though she were trying to explain something to a child.

'Listen, John. You are very ill. You have been ill for a long time. You killed Jim and after his death the evil that was his curse has been your curse. I have known it a long time. My brother has nothing to do with this, nothing at all. Before it is too late, you must be rid of this evil, destroy it, throw it away. I will help you. Stay here with Richard and me. You and I, with God's help, will destroy it together.'

I remember thinking what a silly conversation it was between two grown people. I knew, as I looked at her, that we had lived together and slept together and eaten and drunk together for years and years. At the same time something in me wanted to surrender to her and feel her strong, cool hands on my forehead (I know the touch of her hands so well) and stay with her and, above all, sleep without dreams.

So, lest I should listen to that ridiculous voice inside me (we all have these ridiculous voices), I spoke loud and fast.

'You tell Richard that I'm after him and I'll follow him everywhere and at last I'll get him and he can't escape me. Do you hear? He can't escape me.' And I went out of the room and out of the house, breathing as though I had been running fast.

★★★★★★

Two nights ago, I had Cheeseman to sleep with me. Nothing could be more disagreeable than this, and yet I am beginning to avoid being alone. When Cheeseman was undressing I asked him suddenly whether he saw anyone in the corner of the room. He walked in his shirt and in his bare feet (his toes are bent and red like the claws of crabs) and examined the room from end to end.

'There is no one here,' he said. And yet, even then, I could see, I fancied, a thin figure with bent head, shadowy and yet real.

Cheeseman, I am happy to say, is, in spite of my confiding my secret to him, afraid of me. . . . I was acutely aware that last night he wished desperately not to sleep in the same bed with me. He would give almost his life not to do it but does not dare to refuse me. The Rat does what I tell him. At last he has found a power stronger than his own.

While I was undressing I looked at the upper part of my arm and it seemed to me that I detected a tattoo-mark faintly blue. I made Cheeseman examine it and with all the more pleasure that he hated to touch my body. He could see nothing. I fancy that I can trace a design.

In bed the Rat lay withdrawn, dreading with all his flesh lest I should touch him. I reached out my hand and laid it on his thigh. He trembled from his ears to his toes. This gave me great pleasure and after that I allowed him to sleep.

But last night I refused to surrender to any absurd panic. I had had a wonderful walk in the darkness and I had heard news of Richard. Cheeseman reported to me just before supper that he had that afternoon seen Richard and Leila leave a taxi and enter, each carrying a bag, a little hotel off Soho Square.

I have indeed great powers from my Master, for consider the co-incidence that the Rat, passing through Soho Square, thinking of his own affairs, watches idly a taxi-cab draw up outside the shabby hotel and sees Leila and Richard emerge from it! Such things do happen, of course. Everyone can recall astonishing coincidences. But does not this one convince me that I am indeed assigned this especial task of punishing my fellow human creatures and that I have been granted especial powers? Even a wretched creature like Cheeseman can feel something of this especial divinity in me. When I look at him he lowers his eyes. When I speak the tips of his ugly ears are crimson. When his teeth protrude and his head crouches into his shoulders he is indeed like a rat caught in a trap.

However, last night I slept alone. I awoke abruptly at one-fifteen. Someone was in the room, and, sitting up in bed, I heard once again that pitiful sobbing that had exasperated me so outside Bella's room.

I switched on the light and, staring a little breathlessly, was certain that in the far corner between the looking-glass and the window I saw that thin, shabby, bending figure.

When I write down the dialogue that follows, it is for my own reassurance that I may realise its absurdity. But it seems to me that I talked with the Figure, who answered me.

And yet it may be that I still slept and that I talked to myself in my dream.

★★★★★★

Myself: 'Stop that crying.'

'Let me go, then! Oh, for pity's sake let me go! If I did you once a great harm, I have been punished enough.'

Myself: 'I don't know what you are talking about.'

'You do; you know you do. Ever since we were small boys together you threatened me. You said we were the Siamese twins—that nothing could separate us.'

Myself (chuckling): 'You wouldn't listen. I warned you. What was it I used to call you?'

'Jacko.'

Myself: 'Yes, Jacko. That was it. A silly name.'

'Let me go now. Please, please let me go. And this other man whom you are pursuing has nothing to do with *us*. He may be like me a little, and so the sight of him infuriates you, but he is not *us*.'

Myself: 'I am not so sure.'

'You are carrying me along with you in your dreadful purposes just as you have always done. How ashamed and unhappy you make me—just as you have always done. My poor wife and boy. You struck her and showed Archie indecent drawings. They thought it was me. Oh, the shame, the shame!'

Myself: 'And so it was you, Jacko! For you are me and I am you!'

'I am not! I am not! You said that when we were children together, and it wasn't true then and it isn't true now. Every man's soul is his own, and if he is strong enough, no one can touch his inviolability. But I am not strong enough because of the one evil thing that I did.'

Myself: 'Poor Jacko! The one brave, downright thing you ever did, and see how you are punished for it!'

'Leave me. Leave me. Go your own evil way and meet your own evil destruction. Let me return to my wife and son and beg their pardon and Leila's pardon, too, and show the town that I am just as I used to be. . . .'

Myself: 'Oh, no, Jacko! That would be far too easy an escape. We go on together to the end. One's acts are irrevocable, you know. After all, you were paid the compliment of free will. You really can't blame anybody but yourself. Now stop crying like a baby, Jacko, and let me have some sleep.'

★★★★★★

Dreams! I don't know. As I write down this nonsense I can see myself years and years ago trembling at Jim Tunstall's touch, even as Cheeseman trembled the other night at mine.

4

I have escaped. For a moment only perhaps. Oh, God! Give me time! I know that someone is praying for me and has given me this extra power. I, in my turn, pray to God to keep me free and allow me time for my penitent submission.

Everything is so quiet here. It is as though I had been fighting under turbulent waters. With a dreadful din in my ears and a drive of waves beating at my throat and heart and eyes. Now suddenly I am floating in a blessed silence and the steady beating of my heart. . . .

This room is so still. Why did it seem to me so mocking and sinister? The clock on the stairs has struck two. I went to bed in a kind of madness. A furious hatred of mankind. I was planning some dreadful act. In my dreams it seemed that someone called to me again and again as friends do when they are trying to wake you!

'John . . . John . . . John Talbot, John Talbot . . .' And I struggled as Lazarus must have struggled. It was as though I had to lift a great burden. I was fighting someone and I heard his chuckle: 'Down, Jacko! Down! Keep down!'

In my nightmare I knew that I could never beat this off unless great help was lent me, and I called out, as one does in dreams: 'Help! Help! . . . In God's name help!'

I felt the hands on my shoulders keeping me down, and I felt the hands under my armpits lifting me up. New strength came to me. I cried out—and it is the first time for so long that my voice has been heard—'I am free!' Then I woke. I was sitting up in bed. I switched on the light, put on my dressing-gown, and now I'm sitting, writing this on the dressing-table, writing as once I did, happy, tranquil, quiet. . . .

Early tomorrow morning I will go back to Eve . . . I will catch the first train. . . . Oh, God, forgive me my sins. I have sinned. I have sinned. I will give myself up to justice.

Oh, God, Thou hast punished me enough. Release me now from the possession of evil. Make abhorrent for me these vices that I abhor but am a servant under. Deliver me from Evil. Oh, God—Deliver us from Evil. Raise my head from under this possession.

Oh, God! He is returning—my heart sinks with fear. My breath thickens on the glass. He looks through my eyes again. There is the

325

stink of his breath in my nostrils. Oh, save me, God, save me. . . .

5

So, you thought you had escaped, old fellow, did you? You thought you had escaped? I have read that nonsense. But *was* it, like my fancied dialogue a night or two ago, an imagined dream. Memory? When I dream—and I have dreamed much of late—who am I?

My handwriting does not change. That is simply a trick of habit. But have we not all an imprisoned self? In any case, *my* imprisoned self is a wretched creature with his weeping and wailing and appeals to a God who does not exist. I heard the other day of an old Jew in one of the German prison camps, and when they threatened him with torture he prayed to God. So, they beat him to death with hose-pipes and between every blow they cried: 'Now, Jehovah! Help Thy servant.' The thought of those beatings stirs my blood. So, Jacko, say: 'Now, Jehovah! Help Thy servant!'

My hand trembles as I write. This writing is almost illegible. That does not matter, for no one will ever read it. This is in all probability the last time I shall ever write anything. From words to deeds . . . I feel a conqueror. My heart beats in my breast like the heart of a king. What I did last night I will do again—and again and again. I will terrorize this whole city. I am Hitler's forerunner of vengeance. Maybe I *am* God. Who can deny it? I stretch my arm and it seems to reach into infinity. I stare with my eyes and, as in that pub last night, they are turned to stone.

Last night the wind blew with a fury and all the houses seemed to bow to me. I walked into the darkness like a king.

And tonight, when I have settled my debt with that pitiful murderer, I will begin my campaign of vengeance. The winds of the air, the stones of the streets will aid me.

Well, about last night.

Cheeseman watched and saw him leave his Club off Jermyn Street. He followed him then to a little eating-place at the Knightsbridge end of Sloane Street. Then he met me where we had agreed to meet, at the coffee-stall at Hyde Park Corner.

Strange, isn't it, that I thought by my confession that I had yielded myself into Cheeseman's hands, and it has turned out the exact opposite from that! Cheeseman, the great Cheeseman, the blackmailer and terrorizer, who has held so many men and women at his mercy for so long, strange that he should at last be in the hands of someone

326

else! For he is terrified of me and with every day his terror grows the stronger. Yesterday in my room I asked him: 'Why are you frightened?'

'You look like—'

'Like what?'

'Like the Devil.'

'You are not frightened of a man's looks, Cheeseman. Come here.' And he came. 'Kneel down.' He knelt down. 'Raise your hands and touch my arms.' He could not do it. 'Hold my arms, Cheeseman.'

At last, his body trembling, his head averted, his hands lay on my arms, those pale hands with the thin red hairs.

I bent forward and cupped his chin, forcing his head upwards. His eyes closed.

'Look at me, Cheeseman.'

He would not.

'Look at me, Cheeseman.'

He would not.

'Look at me, Cheeseman.'

His face trembled like a face under moving waters. Then he looked at me.

I feel a deep pleasure as I describe this remembered scene.

I went and stood outside the little restaurant. After a while Richard came out. There was a strong wind now rushing in and out of the restaurant. There was no light from the door of the restaurant, but I flashed my torch. He saw me. For an exciting moment he stared into my eyes. I thought he was going to speak, but he did not. He crossed the road and walked quickly along Knightsbridge. I followed him.

My pleasure was now so intense that I could have suspended it into eternity. I knew what terror there must be in his heart. I wondered whether he would stop at Hyde Park Corner and take an omnibus. But he knew that that would not save him. He knew that there must be that last walk from Piccadilly to Soho Square. If he took a taxi-cab there would be that moment when he stayed on the pavement to pay his fare. Or, perhaps, he wished to end it. Whatever he did, wherever he went, he could not escape. If he appealed to the police, that would not save him, for no one save Leila had heard me threaten him, and in any case the police could not save him for ever. But, Richard, you are only the first. After you there will be many, many others.

As I walked through Knightsbridge, I felt an exquisite, a sensuous pleasure. To feel the revolver in my hand and to know that my power, my great, great power, stretched far beyond my revolver. I could have shouted with joy at my power, calling out, 'Rain down your hailstones of fire, Revenger!' And so, they will rain down and a great fire roar to heaven, and these puny buildings come crashing to the ground.

The wind blew through the darkness, making it vocal. The power of the wind met my own power. We were great together.

By the coffee-stall at Hyde Park Corner he paused. He looked about him, the poor miserable fish. He was considering, I fancy, whether he would not take a taxi. I would be there before him if he did. There was a little crowd round the coffee-stall, which was dimly lit. There was a cheerful hum of voices and laughter. I stood, robed in my darkness, and thought: 'Aye, you may laugh. Soon you will be crying to heaven'—a grand thought that made my heart beat almost to suffocation.

He decided to walk and I followed him down Piccadilly. While I was behind him I was also with him. My hands were on his neck and I had twisted his head round so that his eyes were staring pitifully into mine, begging for mercy.

Along Piccadilly the wind, blowing across the Green Park, was raging. Pedestrians had difficulty in standing steady, and as the wind blew against them I knew that it was my power and I had only to command and the wind would rise until it lifted them off their feet and blasted their bodies against the walls, and then the walls, too, would crash to the ground, buildings, old, beautiful buildings that had been the country's pride and pleasure for hundreds of years, reduced to dust and rubble.

At Half Moon Street he turned up into Curzon Street. Why he did this I do not know. I followed him up that dark little street. By the Christian Science Church, he paused and then struck right. And then—I lost him.

I made a mistake. There is a little public-house on the right and I thought he entered it. I pushed open the door and looked in. The room was brilliantly lit. There was a man behind the bar, a girl serving drinks, some people at the tables.

As I stood in the doorway they all turned and looked at me. Some power compelled them. Some power also held them so that they seemed turned to stone, all staring, not moving. But he was not there. I was out in the street again and began to run. I collided with a man hurrying in front of me. I was enraged at his stopping me. I caught him by the neck. He cried out. I hit at his face with my fist. I hit again and again. He fell to the ground and, with an exultant pleasure,

I stamped on him, on his face, on his belly. I kicked him, bent down and tore at his face with my hands. Ah, but that was a pleasure, a great exultant happiness. I felt his flesh under my hand, I felt his belly quiver as I turned my boots upon him.

I felt all the power of the wind and the darkness in my soul as I ran on, ran till I could run no more, ran until I reached the steps, and there, laughing because I was master of the world, knelt down to tie my bootlace and then stayed to wipe the sweat from my face and steady my beating heart. I had lost him. For this moment I had lost him, but not for long.

★★★★★★

This will be, I fancy, the last time I shall write. . . . Deeds now. Not words.

The little tinny bell has rung for supper. Through my open door I can hear them scurrying down to their food. I will sit with them, eat with them, drink with them. How wonderful that at last, at last, this long-postponed hour has come!

6

Letter from Leila Tunstall to Eve Talbot

My Dear Eve—By now you will have received my telegram. We must wait for the inquest, and as soon as that is over Richard and I will bring John down to you. I want to give you an exact account of what occurred so that you may understand, as though you had been there, just what happened.

First, I must tell you that poor John killed Jim by throwing him over Shining Cliff. This he himself told me, but I knew it long ago. Perhaps you also had guessed it.

A simple explanation of all that occurred after that is that John brooded so deeply on what he had done that he became insane. Nothing more is needed than that, although I think the real explanation is a much more complicated one. You do not know perhaps all that I suffered during my last years with Jim, although you can understand it possibly by all that *you* suffered during these last months with John. We all watched the change in John. It seemed to eat him up, bit by bit, like a disease. I know how you suffered, but I suffered in my own way too, for I loved John—like a mother, a sister—but I loved him always and I love him now. I was not, however, more directly concerned until I found that he hated Richard. Richard is, and has always been, my particular care. When we were children together I tried to look after

329

him and protect him. Physically, Richard resembled very closely what John used to be, and in some curious way this physical resemblance exasperated John. At first Richard thought that he must be imagining this hatred. He had never had anything to do with John, bore him no ill-will although the John of these later months was antipathetic to him in every way, but he knew how fond of him I was and he put up with him for my sake.

However, during this last summer, matters became serious. John insulted him in every possible way, followed him about, and once in Carfax Wood nearly assaulted him. I invited John to come and talk to me about it, but when he came he only talked wildly of hating him.

You know how John's face had changed during these last months, how terribly it had changed. He reminded me often, by his looks and speech, of Jim as he had been during those last years. In that talk I had with him I felt certain that he was in the possession of some evil power, as Jim had been. Here I must ask your patience, for you may consider the power of evil and its possession of human beings as a piece of old-fashioned nonsense, not seriously to be held in these days by any mature, sensible person. It seems to me that if you believe in God you must also believe in Evil and in a constant battle between good and evil. But I am not pretending that I am putting forward here any belief but my own. I am not attempting to force it on to anyone of a different belief. We have each of us our own explanation of the great mystery, an explanation that must come from our own experience of life. No one has the right to say to us that we are speaking falsehood as *we* see truth, nor have we the right to challenge the belief of anyone else.

However, this persecution of Richard by John became so incessant that Richard's health (he has never been very strong) became affected by it and I decided that we should go to town. We went but had been there scarcely any time when Richard was met by John outside his Club. Quite suddenly John appeared at my house. He stood in my doorway and, Eve, I looked at someone so terrible that I shrank as from the presence of the Devil himself. It was *not* John with whom I spoke, but something I had never encountered before, save in *my* most terrible dreams. Something not only incredibly wicked but something also quite dreadfully sad.

I did not know what to do. To inform the police, to insist that John should be medically examined, was hopeless, for what would they, who knew nothing of the inside of our story, see but a quiet, sad-faced man who would talk to them with perfect coherence and deride my fears? But the danger to Richard was most urgent. He felt it himself and yet could not believe in it.

We moved to a small hotel off Soho Square and began to make our plans for going to some other part of England for a time. Richard was against this. He felt it a cowardly surrender to an absurd fear. I on my part was sure that this was no solution.

We had scarcely settled in at this little hotel before John found us. When we were out someone—John or another—would enquire for us. John, of course, had quickly found the number of my brother's room. I cannot describe to you, dear Eve, how strange this experience was. Someone was following us in the dark, drawing ever closer and closer. Wherever he went, whatever he did, Richard felt that he was followed. Sometimes he saw John staring at him out of the darkness.

An evening came when Richard returned to the hotel, his nerves gone, trembling and begging me to protect him. Richard is a brave man and has faced many perils in the East. I had never seen him like this before.

We sat up late that night and decided, after much discussion, that we would trust in God and face the climax of this whatever it might be. I told him that we must be together from this time on and take whatever was coming side by side. I knew that I had some power with John.

We had not long to wait.

On the evening following Richard's collapse, at about half-past nine, Richard went up to his room and I went up with him. I was sitting in an armchair, Richard on the bed. The door opened and John stood there.

I think my first feeling was one of relief that we had all met at last face to face. But at once I, who am not, I think, a nervous or cowardly woman, was stricken with fear. Dear Eve, I want you to understand exactly what followed, but it is far from easy to explain this dreadful moment as I saw and felt it without your feeling it to be exaggerated and false. And yet I fancy there must have been moments in your last weeks with John when you realised something of the same kind. This was John and was *not* John. You know how, when someone you love and have lived with for a long time, falls into a sudden tempestuous rage, how the face, the body even, changes and you feel you are encountering a stranger. It was not that the figure in the doorway was in a rage. It was calm and controlled with a horrible coldness. I am exaggerating nothing when I say that the room seemed to chill around us. Richard himself acknowledged this to me afterwards. The figure looked at us both, and from those eyes came a gaze so cruel and at the same time so distant that it belonged to no time, as we recognise time. Isn't it the worst thing that we feel about Hitler that he has no human passions, no love, no lusts, no sensuous weakness, no bowels of compassion? We are human beings bound all of us together by our common human experience, and we can imagine nothing more awful than encountering someone who has had none of our experience and is bound in no way by our laws, to whom no appeal can ever be made that he will understand.

This figure that faced us was evil because it was not human. The black hat, the dark coat, the gloved hands were a symbol expressing the whole power of inhuman impersonal evil.

At once, for this that takes so long to tell occupied a very brief time, I felt, rising in my breast, beating down my fear, an immeasurable overwhelming pity for John. Something infinitely greater than myself filled my soul. At the same time, I felt a disgust, a sickness of revolt as though I were seeing some appalling cruelty to children or animals.

I prayed to God. I implored Him to give me strength to fight the force confronting us. I knew then, Eve, in a swift impulse of revelation, that everything I had been, done, and suffered was to count now. Had I suffered that much less in the past—mental, spiritual, physical suffering—the less strong would I be now.

I rose and cried out as though I were summoning the dead:

'John! John! John!'

The figure moved forward into the room. In its gloved hand was a revolver. I saw that and Richard saw it, too, but I think neither of us felt the least fear of it, for as the figure stepped further into the light, its face was quite dreadful to see. It was not the cold, passionless stare of the eyes, the pallid, swollen, baglike folds of the flesh, the mouth slightly parted, but sharp like a trap—it was rather the absence of all humanity and the sense of horrible timelessness as though, for ever and ever, it had been exactly thus and would continue for ever so.

Then I fought it. There was, of course, no physical contact. I should have died, I think, had there been. I don't know, Eve, what I said or even if I spoke. But my spirit saw John's spirit struggling to be free. With all that was good in me, with everything that had ever been worthy in my life, I fought for that spirit. My spirit said: 'John, John, I am with you. Don't be afraid. You are escaping! You will soon be free!

You will be free, John! Be brave! I am with you!'

The figure raised its hand. There was no other motion. Into that evil, timeless face there came movement. A fearful struggle. I seemed to have John's body in my hands. It was as though, between my hands, I felt the battle to be free. I cried out to God, and in myself I realised a power I had never known before, like the sun breaking on to a sullen plain, a warmth, a heat, a consciousness of resurrection. The face with which my whole soul was battling broke up. The eyes dulled. The mouth trembled.

A deep, bitter, heart-breaking sigh trembled on the air.

The figure turned on one foot, seemed about to fall, then, with bent hand, directed the revolver into itself.

We heard the report as though from a great way off.

At last Richard came over to the body, and very gently, reverently, turned it over.

There was lying there, Eve, the old John, the face thin and drawn, the eyes staring with a peaceful happiness—John, as you and I for so long knew him and loved him.

I can tell you only, dear Eve, that I have spoken the truth as *I* found it.

We are in God's hands now and always.

Your affectionate friend,

Leila Tunstall.

Lightning Source UK Ltd.
Milton Keynes UK
UKHW04f0604110718

325544UK00001B/86/P